THE HOUSE OF AMFITHERE

THE HOUSE OF AMFITHERE

BOOK 2

CIARA HARTFORD

For Tim and Myra.
My Love and my Moo. Thank you, endlessly.

To my readers!

Thank you for coming back to Rhend for more abuse. I cherish you more than you know. But this book is not for everyone. It is intended for adults and may not be suitable for those under the age of eighteen. As with *The House of Starling*, I've given it a movie rating, somewhere between PG-13 and R, but probably closer to R. Everyone is different in what they enjoy and what they find triggering. Above all else, please protect yourself.

Mature content includes:

» Abduction
» Anxiety
» Child abuse and grooming
» Post-traumatic stress disorder
» Profanity
» References to rape and sexual assault (no actual depictions of)
» Sexual content (fade to black)
» Graphic violence including:
  › Torture
  › Blood and gore
  › Dismemberment
  › Evisceration
  › Decapitation

Welcome Back to Rhend.

N
W
E
S
FORTHA
RAGGATHAN
DAKARAI
HOLD
THE MIDDLELE
THE
WASTELANDS
KEKK
HOLD
GLAZMIN
SEBBETT
HOLD
SORMIRE

VAIL
THE WILDS
KORTHAN
PARTH
THANDOR
THE MOORS
THE EASTERN PASS
DORMSHIRE
OLD ROAD
FOREST
THE HIGHLANDS
REMIRE
DOOSHAWN
SORMIRE
HARMEND
RHEND

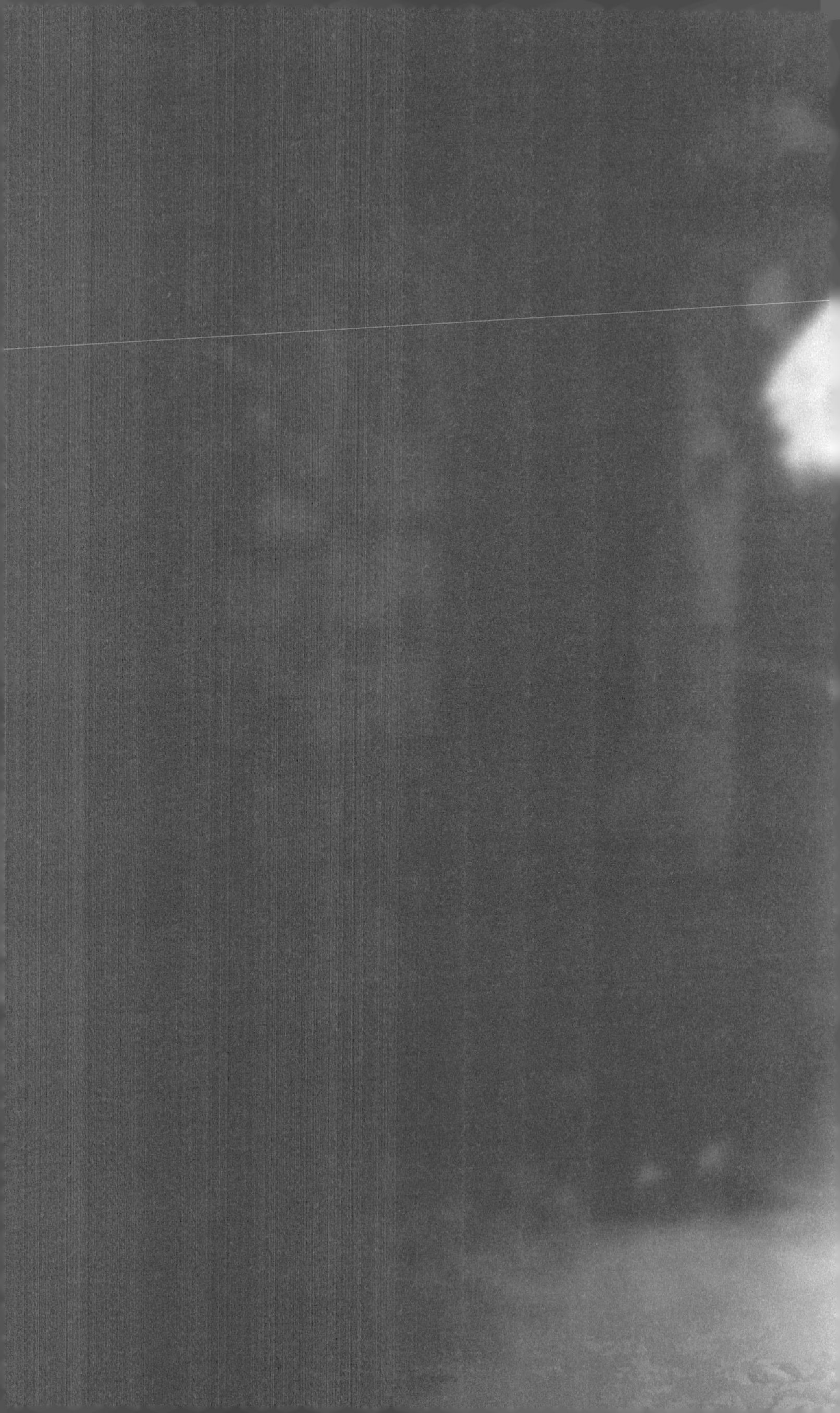

Destroying History

With careful hands, he cut a page from the ancient manuscript, laying it over hot coals and coaxing a meager fire to life. Flames erupted through the parchment, devouring words with ravenous hunger, destroying the age-stained paper in seconds.

History. That's what he destroyed. And he was helpless to change it. He hadn't been asked to do this, he'd been ordered. The ill-tempered mercenary, hovering over his every move, didn't much care for what he wanted.

His hands trembled as he selected the coordinating page from a collection of loose counterfeit documents. From his satchel, he pulled a vial of hide glue; a roll of delicate repair paper; and a thin, flat tool made of bone which had been polished until it shined. It had been his grandfather's bone folder—a precious implement he'd carried with him for centuries. A piece of his life he'd likely keep with him until his death, which he feared would come sooner than anticipated.

He never imagined he'd be ripping pages from books and replacing them with fakes. He'd devoted his life to these manuscripts—studying them, copying them, protecting them—and now?

Destroying them.

Destroying history!

Using the bone folder, he smoothed down his work, the frayed edges of the repair paper disappearing. He sandwiched the new page between sheets of waxed parchment before clamping the manuscript closed to dry smooth and flat.

Grabbing another manuscript from the stack, he leafed to the page that needed to be replaced, cutting it away—another scrap of history held between his fingers.

This time, when he turned to the flames, he hesitated, his thoughts scraping over all the people who could be harmed by altering history. All the elves who would likely be controlled or killed because of his tampering.

"What stops you?"

An impatient, pink-fleshed hand pushed his into the fireplace. The flames caught on the parchment, licking up around his fingers. Yelping, he yanked back, elbowing the mercenary in her chestplate.

"I'll not ask again." She jerked him up by his collar, sending a sharp thread of pain down his spine. "Someone else can be found who knows the passages," she spat, a blade kissing the soft flesh under his chin. "Choice is yours."

Her eyes were cold, immovable. How had he gotten himself into this? He shook his head enough to be seen, but not enough for the dagger to bite into his skin.

"I'll do it. Please...I'll do it!"

He was dropped into a heap beside the manuscripts that had been gathered for him. Books on Great Houses, lineages, and histories. Original copies of the prophecy—ancient texts, dusty after centuries of sitting on shelves at the back of libraries. These were the works of his ancestors, dating back to the time when the Elder Gods still meddled in the lives of common elf-folk.

He collected himself, taking a deep breath before pulling the manuscript he'd been working on back in front of him. Again, he ripped a strip of repair paper. And again, he pasted in a counterfeit page, sandwiching it between waxed parchment.

He said a silent prayer to the Elder Gods that someday someone would notice the tampering. That they'd notice the slightest differences in the artificially-aged paper. The inconsistency in the writing styles and the intensity of the ink. The places where pages had been ripped and not replaced. He hoped he'd left enough discrepancies that a keen eye could catch them. That someone would notice.

Someone had to. For all their sakes.

He eyed the mercenary as she bit her nails out of boredom. When she realized she had an audience, she stood up straight. "Is it done then?"

He flinched at the finality in her question, wondering if when he finished here, he would, in fact, be allowed to go free as promised. Part of him knew the answer—one he'd feared when his bondmate and young elfling had been taken as well.

He wasn't going home after this. But he could do everything in his power to give his family a chance.

"A couple more manuscripts," he said with a confidence he didn't feel.

"Well, stop wasting time and get on with it," she said.

"Of course."

He turned to the stack and slid the next tome from the top.

Veneer of Hope

Gastel met a sea of heather in full bloom from the window of his bedchamber. It was the same view that had greeted him every morning for nearly his entire life. It was familiar, calming—the changing landscape, a reminder of the passage of time. But now he saw it with different eyes. Ones that could see past the veneer of hope and the delirium of the temporary.

He'd read once that only the lost could see through to the decrepit innermost parts, made of tears and blood and ashes. To behold the world as it truly was. Nothing was permanent. The purples and yellows of summer would fade into the reds and golds of autumn. And then it would all be scraped from the surface of Rhend when winter plunged them into blistering cold. Everything that lived would die, just as elves lived and breathed and killed one another.

The sun rose from the opposite side of the castle stronghold, stretching shadows like wraiths across the moors at the feet of the royal gardens—darkness bleeding into the beautiful. It was in these quiet moments that Gastel found solitude, knowing he could see the truth when so much of his life had been lies.

There had to be more than this empty rage that churned in his gut day in and day out. A few weeks ago, he'd burned with the need to continue the work that Raemian Starling had given her life to accomplish. Now, he simmered alone for hours in his quarters, his anger melting into frosty resentment.

Raemian was gone. She'd fallen into the rift after losing her footing, saving his life. And though she wasn't always the first thing he thought of when he woke, there were days he couldn't get her out of his head. He squeezed his eyes closed, willing this day not to be one of them.

Gastel turned and received the harsh reality of his face in the mirror, seeing all of himself at once, past the mask of smooth gray skin and amber eyes. And his hair—Gods, his cursedly short, unruly hair. He was frozen in the moment the disgraced Queen Gemma had sheared away the record of his elflinghood and had thrown his topknot away like trash.

He raised a hand to drag his fingers through the strands and stopped short, the scarred flesh of his fingers unable to stretch open.

"Fuck." The word slipped from his lips.

He instantly regretted saying it. He sounded like the younger of his two brothers, who'd rather the elves of Rhend continue to slaughter one another until the end of time. Roulin had fled shortly after peace had been established between the Shay and Bleck Larin. Now, instead of hearing Roulin's sour words day in and day out, Gastel was tortured by self-reproach so heavy it made it hard to breathe. He had spells of it—shortness of breath, blurred vision, racing heart. His eldest brother,

Belkin, would glare, silently berating him for not having better control of his emotions.

And his father? He was the last person Gastel wanted to speak with. The man had kept so many secrets from him. The prison of lies the king had built around Gastel had collapsed with one fateful decision to take Raemian home. All the mistakes he'd made, every bad decision, could be traced back to the ignorance forced upon him by his father.

And through all of it, he was left with...*this*.

A broken world, scattered in pieces, left to bleach white like bone in the insufferable sun. A world without Raemian Starling.

Turning to pull on a fresh shirt, he stopped. He hadn't been able to dress himself since his hands had been incinerated in the fires of the rift when he'd tried to save her.

When he'd failed to save her.

It was demoralizing. The fact that he was unable to do something as simple as pull on his shirt, fasten his vest, lace up his boots, feed himself properly. It was a constant reminder of what he'd lost. Peace was still too fresh with the Shay to find an Eishtala Master willing to come to Parth to heal him, and conventional remedies had done little more than ease his pain and fend off infection, leaving him with leathery, scarred skin that refused to stretch.

He flopped back down on his bed, glaring up at the exposed beams. He'd wait for the servant who came each morning to help him, but it wouldn't be long before he'd stalk the halls in his undershorts.
Gastel had nearly given up when someone knocked. Frustration bloomed in his chest as he leaned up on his elbows, taking two deep breaths to keep from sounding like the ungrateful, dejected prince he was.

"Come in."

The elf was too short and wide framed to be a Bleck Larin. Even in the shadows of his library, Gastel knew him. Dulanii walked with a familiar swagger, hands on his hips, clothed—as usual—in nothing more than brown pants and worn leather boots.

"Are you ready to kick my ass?"

Bewildered, Gastel blinked up at the man who stood over him. "Excuse me?"

"Wait...are you not dressed?" Dulanii cocked his head to the side, his frosty white eyebrows drawing together in confusion as he took in Gastel's distinct lack of shirt and pants. "But you're always up early."

Gastel lifted his ruined hands. "I'm unable to dress myself." He clenched his teeth in frustration. He hated being incapable. He hated being vulnerable. Gods, he hated so many things he never thought he'd have a reason to hate.

A bright smile broke across Dulanii's face. "Ah. Well, then. Let me help you so you can help me."

"Help you with what?" It was Gastel's turn to be confused as Dulanii searched the wardrobe.

"You know. That thing."

"Thing?"

"Yeah." Dulanii peeked around the wardrobe door. "Where you stop being a sulking elfling and start being the badass I know you have tucked behind that gorgeous face of yours."

Gastel's eyes grew large, and Dulanii roared with laughter, his cheerfulness washing away Gastel's frustrations like a swollen river stripping the debris left by weeks of treacherous storms. It was nearly impossible to resist the mirth that oozed off the Shay.

"Come on, I'll help you," Dulanii said as he motioned for Gastel to sit up.

Dulanii was a paradox. The man had been Raemian's greatest friend and had partnered with her for most of the war. Somehow, he'd managed to pull himself from his melancholy within a week of her death.

Gastel had caught the Shay in moments of sadness, but for the most part, nothing but radiant friendliness emanated from him. It was frustrating that Gastel could not seem to do the same.

"For the Elder Gods' sakes, Gastel, have you never been dressed by someone before?"

He was yanked from his distracted thoughts as Dulanii stood before him, a pair of pants slung over his shoulder and a shirt rolled and ready to pull over Gastel's head.

"Arms up, little elfling," Dulanii said in a singsong voice.

Gastel shook his head but did as he was bidden and let the Shay pull the shirt on, guiding his arms into the sleeves.

"That's better." Dulanii leaned down to slip one of Gastel's feet into a leg of his pants. "Your bare chest is *very* distracting."

"This coming from the man who's never fully dressed."

Dulanii stood straight, a cocky simper gracing his lips. "I need to show off my best attributes. We both know my head's full of wine and honey cakes. Besides…" Dulanii's cheeks brightened as he helped Gastel with the other leg of his pants, motioning for him to stand so he could pull them the rest of the way up. "I'm trying to get your brother to spare me a passing glance."

Gastel placed a bandaged hand on the Shay's shoulder, accentuating how much taller he was than Dulanii. Gastel still couldn't help but notice the physical differences between Shay and Bleck Larin.

"Good luck with that." The words popped out before Gastel had thought them through, and he instantly regretted them as Dulanii's expression fell. "It's not you. I've never known him to have a lover, but I've heard he had many before I was born."

"Perhaps with all his warlording, he hasn't made time for a little fun." Dulanii tucked the shirt in before he stood back from Gastel, hands falling to his hips. "But you? Cooped up here?"

Gastel could only stare at him. He'd had the occasional tryst when he was younger, but at some point, the allure of dalliances with flighty courtesans had faded. He hadn't been interested in anyone in a long time. Not until…"No."

Dulanii must have noticed the moment Gastel's mind firmly affixed on the memory of her.

"Gods, I'm an idiot. I shouldn't have—"

"It's fine."

Dulanii looked up, his crestfallen face a reminder of his genuine concern. That's what Dulanii was—genuine. Unable to hide his emotions behind a mask of stoicism like Bleck Larin were expected to do. He filled a sullen room with cheerful humor. He was the definition of loyalty and friendship, wrapped in an annoyingly muscular, pink-fleshed elf with cropped white hair.

Gastel forced a smile, knowing it never touched his eyes. "Really, don't worry about it."

Dulanii inspected Gastel with a critical gaze. "I'm going to worry about it."

Gastel shook his head. "So stubborn."

"Not any more than you." He turned back to the wardrobe and rummaged through the collection of doublets and vests. "Do you wear nothing but red?"

"Do you ever wear a shirt?"

Dulanii poked his head around the door, glaring with a faux grimace.

"At least I *own* shirts. You have nothing in here but red!" Dulanii pulled out a blood-colored vest with gold embroidery of dragons down the front.

"I'm sure there's some black and gray in there if you look hard enough," Gastel said with a crooked grin.

Dulanii helped him slip the vest on before fastening the toggles, his careful fingers pushing Gastel's hair back from his face.

"Now you look like a Bleck Larin prince." The Shay winked. "I feel better about kicking your ass."

"What did I look like before?"

Dulanii pursed his lips. "A lost little elfling in need of a hug."

Gastel shook his head slowly, unable to stop grinning. He hated admitting how right Dulanii probably was.

As they walked side by side, Gastel realized this was his first time attending training since his hands had been burned. The familiar energy of it buzzed through him as they exited the castle stronghold and emerged into the summer morning, savoring the scent of sun-warmed heather and loam. The manicured gardens were obnoxiously green against the brilliant blue sky. This was why he avoided it. The cheerful gardens around the arena were at odds with what he knew to be true.

Belkin and his soldiers were already paired up and sparring. Once they saw Dulanii, however, they pressed themselves against the edges of the arena, waiting with rapt attention to see what would happen next. Belkin eyed Gastel with heavy suspicion, his glare eventually falling to Dulanii, a single eyebrow raised in question.

Dulanii reached for a discarded practice sword, flipping it around his hand with a flamboyance perfectly matching the shaymarks that danced down his sides. It was Gastel's turn to raise an eyebrow. The Bleck Larin had no use for theatrics, flipping blades, flair for flair's sake. Quick, efficient movements had been railed into Gastel from an early age.

"On second thought, you can't even hold a weapon," Dulanii said, breaking the silence that had settled over the arena.

"That never stopped him before." Belkin's coarse voice answered.

The smile fell from Dulanii's face, his cheeks turning a brilliant pink.

"You've come to learn, haven't you?" Gastel spoke the words before he realized who he sounded like: Effrin Kresha, his heartless instructor from The Vail of Wielders who'd tried to break him during his brief stint of Anam training. He shook it away. This was different. Dulanii was goading him into friendly sparring.

The Shay squared off across from him, still absentmindedly twirling the practice sword. A smirk grew on Gastel's face. There was something about standing across from Dulanii that made him smile. What Dulanii might not realize was that Bleck Larin training went beyond proficiency with weapons. Hand-to-hand was equally as important. Even without usable hands, Gastel was expected to be deadly.

Dulanii's meager attempt at an opening move was easy enough for Gastel to duck away from. Three consecutive swings to the ribs were predictable. Gastel spun forward after the third and elbowed the Shay in the sternum, sending him back several feet.

"Cheap shot," Dulanii gasped. His breath had been knocked from him.

"This coming from the elf wielding a weapon against an unarmed opponent," Gastel said, throwing his hands up in surrender.

Dulanii stood straight, eyes wide, then pointed at Gastel with the practice sword, his brows furrowed in concentration. "Again."

This time, Dulanii was slightly more prepared. The Shay changed direction midswing, letting Gastel pass him before he twisted to bring the practice sword down, but Gastel had assumed as much. Forearm to forearm, he blocked, and Dulanii's practice sword went flying toward Belkin, who caught it as it twirled toward his head.

"Fuck." Dulanii shook his arm out. "How did that not hurt you?"

"I've conditioned my bones for impact." Gastel couldn't help it; he was smiling wider than he had in weeks. Even the fact that he couldn't push his short hair out of his eyes didn't seem to bother him.

Dulanii rubbed his arm, a scowl burning across his usually friendly face. There were snickers from the others along the wall as Belkin handed the Shay his practice sword, the slightest smile softening the high general's typical serious expression.

"Again," Dulanii yelled, frustration tainting the edges of his voice.

Gastel shrugged and leveled his weight on both feet, bandaged hands on hips, waiting for Dulanii to make the first move.

This time, the Shay let Gastel duck in close, forgoing the use of the practice sword and bringing an arm around his throat and tightening. Gastel pushed away a wave of panic. With or without hands, he would need to persevere. He clamped the Shay's arms with his own before flipping Dulanii's burly frame over his shoulder. The Shay was left looking up, bewildered at how he'd gotten there.

More chuckles rippled through the arena, and Gastel held an arm down to help Dulanii up. Instead, the Shay swept Gastel's legs with his practice sword.

The entire arena erupted with laughter as Dulanii stood over Gastel, victorious. After basking in his moment, he reached down and took Gastel's wrist to help him to his feet.

Before the Shay could say anything else, Belkin stepped forward.

"My turn."

The smirk dropped from Dulanii's face.

"What's wrong, Shay?" Belkin's grin was wicked. "Scared?"

Dulanii's eyebrows shot up as he stepped back, letting his practice sword dangle limp at his side. There was something so satisfying about the terror written across his face. Gastel would be sure to poke fun at him about it later.

Belkin reached out a hand, and a practice sword was placed in it.

"I'll pray for your soul, sweet Dulanii," Gastel said, unable to help himself. He knew how serious Belkin was with sparring.

"At least we're using sticks," Belkin said. "For your safety, of course."

Dulanii squared off across from him, intense concentration written in his brows. Good. He would need it. Belkin rarely went easy on anyone. Gastel had been pummeled as an elfling more than once, left with bruises and black eyes.

There was a distinct nod to Raemian that bled through in the way Dulanii seemed to duck in close, causing Belkin to push him away with a kick to the chest. Gastel had only witnessed her fighting prowess a couple times, but it had left an imprint on his memory as sharp as steel. Dulanii was not Raemian, though. Belkin kept himself free and clear, easily controlling the duel in a way that looked effortless.

"Had enough yet, Shay?"

Dulanii straightened, likely realizing Belkin hadn't been putting in full effort.

"Your friend had me disarmed in significantly fewer moves," Belkin said.

A darkness moved across Dulanii's brow, only intensifying Belkin's sneer.

The Shay exploded forward, a primal roar ripping from his chest. Belkin gave him lead, blocking the angry swings with ease and letting Dulanii push him until he was nearly to the edge of the arena. All the while, the smile grew on the eldest prince's lips.

Sweat beaded along Dulanii's forehead, his shoulders rising with each breath as his energy waned. To his credit, Dulanii's stamina was impressive. Gastel could only watch and wait. He knew what was coming.

Belkin's heel touched grass, and his demeanor shifted. He parried and spun in, elbowing Dulanii in the face, then spun back the other way. He slammed the practice sword into the Shay's ribs hard enough to send the elf flying to the ground.

Silence. Belkin's expression had hardened into his typical stoic mask as he stood over Dulanii, who struggled to breathe...again.

Biting his cheek to hide his amusement, Gastel stepped forward, reaching a bandaged hand down so Dulanii could pull himself from the ground.

"Cheap shot," Dulanii gasped, rubbing his ribs.

Belkin doubled over in laughter. "Was it?" Belkin said between his mirth. "Your friend didn't seem to have any issues."

Dulanii glared at Belkin before his scowl melted into a brilliant smile. "Of course she didn't. Rae was the best."

Belkin threw his practice sword to the ground and reached a hand forward, grasping Dulanii's wrist in a earnest shake. It was something Gastel hadn't witnessed from his brother—a warmth Belkin reserved for family and, even then, rarely bestowed.

"Good effort, Shay. Train with Tildimin. I need to speak with my brother."

Dulanii nodded. His cheeks were bright pink, and Gastel wondered if it was from the sparring or his brother's touch. The Shay turned as Belkin's right-hand man materialized from the other training Bleck Larin.

Belkin directed Gastel away from the arena and back toward the castle stronghold, walking for a time without words.

"How exactly did the Shay get you down here?"

Gastel's smile faltered his bandaged hands perched on his hips as he looked down at his feet. "I think it's time I tried to get back to some semblance of normal. You know, before I throw myself at the next rift."

Belkin eyed him. "Still insistent on opening more?" There was a distinct air of concern in his tone.

"It must be done in order to restore balance." Gastel tried to press as much determination into his voice as possible. He needed Belkin to understand. "I'm going to visit someone at the Vail first. She may have a map so I can target the correct ones. Hopefully I'll only need to open two more. I promised Freya I would do this much at the very least."

"Promised Freya?" A snap of frustration colored Belkin's words. "When have you been in communication with the regent?"

"Just because I don't have usable hands doesn't mean I can't send a letter." He spun to walk backward in front of Belkin. "Are you jealous she writes to me and not you?" Gastel couldn't help his teasing. It had been a long time since he wasn't smothered in dark thoughts.

In a snap, Belkin was swinging a playful fist in Gastel's direction. Gastel slid clear, a wide smile spreading across his lips.

"Cheap shot."

Belkin chuckled, shaking his head as they continued walking.

"Father should have sent the Shay to you sooner."

Realization melted over Gastel, and he took a sharp breath. Again, his father had meddled. Could he blame him this time? Gastel had been in a dark place for far too long. He let his frustration roll away.

Belkin must have noticed the change in his demeanor. "He worries, Brother. We all do."

"I know."

Gastel tried to pull together some response that would ease his eldest brother's concerns, but there was none. Gastel was just as concerned as the rest of them that something terrible would befall him by opening a second rift. But if their world had any chance to ward off the Sundering the prophecy spoke of, balance needed to be restored to the magic of Rhend.

TWO

A Teacher

All the levity there had been during training was gone. Gastel needed to speak with his father, which instantly put him in a sour mood. But if he could drag himself to training—even though it'd been with heavy encouragement—he could open the next rift. Too much precious time had slipped past as he'd wallowed in self-pity these last several weeks.

After finding his father's study empty, he headed toward the throne room, but as he passed the library, he was greeted with a familiar voice.

"Gastel."

"Kal?" Gastel practically ran to greet the Anam Wielder. "How are you? What—"

"Am I doing here?" Kalbasen's warm smile eased some of the tension building in Gastel's shoulders. "Your father sent me a letter last week."

That tickle of annoyance warmed the edges of Gastel's consciousness. More meddling.

"He mentioned you might be interested in some Anam tutoring," Kal continued.

Gastel closed his eyes to center himself, letting the waves of frustration wash away. He looked past Kal to his father, who sat on a velvet settee in the library. The king was surrounded with stacks of reading materials and wore his typical impassive expression, hiding his true thoughts.

"I thought maybe I could show you a few skills Inara and I are working on. Some advanced defensive techniques." Kal's enthusiasm was endearing, but not enough to tame the rage building in Gastel's chest. "I've brought Inara as well. After leaving the Vail, I offered to continue her studies, and I thought it'd be perfect to train you both."

Gastel continued to glare at his father, trying desperately to keep from blowing up. This wasn't Kalbasen's fault. He'd answered the king's request. This was his father's doing. More secrets. And yet there was a thread of good intention in this that had been missing from everything his father had kept from him before.

"That would be..." Gastel pried his eyes from his father and gave Kal his full attention. "That would be fantastic, actually."

The genuine smile Kal gave him was something Gastel needed at that moment. The last of his frustration sloughed away. He'd do what he did best and throw himself into something to take his mind off all the other things burning holes in his chest.

"When can we start?"

"In a moment," Mesmal said, drawing Gastel's glare again. His father had crossed the library on silent feet. "I need to speak with you a moment, my son."

Gastel grimaced. Of course. The king would want to continue his campaign to keep Gastel from leaving again. But he'd made promises he wouldn't break. He'd watched Raemian plunge into the rift for him. He wouldn't waste her sacrifice.

"I'll be just outside," Kal said as he bowed and stepped away.

An uncomfortable silence burrowed into Gastel's patience as his father waited for Kal to leave.

"Did I hear correctly?" Mesmal's voice rose with amusement. "Did you venture to the training arena?"

Word had spread fast. Gastel tried to snuff out the momentary current of warmth as he recalled his morning spar. He wasn't ready to admit that something could turn his self-imposed dark mood around so easily.

"Dulanii is persuasive."

"The Shay has been a welcome addition to the castle stronghold," his father said with a gentle upturn of his lips before giving Gastel a pointed look. "You were hunting me down for a reason, no doubt."

Gastel took a deep breath, needing another second to frame his words.

"I'll be leaving soon." He tried to hold eye contact but failed. "I need to open the next rift." His father started shaking his head. "Please understand, I've made a promise. I won't forsake her memory."

"And how exactly do you plan to do it *safely*?" His father was direct, his glare as hot as Gastel's composure. "You gave your hands to open the last one; what will you give for this one?"

"I gave my hands to save Rae—"

"Who sacrificed herself to break the connection to the rift as it drained away your life."

Gastel took a deep breath in through his nose, the muscles in his shoulders tightening. While pieces of information had been given to his father about the events at the rift, it wasn't a subject Gastel had discussed with him directly. Part of him hadn't wanted Mesmal to know all the details.

"Who will be sacrificed this time?"

Gastel clenched his jaw, desperate to rein in the rage. "No one," he said so softly he wasn't sure his father had heard. "I'll not make the same mistake twice."

Mesmal's expression hardened. "I don't think you know what mistake it is you made." His father overenunciated each word, pressing them between clenched teeth.

If his father had been anyone else—and Gastel had usable hands—he'd have yanked him forward by the collar. He took hard breaths to attempt to calm himself, but the consuming fury only burned hotter. He wanted to ball his worthless hands into fists and punch anything that got in his way.

"Why must you always treat me like an elfling?" Gastel's voice rose, no longer able to tame it. "This isn't a whim. This is the future of Rhend...of our world!"

With every word, his patience crumbled. His father must have noticed because he took a cautionary step back as Gastel squeezed his eyes closed, desperate to hold whatever this was inside.

But he failed, and a deluge of white soulfire exploded from him.

"Why can't you see that this is what must be done?"

His voice carried that faraway quality it had the last time he'd been consumed by soulflame, both a single voice and many woven together. Mesmal took a few more steps back and stumbled into the settee he'd been occupying, eyes wide with terror as he looked up at Gastel towering over him. Through the soulflame, all Gastel could see was a withered old man, and it only enraged him further.

"You sit in your stronghold and hide away. I won't hide with you anymore. I'll do what needs to be done."

He turned, letting the fire drip from his flesh as he stormed from the library, unable to draw it back into his body. It was clear that the strength of his Anam had recovered after being almost completely decimated opening the first rift. He hadn't been sure he'd ever need his mother's soul stone again, but now it seemed it might be the only thing that could help him smother the flames.

Gastel had been working with Kal for what seemed like hours. He was exhausted and frustrated. He'd put his soul stone on after blowing up at his father, and while it had calmed the fire, it hadn't cooled his anger.

"He means well." Kal's patient voice broke Gastel's concentration, and he lost the orb of protective soulfire he'd conjured. It burst from around him and dissipated into the cloudless afternoon sky.

Gastel shook his head, trying to push the rage down where it belonged. He couldn't keep getting so upset. Something had to give.

"Please say this anger will go away." Gastel pinched the bridge of his nose.

Kal paused, attention fixed on something behind Gastel. "You learn to channel it. Though with your strength of power? I honestly don't know." His glare returned to Gastel's with a seriousness that caused him to stand a little straighter. "It's possible you'll have to work harder or risk being consumed by your own Anam."

How was that even possible? Gastel didn't remember reading anything about this in his Uncle Dormel Amfithere's journal or any of the manuscripts he'd devoured while recovering. He made a mental note to scour the journal again. It contained a plethora of entries detailing Dormel's quest to help Gastel's mother as she struggled with her own immense power.

"Try it again," Kal said, his voice stern yet friendly.

Gastel took several steps back and reined in his emotions. Preparing defensive soulflame was different from the way he usually summoned Anam. His eyes slipped closed, pushing the world around him away, focusing on the warmth of the sun heating his hair. He took a deep breath, savoring the smell of blooming heather. A wave of calm washed the last vestiges of his anger into the soil beneath his feet.

Another breath. At the back of his mind, it waited. The calm Anam that didn't feed on his frustrations. It was like a separate entity that hid in the shadows of his consciousness. Like an elder brother, he held out his hand, guiding it forward until it stood beside him. Together, they gazed across the moors until nothing existed besides Gastel and waves of heather swaying from the ripples of gentle Anam.

When he opened his eyes, Kal was no longer in front of him. As he'd been shown, Gastel lifted his hands in a circular motion. He pressed the timid presence forward, letting it flow from him into a brilliant, white blossom that opened back upon itself, enclosing Gastel in an orb of fragile soulfire. He twisted his wrists, ignoring the way his scarred skin pulled tight, guiding the force into swirls that solidified into concentric rings, rolling and overlapping in a dance of endless knots.

He held it, like the longest note at the end of a song, sweat beading on his brow. When he couldn't hold it any longer, he let it shatter around him in millions of bright, white shards.

"That...was incredible." At some point, Dulanii had snuck over from wherever he'd been hiding and sat cross-legged in the grass, his face alight with wonder. "Why have I never seen this magic on the battlefield?"

Kal's attention shifted to the Shay. For a moment, Gastel wasn't sure how Kal would react to Dulanii, but he shouldn't have worried. At the Vail, the Eishtala Master, Lorilay, would have likely healed Kal at some point.

"Because it's draining," Kal said, pure admiration in his voice. "A lot of Anam Wielders don't realize how much of their life force they've used. Especially Gastel. That was..." Kal took a timid step toward Gastel, his eyes searching his face. "I've never seen Anam of that level before."

Gastel reached for the soul stone around his neck. What could he do without its suppressive powers helping him control the full force?

"All that's left for you to master with that technique is calming your mind."

Kal gave Dulanii a curious glance, and the Shay was on his feet in an instant.

"I'm Dulanii." His cheeks were burning a brilliant shade of pink as he bowed, refusing to come any closer, his eyes seeming to snag on Kal's height.

"Yes, sorry." Gastel stepped forward, gesturing to Dulanii. "Kal, this is Dulanii. He's..."

"I'm a friend." Dulanii said.

"More than a friend," Gastel said with a wide grin. "You're a brother."

Dulanii's cheeks grew even brighter as he rubbed the back of his neck.

"And this is Kalbasen, my Effrin from the Vail."

"Call me Kal, and I'm no longer an Effrin. I lost that title when I left with Gastel," Kal said with a smirk. "Pleasure to meet you, Dulanii."

Gastel returned to the training arena with Dulanii the next morning, sparring until they were exhausted. He was sweaty and spent, lying on his back in the grass beside an uncharacteristically quiet Dulanii, when Belkin showed up. The eldest prince sauntered over and gazed down at them.

"The two of you are a sight."

Gastel shielded the sun with his arm so he could see his brother. "Good morning to you, too."

"When do you sneak away on your little quest?"

A hot blade of frustration rippled through Gastel as he glared up at Belkin. He wondered if his brother realized how condescending he sounded. How he *always* sounded.

"Trying to get rid of me?"

"I leave for Korthan." Belkin glanced out over the moors. "Roulin sent a curious summons, and I've decided to indulge him."

Gastel struggled to push himself up. "Alone?"

Belkin's face hardened, but he ignored Gastel's question "I assume you intend to leave before I return?"

Gastel held his brother's eyes for a long time. What was Belkin trying to say? Was he asking him to wait? This new, almost caring brother was not someone Gastel was used to dealing with. He was better at predicting the Belkin who ignored him until there was a lesson to be taught...or break him down while wearing the impenetrable mask of indifference expected of the high general.

"Shay."

Dulanii perked up at Belkin's stern address.

"Do you intend to accompany my brother?"

Dulanii glanced from Belkin to Gastel and back, his eyebrows raised. "I believe that's the plan, Highness."

Belkin nodded in thought as Gastel managed to climb to his feet, the anger growing and blistering his insides.

"First of all, Dulanii has a name, and last I checked, it wasn't Shay." Gastel glared at his older brother, whose expression had eased into one of tempered amusement. "Second, if Father wishes me to stay until you've returned, he can ask me himself."

A smile grew across Belkin's lips. "First of all, *Little Brother*, I'm well aware of Dulanii's name, and I'll refer to him however I'd like. And second, I'm the one who'd rather you wait until I return." Belkin's expression evened out. "Our father is not as young as he used to be, and if Roulin has something planned, I'd rather you be with Father, should something happen to me."

Gastel hadn't expected this response. If there was anyone who seemed not to notice that their father had aged more rapidly over the last few months, it was Belkin. Gastel nodded, realizing Belkin hadn't been oblivious; he'd just not bothered to draw attention to what everyone could plainly see.

"I'll wait then," Gastel said, swallowing hard. If anything, it would give him a few more days to train before leaving.

Belkin nodded before he turned and left.

"He can call me Shay all day and night if he wishes," Dulanii said under his breath. When Gastel glanced over at him, he wore a crooked smile, his eyes following Belkin.

"He's an asshole."

Dulanii shook his head slowly, his smile widening. "But that soft spot for your father is…" He hummed as he bit his index finger.

Gastel rolled his eyes. He'd never understand.

THREE

The Usual

Belkin hadn't had an opportunity to leave Parth in several weeks, and as the city faded away behind him, he relaxed into Jore's easy rhythm. After decades of weekly campaigns to assure the security of the Bleck Larin border, being cooped up in the castle stronghold had him stir-crazy. Just the feel of the saddle beneath him was enough to bring a smile to his lips.

Roulin had requested an audience with Belkin, alone, at the stronghold in Korthan. It was an ominous request that he only considered entertaining out of curiosity, bearing in mind the way they'd left their last conversation. It had consisted almost entirely of angry words ripped from the rage Roulin nurtured in his heart that had turned his tongue black with bitterness.

The ride to Korthan was almost always uneventful, and now that the Bleck Larin were at peace with the Shay, there was even less concern of running into trouble. Belkin turned Jore toward the east, in no real hurry to deal with Roulin. He'd enjoy the silence and solitude with his most trusted companion as he worked through the meaning of the summons' words.

Even Jore seemed to know there was something not so savory about the way Roulin had all but ordered his elder brother to Korthan. Before the abdication of Queen Gemma, the death of Raemian Starling, and the peace their father had ordered them to endure, Roulin never would have dared to use such language. Not against the king, and most certainly not against Belkin.

Jore veered hard to the southeast, and eventually, Belkin stopped resisting, letting the horse pick their way across the wilds. The stretches of grassless clay left no place for roots to take. Trees clung together in clusters along the sides of creeks that slithered down from the mountains. The streams brought cold runoff from snow, writing maps across the wilds until they died like suffocating worms after a hard rain.

Like the highlands that split Rhend south of the Middlelend Forest, the wilds had very little game to hunt and soil unsuitable for farming. At least the open expanse was peaceful and pure with the color of autumn leaves and the smell of warm earth and lavender, which thrived along the slips of trees.

As evening approached, Belkin and Jore drew closer to the outskirts of Thandor, a small village nestled tight against the foothills on the north side of the Eastern Pass. It was quaint, no stronghold. Over the years of warring, it'd taken damage to the outer wall from roving bands of Shay, but the residents had always rebuilt quickly.

Belkin steered Jore through the main gate, knowing the exact place he planned to stay. It wasn't his first time through here. If given a choice, he'd find a more permanent residence. The town was quiet, endearing. The homes were modest dwellings made of stone bricks cut from the leftovers used to build the great strongholds of the Bleck Larin cities, quarried from the sides of the mountains that cradled Rhend on the east.

These were hardy people. Not afraid of battle, invaders, or beasts that wandered down from the massifs. They were miners, quarriers, soldiers—honed from the stone they carved and shaped. They took pride in themselves and their craftsmanship, and to Belkin, they represented all that was wholesome about the Bleck Larin culture.

He swung down from Jore, giving the horse a kind nudge to his muzzle before ducking through the rustic door of the inn. He was immediately assaulted with the familiar din of chatter and clinking glasses, and the bitter fragrance of spilled ale. These were the charming vestiges of the establishment simply known as The Aubridge. No one turned to look in his direction. He was just another traveler, and he liked it that way. Anonymity. The reason he wore the same armor as all the other soldiers on the battlefield. And the reason he donned a simple riding cloak and jerkin today. He was a prince disguised as a commoner in a common place. The only distinguisher, the cuff that held his topknot.

The innkeeper knew him on sight, however, and as Belkin sidled up to the bar, the man had already poured him a tankard and placed it in front of him.

"Needing a room, Highness?" Sebinson was always business. He was a simple man, trustworthy and pragmatic.

"Just for the night. I pass through for Korthan."

The innkeeper nodded and disappeared into a room behind the bar. It gave Belkin a moment to glance around at the regulars. They were faces he recognized. All but a small, dark, armored group pressed into their seats with their heads down in the far corner.

When Sebinson returned with a key, Belkin leaned forward. "How long have they been here?"

Sebinson didn't need to ask whom Belkin referred to. "A couple weeks now. They're camped along the south wall. Just pitched their tents and settled in like they intend to stay."

Belkin took several hardy gulps of his ale as he worked through the words, then slid the key across the bar top until it dropped into his other hand.

"Have they been trouble?"

Sebinson shook his head. "Not to us. Though word is they've been stirring things up with the Shay. And I think we all know how your father feels about that."

Belkin took another long draw of his tankard and nodded good evening before turning toward the long staircase that led up to the guest rooms.

"Will you be needin' your usual, Highness?"

Belkin faced the man, giving him a rather perplexed look before a smile crept across his face. He wasn't entirely sure he was in the mood, but things could change before he'd be ready for sleep.

"Please."

Belkin woke with the morning light, lying on his back with the delicate arm of a woman draped over his chest. His "usual" had graced him with her presence the entire night. A pang of guilt faded quickly. He was a man with needs, and she was a woman more than willing to provide them. It wasn't the first time, and it wouldn't be the last he'd pay for her company. There was a reciprocal familiarity between them that was irreplaceable.

He smoothed his hand up her arm to her shoulder, her skin impossibly soft.

"Don't keep your cranky brother waiting on my account." Her teasing voice was full of sleep as she snuggled against him, gliding her fingertips over his stomach. Belkin glanced at her closed eyes, heavy with dark lashes. She smiled, knowing full well that he was looking at her. "You've told me about his temper," she said.

"You make it hard to leave, Venna."

She knew what the feel of her naked form against his skin did to him. She giggled, opening her sultry amber eyes. As difficult as it was to pull away from her lithe body, he needed to leave. Perhaps he'd stop through on his way back. He reluctantly slipped away. Goosebumps rose on his arms against the chilled morning air as he sat on the edge of the bed, building the motivation to gather his clothes from the various locations they'd been deposited the night before.

He could be to Korthan well in advance of the midday meal if he left soon.

Venna's tempting hands crept over his shoulders and around to his chest, fingers meandering down his abdomen, her breasts pressing against his back.

"The Madam will be mad enough with you for staying all night," he said, his voice breathier than he'd intended.

Her lips were like fire on his neck. He closed his eyes, tipping his head back. He begged for more time as her hands traveled lower. She drew a moan from deep within him. *Gods, those hands.*

"She knows whose company I keep."

The soft tendrils of her breath brushed over his skin before she nibbled his earlobe, teasing, torturing. Her fingers left trails of molten fire as they traveled the length of him, muscles tightening under her touch as she traced the lines along his neck and jaw. She ran a hand down his braided hair. Two hundred and eighty-four years of hair. Still rather young for a Bleck Larin. He had many more years before he'd need to abandon these pursuits of pleasure and find a bondmate.

He turned to meet her, her own midnight locks loose around her shoulders, partially concealing her nakedness in an alluring way. She wore a seductive simper, a coy tilt to her long face, slender legs on either side of him. Venna was easily a hundred years younger than him, but old enough to know a great many things he found exceedingly enjoyable. He pushed her down to the bed and followed her lips with his own.

Roulin could wait a little longer.

Belkin arrived at the front gate of the stronghold in Korthan before the midday meal. He didn't mince words, no small talk with the overly friendly usher. He knew where he was going. He found Roulin seated alone in the dining hall, dark circles under his eyes as though he hadn't slept in days. He wore an unadorned black doublet and sat with a single, sad glass of wine resting before him. It was clear this wasn't a friendly visit, or Roulin might have thought of having a second glass ready for his travel-weary brother.

"What kept you, dear Belkin? It's not like you to oversleep." Roulin's tone had an unnecessary bite that Belkin didn't appreciate, but he hoped he hid his frustration behind the mask he'd carefully cultivated since elflinghood. He hadn't seen Roulin since their heated exchange in the strategy room at the castle stronghold. The challenge Roulin had laid down was still thick between them.

"More enjoyable company than what you can provide entertained me into the morning hours." He plopped down across from Roulin, crossing one leg over the other and placing a hand on the top of the table before meeting Roulin's cranky yellow eyes. "I thought you'd be waiting for me on the battlefield?" Sarcasm dripped from every word, but Belkin wanted to eliminate any chance that Roulin thought he might have forgotten their last conversation.

Roulin's disingenuous smile spoke for him. He was still angry, but when wasn't he? He'd been angry for years. Perhaps as far back as the day Belkin had been named high general of their father's army. Most definitely since the day Gastel had been born. For some inexplicable reason, Roulin had always harbored intense animosity toward their younger brother. Gastel was harmless. Incredibly skilled with a blade before the demise of his hands, perhaps dangerously trusted by their father, intelligent enough to get into a fair amount of trouble, but still... harmless. And, at the moment, lost in a war with his own demons.

"The Shay have not backed down. They are not keeping their end of the agreement. You need to fix this..." Roulin slammed a fist on the tabletop for emphasis. "Or I'll fix it."

Roulin seemed to forget that Belkin wasn't their father. Theatrics, especially related to diplomatic matters, weren't something he tolerated. From anyone. He leaned forward with what he hoped was a hint of anger in his eyes.

"If you can't control the border *peacefully*, I'll find someone who can." Belkin's voice was a cool blade of levelheadedness. He rose from his chair and stepped away, turning his back to Roulin before glancing over his shoulder. "If this is the only reason you called me here, I thank you for finally getting me back on my horse."

The legs of Roulin's chair scraped across the stone floor.

"You're a fucking coward. You're just like our pathetic, worthless fraud of a father who likes to play the part of a king."

Rage ripped through Belkin. Not because Roulin had called him a coward. He wasn't so insecure that casual name-calling could break him. No, it was the disrespectful way he spoke of their father.

Mesmal was the king. Yes, the man was soft and terrible at planning, but he was also calm and fair and the most beloved and respected king in Bleck Larin history.

Belkin faced his brother, barely able to suppress the burning anger that boiled in his gut.

"You let your hatred blind you, Roulin." He centered his weight, meeting Roulin's fury with cool confidence. He didn't fear him. There wasn't anyone he truly felt he couldn't beat in one-on-one combat. Not anymore. She was dead, and Gastel was far too intelligent to challenge him. "There was peace once, and there can be peace again. This is the harder path we travel now. The braver one. If you can't wash your hands clean of the blood you've shed—"

"Do you even know what you sound like?" Roulin said, taking a few steps closer to Belkin, his hand dropping to the grip of his sword. "You sound like every other idiot who thinks these pigs deserve our kindness. They've invaded our lands, taken our cities, killed our civilians...for years!"

"Because we've done the same to them. There's anger on both sides. That's the price of war."

Roulin drew his sword. Stupid move. Roulin had never been able to beat Belkin in a duel. The corners of Belkin's lips tugged in amusement. Who was the idiot exactly?

"Settle down, Roulin. You'll hurt yourself."

Roulin thrust forward, a poor attempt at an opening attack, and Belkin easily defended. He let Roulin recover, bringing his blade back to center.

"Brainwashed, every one of you," Roulin spat as he sidestepped, swinging up in an attempt to catch Belkin on his less protected left side, but Belkin had only to lean out of the way and slap Roulin's sword with the flat of his saber to knock him off balance.

Perhaps Roulin hadn't entirely realized what he was doing. Or maybe he thought that the last several weeks cooped up in the castle stronghold had been enough to soften Belkin's reflexes. Either way, it seemed he'd misplaced his senses. Roulin's third attempt was the worst of all, and Belkin spun past Roulin's pathetic swing and elbowed his brother hard enough in the sternum to send him back into the table.

Again, Belkin stood back and let Roulin recover. Any other man who'd have stupidly thought to challenge Belkin would be dead or, at the very least, grievously injured. The blow to Roulin's sternum had thankfully tamed his inflated ego, and he dropped his sword, clutching the edge of the table as he gasped for breath. Belkin brought the tip of his blade level with Roulin's throat, still a couple feet away—no real threat.

"Draw on me again, and you won't be standing afterward."

Their eyes locked and held. Roulin knew what Belkin was capable of; he'd seen it countless times. He also knew Belkin didn't throw around meaningless threats or mince words. And he, sure as the sun rose in the east, wouldn't spare his brother if he felt truly threatened. Belkin was giving him a second chance. His only chance, and he should bless the Elder Gods he was given that.

"I'll refrain from telling our father of your treasonous words, but if I hear them again..." Belkin said.

Roulin's face was an emotionless mask as Belkin lowered his sword to his side. Hopefully he'd tempered Roulin's hatred enough to spare Belkin from having to take more drastic measures.

"Was there anything else you wished to discuss with me?"

Roulin shook his head.

"Good. If I hear that you've sanctioned violence against Shay, you'll see me again far sooner than you'd like." Belkin's glare burned past whatever mask Roulin attempted to wear. His brother swallowed hard and failed to hold his eye contact.

Sword in hand, Belkin left. He could feel Roulin's eyes burning into the back of his head. He purposefully didn't look back, wanting Roulin to know he never feared him. He didn't sheath his weapon until he was back to the stables to retrieve Jore, however, unsure if perhaps Roulin had rallied the guards at the stronghold to his treachery.

Jore nickered, sensing the frustration that rolled off him.

"Sorry, old friend. We aren't staying."

FOUR

Focusing Anger

Gastel stormed through the castle stronghold, his skin itching from the heat of anger building in his stomach. He'd been asked to perform the citizen hearings alone. After he'd trained with Dulanii in the early morning, he'd been thrust into his formal doublet and a pathetic attempt had been made to pull his short hair back from his face. Having been forced to listen to petty grievances and selfish complaints for the better part of the day, his temper was crumbling. He didn't bother knocking before barging into his father's study, finding Mesmal leaning over a leather case as he slipped a stack of old correspondence back into it.

"I wondered when you'd drop in," Mesmal said without looking up. Instead, he buckled the case and set it aside, then picked up a second and shoved another stack of aged letters into it.

"Couldn't you have a servant put these away for you?"

This drew a sharp look from his father. "I could," Mesmal said. "But I could just as easily do it myself."

"And force your son to do what *you* should be doing?" Gastel asked as he rested his worthless hands on the back of the chair he usually occupied.

A sly smile slipped across Mesmal's face before he settled into his mask of indifference. "And spare you the trouble? Have you learned nothing from me?"

Gastel took a deep breath, desperate to calm the fury before it exploded from him in white-hot soulfire. If his father had any idea how close he was to tearing the castle stronghold to the ground, he didn't show it.

"Were there any interesting complaints?" Mesmal closed another case before he plopped down in his own chair and looked up at Gastel. "Anything notable I should be aware of?"

"Perhaps if you'd attended, you wouldn't need to ask."

His father nodded, closing his eyes in thought before he met Gastel's glare and motioned for him to sit.

"I'd rather stand," Gastel spat.

Mesmal tipped his chin up, narrowing his eyes. "What have you hunted me down for this time?"

"I should be training with Kal instead of running your worthless hearings. Wasn't it you who sent for him in the first place? You're wasting his time."

"That can't be your only reason. You've avoided me rather thoroughly since you opened the rift."

Gastel glanced at the dark fireplace and took a deep breath. All of this had seemed so much more grievous a moment ago. His father made his frustrations sound pathetic, selfish. Just like the complaints he'd spent hours listening to.

"Please tell me I'm not to do this again tomorrow?"

Mesmal only stared at him, his face a blank mask.

"Father, I'm not equip—"

"You are far more equipped than you realize."

"Why must I do this? What lesson is there?"

"*Patience.*"

Something snapped deep in Gastel's mind, and he stood up straight, his hands slipping from the leather chair. It took all his energy to hold his tongue. He turned away, ready to remove himself from his father's study as quickly as he could. This room had been such a haven once, a place he could spend hours in candid conversation with the only person he thought he could truly trust. Now? He'd rather be in the dungeons of Tremire, waiting for his execution.

"I'd hoped the hearings would help you control this anger you seem to be cultivating."

Gastel stopped short, turning just enough that he could see his father from the corner of his eye.

"I know you struggle with it and that you don't trust me after everything I failed to share with you." Mesmal's calm mask contrasted with the sadness in his voice.

Gastel's frustration bloomed into a burning rage. How could his father not understand how this whole thing felt like another lie, another omission? He swallowed his angry words, slamming the door behind him as he fled.

Rage still festered like an open wound when Gastel found Kal. By the grace of the Gods alone, he'd been able to contain it beneath his skin, but he knew it was a matter of time.

"I know that look," Kal said, drawing Inara's attention and causing her to lose her sphere of protective soulfire.

"I'm done with my father's games. His lies. I can't...I can't do this anymore." Gastel stopped a few feet from Kal, facing the moors, and swept his hand in an arcing motion. As if ripping Anam from the air, white soulfire exploded around him, no longer able to remain beneath his flesh. Both Kal and Inara took several steps back.

Almost instantly, he realized his error. He hadn't brought his soul stone with him today. He'd stupidly thought he wouldn't need it. Plus, he'd wanted to train as much as possible without it.

He turned to Kal, sending the man back a few more steps. "There must be a way to control this."

"I...I don't know if there is," Kal said, the fear ripe in his voice.

Gastel turned away, his eyes searching the moors for something to glare at, taking deep breaths as he attempted to drag the anger back down into the pit of his stomach, where it couldn't do so much damage.

"Try centering all of your Anam into a ball in front of you." Kal walked around Gastel to stand in front of him, determination fighting the fear still written in the arch of his eyebrows. "Perhaps it's less about controlling your anger and more about focusing it into a single place."

With a deep breath, Gastel pressed soulfire into a ball in front of him, straining to keep it contained in a simple form while the rest of him continued to burn with wispy, white soulflames. He closed his eyes, focusing on the center, coaxing his Anam to a single point in space, forcing the hungry fury smaller and smaller until he could see it in his mind as a solid thing before him.

It was akin to chasing a rabbit on a hunt. The soulfire was sneaky and slipped between the crevices of his concentration, oozing around thoughts of his father's stoic mask, Belkin's unyielding sternness, his own self-loathing.

Slowly, so slowly, his Anam seemed to submit. The roaring of anger faded to whispers. Gastel opened his eyes, finding a ball of soulfire so tightly compressed it was black at the center.

"Now release it."

"At what?" Gastel asked, his voice shaking with the strength needed to contain his power into such a condensed form.

"Anywhere, really. Preferably not at me," Kal said with a slight smirk.

Gastel thrust the fire across the moors, sending it searing through the heather and stripping a massive swath of earth bare. For a long moment, he stared in disbelief at the charred soil and the nubs of burnt bushes, stretching until they touched the horizon.

"How in the Gods' names..." It was Belkin's awed voice.

He turned to meet three pale faces, eyes wide with fear. At some point while Gastel had been focusing on pressing his Anam into the sphere, Belkin had found him. His eldest brother couldn't have been home long, as he was still wearing his riding cloak.

Gastel took a timid step toward Belkin, but exhaustion grabbed hold and yanked him down to one knee. The world spun, even as he tried to steady himself with his hands in the grass. Instead, he fell over and rolled onto his back, no longer able to keep himself upright.

Belkin stood over him, an amused expression plastered across his face. "I assume ending up on the ground isn't ideal."

"Not really," Kal said as he stood across from Belkin, peering down at Gastel as well. "But until he masters focusing his anger, it may be unavoidable."

Belkin glanced at Kal with sharp eyes. "I prefer you refrain from helping my brother kill himself. He does a fine job of that on his own." He looked back to Gastel. "I came to speak with you regarding Roulin, but we can discuss matters once you've...recovered."

Gastel could only blink up at his brother. He needed to figure out how to do more than focus his anger. He needed to learn how to smother it entirely—or he'd be spending a lot of time recovering.

Though still beyond weary, Gastel dragged himself to the strategy room before the evening meal. As he'd assumed, Belkin was there, deep in discussion with Tildimin.

"Ah! Brother." Belkin seemed almost cheerful, which grated against Gastel's exhaustion. "Regent Freya has invited Father to Tremire to discuss further peaceful advancements between our people."

Belkin handed Gastel a letter, the handwriting instantly recognizable from the letters he'd exchanged with the regent. He couldn't read it fast enough. His mind seemed to blur the words together, leaving a mushy softness to his thoughts.

"But first, Roulin." The distinct shift in Belkin's tone drew Gastel's eyes. "It seems the fire of his hatred continues to burn. I may need your and Father's thoughts on how best to snuff it out. He can't just lob a massive ball of Anam across the moors and feel better."

Gastel side-eyed his brother. Thank the Gods Roulin wasn't able to. He could only imagine what their world would be like if Roulin possessed even a smidge of Anam capabilities. He shivered at the thought of Roulin being trained by Kresha...or Rayken!

"At any rate, I can't ask you to postpone your quest any longer," Belkin said, drawing Gastel's full attention. "But I do want you to be aware that I plan to go in Father's place to Tremire."

"Excuse me?" The words burst from Gastel before he could stop them.

"Unless you'd rather go yourself?"

"Why wouldn't Father go?"

Belkin took a deep breath, letting it out slowly as he glanced at Tildimin, who had thus far kept himself tucked against the wall. "He said he felt it would be better if one of us went in his place."

"That's not a good reason."

"He's the king. He doesn't need a good reason," Belkin snapped.

Gastel glared at Belkin, that tickle of frustration igniting in his chest again. There was something else Belkin and his father weren't telling him, but he didn't have the energy to argue. And Belkin was right. Mesmal didn't need a reason. He could send whomever he wanted.

"Fine. But I leave in two days to open the second rift."

Belkin nodded, glancing down at his feet as a muscle feathered in his jaw. There was definitely more Belkin wasn't saying.

Things hadn't gone as well as Roulin would have liked during Belkin's visit. It wasn't so much that he thought he could threaten his eldest brother. No, Belkin was indomitable. Roulin knew where he stood when it came to fighting prowess and sheer strength. However, he'd hoped to get more words in before Belkin shut him down. It was that superiority that would be Belkin's undoing.

Roulin glared at his glass of wine in the dying light of another day. He was several glasses in, lounging in a massive chair in his bedchamber with a letter abandoned in his lap. He'd received news that Belkin was venturing to Tremire on the first official peaceful visit to the Shaylands in thirty-two years. Things were moving again, and soon, Roulin would need to make decisions that would affect not only his future but the future of Rhend.

A soft knock broke him from his thoughts.

"Enter."

The door was silent as it swung in, the familiar sound of Tace's boots slapping the stone floor.

"She was easy enough to find."

Roulin stood, facing Tace, who led a delicate Bleck Larin woman into his bedchamber. Her hands were unbound, but judging by how

Tace's fingers sank into her upper arm, Roulin could assume she was not overly excited to be there.

"Exactly where you said she'd be, at the little place in Thandor."

She was not a warrior, as Roulin had anticipated. She was an escort, a divinely attractive one at that. No wonder Belkin had always returned to her. He grasped her chin, forcing her to look at him, her face calm, sultry. She wore no kohl to accentuate her eyes, no adornments, just a natural beauty that Roulin could fully appreciate. Her dress was plain, modest even.

"It seems Belkin has a taste for simplicity."

A flash of anger crossed her face as she tipped her chin higher, allowing her to look down her nose at Roulin.

Feisty. How delightful. Roulin turned away, his eyes falling to the fire. It would be hard to do what he needed to do. This woman had qualities he hadn't been prepared for. He'd assumed when Tace informed him that Belkin had a mistress, he'd find either a soldier or the typical prostitute bedecked with jewels she couldn't afford, flaunting attributes that tempted her patrons. This woman could pass as gentry.

"Where are you from?"

"I should think that obvious. I was, after all, taken from my home."

Her words were stained with derision. Roulin would pretend it was unhappiness at being taken from her home rather than any disdain for him that he, as of yet, did not deserve.

"I don't remember you from my various times staying with Belkin at The Aubridge."

"Why would you?"

"Are you not paid for the services you provide him?"

She glared, a hot anger simmering in those glorious, amber eyes. "I am."

"Then surely you would have presented yourself to me at some point."

"My company is always reserved for Belkin. That is his agreement with my Madam."

"Exclusivity. He must pay a heavy price for this. I wonder if Mesmal was ever aware of such misuse of royal funds." Roulin approached her again, waving Tace away. "I find a distinct lack of Belkin present here this evening. No need to *reserve* yourself."

The muscles in her shoulders tightened. Fear? Or anticipation? Perhaps some part of her thought she was above entertaining Roulin because she'd shared Belkin's bed? She lifted her chin with confidence, her slender, unadorned neck drawing a flash of heat from deep in Roulin's core. His fingers itched to wrap around it, to hold her in place.

To taste the fruit Belkin had so lovingly harvested.

FIVE

Waking

Struggling to piece together what had happened, she pushed herself to her knees. She knew there was something important she was doing, but like a strange passing dream, the memory of it was just out of reach. A gray-fleshed face, the glare of bright light, an overwhelming sense of terror—emotions, disjointed details, pieces of truth, all gone in an instant.

Her eyes raked across the unending white sand. Had she been here before? It was both foreign and familiar. She stood, her boots sinking into the sand as she fought to take in all the details at once. The rosy sky with occasional creamy tufts of cloud. The smell of hot stone. The gentle breeze that pushed her hair from her face. It was so bright, yet there was no sun. She spun in place, the sameness stretching in all directions until she spotted a massive monolith jutting up from the sand in the distance. Had it been there a moment ago?

Where the dunes met the sky, a figure interrupted the horizon, moving toward her faster than she thought possible. A tall, genderless being with pale-pink flesh, broad shoulders, and long, pointed ears. Perhaps a man? It was hard to say. They wore their silver hair long and loose. Flowing robes disguised any physical attributes other than a slender neck and angular face with crystal-blue eyes. Calm and kind.

"I thought you might have finally come."

Definitely a man. The deep timbre of his voice was like a balm over shadowy scars. Her eyebrows knitted together in confusion. She wasn't even sure where she was; how could this person have known she was coming?

"Who are you?" Her voice was gravelly, unused. Had she ever used it before? Had there ever been a before? How did she even know what words to use? "Who am...I?" There were suddenly hundreds of questions flooding the cracks of her mind.

"You will learn your name." The sharp edges of his face melted into soft kindness. "Among other things."

"What is this place?"

"It is my home. Do you like it?"

What a strange question. She wasn't sure what she liked. She held his pleasant stare, trying to put the words together to answer him.

"My name is Noe-eb."

"Noe-eb," she repeated in a whisper.

He stared at her, unyielding, expectant, as if his name should elicit some slice of a memory. After an impossibly long moment, he reached a hand in her direction. She hesitated. Her lack of trust only made him smile more widely.

"Come then. I have waited long enough for you." Noe-eb turned toward the monolith, and she followed.

SIX

Healing Hands

Gastel sat up, a cry leaving his lips before he could stop it. It was the same nightmare every night since he'd opened the rift. The pain of Anam shredding his insides before he watched her plunge into white fire. The smell of burning flesh as he reached to save her.

Goosebumps bloomed across his arms where the cool night air kissed his sweaty flesh. The last embers from the fire cast angry apparitions over the cracked earth around him—a reminder that he wasn't at the castle stronghold.

"Are you all right?" It was Kalbasen's sleep-thick voice.

Guilt immediately tightened in Gastel's stomach. He hated disrupting his travel companions' precious sleep. When he was in the privacy of his personal quarters, it didn't matter how many times he woke screaming in the night; he only ever inconvenienced himself.

"I'm sorry." He struggled to pull the blanket back over himself with his ruined hands.

"It takes time to heal, especially wounds we can't see." Kal stirred the fire with a log, throwing sparks and catching the flames anew. "It's only a couple of hours before sunrise anyway."

Gastel sat up on his elbows and watched the man. Kal had insisted he and Inara accompany him to the rift. Gastel wondered how much of this was at his father's request. Other than the few sessions of Anam practice before this trek, he hadn't spent much meaningful time with Kal.

The Wielder watched Gastel, his silhouette illuminated by the timid flames. "Hopefully Master Lorilay can help you." Kal finally settled back down where he'd been sleeping between Inara and Dulanii. "I'm sure you'd feel more yourself if you could hold a sword again."

Gastel wasn't so sure. It had taken him weeks to make his way back to the training arena, and even then, only because Dulanii had coaxed him. But there was hungry strength in his muscles. The vicious anger, simmering like lava in his core, had no place on the edge of his blade. Not to mention, he didn't need to hold a sword to use Anam.

No, the only obtainable thing he wanted was information on the rifts: where to find them and whether there was any hope of opening another without incident. Lorilay, the Vail's Eishtala Master, would know something. She'd been bondmates with Gastel's Uncle Dormel, who'd been a powerful Wielder of his mother's time.

Dormel Amfithere had been a member of the Anam Guild, giving his life closing one of the rifts. The guild hadn't realized what damage they were doing to Rhend at the time—the role they were playing in inciting the Sundering. Now that Gastel was more acquainted with the prophecy's confusing, usually contradictory writings, he better understood how they could have made this mistake.

Gastel eased onto his back, glaring up at the ocean of emptiness above him. Stars winked in and out of existence, but it was the vast space that he found comforting. Black and endless. He closed his eyes, the constant push and pull of time sticky around the edges of his consciousness. One moment, it was honey, cloyingly sweet and desperately clinging; the next, it was a raging fire consuming everything.

He tried to push away the anxiety by taking deep, long breaths. The Sundering refused to leave him alone. It was the uncertainty of if, how, when, or why. He squeezed his eyes closed and focused on trying to get another hour or so of rest before his body begged to go through the usual routine, the risk of returning to the nightmare waiting on the cusp of slumber. A pair of ocean-blue eyes forever burning inside his mind.

They arrived at the Vail early the next day. If they were lucky, everyone would still be in training, and it would be easy enough to slip unnoticed to the infirmary and obtain what they needed.

"I honestly never thought I'd return." Inara said.

She'd been quiet since they'd left Parth, speaking so infrequently that Gastel worried she was offended by Dulanii's presence. It was still a new thing for Bleck Larin born within the last thirty years to be around Shay, and Dulanii was a particularly exuberant and excessively friendly Shay at that. Personal space wasn't exactly something he adhered to.

She looked over at Gastel and smiled weakly. "But then again, I never thought I'd leave on my own two feet in the first place." She shrugged, and Gastel realized that her silence may have been entirely related to the same apprehension he felt.

In another time, he would have returned her smile, but all he could do was look up at the great doors that greeted them, frustrated with the entire situation, a guilty finger pointed in his direction. It was his fault they were here.

And it was his fault Raemian was not.

"What did you say they do here again?" Dulanii's eyes wandered along the surface of the stone with a careful hesitation, eyes wide with cautious wonder.

"Most Anam Wielders are trained here." Kal's tone was sharp, his eyes darting to surprisingly empty parapets where there'd been archers positioned the last time Gastel had come. It was clear he felt as Gastel and Inara did. The last thing any of them wanted was to lay eyes upon these doors so soon after the way they'd left.

A biting wind whipped off the Rahven Sea to the north as if they needed reminding of where they were. Gastel struggled to pull the cloak around himself a little tighter. The damn cold was the worst part. There was nothing that could keep it out, no fire hot enough, no blanket thick enough. He shivered and approached the doors, forgetting that he couldn't curl his fingers around the handle as he placed one of his bandaged hands on it. Dulanii stepped forward to help without acknowledging Gastel's potentially embarrassing mistake.

Bless the man; he never said a word of complaint and always seemed to know exactly what Gastel needed. Someday, when he was no longer lost in his own sorrows, he'd thank Dulanii properly. The Shay was, after all, experiencing the same loss he was, but doing it with significantly more grace.

They moved through the halls with purpose, Gastel and Dulanii capable of complete silence from years of battle training. Inara and Kal fell farther behind as they focused on quiet footsteps and failed. It didn't matter. Gastel only needed one person to help him open the slide lock to the infirmary.

"Here." Gastel stood before the door and waited for Dulanii to let him in. The sound of the heavy lock clicking open seemed twice as loud as Gastel remembered.

A rush of fresh, warm air greeted them. Gods, he'd missed this place and its perpetual summer—its promise of life and healing. The vines of leaves were exactly as they'd been before, strung from hundreds of hooks along the rafters and dangling in glorious, living curtains.

"Oh," Dulanii blurted out.

It was a spontaneous reaction, one Gastel completely understood. There was such a contrast between the empty stone walls of the Vail and the comfort that radiated within the infirmary.

"Gastel?" Her voice was like music, but how she knew it was him was puzzling.

Master Lorilay poked her head from the backroom, her wavy, white hair tied in locks around her head. "What in the Gods' names?" She came forward with such joy and love in her eyes that Gastel felt his own beginning to tear up. She took him into a warm embrace before holding him out at arm's length. "What are you doing here?" She took up his hands and looked down with concern at the bandages.

"I've come for your help."

She looked up at him sharply. "I should think so."

He smiled. "Not for my hands. I need a map."

She held his eyes with an immovable question of his sanity.

"A map of the rifts."

"No one should have that knowledge," she said.

He shook his head, the smile fading. "I need to open them. You know I need to open them."

She hesitated, watching his face, waiting for him to say more, then finally giving up and looking down at his ruined hands again.

"Dormel must have had a map," he said, trying to disguise the anguish—the desperation—in his voice, but he wasn't sure he could hide from Lorilay.

"There are maps, but it doesn't look like you had much luck with the first one." She pulled at the bandage of one hand and started unraveling it. What harm would there be in letting her look? Nothing could be done for them now. He should have been brought to her immediately if he'd wanted to save his hands.

She peeled the last of the bandage away, revealing his withered fingers, covered in leathery, scarred skin.

"I lost her." His breath caught in his throat. "She fell into the rift trying to save me from its hunger. I tried to reach for her…"

He hadn't cried since it had happened, but now, under Lorilay's heavy appraisal, he felt hot, wretched tears squeezed from his very soul. So much anguish and hatred toward himself was hidden behind those tears. Guilt that he'd failed, that he should have done more. He let them roll down his cheeks as he stared helplessly into her eyes.

"Oh, Gastel." She wiped his cheeks with her thumbs, then began to unwrap his other hand, turning both of them in her own to look at them from every angle. "I can try to heal these, but I know I won't be entirely successful."

She ran her fingers up his arms to where the scarring ended on his forearms, her eyes snagging on the Starling bracelet he wore. Her fingertips felt strange as they traced across his scarred, numb skin. It took all his strength not to yank them from her grasp.

"It will be excruciating, but I'm willing to try if you are," she said.

He thought to say no, to push her away, to refuse to fix that which he'd destroyed trying to save Raemian. To force himself to have the reminder of what he'd lost for the rest of his life. But he was young; and his life as a Bleck Larin was just starting. He nodded.

Lorilay leaned so she could look back at Dulanii. "You, young man. I'll need your help."

Dulanii stepped forward, determination in his stance. "I'll do what I can."

"I guess that's all that can be asked," she said, a sly wink passing between them.

"This is Dulanii. He's—"

"A dear friend. I can tell." The glimmer of knowing touched the corners of her eyes.

As before, when Gastel had brought Jad to Master Lorilay after a training injury, he felt the Eishtala building and moving across him as she drew it into herself. At first, that was all he could feel—a gentle sigh as the leaves closest to Lorilay withered and died away, dropping from the vines like crumpled parchment. She took his hands in hers and drew him closer so he shared her breath.

"Place your hands on his shoulders, please, Dulanii," she directed, then took in a deep breath, let it out slowly, then looked up at Gastel. "Are you ready?"

He nodded.

The will to live is a strange thing. Something that Gastel had always managed to find. Until he'd opened the first rift. Until he'd felt searing pain rip through his body as his soul was being sucked away. Until he'd watched Raemian's blue eyes disappear into the flames. He knew what it felt like to wish for death. To beg for it. To barter with the Gods. And as the Eishtala magic from Lorilay's fingertips began to boil into his hands, it was there again.

The icy atmosphere of the Vail pushed in around them, leaving their breath solid in the air. Hands tightened on Gastel's shoulders. His initial instinct to pull away threatened to override his better judgment. But he managed to allow himself to ease into Dulanii, pushing against the man's strength.

At first, he thought he could bear the pain. It couldn't be nearly as excruciating as the searing flames he'd plunged his hands into in the first place, could it? He buckled down, clenching his teeth so hard the muscles in his jaw strained. The agony grew. The fiery heat shredded through the palms of his hands, down each finger, clinging to what was left of his nail beds before reversing direction and searing up across his knuckles, the back of his hands, and up his arms. He squeezed his eyes closed but couldn't keep a cry of desperation from escaping his lips.

"Almost, Gastel." He heard Lorilay's voice through the haze of pain. It ebbed as the Eishtala moved across him again, Lorilay taking another deep breath. Just when he was about to open his eyes, the searing heat ignited. This time, it had redoubled, and he pulled away hard. Thank the Elder Gods, Dulanii held him, pushing against him, not allowing him to move away from Lorilay as her hands traveled up the length of his arms to his chest and down to his abdomen. A boiling fever followed until it was gone as suddenly as it started.

Lorilay stepped back, taking heavy, ragged breaths as though she'd just run across the wilds. The warmth of the infirmary air flooded back in a wave of sultry summer breeze.

"They are as good as I can make them." Lorilay's voice was hardly above a whisper.

He hesitated. Gastel wasn't sure he could look, too scared that the thread of hope at having usable hands would be severed by disappointment.

"Move them and see." Lorilay lifted them higher before turning them over, palms up. He could already notice the difference in the way her fingertips felt on his skin.

Timidly at first, he tried to stretch them, feeling his fingers extending for the first time in weeks. There was no pain, no tightness. He looked down and took in a sharp breath.

They were the color of Trove flesh, his stone-gray skin fading to pure white fingertips. Like a burning tree, the trunks of his arms charred from a forest fire and the white branches of his fingers only a gentle breeze away from blowing into oblivion.

"Whoa." Dulanii peeked over his shoulder as Gastel turned his hands over and looked at the backs, stretching his fingers wide.

So strange how the tracks of the scars had vanished, replaced with the same smoothness as before. He couldn't shake the dysmorphic feeling. These were not his hands, though they were the shape they'd always been before opening the rift. How was it he'd been able to accept the scarred, ruined versions better than what he saw now? He curled his fingers back into his palms, half expecting them to crumble to ashes before his eyes, but instead, he was left with two perfect fists.

He met Lorilay's hesitant gaze.

"I'm sorry I couldn't fix them entirely."

He shook his head, and without realizing, he reached and placed one of his restored hands on her shoulder. He had no words, only a smile and eyes filling with tears for a second time. The joy wicking through him was such a strong contrast to how he'd felt when they first arrived—and something he didn't think he'd have been capable of again.

"Now then. A map," Lorilay said with a twinkle of excitement in her eyes.

Before she could retrieve anything for him, Kalbasen and Inara stepped in.

"He knows we're here." Kal's voice was dark with misgiving.

When Gastel turned to face them, he saw genuine fear in both their faces.

Lorilay put her hands on her hips. "He can come and take you if he wants, but not until we're done here." She gave them each a reassuring look before ducking into the backroom.

"Gastel!" Inara reached for one of his hands, and he didn't pull away as much as he wanted to. She held it, running her fingers over his knuckles, sending a shiver up his arm. "Your hands!"

He swallowed hard as Kal leaned to get a better look.

"She did what she could." He lifted his hand from her grasp and flexed his fingers before reaching for his sword and curling them one by one around the grip.

Gods.

He was sure Kal saw it in his expression, the way his shoulders relaxed at the comfort of a sword in his hand. Before anyone could say more, however, Master Lorilay ducked back out with a handful of scrolls and what looked like a journal of some sort.

"This is all I have," she said as Dulanii stepped forward to take them for him.

He paused when Gastel was able to clutch the items himself, a warm nod passing between them.

"One of the Bleck Larin territories, one of the Shaylands, and one of the Trove holds, with notes." She held the journal up before him, and her eyes grew misty. "I found this after you left. I wish I'd found it before. This was Niminea's."

His heart twisted at the mention of his mother. So much he hadn't known about her until recently. He'd hungrily absorbed every ounce of information, trying desperately to build a picture of the woman she must have been. To know the woman who'd protected him long after her death.

He'd come to the Vail with hopes of obtaining a map that would guide them to what was left of the rifts, but here in this woman's blessed hands was so very, very much more. Dare he say he felt a pang of hope as he took the journal from Lorilay—*took the journal with his own hand*—curling his fingers around the leather binding. Strange how this place always seemed to change him in one way or another.

"We need to go." Kal's concerned tone brought Gastel from his ruminations.

They had to address the growing problem outside the infirmary. Master Rayken would likely not let them casually leave the Vail. Gastel could see in Kal's eyes that he agreed.

"One more thing," Gastel said, turning to Lorilay. "Was my mother the Great Wielder?"

She tipped her chin up, searching his face for something, letting the moment drag out between them.

"I believe she was. And I believe her strength now lives in you." She put a hand to his face, a gentle touch—caring, loving. "Go...before Rayken comes for you. He has ways of keeping those he wants. And now that he knows what you're capable of..."

Gastel looked back to Kal and Inara, their expressions hard.

There was a good chance it was time for Gastel to test his freshly healed hands.

SEVEN

Fairy Tales

Belkin couldn't remember the last time he'd stepped foot in the City of Tremire. He'd been close when he'd helped recover his stupid, selfish youngest brother from the clutches of the disgraced queen of the Shay. Now, Belkin was here for a much different reason—a formal visit in his father's place. He might have brought Gastel, but his brother was eager to start his quest. Part of some prophetic fairy tale about rifts and the Sundering.

Belkin found the entire affair overly dramatic. The state of Rhend was fragile. It needed solid decision-making, a firm hand, and confident rulers. His father was a mess, so Belkin had taken the reins on many things for the time being, hoping to instill some sense of strength and consistency. Regent Freya was inexperienced, though she'd thus far proven herself to be capable, intelligent, and possessing more than enough wherewithal to learn quickly. It was still a process. One that needed vigilant guidance.

Jore nickered as the small group split the tide of people on the busy road into the heart of the city. Belkin and his small retainer of four elite fighters waded their way to the Court of Tremire, bedecked in Bleck Larin red attire. He'd left Tildimin at his father's side. Between his right-hand man and the walls of the castle stronghold, Belkin was moderately satisfied his father would be protected should someone wish him ill.

His fighters were less about protection than they were about a show of strength. They were but five Bleck Larin in a sea of Shay within the capital city only weeks after an anticlimactic conclusion to a thirty-year-long war. Belkin knew where he stood with these people. There was a thin membrane of peace between the elven races but still a river of boiling tension—an undercurrent of anger that Belkin saw in the eyes of these civilians. Some of them had surely lost loved ones on the end of his sword.

Still, the city was charming. The great ironwood trees were a true testament to the power of nature, beautifully manipulated into magnificent works of living art. Eishtala magic was an amazing skill. One that Belkin had found himself coveting more than once in his life. He'd seen Tremire before when he'd been much younger. Seeing it now through more mature eyes, he was able to better appreciate the craftsmanship.

He gave Jore a pat as they approached the steps to the Court of Tremire, exchanging knowing glances with his guards before his eyes fell again to the great doors. They were swinging open before his feet touched the ground. He wasn't entirely sure what to expect. He'd never met Freya in person, only through correspondence, but knowing that Raemian Starling had personally selected the woman gave him confidence. Where once he'd despised the Shay knight, he'd seen her in a new light, learning that much like Gastel, Raemian had never been given all of the information about her heritage. Thinking of her now left an empty place in his gut. If she hadn't fallen into the rift, it might have been her greeting him instead of Freya.

He mounted the steps without hesitation, followed by his men at arms. As they entered the court, he found himself face-to-face with a man he'd not spoken with in person for better than six decades. A man he'd struggled to keep one step ahead of. He clenched his jaw and bit his tongue. Bowrhem, legion of the Shay army, was not his enemy. Not anymore.

"Your Highness." The legion was beyond gracious, bowing deeply, his eyes never leaving Belkin's. Of course, the Shay would be leery of the Bleck Larin prince, heir to the throne—high general of the king's army. Good. Caution was important. One was more likely to question one's actions if there was caution. Belkin bowed in return and glanced up to the woman who sat upon an ornate ironwood throne, a single royal guard to her left.

She had gentle blue eyes and a warm expression. She seemed small for a Shay woman, thinner perhaps. It was clear she was not a warrior. She was dressed modestly enough, which was more than what could've been said for Gemma. The last time he'd seen the former queen, she'd worn a rather unforgettable neckline so low it did little to conceal her perfect breasts.

"Your Excellency." Belkin stepped forward and bowed to Regent Freya as the woman stood and approached him. Freya took the few steps down, letting him tower over her, seeming unintimidated by Belkin's height.

Her fiery red hair was loose and wild, and he couldn't help but compare her to Raemian. She looked as though she could have been the girl's relative. Her shaymarks were soft, not as vibrant as others. They danced tight along the sides of her temples, wrapping around her forehead and down her neck. He didn't always find Shay women attractive, but she was gorgeous—voluptuous in a way that caused him to stand a little straighter. No tattoos, no outlandish diadems on her head as Gemma may have worn. Just calm intelligence wrapped in petal-pink softness.

"Prince Belkin, it's a pleasure to finally meet you. You look so much like your brother."

"Even with his terrible hair?" Belkin couldn't help himself. Gastel's hair was atrocious. Thankfully, his sarcastic humor was well-received.

"You could be twins," she said with a smirk.

She could cause him a lot of trouble. Not as timid and reserved as Raemian but just as quick-witted and significantly more confident. She let the moment hang for a split second longer than necessary, commanding the conversation.

He smoothed his hair back with his hand as Freya's eyes lingered on his topknot, his age prominently displayed and twisted around an intricate dragon wing cuff that held the bulk of his hair.

"I don't want to keep you longer than I have to, but we have much to discuss and a banquet in your honor to attend." She gestured to the side. "Shall we?"

She directed him to a small room off to the side of the dais that contained a long table with several chairs all neatly pushed in. A number of manuscripts were strewn about, some left open or with places clearly marked. Bowrhem and the royal guard followed them in but stood like sentinels at the door. Bowrhem, with his hands crossed behind his back, and the guard with her long white hair pulled into a braided ponytail. Belkin was certain this was more for Bowrhem's comfort than Freya's.

"How much experience do you have with the prophecy of the Elder Gods? Do you have knowledge of the Sundering?"

He took a sharp breath, desperate to control the frustration that creased his brow. He'd not come all this way to discuss the same nonsense that Gastel was traversing the whole of Rhend for. But he caught himself before rolling his eyes. This woman wouldn't waste his time any more than she'd waste her own. He owed it to them both to at least hear what she had to say.

"Gastel has mentioned it a fair amount in recent weeks, and I read about it when I was an elfling a good many years ago. But it has always seemed like nothing more than a fairy tale."

She shook her head slowly. "Unfortunately, I can assure you it's not a fairy tale." Her eyes flowed across the stacks of books that littered the table. "We have...a large problem. There's a strange warping to the atmosphere over the Wastelands. It was discovered a few weeks ago, but I needed to see it with my own eyes. It's as if the world just ends." She let her gaze settle on Belkin, her blue eyes swimming with guarded anxiety.

"The magic of the Wastelands holds?" Belkin's mind turned her words inside out, not sure what to do with the information. But if something had damaged the magic that maintained the barrier of the Wastelands, there would be nothing to keep humans from crossing other than the fear of the blades of elves on the other side. And they had enough problems right now. They didn't need to add humans to the list.

"So far as I can tell, yes. But without knowing exactly what's happening..."

He looked down at the manuscripts. "And you think this is related to the prophecy?"

"I believe it's related to the Sundering, yes." She took a deep breath. "The last time I saw your brother, he was doing the only thing we knew to try. He opened a rift." She looked down at her hands, hints of sorrow touching the corners of her eyes, and her lips turned down ever so slightly. "When our world lost its Rae of sunshine."

Belkin nodded. It was an apt way of describing her. "Gastel quests as we speak to find more of these rifts, but what if opening them does nothing?"

She shook her head slowly, mournful. "We don't know. My advisor, Tor, and I have scoured countless manuscripts, old documents, anything we can get our hands on, but there is nothing that speaks of what the Sundering actually is. Of what will actually *happen*. Only that our world as we know it will cease to exist."

"So, there's room to believe it could still exist, only not as it currently is."

"That's not what's implied."

There was a heavy silence between them, not uncomfortable, but it forced Belkin to turn his thoughts inward. Something he didn't tend to do in the presence of strangers.

Why exactly had this woman called him here? To give him the news of their world's impending doom in person? Or was there some other goal in mind? There was a fair amount of speculation surrounding the writings of the prophecy. It seemed rather clear to him now that it was the unknown that was so terrifying.

"Now then, with the impending end of our world looming heavy over our heads," Belkin's attention snapped back with Freya's words, "the other reason I needed to speak with you in person is more...delicate. While I am more than at ease standing in a room with a Bleck Larin, I fear most Shay do not share my level of comfort." Freya took a few steps closer to Belkin, punctuating her words with actions, further proving she had no fear of him.

Of course, this woman would have been given information on Belkin, his reputation, and his battle exploits. These didn't seem to trouble her. Her fearlessness was endearing, but he could hear Bowrhem shift his weight behind them.

"There have been a number of incidents between Shay and Bleck Larin near Dormshire and the Eastern Pass. More along the Old Road and within the Middlelend Forest. I assure you I've pulled back all scouting missions and replaced them with peacekeeping efforts, but Bowrhem's forces can't be everywhere all at once, and there are many who have yet to accept the end of the fighting." She looked down at the sword on Belkin's hip, her eyes lingering there for longer than they should have. "What else can be done to make our people more amicable toward one another? Do you have any thoughts? Has your father made similar efforts to stave off continued fighting?"

Belkin glanced over his shoulder at Bowrhem, a moment of apprehension tightening his chest. Two war generals from opposing armies in the same room now forced to be allies. He felt he was being baited for information.

He shook his worries away. This was the cost of peace. Sharing strategy rather than shrouding it in secrecy.

"We have pulled forces back with strict instructions for defensive measures, only if needed. My father sent out an edict across the Bleck Larin territories. Any senseless killing of Shay is punishable by death. The king has given no leniency in this."

"And what about you? I know of your reputation." Again, her eyes touched his sword. "You take no prisoners."

Belkin was somewhat taken aback by Freya's directness, but he couldn't help cocking his head to the side. She was a brave woman—clever, likable.

"I am no longer at war and, therefore, would no longer have a need to take prisoners." He lifted a single eyebrow as a smug smile crossed his face.

"I've been given information that one of the Bleck Larin that has led these skirmishes looks much like you. Same cuff holding his topknot. Approximately your age."

A moment of hot rage ignited the pit of his stomach, but he schooled his emotions, locking his expression into a mask of indifference. Would Roulin go so far as to shirk his father's edict? Especially after the words he'd had with him in Korthan? He closed his eyes a moment, taking a deep, soothing breath, channeling his father's stoic calm and dousing the fire that burned behind his eyes.

"I have not drawn my sword against a Shay since the queen was removed from her throne."

"Abdicated. Rae was careful in this."

Belkin smiled, showing his teeth. The woman was delightfully candid and completely unintimidated by him. It was refreshing.

"Raemian Starling was careful in most things." He took a deep breath through his nose, letting it out long and slow, relaxing his shoulders, his smile fading. "Three decades of war is not so long when we have thousands of years of peaceful history between our people."

He tried to keep his tone friendly, doing his best to restrain the condescension that may have otherwise punctuated his words had he been speaking to one of his brothers.

"However, it has only been a handful of weeks. You cannot ask your people to forget their prejudice overnight. You can only provide them with the guidance and encouragement they need to make the right decisions." He looked down at the inlaid wooden floor at his feet. Allowed himself to ponder the countless Shay that had walked over its smooth surface. The Bleck Larin that had graced it in the peaceful times of old.

Freya took another step closer, drawing Belkin's attention. He could see the conviction in those blue eyes. The determination. Her age was a mystery, but he could confidently say she was as old if not older than he. She'd known the same times of peace and had seen what hatred could do to their world. He sensed she probably had her own harrowing story of how the war had devastated her family.

"Forgive me if I'm rushing the process." She lifted her chin to look at him more severely, and he dipped his own in response. Even at her short stature, she could probably be intimidating. Belkin wasn't in the slightest, but he could see where others might. Confidence was a strange thing. "Rae gave me a task, and I shall succeed in it."

"Your Excellency, you have already been quite successful. I'd like to think my hopefully amicable presence within the Court of Tremire illustrates this."

She walked back to the head of the table, her fingers barely missing the stacks of books as she passed.

"I'll not rest in my efforts toward ensuring a conflict-free Rhend until I am satisfied that she would be pleased with our results," Freya said.

Belkin nodded. Even for him, scrubbing the preconceptions of the Shay that had polluted his mind over the last three decades was difficult. Difficult, but not impossible.

He caught and held Freya's easy gaze, silently thanking Raemian Starling. She'd saved his life on the Old Road. She'd been a catalyst in ending more than thirty years of war. And she'd given him the perfect Shay to usher in this new era.

Banquet of Monsters

Belkin wasn't one for gatherings. Royal events were tedious, but he understood the necessity of decorum. So it was with thinly veiled boredom that he sat to Freya's right and allowed platters piled high with all manner of roasted delectables to be placed before him. As long as his tankard was full, he'd gladly indulge the regent's insistence on making the public appearance.

"Tell me, Belkin. How does a prince find himself commanding the king's army?" Freya had peppered him with questions all day, but this one seemed the most out of place for her. She wasn't interested in war—was clearly more concerned with the preservation of lives. But then again, perhaps this wasn't about war. Perhaps this was a means for her to understand what would drive him to take such a dangerous responsibility. A way for her to get to know who he was under the rigid confidence he wore.

"For the Bleck Larin, serving the king in battle is an honor. The high general is often a member of the royal family." He smiled as he thought of the day he'd taken the responsibility from an elder cousin. "Not the heir to the throne—I am the first in that regard—but my father felt I was adequately suited."

He kept his eyes directed toward the Shay dancing and moving through the strange open-air dining area created with twisted trees that had been planted to surround the vast space. Older Shay elflings brought food and filled cups of wine for diners lounging at gorgeously crafted tables manipulated by Eishtala from living branches. Musicians shuffled through as they played, wooing couples with songs and filling the hall with music that wafted into the canopy.

"Didn't he fear putting you in danger?"

"He has two other sons." He glanced at her from the corner of his eye. She hadn't picked up on his dark sarcasm. He'd given the wrong impression of his gentle, calm father. "I requested the position, and after much consideration...and arguing...he relented."

She eased back into her chair, the muscles in her neck still tight. "I lost my son in the Culling. I can't imagine having sent him to war."

It took a moment for her words to sink in. Belkin snapped his head in her direction. If she had a son killed in the Culling...

She met his eyes with a firmness he wasn't expecting. "Your father is brave."

He held her gaze, unsure why she'd give him this family history. Was there some hidden importance to him knowing she'd built a family with a Bleck Larin? He broke first and looked out at the sea of Shay that surrounded them. Whatever her reason, it would stay a mystery.

A disruption started at the back of the dining hall with a sound Belkin was well acquainted with. Blades rasping from scabbards sliced through the din of music and conversation. He perked up, and from his peripheral, he could see that Bowrhem had done the same.

There were a good number of shouts. A handful of royal guards stepped forward to cull the ruckus, but a few heavily armored Shay broke through the revelers and stepped out into the area reserved for dancing. With a vengeful sneer, the forwardmost Shay pointed his sword at Belkin with a war cry that sliced through the music, drawing screams from some of the nearest guests.

Bowrhem was on his feet, motioning for additional guards to step in, but they were finding it hard to cut through the other guests fast enough. The three Shay parted the dancers as they advanced on the head table.

Belkin didn't move. He knew their target, and he invited them— welcomed them. Knowing full well, if they made it to him, they wouldn't make it any farther.

"Belkin..." Freya's hand on his shoulder reminded him that he was not in battle armor but rather a formal doublet, soft and useless. Her concern was endearing but misplaced.

At the last possible second, Belkin reacted. With perfect precision, he rose from his seat as he drew his saber to block the solid cleave intended for his neck. The sound of swords clanging together brought the last of the banquet guests to silence.

Belkin was taller than the Shay but easily a foot and a half narrower. Without his plate armor, he must have looked pathetic in comparison to this muscly meathead. It didn't matter what he looked like, though. He met the Shay's glare with emotionless confidence. The Shay didn't need words to punctuate the error he'd made. Belkin was quite certain it burned in his eyes.

He slammed the Shay's sword away, throwing the man against the others being restrained behind him. The Shay was strong, like most, but

Belkin was built on decades of combat and training, proof that the size of the man did little to dictate his strength.

He let the guards rip the sword from the Shay's hand to pull his arms behind his back. Belkin sheathed his saber as he watched. He wouldn't draw blood. Not here. Even if his own blood boiled with the need for it. Instead, he'd settle for eliminating any doubt about his ability to conduct himself. This was what peace meant. He'd let these warriors' public actions be dealt with by the laws of the Shay people.

He returned to his seat, propping his elbows on the tabletop and folding his hands before his face, touching his lips to his knuckles. He could feel Freya's eyes on him, but his own followed the royal guards dragging the handful of miscreants from the dining hall. Once they'd left, he risked glancing over at her and found Bowrhem's glare as well.

"Have I offended?" Belkin asked.

Freya shook her head and sat back down, glancing out over the disheveled crowd of Shay, who were doing their best to put the party back together. Servants collected broken dishes and cleaned spilled beverages. Musicians tuned their instruments.

"No. I...I thought..."

He couldn't help the grin spreading across his face. He looked to Bowrhem, who slowly sat back down as well, without letting his eyes leave Belkin. Wearing an amused smirk, Belkin finished Freya's sentence: "That I'd kill him?" With a raised eyebrow, he met her wide-eyed stare.

"I...I'm sorry." Her cheeks turned a brilliant shade of pink, which only intensified Belkin's humor regarding the situation. He was entertained that these people thought him such a monster that he would hack down a Shay at a peace banquet. Even though, in actuality, he would have been defending himself. He let his gaze traverse the hall again, touching some of the other startled faces still turned in his direction, their eyes resting quite menacingly on his own.

His smile faded.

They saw a monster. A dark, evil Bleck Larin. Some of them would be more like Freya, but he was certain most would be disappointed that the attempt on his life had failed. Belkin glanced over his shoulder at his sentinels behind him. His fighters had likely not moved a muscle, fully aware of Belkin's capabilities. One Shay? Even if all three had made it the full distance, he'd have been fine. There had been no reason to intervene, and he silently thanked them for their confidence.

Roulin hated the ripeness of the lower district of Raggethan. It was downright pungent. But he understood the importance of the anonymity it gave him for this particular visit to the city. Tace had taken every precaution setting up this rendezvous, and the last thing Roulin needed was for word to filter back to his father. Or Belkin. Especially Belkin. He needed allies before he was ready to deal with his elder brother.

With his hood pulled over his topknot, he stalked through the streets, weaving between nefarious hoodlums and beggars until he found the correct building. The corners were decorated with roughly carved depictions of mermaids painted purple with silver eyes. He ducked down the alley, counting the doors as inconspicuously as possible until he came to the eighth door. Three knocks, a pause, and three more. Then he waited.

He was about to turn around when the door cracked open, and a blade of light sliced into the alley and across his boots.

A throat cleared before a gravelly voice spoke: "For the age of power..."

"...and the dawn of blood," Roulin finished.

The door swung wide, revealing a man in black armor, the lower half of his face covered with a mask—one of Tace's men.

"This way, Highness. They're waiting for you."

The halls of the building were a maze of crudely constructed timber. Gaps between boards revealed the contents of rooms on the other side. Movement from one such room caught Roulin's eye—a woman brushing long, black hair. She was young, perhaps only as old as Gastel. As they passed, she glanced over her shoulder, following him with her eyes before she finally turned away and continued to brush.

Down another hall, the lower half of the walls were constructed of uneven stone blocks—perhaps the leftovers of buildings in Raggethan. The top half were thankfully solid walls, plastered and painted a warm cream color. There were braziers hung from the wall outside the few doors they passed.

At the end of the hall, Roulin's guide directed him into a room lit by a roaring fire in a massive fireplace on the far side. A table had been positioned in the middle with chairs crowded around. All of them were occupied except for one at the end, closest to the fire.

Roulin gave the guide a curt bow as the man stepped out and closed the door behind him. He took a breath. There was no turning back now. He walked with impetus toward the empty chair, plopping down and crossing one leg over the other. He took a long draw from the glass of wine that had been set at his place as he made eye contact with each of the elves that sat at the table: members of the council, a handful of lesser generals, representatives of powerful families in Raggethan. Their posture straightened as his eyes fell upon them. He might have liked more, but he would start with these ten.

"First of all, I assume that if you're here, you've made the critical decision that the crown no longer shares the will of the Bleck Larin people." Roulin took another sip of wine, drawing the moment long, waiting for every set of eyes to firmly affix to him.

This was the moment that would either make the next phase of his planning possible or would destroy everything he'd set in motion over the last sixty years. Long before he'd hired Tace to capture the Starling girl or started negotiations with Gemma. Before the whore Wielder Niminea had brainwashed Mesmal. As far back as the moment his father had chosen to name Belkin the high general—his heir apparent— like an idiot.

That was supposed to be Roulin's responsibility. *His only responsibility.* He was otherwise a useless second son, a disposable heir waiting for his elder brother to be killed in battle. Once his father was dead, Belkin would wear the crown, and Roulin would be nothing unless he would be so lucky as to have his new king bestow him with some meaningless title, like advisor or high councilor.

It was now or never.

"Second, I assume you're ready to do something about it."

Rayken

own the first hall, there was no one. Gastel glanced back at Kal and Inara, finding the same confusion in their eyes. At this time of day, there should have been a buzz of activity coming from the training hall. Perhaps the students had been released early, but that seemed unlikely. Gastel had only spent a few torturous days within these cold walls, but he hadn't heard of training being cut short.

He placed his hand on his blade, savoring how wonderful it felt to curl his fingers around the grip before looking over at Dulanii. The Shay seemed in heavy concentration, his hand in the exact same position, ready to draw should the need arise.

As they turned down the main hall, Master Rayken was waiting. He stood alone before the great doors of the Vail with simmering yellow eyes. Those same eyes that had challenged Gastel when he'd left this forsaken place, down to the same scowl on his lips and likely the same wretched hatred in his heart. One by one, his glare fell on each of them, finally coming to rest on Gastel.

"Back so soon, Princeling?" The condescension in the old Wielder's words oozed from his puckered lips with vicious spite. "We've missed your spoiled attitude and desecrated hair."

Gastel's face grew hot. He hated this man almost as much as he hated Gemma. He clenched his teeth, trying to control the rage building in his gut.

"Come to steal my healer, have you?"

Gastel took a deep breath and let it out slowly, releasing the tension between his shoulders. It wasn't worth all this. He wondered if Rayken even understood what he was doing and whom he was hurting. Whether he knew how monstrous it was to keep an Eishtala Master and a Svet Priest captive within the Vail or drive his students to essentially kill one another.

"I've stolen nothing from you." Gastel let his hand fall from his sword. He hated the man, but he pitied him more. Rayken had nothing but the Vail and his sadistic teachings. Gastel had larger things to deal with. "I needed to speak with Lorilay, nothing more."

He took several steps toward Rayken, his heart pounding so hard he wondered if anyone else could hear it. The vision of the old Wielder reducing him to a charred mound of flesh on the floor swam through his mind.

"We wish to leave in peace."

"Like you did last time when you dragged half my students with you?"

"Rayken—"

"I could have taught you how to control your power. You could have been my protégé!" The old Wielder took a step forward to emphasize his words, a wild light glimmering in his eyes. "Such raw potential wasted. Like your mother, who thought it was more honorable to join the guild than help me establish the next generation of extraordinary Wielders."

Gastel shook his head. He'd heard enough. He hadn't come to rehash what might have been if he'd stayed and finished his training. Or to be berated for what his mother had done. He had enough of her past mistakes to deal with.

"I know someone else who had such high hopes for you," Rayken said, a hint of bitter sarcasm in his voice. He flipped his hand, and a woman stepped from an adjacent room. Her familiar swagger and skin-tight robes should have given away her identity immediately, but her face ...It didn't match Gastel's memory. Effrin Kresha was indiscernible.

"Gods, Kresha," Kal said. His voice withered with shock. "What happened?"

She didn't respond; she just stood between them and Rayken. The entire left side of her face had been melted off. All that was left was a scarred, sunken hole her eye had once occupied and an empty hollow for a cheek. Gastel's stomach lurched. The scent of singed flesh was such an overpowering memory. Why had Kresha not been taken to Lorilay to be healed?

"Effrin Kresha has missed you. She wears her failure well, don't you think? A badge of honor."

Bile rose in his throat as Gastel realized she'd not been *allowed* to be healed. Rayken had punished Kresha for failing to break him when he'd trained at the Vail. And now the horror of that punishment was real, terrible, and all his fault—hatred burned in her remaining eye.

"What's the matter, Highness? Feeling guilty?" A murderous twinkle in Rayken's eyes sealed his fate.

Where Gastel would have left the man alive, a horrible longing to inflict every punishment, every lesson this man had subjected his students to simmered to the surface of Gastel's being. He pushed away a flash of guilt for having such thoughts. Perhaps later, he could reflect on how monstrous they were, but right now, he could only focus on the monster in front of him.

"Kresha, I'm sorry." Gastel pried his eyes from Rayken and met her bitter glare. "I never...*never* would have let him do this to you." He spoke as calmly as he could, but his heart was racing.

He would have said more, but he was pushed to the side by Kal, who threw a stone-shattering blast, meeting a sneak attack Kresha had been preparing. She barely managed to deflect Kal's Anam into the wall, sending shards of granite across the hall.

"I'll handle Kresha," Kal said, stepping forward, already building his next attack as Kresha scrambled to her feet.

Dulanii yanked Gastel back by his arm, his terrified eyes unable to rip away from Rayken as the old Wielder built a massive soulfire blade taller than any elf. "Get behind me—"

"This isn't your fight, Dulanii."

"Your fight is my fight."

Gastel met the Shay's glare, shaking his head. "No. Anam is—"

A feral growl ripped from Rayken's lips as he lunged. In a smooth motion, Gastel elbowed Dulanii out of the way, drawing his sword and igniting it with soulfire. He had only enough time to react, slicing up to block the Anam blade as it cut a path through the frigid air. What he hadn't expected was for his sword to slice completely through Rayken's Anam, shredding it into wispy threads of fire.

Rayken was fast to recover, lashing out with bolts of soulflame that Gastel was hard-pressed to dodge. They slammed into the floor and the wall, barely missing Kal, who fought his own battle of Anam spears with Kresha. Hunks of stone were shaved away as Gastel twisted and dodged another bolt. He sliced through another, splitting it in half and sending one part into the wall inches from Inara and the other to the rafters overhead.

Gastel glanced over his shoulder, finding Inara holding a sphere of protection around herself and Dulanii, the two of them huddling behind him. Thank the Elder Gods. He'd never forgive himself if something happened to either of them in the chaos.

With every step closer to Rayken, Gastel grew more confident. The old Wielder was slowing. Gastel had taken an entirely defensive stance thus far, letting Rayken exhaust his life force. Two more bolts, two more loud crashes as Gastel deflected them away.

"I should have known you'd be a coward," Rayken said, deep loathing tainting his already gravelly voice. "Attack me."

"I will when I need to," Gastel said through clenched teeth. The weaving and dodging were starting to wear him down, sweat beading on his brow.

Rayken twisted his hands in front of him as they ignited with soulflame before he pressed it into a tiny, brilliant ball so small it was almost black at the center. Gastel knew how powerful that ball of Anam could be. He'd left a swath through the moors from something that had looked very similar. It was the manifestation of pure rage compressed into a sphere of destruction.

He risked glancing at Kal from the corner of his eye. The Wielder had managed to restrain Kresha with strange rope-like structures that wrapped around her and held her arms against her body.

"Use your power, boy."

His attention snapped back to Rayken.

"I will when I need—"

The concentrated ball of Anam exploded out from the old Wielder, and Gastel could do little more than block with a feeble shield he'd hastily tore from his very soul. The force of the blast was strong enough that it blew Gastel off his feet, ripping his sword from his grip.

For a moment, he couldn't remember where he was. Somewhere cold with high ceilings. Smoke wafted up from his clothes in mesmerizing, delicate tendrils. The sulfuric scent of hot iron burned his nostrils. He tried to wrap his mind around what had just happened, but a ringing in his ears made his thoughts seem translucent and slippery.

Rayken's cruel laughter, thick with anger, echoed through the hall. When Gastel lifted his head, he found the old Wielder hunched over, his shoulders shaking from the effort it took to stand.

Gastel's eyes met Kal's. He'd been thrown against the wall and was trying to scrape himself together. Kresha was doing the same; both seemed to sway as they stood.

Dulanii dragged Gastel to his feet. "He'll kill you if you don't—"

"Where's my sword?" Gastel asked as he glanced around, his head still swimming.

"Forget your sword; use your Anam."

Gastel pushed Dulanii back. "Just get Inara out of here."

"Such power..." Every breath rasped past Rayken's brittle lips. "And you waste it...on swords and stupidity." The old Wielder stood straight, holding up his hands and starting to draw his Anam out again.

Gastel scrambled to find his broadsword, knowing full well he couldn't clear his head quickly enough to create one of the defensive shields Kal had been helping him master. There wasn't time; Rayken swung a sickle-shaped blade of Anam over his shoulder.

He couldn't dodge; he couldn't think. Gastel could only react, releasing raw, unfocused Anam from beneath his skin and lobbing it toward Rayken's sickle. It shredded the old Wielder's Anam and continued toward Rayken. But it never hit its mark. Instead, it blasted through Kresha's chest, flames exploding out the other side and sending Rayken sprawling on his back.

A soul-wrenching screech ripped from her throat as smoke began to erupt from every inch of Kresha's flesh. Soulfire belched from cracks in her skin and lapped around her body until she was nothing but a pillar of white flames. Her outstretched arms shook in agony as she burned, her screams stretching thin until they faded into a whispery gasp.

Gastel couldn't look away, no matter how much he begged himself to do so. Not until Kresha crumpled into a pile of ash at his feet, the last wisps of soulfire twisting away as if they'd never existed.

Inara whimpered behind him and then emptied her stomach. A part of Gastel might have done the same, but a soul-searing fury was building within him that tamped down any other emotions he might have had. It hadn't registered that Dulanii was dragging Inara back down the hall the other way or that Kal was a stone statue beside him, eyes unable to move from the brittle corpse of Effrin Kresha.

Or that Rayken had managed to drag himself to his feet.

"Finally!" Rayken said as he started to spin soulfire around himself, sending lassos wide into rings of fire. They twisted and encased Gastel, creating a prison, the Anam crossing over itself as it solidified. "Finally, you embrace it!"

There was no remorse for the woman who'd just saved his life in the old Wielder's voice. His face was a grotesque mask of elation that only fed the wrath building in Gastel's chest.

"I want all of it, boy! Give me everything you have!"

The dome Rayken had created roared with a thickness that made Gastel's teeth set. He growled with rage. He would not be imprisoned. Not here, not ever.

He caught sight of his sword, but it was too far away to reach. He needed a new idea. A new technique. What better time to learn than when the cage of soulfire began to shrink around him.

The air grew thin. If he didn't do something soon, he'd suffocate before he burned to death. He wasn't particularly interested in either option. Crouching to give himself a little more space, he twisted a thread of soulflame from one hand to the other, drawing it out into a whip. Unsure if he had enough room to do what he wanted, he took the deepest breath he could of the dwindling air as he focused his rage on the Anam at his fingertips.

"Gastel!" Kal's urgent voice sounded muffled.

"Stay back." He hoped Kal could hear him over the roar of the dome slowly shrinking in on him.

There was a splintering blast, drawing Gastel's attention from his concentration in time to see Kal scrambling out of the way of falling debris.

"Stupid boy." Rayken's voice sounded as though he were nearly within reaching distance. *Good.* Gastel needed him as close as possible.

He snapped the soulflame whip in the direction of Rayken's voice, slicing through the cage as it twisted. Sparks showered down on him, leaving tiny holes in the shoulders of his tunic. Rayken's cry of alarm was all Gastel needed. He yanked and felt the weight of the man coming toward him. A puff of smoke and white flames later, Gastel shared the space in the dome with the old Wielder, his robes steaming from passing through, his arm seared black where Gastel's whip was twined.

Seconds. He needed seconds, but he didn't know if he had them. As he released the whip and grabbed for his dagger, the soulfire around them shattered, leaving him and Rayken hunched over in the center of the hall. He pressed the blade against Rayken's Adam's apple, glaring into the old Wielder's hateful eyes.

Gastel would have loved to give a grand speech, something about teaching hate and horror, but the words were gone. In their place was only disgust, putrid rage that festered under his skin. It was so dirty, so wrong, and so delicious. Gastel released his soul, igniting himself and his dagger; the flesh at Rayken's throat blistered and cracked before turning black.

"Just like your mother."

They'd be Rayken's last words. Gastel sliced deep, hitting vertebrae at the back of the man's neck. The flaming blade had cauterized the wound as it sank through flesh and muscle, leaving the old Wielder's mouth gaping open, his eyes wide. Gastel pushed him away, and he fell to his knees, one hand catching the floor, the other reaching for his throat, the last of his breaths nothing but wretched gurgling.

It was a slow death as he suffocated and slumped to the side, the light in his eyes fading. And Gastel stood over him, fury still boiling in his blood, watching with beautiful, morbid pleasure—so much satisfaction in seeing this man reduced to a pile of lifeless flesh.

He turned, meeting Kal's wide eyes.

"Gods."

Gods indeed. What monster had Gastel become?

The monster that Rayken wanted him to be.

He yanked on his Anam, trying to draw it back into himself, but was unsuccessful and was thankful he'd had the forethought to bring his mother's soul stone just in case. He pulled the precious pendant from his pocket and slipped it over his neck, instantly dousing the soulfire from his flesh.

Gastel should have felt the familiar exhaustion that clung to his bones after using so much of his life force, but he didn't. He felt electric with power, exhilarated, and ready to let the fury and white flames loose, destroying everything in sight. It was so much louder than it had ever been before, fighting against the gentle calm of his mother's soul. He swallowed the new fear bubbling up in his stomach.

Fear of himself.

As the chill of the Vail washed back through the hall, Dulanii and Inara rounded the corner with Lorilay at their heels. The Eishtala Master's eyes moved from Rayken's still form to Gastel, growing wider as she realized what had happened.

"What…" Lorilay took several hesitant steps closer, clutching Inara's trembling arm before her eyes went to the pile of ashes that had once been Kresha. "What have you done?"

Gastel watched the moment wash over her. Her expression hardened as her eyes met his again. He'd chosen violence. He should have let Rayken tire himself instead of attacking back and cutting his throat.

"Go. *Now*." Lorilay's tone was stern, unyielding. As cold as the Vail itself.

Kal took Lorilay's arm as the Eishtala Master tried to push past. "Rayken wouldn't let us leave in peace. Gastel tried—"

"There are ways other than violence." Her eyes burned with anger as they touched Gastel. "This place has built so many monsters."

Dulanii stepped between him and Lorilay. "Aren't those who do nothing just as much to blame as those who would try and fail to do things the peaceful way?" An undercurrent of resentment stained Dulanii's otherwise cheerful voice. "There's not a monstrous bone in this man's body."

Lorilay held Dulanii's glare, finally softening until she looked away from the devastation in the hall.

"Go. And don't come back here, Highness." Lorilay glanced at the mound that had been Kresha before she shook her head. "The Svet Master can resurrect Rayken."

Gastel's eyes stung with a vicious mix of shame and anger. He straightened and turned to the door, hoping the others would follow because he wasn't able to speak.

TEN

Seeing

S he stood against a terrifying backdrop at the monolith's edge, eyes closed, breathing slowly, deliberately. Strangeness moved around her, but she dared not speak. Not yet. She'd made this mistake before, and Noe-eb had chastised her. The last thing she wanted was to anger him again. Not when he was doing so much to teach her.

"Feel it move through you, around you, into you." He took another breath, deeper this time.

She could feel it, but she could feel other things, too. The hot breeze that ripped at her clothes. The hunger that nagged at the pit of her stomach. She hadn't eaten since she'd woken up in this strange place. She felt apprehension every time she tried to take the strangeness into herself. It left her feeling exhilarated and terribly exposed at once.

She clutched at the bottom of her jerkin and pulled hard. She did this often enough; she wondered if she'd always done it. She didn't even know her own name, much less her idiosyncrasies. Who she was and why she was here. And when she would have answers to her questions. And why was Noe-eb helping her? And—

"Clear your mind." His tone was clipped—sharper than usual.

Could he read her thoughts? Could he see she was distracted? He could have eliminated all of it by answering the one question that burned on her tongue.

"It doesn't matter who you were. It only matters who you will be." It wasn't until he opened his eyes and glared at her that she realized her error.

Noe-eb knew exactly who she was. This was a test that she'd need to pass before he would tell her.

She closed her eyes again, clenching her jaw as she tried to clear her mind. Without sight, her other senses seemed to heighten. The crisp slapping of Noe-eb's robes as the wind yanked at them. The sharp smell of heat from the sand. The faintest taste of sweetness as the sourceless light began to dim with the promise of twilight.

"The first step to learning who you are is to clear your mind." Noe-eb's soft slippers scuffing along the stone to the opening where stairs descended into the depths of the monolith.

She didn't follow. Instead, she turned away, facing the expanse of white sand, taking a deep breath through her nose. Smelling the world, feeling the space around her. Seeing it in her mind as she had with her eyes.

She let her mind free, her questions exploding over the edges of her consciousness. Like spilled blood, they oozed out, pouring down into the same dark stairwell where Noe-eb had just retreated, flowing over the edge of the monolith and plunging to the sand below.

With invisible fingers, she tried to grasp anything and everything. It wasn't much, and it had the viscosity of smoke, but she pulled at something, slowly drawing it back and into her nostrils as she had the rest of this world. She held it in her lungs a little longer than usual before exhaling it out in a burst of power.

Her eyes popped open. A raw laugh ripped from her lips. She hadn't expected any response, any change in the world around her, but something had been there, and she'd moved it.

With her mind!

Noe-eb emerged in a mad rush. "What did you do?" His tone was both accusatory and curious, but she turned to face him, shaking her head.

"I...I don't know. I felt it. I gathered it up and pulled."

"What did you feel?" Noe-eb took another step toward her.

"I don't know...everything. The wind, the sand, the sky. Everything." The light was fading fast. She stepped away from the cliff's edge, her heart still racing from whatever it was she'd done. "What was that?"

"Eishtala."

The word was strange as it rolled around in her mind—heavy on her tongue. Hot. She couldn't repeat it. She should know what it was, this strange force. Noe-eb smiled and held out his hand, lanky fingers cradling a circle of silver metal, its surface polished and etched with intricate vines that laced around what looked like a bird in flight. It was beautiful.

"Take it. It's yours. A gift for your hard work today. A piece of your past."

She held the cool silver band in her hands, then pressed it against her chest. It was a precious sliver of that which she craved more than air or sleep or food.

"Come. You must eat." She followed with confidence, his tone having changed to one of tenderness.

She knew he'd bring her back here. That she'd do as he asked. He held all the answers, and she wanted them. More and more, with each passing moment, she wanted them.

Imitation

Belkin excused himself from the banquet as soon as it was polite to do so. He had a lot to think through and wasn't interested in doing his thinking in public. He bid his guards good night after they were led to a cluster of dwellings deep in the eastern residential section of Tremire, far from the court and the open-air gathering hall.

A mild evening turned into a cool night. He'd pushed the shutters open to let in the breeze and the rhythmic sound of insects tapping out the chorus of twilight. He needed the chill to keep his mind sharp a little longer.

Roulin. How was he going to deal with Roulin? He would need to address the problem with his father, but he'd first need to assure Freya that things were being handled, even if he wasn't entirely sure how or when. It was clear Roulin was no longer interested in upholding the edicts of their father. Not that this surprised Belkin...but what *did* surprise him was that Roulin had chosen to do it so publicly.

A soft knock brought Belkin's head up. He crossed the sitting area, only vaguely considering that the person on the other side of the door might not be friendly. He wasn't dressed for company. He'd already removed his blades and formal doublet and wore nothing but pants and a shirt with sleeves rolled to his elbows.

Freya's gentle grin met him on the other side. Unexpected. It was late, and when he'd left her, she'd been retiring for the night. All the resplendence of her banquet attire had been sloughed off, replaced with a casual red tunic that nearly matched her hair color. The simplicity gave her a beauty that he couldn't help but appreciate, letting his eyes slip down the length of her. Appreciation she noticed and returned, her gaze falling to the open laces of his shirt.

"Pardon my interruption, Highness." She tipped her head to the side. "If you're in no mood for company, this can certainly wait until tomorrow."

Belkin stepped to the side, letting her enter before he closed the door behind her, a momentary concern at being with the woman alone—no Bowrhem to watch over her, no guard in sight. After seeing how heavily protected she usually was, he hoped this wasn't some elaborate scheme to put him in a compromising situation. The peace between their people was still very tender.

Her steps were calculated, cautious. She seated herself on one of the raised futons and folded her hands in her lap, following him with her eyes as he joined her.

"Late for a casual conversation." He kept his tone soft. "You have my curiosity piqued, Excellency."

"As you said. Casual conversation. Please, call me Freya."

Belkin's eyebrows raised. "In that case, Freya, my undivided attention is yours."

She smiled, her eyes two drops of ocean depths. "I have a personal question to ask."

Belkin nodded for her to continue, trying his best not to rush her, but at the same time, he burned to know what could have brought her before him at this hour.

She hesitated as if ripping the words from her soul. He could see the anguish on her face as she pulled them forward. "My bondmate...He ..."

Belkin was unable to predict where she might be headed with this topic. It was clear from her comment at the banquet about her son that she'd at least loved a Bleck Larin enough to have a family with one.

"You likely knew him." The color had drained from her face.

"Please, if this pains you—"

"It's fine...I mean, it does pain me, but..." She closed her eyes and collected herself. "He was close with your brother." She finally opened her eyes again. "In constant communication with him, actually. Before Gemma took things too far."

Belkin tipped his head, furrowing his brow. Roulin hadn't been close with anyone that Belkin was aware of, and least of all, a Bleck Larin bonded to a Shay. Roulin's frustration with the Shay had started in advance of the conflict between their people. Or so it had seemed.

"I'm sorry if this seems strange. Edrist was a courier. Not an ambassador, per se, but he was always traveling between our kingdoms." She studied her hands as she spoke. "I'm not sure why Roulin seemed so attached to him, but he trusted no one else with his correspondence, and Roulin seemed to have a lot flowing back and forth before the Culling."

Belkin swallowed hard, turning over her words and trying to figure out exactly what they meant and why they were important.

"Is Roulin behind these attacks on the Shay?"

The cold truth of what she was asking washed over Belkin. She likely already knew the answer. She wanted to know the same thing Belkin was trying to figure out. *Why* was Roulin behind them?

He looked away, which was as good as saying yes. Part of him was not ready to admit that Roulin could be so stupid. Being hotheaded was one thing. This was treason.

"I'm not certain." Belkin met her glare. "Though in the essence of fostering trust between us, I will say this." Belkin lowered his chin, directing all his attention at the woman who seemed to ease away from his heavy glare. "When I have proof, he will be punished for his actions in whatever way my father deems appropriate." He felt the power of his own words wrapping around him. "If that means the ultimate price, it shall be paid. But I must have irrefutable evidence to accuse a prince of treason."

She blinked a few times before glancing down at the open laces of Belkin's shirt. "Thank you, Highness."

"Please, Freya, call me Belkin."

"I appreciate your candor more than you know." She glanced at the door, squinting her eyes in annoyance. "There's so much seriousness surrounding us these days. It's nice to just talk with someone."

There was something immeasurably humble about her words that he couldn't ignore. "Bowrhem keeps an eye on you for your safety, I'm sure."

Her glare snapped back to Belkin, frustration scrunching her eyebrows in an adorable way. "He's a chore."

Belkin smirked. "In this, I can only agree."

She chuckled. "I'm sure you do. He was certain your father sent you to kill me."

"He should know my father better than that." Belkin scoffed.

"Thirty years of war has hardened him."

Belkin nodded, trying to smooth the emotions from his face. He was sure he'd already failed at being the stoic Bleck Larin. Something about this woman broke down his walls in a delightful way. "Thirty years of war will harden anyone."

"You don't have to defend him, you know," she said with a smile.

"I'm not. I'm defending myself."

Freya's eyes grew round for a moment, the smile slipping from her lips. "You remind me of Edrist." Her eyes mapped Belkin's shoulders before returning to his gaze. "Hard exterior. A mask of indifference." She took a deep breath, her gaze intensifying. "He let battle training dictate so much of his life."

"True of most Bleck Larin fighters, I'm afraid." Belkin couldn't help the left side of his lips from turning up.

"I found the softness beneath his rigid exterior." Her eyes seemed to sear into Belkin, seeing all of him. "I could find yours."

The smirk slipped from Belkin's lips.

She stood, her face turning a brilliant shade of pink. "I…" Her shoulders were stiff. "I…I'll go."

But Belkin stopped her; he was on his feet lightning fast, his hand taking hold of her forearm tighter than he'd intended. He was at a loss for words, not entirely sure why he'd stopped her in the first place.

Her eyes were wide with shock. "I overstepped, Highness. I'm sorry."

"No." He left the word jagged and open for her to wonder if he refused her apology. Instead, he closed the distance between them, taking hold of her chin and tipping her face up to his.

There was no fear in her eyes as he eased closer, leaving hardly enough space for the cool breeze to pass between them.

"What did you actually come here for, Freya?"

She opened her mouth to speak and closed it again, her gaze slipping to his lips. It wasn't the first time a Shay woman had found him attractive. The hard lines of Bleck Larin were so very different from the muscled burliness of the Shay.

He let his fingers trail down her arm, her skin agonizingly soft. One of her hands wandered over the plains of his chest, drawing a ribbon of longing from his depths. They were careful hands. Gentle.

She tipped her head back, and he leaned forward, following the muscles of her neck with his lips, drawing a soft moan from her. The sound pulled him from the moment, and he leaned away from her, every muscle in his body tense as he searched her eyes.

Gods, this was not what he'd intended—and certainly not appropriate. He'd lost himself in a moment of weakness, in the eyes of a beautiful woman. He hated how this felt like he was taking advantage of his status—a prince over a regent—whether her attraction was earnest or she tried to bait him into something he might regret. Yet the way her eyes saw every part of him was so similar to...

He yanked away from her as the thought dragged across his mind like a dagger across his throat. *Raemian.*

She reminded him of Raemian.

The knowing look in her eyes. The slightest upturn of her nose. The way she tried to hide behind a mask and failed.

Her face burned an even brighter shade of magenta. "I'm...so sorry. I shouldn't have—"

"Not entirely your fault. But we can't." He ran a hand over his hair, smoothing it back to his topknot. "This isn't—"

"Appropriate. I know. Forgive me, Belkin." She backed away, tucking her hair behind her ears as she moved toward the door. "I let my emotions get the better of me."

"We both did." His words were like a thousand nails through his heart. Whether Freya noticed or not...Gods, he hoped she hadn't. His embarrassment was already unbearable. He found Freya an imitation of whom he truly desired. He pined for a dead woman who never belonged to him in the first place.

Simple Plans

Gastel couldn't help but smile. Dulanii's desperate attempt to make sense of the map of the Bleck Larin territories was immensely entertaining. The Shay kept turning it this way and that, trying to orient himself.

"Put you in the world, and you know exactly where to go. Give you a map, and you're completely lost." He spun the map and pointed. "We're here."

Dulanii gave him a cold look before he softened, making a strange, scrunched face as he tried not to laugh at himself. "This was always…" Dulanii paused mid-sentence, unable to continue.

"I know," Gastel said.

Saying her name was hard for both of them. Gastel clenched his jaw. He wasn't the only one who felt it. Dulanii suffered with him. He'd known her longer, more history, more life with her. The love that

Dulanii and Raemian had shared was different, but it had still been love and, honestly, far stronger.

Gastel tucked the emptiness away for another time. Right now, they needed to focus on finding the Gods forsaken Anam rift.

The four of them had found temporary lodging in Thandor at a quiet inn on the edge of the village. They'd spent just enough time to get their bearings, rest, and enjoyment of the fruits of civilization a little longer before plunging into the wilderness.

Kal rose from the comfortable chair he'd been occupying; his eyes moved along the map to the location marked as a rift of Anam. Jaw clenching and unclenching, Kal finally looked up with brutal, open honesty in his countenance.

"Opening the first rift nearly killed you, and you have immense power. Untamed, raw power the likes of which I've never seen." Kal absentmindedly ran a hand over his hair, smoothing it back toward his topknot like Belkin always did. "You said it yourself: it tempered your Anam. How do you know it won't kill you this time?"

"I don't. But this has to be done."

Kal rolled his eyes and stepped away, hands on his hips and head cast down toward his feet as he paced. "What *do* you know?" He gave Gastel a bitter smile. "You could be solidifying our doom by opening them."

It wasn't the first time they'd argued over the rifts. The Sundering was open to too much interpretation. The prophecy had been shrouded in convoluted texts and flowery exposition, making its proper transla-tion difficult. Not to mention conflicting descriptions of what it would actually entail. It seemed every copy was different.

Gastel remembered discussing some of the discrepancies with Freya and Tor as he waited among the Aequus while Raemian put herself in devastating danger to stop the war. He'd had too much time since then to dwell on the information further.

"There can't be harm in opening one rift for each magic to hold the balance. I'll open a Svet rift after this one."

"If you live through opening this one," Kal spat.

Gastel was the one turning away this time. It was impossible to make him see. He'd promised to do this. To undo the imbalance his mother had unwittingly helped create.

He bit the inside of his cheeks to keep from yelling. Arguing wouldn't help. He wished Raemian were with them. She'd have already been able to explain everything with enough clarity and conviction that no one would have argued.

"I appreciate your concern, Kal, I do. But I'm going to open this rift."

He gave Kal the full force of his glare, every ounce of confidence and certainty he possessed in that look. It had the effect he'd hoped for. Kal eased away, plopping himself into the same chair he'd previously occupied.

After a long moment, Gastel looked back down at the map, spreading his fingers over the curved parchment. He couldn't help but trace the outlines of his Trove-white hands with his eyes. That dysmorphic feeling that they were not his own still haunted him. But they moved when he commanded them. They held his sword when he drew it. They did everything he needed them to do.

"It's dangerous for Dulanii, even with this tentative peace," Kal said.

Gastel gave the man a firm look. "Is that honestly your concern? Or is there another reason you'd rather not travel with him?" He met Kal's glare once again, wondering if Kal had been uncomfortable traveling with a Shay this whole time.

"We're not exactly inconspicuous," he finally replied.

Dulanii cleared his throat, drawing their attention. "Perhaps I should stay behind if Kal's concerned. I would hate to put anyone in danger with my presence."

Gastel was shaking his head before Dulanii had finished. "I need you with me."

Surely Dulanii understood? Gastel needed him. It was selfish, but he refused to go without him. He had to ensure no harm came to the man. Not after all Dulanii had done for him—all Dulanii had lost. Gastel could not guarantee his safety several leagues away. Plus, he'd grown immensely fond of him. Leaving Dulanii behind was not an option. Not for Gastel.

A strange smile spread across the Shay's face, warm and knowing. His cheeks burned with that delightful blush all Shay seemed to possess. Gastel pressed his lips together before looking back at the map. No, the only one in any real danger was himself, and he liked it that way.

A soft knock at the door brought Dulanii around the table to answer it, but Gastel stopped him with a sharp look. They were, after all, in a Bleck Larin town, and even with the precarious peace terms established, Gastel felt a current of concern for the Shay's safety.

Gastel pulled the door open for Inara to enter, her timid eyes passing between Gastel and Kal before falling to Dulanii, as they always seemed to. Her cheeks brightened before she looked away. Gastel knew that look. The eyes of a shy young woman surrounded by confident, mature men—and Dulanii's frustrating distaste for fabric covering his upper half.

"When do we leave since you're set on throwing yourself into this?" Kal said, his voice dripping with derision.

"As early as tomorrow if everyone is ready."

"The only person who needs to be ready is you." It was clear Kal was still irritated.

Dulanii distracted himself by refolding the same shirt for a fourth time. Why he'd packed a shirt was a mystery. Gastel had never seen him wear one. Inara appeared to be forcing herself to focus on something other than the three men, her cheeks turning more violet by the second.

A stomach grumbled loudly enough to draw a raised eyebrow from Dulanii.

"We'd be better off making decisions with full stomachs," Gastel said.

Desperately trying to put his own worries aside, he hoped he'd given his friends the time they needed to recover from what had happened at the Vail. He'd ripped Kal and Inara from their home, then thrown them back in long enough for Gastel to kill a fellow student and the man they'd respected as their master. That couldn't be easy for them. He hoped they knew this whole quest wasn't a frivolous whim but for the better of Rhend. Based on Kal's resistance, though, he wasn't so sure.

The four of them made their way down to the inn's common area, where the innkeeper was more than happy to take their money for some food. They picked a table out of the way, but eyes followed them from all directions, causing the hair on Gastel's neck to stand on end. He didn't like the attention they received traveling with a Shay. His hair likely garnered a fair amount of its own curiosity as well.

After they'd seated themselves, Dulanii leaned toward Gastel, nudging him with his shoulder. "The crew at the back, in all black."

He knew to whom Dulanii referred. He'd noticed them on the way in. They were hard to miss with their coordinating attire.

"They've been in here every time we've been here," Dulanii said under his breath.

"Perhaps they keep the same schedule?"

"Just strange that they're *always* here. Same schedule or not."

Gastel glanced at Dulanii from the corner of his eye. "Maybe they have nothing else to do with themselves but gawk at a Shay."

"They aren't staring at me."

Gastel couldn't help but glance over at the black-clad crew, causing multiple members to look away quickly.

"Always a good sign when the locals can't stop staring," Kal said as he leaned forward.

There was a shuffling under the table before Kal and Dulanii shared a long glance.

"Sorry…" Dulanii visibly struggled to find the right words.

"Not used to such long legs on an elf?" Kal said with a wink, drawing rosiness out on Dulanii's cheeks.

As the food was set before each of them, Kal still gazed at Dulanii, who seemed to find his hands more interesting than the rest of the inn. Gastel had been mistaken. Kal didn't dislike Dulanii. Quite the opposite. There was curiosity there. A need to learn more about these strange elves, the Shay.

Gastel couldn't help but smile as he brought a bite to his mouth.

They left early the next morning. Gastel was antsy to be done with the second rift and on their way to the third and hopefully the final one he'd need to open. A tingle of anticipation simmered under his flesh, drawing a strange yearning across his arms. Yearning for white flames to smother him in glorious, burning Anam, both terrifying and exhilarating.

The rolling hills made for rough hiking, especially for Inara. She wasn't used to walking for leagues on end up and down inclines, over jutting outcroppings, and along ledges. Their pace was dreadfully slow for it, which didn't help Gastel's anxiety. He'd never speak of it. He would hate to embarrass her. She was young and a Wielder. She didn't need the same physical stamina. Even Kal struggled at times with the pace, and Gastel and Dulanii would slow to let them catch up.

As they dove farther into the wilderness, Gastel grew more comfortable letting his thoughts wander. He was reminded more than once of his treks through the Middlelend Forest, but this place was distinctly different. The trees were shorter and twisted into chaotic, angry shapes as they struggled to find places to grow in the cracks between granite slopes and rocks. The craggy path left sections of land completely barren, like jagged scars in the earth itself. Scruffy bushes clung to cliffsides, sharing meager soil with wispy clumps of grass.

Water seemed precious. They found plenty of dry riverbeds that looked as though they hadn't seen rain in months. Eventually, they found a stream that meandered between the same cracks as the trees. They followed it until it grew into a pool large enough to refill their waterskins.

Thankfully, the sun kept them warm, but when they made camp, Gastel scooted closer to the fire. Inara was bundled with her blanket and Dulanii's unused cloak.

"Strange forest," Dulanii said as they settled in for the night. He'd managed to kill a couple of lanky rabbits with massive ears. It didn't provide much meat, but Gastel learned Dulanii was a far better wilderness cook than he could ever hope to be.

"Rumor has it these lands are rarely traveled. That monsters keep the treasures of the mountains protected." Kal gave Dulanii a wide grin as the Shay's eyes grew round.

"Fairy tales," Inara whispered through chattering teeth.

Dulanii looked between them before he glared over at Gastel. "Tell me there aren't monsters here."

Gastel knew the stories. They were told to elflings to keep them from climbing much higher than the foothills. He leaned back onto the palms of his hands.

"I've heard the stories." Gastel bit his lower lip as Dulanii shook his head and stood. "Scary stories told to elflings, Dulanii. They aren't real."

"You're both a couple of monsters yourselves," he said as he sat next to Inara, wrapping an arm around the girl to keep her warm. "Inara is the only reasonable one here."

Gastel couldn't deny that Dulanii was probably right. The biggest monsters here were themselves.

On the second day, the forest changed. The soil was soft under their feet, and the trees grew closer together. Their twisted trunks looked more like wraiths with hands outstretched to the sky, scarcely dressed in scraggly needles instead of leaves.

Gastel could sense a change in Dulanii's demeanor. He'd hurry ahead, then double back, all the while keeping eyes on the trees around them. After an hour of this, Gastel pulled him aside while the two of them were ahead of the others.

"What troubles you?"

Dulanii leaned in and whispered, "We're being followed. There's at least four, maybe more. I assume Bleck Larin. And I think we can assume their reason for tracking us."

"How far back?"

Dulanii's eyes roamed the forest, catching and narrowing on a handful of unseen objects before he looked back at Kal and Inara. "Too close."

Gastel nodded.

He fell back, and Dulanii led at a much slower pace, sandwiching the Wielders between them on the path. The silence was deafening. Tension built in his shoulders. Not even the gentle sound of birdsong broke their forced quiet.

The hair stood up on the back of Gastel's neck, and his hand dropped to his sword hilt. He turned at the softest sound of a blade being slid from its scabbard.

THIRTEEN

Fading

She woke with the remnants of a dream on the edge of her mind. Cool, gray skin, amber eyes, raven hair in a messy mop around his face. Something about him was familiar, but his name would not come to her no matter how hard she tried to remember. And the longer she was awake, the further it slipped from her grasp, fading like her hope of ever knowing who she was or why she was in this place.

"He is your balance." Noe-eb's voice yanked her from her half-asleep thoughts. Balance? That word held weight.

Noe-eb stood against the wall, his gaze never wavering from her. He could see her dreams, her thoughts, everything. She already knew this, but it troubled her to be so firmly reminded that she had no privacy.

She pulled herself from bed, ignoring him as she stretched in the darkness and willed her weary legs to put one foot in front of the other until she ascended the stairs to the top of the monolith.

It was early. The pink sky had yet to illuminate. She sat cross-legged, shoulders back, hands resting on her knees. Noe-eb called it meditation. He wanted her to clear her mind—to recall how she'd moved the magic before. To push and pull the forces she'd manipulated. He called it Eishtala. And as she tried to remember the feeling she'd experienced, she realized it wasn't so much a feeling as a desperation.

The longer she was in this place without knowing who she was—who *he* was—the more likely she'd never recover those memories. Some sense that she needed to do something, go somewhere, help some-one—and soon—was overwhelming. Even now, as she tried to calm her thoughts and smooth her breathing, the urgency poured into her. There was something important she was meant to do.

She closed her eyes and imagined the flow of the wind. To see its weight as it moved over her skin. To hold its viscous form in her hands like the white sands that spread to the horizon. But like the sand, it slipped through her fingers and twisted away, taking any hope of know-ing the name of the man who owned those eyes with it.

The Wyvern King

Gastel drew his blade in time to slap away the broadsword swinging at his head and drove it to the ground. He stepped onto the Bleck Larin's hand, drawing a grunt of pain from the man.

He was in familiar black armor, his face concealed behind a mask. Nothing but burning amber eyes peeked from under a hood. Gastel grabbed the man by the collar, yanking him up and pressing his blade to his throat.

"Who are you?"

The man stared in silence as fury grew in Gastel's chest like a ball of soulflame. Inara cried out; the sharp pang of steel met steel, but Gastel couldn't risk looking. The weight of his dagger eased from where it was sheathed on his waist. Before his assailant could stab him with his own knife, he sliced his sword across the man's throat.

The smell of blood instantly drew dark memories from the depths of Gastel's mind. Blue eyes. Pink flesh. The first man he'd ever killed. Kresha's burning form. Rayken's brittle gurgling as he suffocated.

The black-clad elf sank to the earth in a heap of leather. Before Gastel could dwell on it, he swung in time to block a blow meant for Kal's neck. It was all happening so fast—a nightmare cut into fragments. This Bleck Larin was taller and much thinner than the others. She fought with her hood down; her braid looped several times at the end of her topknot. She had age and experience and put Gastel on the defensive almost immediately.

He hesitated. Only blocking, not attacking, desperate to push from his mind how easy it'd been for him to kill again.

"What do you want with us?" he asked between clenched teeth.

Her eyes narrowed, reducing to two blazing slits across her face. A snarl moved her lips beneath her mask.

"You travel with a Shay pig. That makes you no better than a pig yourself."

She threw all her strength into every swing, and Gastel wondered how long she could fight with such voracity.

"The king has called for peace."

"Mesmal is not my king. I answer only to the Wyvern King," she hissed. "He will sit upon the Bleck Larin throne soon enough."

"Wyvern King?" His backside slammed into the trunk of a tree, pressing the breath from his lungs in a rush. She pinned him there, her blade crossed with his mere inches from his throat.

"The true heir."

A shiver rippled up Gastel's spine. Did she speak of Belkin? Roulin? Some other unnamed Bleck Larin who would lay claim to the throne after centuries under Mesmal's rule? Countless questions flooded through him as he held her aloft, their eyes locked in murderous rage.

The sound of Inara's warning yelp and more blades colliding brought Gastel to his senses. He couldn't defend himself indefinitely and feared the others needed his assistance more than he needed to spare himself from killing another elf. He set his teeth and took a deep breath, reaching for the edges of his Anam.

"He will have your head to decorate his throne room, *Highness*."

Confirmation that she knew exactly who he was.

He let his apprehensions go, exploding forward with a rage he'd held in for far too long. She stumbled back but managed to keep her footing, the narrowed slits of her eyes growing wide. If she knew who he was, she should have known what he was capable of.

He took two confident steps, letting soulflame ignite his blade before swinging over his right shoulder, leaving a trail of white fire in its wake. They exchanged blows as she backed away with terror in her eyes. Her strikes weakened, and her recovery slowed until he felt his blade hit bone. Her sword clattered at their feet, and she clutched her arm; a cauterized stump remained where her hand had been.

Her shoulders rose with each breath as she tipped her chin up. "He said you were soft. That you couldn't kill a soul."

Roulin.

"Tell your Wyvern King he was mistaken." Gastel yanked his Anam back into himself, and it responded for the first time, extinguishing the soulfire from his sword. "When you see him on the Great Sheol."

It was terrifying how easily his broadsword sank into flesh, plunging into her chest. Blood poured from her mouth, choking her as her lungs filled. With the same ease, he drew the blade out from between her ribs as he'd seen Belkin do on the Old Road. A revolting satisfaction filled him as he watched her take her last breath and slump to the ground.

This is war, Brother. Welcome to the battlefield.

Belkin's words vibrated through him, sending a wave of something rich and hot into his core. He snapped his head up, searching for Dulanii's white hair. What he found were two additional dead Bleck Larin, two terrified Wielders, and one Shay leaning against a tree.

Inara's eyes were wild. If she hugged Kal any tighter, she might crack his ribs.

"It's done, Inara. It's okay," Dulanii said as he moved to extract her from Kal's torso and examined her for any injuries. He stooped to one knee, looking up at her as he checked her neck and face—such a paternal thing, tipping her head from side to side. "You're safe now."

Gastel wiped his broadsword on the dead woman's pants and sheathed it before retrieving his dagger from beside his first assailant.

"Gods. The two of you are..." Kal's voice shook as he looked between them, his eyes finally holding on Dulanii. "That was incredible."

Dulanii winked up at Kal. "I noticed them earlier, so we were ready."

"Excuse me, *what*?" Inara's words rushed out of her in a broken, sharp squeal.

Dulanii bent over in a hard laugh, drawing an exasperated frown from Inara, who balled her fists at her side.

"That was truly terrifying. Why would you—"

"We'd hoped they'd leave us alone," Gastel said before she could continue. "Perhaps the incident with Rayken has given you the wrong impression, but I, for one, don't exactly enjoy killing people." Gastel smirked. "I can't speak for Dulanii, though. Killing Bleck Larin isn't exactly new to him."

Inara and Kal looked at the Shay simutaneously with wide eyes.

"Hey, now," Dulanii said, giving Gastel an incredulous look. "I'm reformed, I promise."

The two Wielders stared at the Shay for another moment before Kal squeezed his eyes closed to clear his mind. He turned to Gastel.

"What did the woman say about a Wyvern King?"

Gastel wasn't ready to implicate his brother in something so sinister as treason. Instead, he shook his head, glancing out into the trees around them.

"They knew who I was."

"I think they were from the same group of Bleck Larin that took Rae from the Middlelend Forest," Dulanii said. "Who are they?"

"Mercenaries." Thick silence filled the space around them. "They follow a man named Tace, and they're notorious for their disinterest in following my father's kind suggestions regarding their conduct."

Kal let out a huff of air. "It appears nothing has changed."

They set up camp within visual distance of the dark rift. It'd taken considerably longer than Gastel had liked to find it, even with a map to guide them. Yet, through the unfortunate run-in with the trackers and all the other delays, Gastel found himself hopeful for the first time in weeks. Hopeful that he could open the rift without further incident and get the four of them headed to their next destination.

Kal had been uncharacteristically quiet the rest of the trip, which left Dulanii to fill the void in conversation, but as twilight settled over them, even he fell silent. The heaviness of what they were there to do weighed on them like the smothering, overcast sky.

"He worries about you," Inara said as she sat beside Gastel at the fireside. She'd been quiet the entire day. "Kal worries you won't know how to hold back. That you'll sacrifice yourself. I've never seen him argue with anyone like how he argues with you. But it's because he's scared, and he respects you." She put a hand on Gastel's shoulder and met his eyes with more confidence than he'd ever seen from her, the shyness replaced with purpose. "You need to be careful tomorrow."

He nodded, rolling the silver Starling bracelet around his wrist. It reminded him of everything that could go wrong with what they had planned—of everything he could give if he wasn't careful.

The plan was simple. Gastel would attempt to open the rift as he had in the Middlelend Forest, but the moment any one of them sensed things were going wrong, Dulanii would pull him away and break the connection. Dulanii could be burned, but he insisted on being the one to do it. The hope was that while it would draw a heavy price from Gastel's soul, it wouldn't kill him, and they'd pray to the Elder Gods that there would be an open rift at the end.

It was what he should have done in the first place. It might have saved Raemian from the reckless way in which she'd broken the rift's hold on him the first time.

If he failed, Kal and Inara could step in and try to finish what he started. He'd been working with them on different Anam techniques as they'd traveled, but they didn't understand. It was hard to explain the level of pain he'd have to endure, and he knew if he shared this now, they would all flatly refuse to allow him to even attempt it.

"I'll do everything in my power."

She nudged him with her shoulder, drawing his attention to her eyes, dewy with unshed tears. "That's the problem." She glanced over at Kal, who glared at them across the fire. "Your power is so strong. So… consuming." She snaked her fingers into one of his hands and squeezed. "We'd rather not carry you home."

He took a deep breath, letting it out long and slow, nodding to her as she stood and left him to his thoughts. If there was one thing he didn't want to focus on, it was his thoughts. They had nothing but doubt and terror written in them.

Gastel met each of his companions' stares, realizing they were watching him now. Inara with sullen worry, Kal with frustration, and

Dulanii with a strange, anguished pinch to his eyebrows. The Shay was the only other elf here who knew what to expect. Gastel swallowed hard, shoving his nervousness down into the pit of his being.

He'd wear his father's stoic mask. He had to—for himself and his friends. But his Trove-white hands wouldn't stop trembling.

FIFTEEN

The Deepest Darkness

Neith's hair floated on the surface of the reflecting pool as she washed blood from her upper lip. Her father had struck her again. Harder this time. In the pale purple light of the Netherfields, she could finally appraise her injuries. It wasn't the first time she'd run from her father, but it was the first time she hadn't returned after an hour.

She stared at the hollow eyes of her reflection. Pale white, almost translucent flesh stretched thin over round cheekbones. A deep violet bruise bloomed across her left eye. Through the image of her sad face, she saw her white hands splayed across the bottom of the pool, holding her weight as she hovered. The lanky fingers were bright against the basalt that surrounded her.

Pulling a hand from the water, Neith let the liquid drip down the front of her loose frock as she rubbed the last tears from her eyes. Did she dare go back? The last time she ran, he'd thrashed her with a leather strap and locked her in the lavatory for a full two cycles of the light to teach her a lesson. The only lesson she'd learned was that there was, in fact, no lesson. There was truly nothing she could do to please her father. Nothing she could do to change who she was—to make herself normal. To rid herself of the strangeness that he hated.

There had to be a better life than this. Neith's dearest friend, Adott, had never had a hand laid upon her in such a violent way. Adott's mothers were kindhearted, caring parents. How was it that Neith had been given such cruelty to endure? What had she done to anger the Elder Gods?

Neith squeezed her tears back. Crying about it wouldn't change her circumstances. Unfortunately, running into the Netherfields wouldn't either. She picked herself up, her eyes never leaving her reflection as she dusted herself off. Ripples glittered and crisscrossed the pool's surface where the sopping ends of her hair dripped. It distorted the image of herself into an otherworldly thing.

She glanced out across the landscape. The ambient light of the world of Noor Above was strong here, amplified by bioluminescent vegetation. It marked the edge of the hold of Dakarai, the last of the Trove settlements before the world ended at the Rahven Sea. From here, the winding caves reached in many directions. One led to the central hold of Kekk. Still others to the world of Noor Above—the place she dared not go—not in these times of warring between the other elven races. Her kind was the most shunned, the most feared. Perhaps if she'd been born a Shay or a Bleck Larin, her father would not have been so terribly cruel. Perhaps if only she'd been born normal.

Neith plucked a delicate flower from a vine that entwined one of the countless stalagmites rising like desperate statues to the cavern's ceiling. She crushed the petals between her fingers until she was left with a fragrant, powdery paste. Like her, the stalagmites would never reach their destination, not in Neith's lifetime.

Not in five of her lifetimes.

Yet, they tried.

She wriggled one of her fingers under the vine to touch the surface of the calcium-rich stone. It was cold and moist and strong.

If only she had the strength of will to be like a stalagmite. To forge on without worrying about how long or hard her journey would be. She could leave this place and not fear the dangers of the caves, the unknown, or even the world of Noor Above. She could go somewhere else. Somewhere her father and her cowardly mother were not. She would miss Adott, but she wouldn't be nursing bruises and broken noses anymore.

Tears threatened again. Was she strong enough to trek out on her own? She looked at the stalagmite through watery eyes. So sturdy. She was not so well-built for the struggles of life. Trove were small and fragile and shunned, or so she'd been told all her life. She, a particularly peculiar Trove, feared retribution even more. Her unusual ability to feel the presence of others was not welcomed. The name of such magic was forbidden to say aloud.

Neith crouched down along the side of the stalagmite and nuzzled into it, pulling her bony knees to her chest and hugging them tightly. She'd stay here, avoiding another beating, a little longer. She'd marvel at the luminescence of the cavern walls as it slowly grew darker, another cycle of the light complete.

Would they even bother searching for her? Or would they be pleased to finally be rid of their undesirable daughter? The strange one. The one who foresaw the coming of the Shay elf before he'd appeared and presented himself to the Ethnarch of Dakarai. She'd sensed the word before anyone had ever heard it spoken. *Aequus:* neutral elf. One who seeks peace among the races.

He'd come alone but with much courage. Neith's father had sequestered and forbidden her from seeing the man as he'd been led through the roving paths of Dakarai. No one had seen a Shay in over three decades. All the maps of the tunnels that led out to the world of Noor Above from Dakarai had been destroyed. The ones who still held the knowledge kept it tucked away in their deepest memories.

Neith glanced in the direction of the tunnel to Kekk, the only one that remained open. That would be her answer if she chose to leave. It was a long voyage through barren, solid rock. She'd heard the stories. She would need provisions to make the trek, and even then, it was dangerous to go alone.

She pulled herself up. The cycle of light was complete. There was no going home now. She said a prayer to the Elder Gods. May they see her through the cycle of dark safe and sound. May they give her the courage to be like the Shay Aequus or the stalagmite. May they help her to find a new start in Kekk. And may they curse the man she called father to a life wrought with the same cruelty he'd doled out on her.

SIXTEEN

The Price

Gastel found Dulanii standing at the edge of the dark rift, eyes cast down into its black depths. He dared not ask his thoughts. He knew them well enough already because he shared them. Dulanii looked for her, not truly thinking she'd be there but hoping that she might be.

"Some days, I wake, hoping it was all just a nightmare, and she'll come swinging through the trees with that silly smile of hers." Dulanii let his arms sag at his sides; his shoulders slumped. "Then I shake it off and realize it's not a dream. She's really gone. And I need to figure out how to move on."

Gastel nodded but wasn't sure he was ready for the latter. He had no words to express the roiling emotions hollowing out his chest. He knew he needed to find better ways of coping with the sorrow. He needed to get back to being himself rather than the angry person he was becoming.

Part of him hoped that opening this rift would help, but every time he tried to mentally prepare himself for the pain he would endure, he was reminded of how he'd survived the last one. The rift would have taken all of him if she hadn't sacrificed herself. Perhaps his father was right to ask what he'd sacrifice this time.

Had he been spared because she'd fallen in?

He wrapped his arms around himself as he stood beside his solemn friend, the greatest friend he'd ever had other than his father. He thanked Raemian again because he would never have known Dulanii and his unfaltering kindness without her. Gods, he might not have ever known a world with Shay. He'd likely still be oblivious to Rhend outside of Parth.

"I miss her," Dulanii whispered.

Gastel's heart broke all over again. "I miss her, too."

It was his fault. Dulanii didn't deserve this, and as if the Shay sensed Gastel's guilt, he turned and placed a gentle hand on his shoulder.

"You couldn't have stopped her, you know. No one could once she made up her mind."

So much truth, yet it brought Gastel little comfort in that moment. There was so much sorrow and pain he didn't know how to deal with. He took a deep breath, letting it out long and slow. He needed to focus. He needed to open this rift. Whatever else he wanted or thought he needed had to be driven from his mind until this task was completed.

"I could have trusted her, though. I could have listened."

"And I could have put a sword in your gut the moment I saw you, Gastel."

His head snapped in Dulanii's direction, catching a glimmer of a grin on the Shay's lips.

"We can't dwell on what we could have done," Dulanii said, glancing over at the sleeping elf-shaped lumps of Kal and Inara near the cold fire.

Gastel shook his head with a smirk. "I'm glad you didn't."

Dulanii held a genuine smile. "Me too."

They had a silent breakfast of cheese and the last of their bread. More than once, Gastel caught Kal or Inara watching him, but he had nothing to say to them. He'd do what he had to do. So, when they'd finished, and there was nothing to delay him further, he walked to the rift. He pulled the soul stone over his head and tucked it into his pocket.

Gastel cleared his mind as much as possible, but he could feel their eyes on him as he stood with the toes of his boots at the rift's edge. Looking down into the darkness pulled such strong memories. He pressed his lips together, the vision of her sinking into white fire flashing before him.

It was time to let her go. He had to. He squeezed his eyes closed. He could see her face, her sweet smile. He pushed her away, a tear slipping down his cheek. He held his hands out, palms down, and sought the presence within.

It was waiting for him. Anticipating his every need, his every desire. This time, it knew what to do—it had done it before. His soul exploded out from him in a wave of delicious, hot strength. The white light bled through his eyelids, engulfing his body—ready and burning.

This time, without hesitation, he directed his soulflame into the rift, letting his Anam control the flow of power. Within seconds, the burning started to build in his chest as the rift took over. Every muscle in his body grew taut as the searing agony began to riffle through him, drawing his life away, painful sliver by painful sliver.

Gastel clenched his teeth, bearing down and holding firm as he dared to open his eyes. He was helpless as the flames faded away from his head and feet, leaving only his arms and torso engulfed. He tried to pull away from the crescendo of agony battering him, washing through him, locking him in terrifying panic. But the rift held him. Thirsty for more. Taking more. Wanting more.

He tried again to pull away; a wretched cry escaped his lips as he failed. As though on cue, firm hands clasped his shoulders and pulled him away. The connection broke, the pain vanishing as though it had never been. He fell back against Dulanii, unable to stand or speak. He was lowered to the ground, his eyes filling with tears, smothering his vision, like looking through stained glass.

After a few seconds, he managed to free his voice. "Is it done?" He looked up at the shadows of people above but couldn't make out any of their faces. "Gods, please...let it be done."

The light from the sun itself seemed to fade. He just wanted to know if it was done—if he'd managed to open another rift. He couldn't keep his eyes open. Instead, his soul seemed to slink to the depths of his mind, and he could do nothing but follow it into the darkness.

SEVENTEEN

Finding

The days and nights blended together. She struggled to keep track. It hadn't been long, but it felt like a lifetime. She'd tried to mark the days in the loose sand on the bedchamber floor, but it didn't make sense. Had it only been four? Her index finger hovered over the hash marks as though it knew better than she. And it probably did. She couldn't trust her mind to give her accurate information.

Today, when she woke, Noe-eb was not in his usual place. He'd not been there to help her sort through this latest dream. It was him again, of course. It was always him. But this time, he was hurting. She could see him lying amongst leaves and debris. His face was twisted in anguish.

She'd tried to reach for him and help him, but he couldn't hear her. Of course he couldn't. It wasn't real. For all she knew, he didn't exist at all. But even that would need to be based on some reality, wouldn't it?

Some person who did exist. She couldn't have created him within her mind, could she?

Like all the other dreams, it faded quickly, and now she was left with the same empty feeling that she should be doing something or going somewhere. That she should know who she was and who the man with the amber eyes was. Instead, she left her dream with the hash marks on the sandy floor of the room and went in search of Noe-eb.

Today, she promised herself she'd find the Eishtala within. Just as Noe-eb said she could.

She sat alone at the top of the monolith—again—her heart full of failure and frustration. The wind had died to a gentle breeze, the pink sky fading into a rich violet as the light dwindled. Another day was gone, and nothing.

Hot tears ran down her cheeks as she cried in silence, a wretched longing to know. Noe-eb had given her all the tools, and yet she couldn't figure out how to use them.

She was a failure.

She closed her eyes, wiping away the tears and relaxing into a meditative position. This time, she let her hands touch the monolith itself, her fingertips tracing the rough sandstone surface as granules sloughed away under her caress. It was soft and malleable, like a mind, a memory. She could carve her name into it if only she knew what it was.

She was sick of the endless expanse of sky, the constant wind, the white sand that stretched forever. Gods, the sand. *So much sand.* And yet, as she thought of the sand, it occurred to her—each granule was like a question. Countless. Like souls piling into dunes of memories and dreams.

The sand.

Something about the white sand was significant. She ran her hand over the surface of the monolith and brought it to her face. Several minuscule particles had collected in the creases of her palm. All the lives she'd touched, all the people she'd forgotten. A gust of wind blew them away, lost to the world far below.

She sent her mind out to follow, flowing over the edge of the monolith and down, pressing the world around her to a stop as if time itself froze. She could see the sand in slow motion as it fell, blowing and twisting on its journey to the ground. Her consciousness drifted with it in an aimless tumbling until she hovered above the sandy dunes.

"Find him, Raemian." Noe-eb's voice cut through the fog, but she dared not open her eyes.

Who was Raemian?

Was that her name? It left a warm numbness in her extremities. She pushed her thoughts out as he had bidden. Searching over the dunes of unending sand, looking for a single granule—one specific granule— because she was right.

It wasn't sand at all.

The fingers of her mind took up vast swaths, letting it flow between them like waterfalls of snowy heat. She sifted through whole dunes until he was there. A single piece of beautiful, amber sand.

When she opened her eyes, Noe-eb faced her, sitting cross-legged in front of her. His smile was tender. She looked down at her closed hand, scared to open it, scared of what she'd see. Then, finally, she peeled her fingers back, revealing a single piece of brown sand.

"Today, you found him. His soul among the vast dunes of my Sheol." Noe-eb held his outstretched arms to the endless desert below. "Now, you must let him go."

But she couldn't. He was hers.

This tiny piece of sand was hers. She wasn't sure how it had come to be in her hand when her body had done little more than breathe and exist in the space at the top of the monolith, *but he was hers.*

"No."

Noe-eb's smile intensified, a knowing behind his upturned lips. "I have given you your name. Now let him go, Raemian. He is for another day."

Goosebumps bloomed on her arms at the sound of the name.

Raemian.

She placed her free hand around her wrist, feeling for something that wasn't there. Some other part of her. Raemian was not all of her name.

"That is all I shall give you today."

Again, he'd entered her mind and seen her thoughts. She closed her eyes and took a deep breath before looking down at the tiny piece of sand nestled in her palm. He was hers. Eyes wet with tears, she didn't want to let him go. She was so close.

She turned her hand over and let the granule loose upon the breeze, knowing it would blow over the edge of the monolith, falling and twisting until it again found its place amongst the other souls.

EIGHTEEN

Lost and Lifeless

Belkin glared over at his unconscious brother. Gastel had returned home broken, this time with strangely healed hands manipulated by Eishtala. They were usable again, at least, but the color of Trove flesh. The dim light of Gastel's bedchamber gave them an eerie tint of violet that made them look as though they were made of glass.

He wasn't sure what to do. Leave Gastel to wallow? Put him out of his misery? Something nagged at him. Something Freya had mentioned when he'd been in Tremire: Wielders were a strange lot of elves who could control faculties that other Bleck Larin could not. All the questions she'd asked him dredged up memories of the peaceful time before the start of the warring when Gastel's mother had hovered around the castle stronghold.

Niminea had been a kind woman. Beautiful beyond reason. It was understandable that his sappy romantic of a father had fallen so hard for her. But she'd been secretive, hiding things from Mesmal. Hiding her pregnancy and her true Anam powers.

Everything happened so fast after Gemma called for the Culling. Belkin hadn't had time to hate Niminea for how much she'd destroyed his family. And then there was the elfling. The way his father doted on Gastel with more love than Belkin had ever received. It made Roulin's immediate hatred for the elfling more understandable. What was it about Gastel that made him Mesmal's favorite?

Freya had said that Niminea was not only a powerful Anam Wielder but the Great Wielder. The one who'd thrown their world off course—the catalyst of the Sundering the prophecy warned of. It made sense that the balance would be restored by her son, an Anam Wielder, who possessed her power and so much more. That within him lived the souls of Niminea and all the ancestors before her. A family of impossibly strong Wielders growing stronger each time they passed their power to the next generation. Their deaths intentional in order to strengthen the line.

"He'll be all right...right?" Dulanii asked, breaking Belkin's train of thought. The Shay hadn't left Gastel's side, going so far as insisting food be brought to him in Gastel's bedchamber.

"You say he's been unconscious since he opened the rift?"

Dulanii nodded. "I pulled him away like we planned, but I think it was too late." Dulanii ran his fingers through his white hair, which had grown out a bit longer than he usually kept it. His face was pinched with worry. "I'm sorry, Belkin. I failed at keeping him safe."

The Shay looked over with anguished eyes. The man had invested so much of himself in Gastel. It reminded Belkin of before the war when it was common for Bleck Larin and Shay to befriend one another. Perhaps there was hope that peace could work between their people better than he'd anticipated.

"You didn't fail," Belkin said, drawing Dulanii's attention. "Thank you for saving his life."

Belkin sat back in the chair at the foot of Gastel's bed.

"I wish I would have pulled him back sooner." Dulanii seated himself at Gastel's side and placed a single hand on his forehead.

These Shay were so emotional. A flash of a memory. Raemian's face as she confessed that she'd not known who her mother was. A tear slipping from her eye. So vulnerable in that moment. So genuine and beautiful. Belkin could tell she'd hated it. He could see her struggling to keep her hardened exterior intact.

Something in that moment had changed the way he'd seen her—a seed had been firmly planted. Despite her death, it had grown and bloomed.

"I'm sure you can apologize when he wakes," Belkin said.

Dulanii looked up at him with questioning eyes.

"I doubt something like a little rift could kill Gastel." Belkin couldn't help the left side of his lips from curling up. "Roulin and I have been trying to end him since he was an elfling."

There was truth in those words, but Dulanii didn't need to know that.

He sat for a moment longer, glancing over at the unconscious form of his youngest brother. Stupid, selfish youngest brother.

No. Belkin corrected himself. Stupid, yes, but not selfish. Gastel had thrown himself at this task because he'd been told he was the only one who could do it and that the fate of all elvenkind rested on his shoulders.

He was the furthest thing from selfish.

If anything, he was to be commended. That he willingly tried to open a second rift after having given his hands to open the first. Stupid, reckless, but terribly brave.

Belkin's thoughts turned to darker things. If he'd given his hands opening the first rift, what had he given this time?

He furrowed his brows as his eyes swept over what he could see of Gastel. His face, neck, and shoulders seemed fine. His horrible hair, just as short and terrible. His arms were laid out on either side with those foreign hands resting palms down. Other than his hands, he looked normal.

Gods, what price had he paid?

— — —

The way had seemed clear at first, Neith's feet were sure. She'd found the correct passage easily enough. *Always take the right-hand fork, never the left; follow the luminous gems along the way.* She'd repeated the instructions to herself until she was certain she wouldn't forget and struck out with enough supplies to reach Kekk.

She quickly learned she was used to the open caverns of Dakarai. Massive spaces filled with ambient light from the world of Noor Above, but here? It was closed in, pressing down on her from all sides; the tightness in her lungs mirrored the tightness of the passage. The air was thick and stale. There was little ambient light, and the luminous gems were spaced so far apart that Neith ran her hand along the wall to guide her. Even with exceptional low-light vision, total darkness was paralyzing.

After only a single cycle of light, Neith began to feel wretchedly lonely. While she'd longed for such solitude around her father, here it was agonizing. She wished she'd have stolen Adott away to journey with her. Instead, Neith began to talk to herself in the darkness, holding full conversations about how her father would fall victim to various horrible tortures until his death. It was morbid but comforting, and it helped her pass the time as she forced herself to put one foot in front of the other.

After the second cycle of light, she wondered if she'd taken a wrong turn. Perhaps she'd been misinformed? Maybe she'd taken a left by accident? She cast her thoughts back, trying to trace each time she'd come to a fork in the path. But she was certain she'd always taken the right. Not to mention the constant luminous gems that would come into view when she was about to lose all hope of ever finding her way to Kekk.

The third cycle of light instilled new hope. She'd been told if she was quick, if she didn't stop for breaks unless absolutely necessary, she would find herself in the outer gallery at the end of the third cycle. The gallery was a monstrous cathedral of stone that housed the whole of Kekk, nestled upon an island in a massive reflecting pool, only crossable by two bridges made of hand-hewn basalt. The Trove of old had fortified their most sacred Hold, protecting it from the denizens of the deep and the true monsters, the elves of the world of Noor Above.

But as the cycle waned and she hadn't found the gallery, she began to panic. Had she taken the wrong cave? Perhaps she'd been misinformed on purpose, with the whole of Dakarai ready to be rid of her permanently. She froze in fear, knowing full well she'd have to endure another cycle of dark in the loneliness of the tunnel.

The blackness was so heavy, so smothering. Neith pressed her back against the cave wall and slipped down until she sat on the cold, rough stone. She closed her eyes, the stagnant air wrapping around her with its thick arms. She was on the last of her food and water, having only packed enough for four cycles. If she didn't find Kekk in the next cycle of light, how quickly would she starve? Alone. In the heart of the earth. The very place she'd called home her entire life.

With her eyes closed, Neith cast her mind back, feeling along the passage, retracing the way she'd come, searching for the forks in the tunnel to make sure she'd always taken the correct one.

This was the ability that had caused her so much strife and to be shunned by her people and called a freak, an abomination. This was how her father justified his treatment of her. The power to see with her mind what her eyes could not—Trove, the Shay Aequus, animals of the deep. Their souls spoke to her in a language older than the rock that entombed her.

It had been nearly as long as the warring between the Shay and Bleck Larin that Dakarai had housed a Svet Priest. He'd been driven away, his ability to see souls considered filthy, truly evil. As she grew older, her parents realized she had the curse. They'd forced her to hide it or be sent away as well.

Now, she was trying to escape from those same parents.

She let her mind drift deeper, lost in the way searching eased her loneliness. It was calming. Familiar.

She froze.

There was someone there. Not someone. *Something.* A living thing, but it wasn't Trove. It wasn't elven at all, and her blood ran cold. She had no weapons or training in combat. Trove didn't fight. Some carried knives for their professions, but most were at the whim of life, casting their fortunes at the feet of the Elder Gods and the basalt. She felt the thing moving in the darkness, slowly at first, before it seemed to turn in her direction, as if it felt her mind touch its life force.

It moved faster. *Much faster.* Heading in her direction at shocking speed.

She stood, not knowing what to do, but she yanked her consciousness back. It didn't matter how quickly the thing approached; it was coming, and there was nothing she could do but run.

Noor Above

Neith ran toward Kekk. She opened her eyes as widely as possible. She'd need every scrap of light to see, praying to the Elder Gods she didn't catch an uneven patch on the floor and trip. Sheer terror took over as she sprinted with every fiber of her endurance. She'd never run for so long or so hard, but she dared not stop. Not until she broke the border of the gallery. Even then, she might not be safe from whatever pursued her.

She risked reaching her consciousness back and found the creature gaining at an alarming rate. A clearer picture of the thing flashed through her mind, turning her insides to shards of shattered basalt. She feared many things: her father's rage, speaking of her filthy curse aloud, and the denizens of the deep. They never approached so close to Dakarai, but here? This was their domain. And this one was no less terrifying. May the Elder Gods save her, she could see its life force in her mind. Eight spindly extremities protruding from an armored thorax. A head equipped with fangs the size of her torso.

A luminous gem was coming into view. Another fork in the path. She'd hoped she'd have come to the gallery; the Gods only knew how far she truly was from it. She cast her mind ahead, avoiding the danger that gained. There was nothing for as far as she could feel, and drawing breath was becoming too painful. Her legs were giving out; the pain in her muscles growing unbearable.

She slowed, her body no longer physically capable of maintaining a hard sprint. Perhaps if she kept moving, she could stay ahead of the beast. But that was wishful thinking. It was close enough now that she could hear it. A wretched clicking sound it used to see in the darkness.

Both exhausted and petrified, tears obscured what little vision she had. She slid her hand along the cave wall, trying to keep herself upright, scraping her palms raw. She'd never feared her father's rage like this. He'd promised anger, a beating, insults. This promised a painful death.

She felt the thing's stone-slicing extremities vibrating through the rock around her. It was only twenty or thirty yards behind. The fork in the path loomed ahead, and for the first time, she dared consider the left tunnel. If she veered from the obvious direction, it was possible the thing would continue for a time, and she could keep ahead of it a little longer. She had precious seconds to consider, but it came down to one thing. She couldn't outrun it if she continued straight.

Neith took the left, pushing herself hard off the wall at the last second. The air moved as the thing passed harmlessly down the straightaway. It had been only a few feet from her.

Without looking back, without casting her mind out, she started sprinting again with renewed energy as adrenaline took over. The way was rougher and unused, and she worried she was running into an entire den of monsters. Ones she'd never have the pleasure of seeing, as there'd be no more luminous gems to light her way.

Neith's outstretched arms reached both sides of the tunnel as it narrowed, her chest tightening with fear. She slowed to a swift walk. Any faster, and she risked twisting an ankle or, at the rate the cave constricted, running smack into the unyielding stone.

For better or worse, this was the path she'd chosen. Most assuredly worse, she needed to duck as the cave tapered more, slowing her pace further. Then, as if the Gods were playing some horrendous prank on her, she heard it. That wretched clicking. The thing had doubled back when it hadn't found its meal down the main tunnel and was gaining. Her slowed pace helped to speed her inevitable death closer.

Panic rose in her chest as she panted, out of breath, out of energy, and out of time. The only blessing was a glint of light ahead. Perhaps a luminous gem mounted on the far side of an outcrop of stone? Neith scrambled as quickly as she could, hunched over, her chafed hands guiding the way, listening to the forsaken clicking as it grew louder. It would likely be the last sound she heard. But the light grew stronger. Unlike the luminous gems that left a pale glow, this came from a distinct direction, obstructed by craggy rocks that jutted into the tunnel. She weaved around one only to find more, making her already lethargic pace slower.

As if it knew Neith had found hope of escape, the thing released a bloodcurdling screech that seemed to vibrate Neith's teeth and paralyze her muscles. It was so close, perhaps ten or so yards. The light ahead streamed painfully bright, and Neith risked looking back over her shoulder.

Elder Gods be damned. In all its horror, she saw it. As pale and white as she. No eyes; instead, every inch of its head was dedicated to those deadly fangs that could move on their own, like appendages. They framed a mouth lined with tiny teeth that seemed to stretch apart as it opened, gaping, dripping with saliva as it sensed an impending meal. It was only a few yards behind; Neith's fear renewed her energy, and she ran as best as possible while hunched over. The opening was hardly large enough for her to fit through. Not nearly big enough for the thing behind.

She grabbed both sides of the opening with her trembling hands and dragged herself up through with the last of her strength, leaving her legs dangling. Hot, wet pain lanced through her as a fang sank deep into the soft flesh of her calf. A withered screech escaped her as she jerked her leg loose, ripping the muscle free so she could drag her now useless leg the rest of the way through the hole. Her nails splintered as she dug her fingers into the solid rock around her, pulling herself farther through the opening.

The thing clawed at the entrance in a craze, chipping stone away as it tried to follow. She needed to close her eyes against the piercing light as she continued to drag herself through the rip in the rock. Jagged edges of stone bit into her flesh as she squeezed, desperate, terrified, yet hopeful. She pulled herself farther into a cavern that seemed to sit above the tunnel below.

She could still hear the thing as it tried to follow, but the sound grew more distant as she heaved herself all the way through and continued with eyes closed. She felt with her hands until she came to a sharp cliff's edge. Here, she worked her way until she was able to lean against a rock wall and draw her legs tightly against her chest. Gently, tenderly, she searched her leg with her fingers. She pulled away with a new fear, her hand moist, the familiar metallic smell of blood filling her nostrils.

The light was too bright to peel her eyes apart and see the damage. She pulled her nearly empty pack from her back and rifled through it blindly, feeling for the piece of cloth she'd brought in case she needed to cover her eyes.

"Hello?"

She froze at the sound of a man's voice—a new danger she couldn't see. She sent her mind out. Not a Trove, a Shay, several yards on the other side of the cavern. He was running in her direction with conviction. She couldn't help a whimper from escaping her lips. She'd just gone from one monster to another. And while she'd been promised a quick death with the beast, there was no telling what a Shay would do with her.

"Are you hurt?"

He was so close. She pulled her legs up tighter, feeling the pain shoot up her thigh from her injury.

"It's okay; I won't hurt you." His voice was beside her. The light emanating from his lightsource burned her eyes through the cloth she'd just pulled over them.

She held her arms up around her head in a pathetic attempt to protect herself. The sound of metal clanging as something was dropped onto the stone was the only warning she had before a warm hand took hold of her wrist and drew it away from her face, but she had no energy to fight off this new enemy.

"I promise I won't hurt you. Let me see your leg."

She struggled against his hands but felt her consciousness waning. Either from the shock of injury or the fear of this Shay, she wasn't sure, but her world narrowed to those warm hands and the pain radiating up her leg.

He sucked in a breath between his teeth. "You've been bitten."

Shaking her head and pushing as hard as she could against him, she tried melting into the rock behind her.

"Let me help you. Their bite is venomous. You need the antidote."

His strong arms took her under her legs as she went limp, a cold numbness flowing up from her injury and into her abdomen.

"Help" was all she could say as he lifted her from the cave floor.

"I've got you."

Maybe it was the motion as he walked with her in his arms, tucked against his warm chest, or the smell of his skin clouding her senses. It was the scent of soil and growing and something strange she'd never experienced. It was soothing and terrifying all at once. And it was the last thing she thought of before her world went darker than the deepest blackness she'd ever known.

Belkin sat alone in the strategy room. It had been a week, and there was still no sign that Gastel would wake. He was beginning to think he should have put him out of his misery when the Shay and the Wielders had returned with him. To wither away in a bed seemed so much worse.

"Your Highness?" Kalbasen broke Belkin's concentration.

He glanced at the man, certain his face was an emotionless mask of perfection.

"I wanted to speak with you before leaving."

"Ah, yes. I'd heard the Shay mention you'd be returning your elfling apprentice to her home." Belkin let his mask slip a little, a tiny grin turning up one side of his lips.

There was something so genuinely wholesome about the way Kalbasen treated Inara like his daughter. The castle stronghold wasn't home to many women. Perhaps it was because of a royal family dominated by men. Regardless of the reason, having the girl around had been a welcome change, but, more so, because of how the Wielder doted on her.

"I promised her mother I'd only have her away for a few weeks."

"I see."

"I was hoping Gastel would wake before I left." Kalbasen's attention wandered to the topographic map of Rhend. It had always drawn

Raemian's attention as well. "Will you give him this for me when he finally finds his way home?"

Kalbasen handed Belkin a letter sealed with purple wax, the symbol of a flame over the open palm of a slender hand.

"Of course." He let his eyes rest on the seal. It was vaguely familiar. "Finds his way home?"

Kalbasen smiled, but it never touched his eyes. "I fear he used so much of himself that his soul retreated into the depths of his mind." He glanced back down at the map, unable to hold Belkin's eye contact. "Now he needs to find his way out."

"Is it possible he could be lost indefinitely?"

"No." Kalbasen's attention snapped back to Belkin. He shook his head with vehemence. "The fact that his body sustains is a good sign. If there was nothing left of his soul, he would have expired at the rift." The Wielder ran his fingers over the rim of the map, following the edge of the Rahven Sea without looking down. "But I don't know how long it will take him. I had the healers make sure his mother's soul stone was nowhere near him to avoid any restrictions to his Anam."

Belkin schooled his emotions as best as he could. Anam was a strange subject for him, but this insight was invaluable. It made it even more disconcerting that his brother hadn't woken, though. How much had he given to the rift before Dulanii managed to pull him away?

"We leave after the morning meal tomorrow."

Belkin nodded before glancing back at the sealed letter. "Be sure you speak with the Shay. He's grown fond of you."

The silence between them was thick, and Belkin settled his attention back on Kalbasen's serious expression. The Wielder seemed to struggle to hold his feelings in check as he stared at nothing in particular. Finally, his eyes flicked to Belkin's, and he nodded before turning to leave.

"Kalbasen." The Wielder glanced at Belkin over his shoulder. "Thank you. For helping Gastel with this quest."

The Wielder gazed at Belkin for a long moment before his eyes dropped to his feet. He departed without another word, leaving Belkin holding a mystery letter.

TWENTY

Giving

Raemian woke with tears streaming down her cheeks. He was alone yet not alone, set within some strange prison that encased him. She'd felt his panic and pain, her heart racing with his. Her tears were his tears.

The dream was slipping away, but not before she recognized something. A band of silver was on his wrist, much like the circle of silver that Noe-eb had given her.

She pushed away the coverings of her bed, finding it where she'd placed it beneath her pillow. It was warm from her body heat as she held it in her hand. She turned it over to inspect the designs until the last of the dream slipped away; she was no longer certain why she'd needed to see it. For some reason, she'd felt compelled. She slipped her hand through the circle.

Like gears that clicked into place.

Starling.

The bird was a starling. Something significant about that word. She covered it with her other hand and closed her eyes, trying to remember, but it was gone. The dream, the strange remembrance, all of it slipping away.

"It's time." Noe-eb had entered without her hearing him. He had a way of seeming to appear out of nowhere sometimes, then allowing her to hear him approach at others. She met his steely blue eyes—the same kindness as before. She stood, the weight of the circle of silver on her wrist a familiar comfort. "Leave the bracelet. I would hate for you to lose it." He turned and left.

She set the bracelet on the ground and drew a sixth line in the sand.

Raemian followed the curve of the dunes with her mind, tumbling over each like the granules that rolled and collected. She no longer needed to see them to know them. She breathed in through her nose, tasting the sharpness of the day's heat, clearing everything from her thoughts.

"Draw it into yourself."

She pulled at the world around her, filling her being until it ran through her veins and simmered in her muscles. Cradling it in her chest, she held it, worried if she lost control she might burst, but Noe-eb had not instructed her to let go.

"Now release it into me."

She did as she was bidden, laying a hand on his arm and letting it explode out of her all at once, pouring over the edge of the monolith like invisible water. She wasn't sure if any of it was actually released into Noe-eb, and considering his silence, she assumed the answer was no.

Waiting for Noe-eb's approval was torture. After a long moment, he placed a warm hand on her shoulder, and she chanced peeking up at him. His face gave nothing away. Expressionless, dull eyes, as though he slept sitting up.

It was midday, the heat at its highest. She'd meditated and practiced drawing the strange magic into herself since early morning. She was weary. Surely, he could see that her failure was less about skill and more about exhaustion.

He closed his eyes, lowering his chin in disappointment.

"We have such little time left."

"Perhaps if you explained it again—"

"You know how to do this, Raemian. You've done it before when you didn't know what you were doing. You need to focus." Noe-eb's voice was sharp, and she flinched away from him. He closed his eyes and took a deep breath as if to calm his frustrations. When he opened his eyes again, there was a sadness that she'd never seen before.

"You are perhaps the most capable vessel I have ever known," Noe-eb said, his voice softening. "You have only to realize this."

But she didn't understand what this meant, and she was too scared to ask. He likely knew her thoughts already, anyway.

"Meditate. I shall return shortly." He left her on the top of the monolith as he always did to send herself out in search of that single grain of amber sand amongst the countless white silica granules.

She focused on her breathing, her shoulders rising and falling with each breath. Such a strange, involuntary action. After a while, she grew bored and let her mind drift back to those eyes that seemed to haunt her more and more. The rest of him was little more than a whisper of a memory, but his eyes? She opened her own and looked out at the ocean of white stretching to the horizon. He could be anywhere, blown to the farthest reaches of this place on the merciless winds.

"You'll know him again soon. You need to put him from your mind for now." Noe-eb had snuck up on her and extended a curious object in her direction. "Take this." She wrapped her fingers around the handle, instinct clicking into place. It was a delicate falchion made of layered steel and a rose-gold-colored alloy that sparkled in the pink light of day. Electricity writhed up her arm, and she straightened, tightening her shoulders back.

"Of all my acolytes, you have a talent that no others have had." Noe-eb smiled. "Now you must combine it with Eishtala and hone it to perfection."

Noe-eb turned away and drew the world into himself as he had when he'd illustrated what he wished for her to replicate. With a wave of his hand, five figures wafted into existence.

They were tall, sneering creatures. Dark as the bottomless shadows within the monolith, with stars for eyes that glowed an angry pink. They spread out around her as Noe-eb walked toward the stairway.

"Their talons have the power to destroy your soul, and if you're killed here, you can never be resurrected."

She spun on the balls of her feet to face the wraiths, cold fear freezing her limbs in place.

"They can't be killed with a blade alone. You must use Eishtala. Remember what you've learned and who you are."

And he left her to face down five wraiths, alone, on the top of a monolith.

Changing of the Guard

Weeks. It had been weeks since Gastel had returned unconscious from opening the second rift. Belkin tried not to think about what it would mean if Kalbasen was wrong and his youngest brother never woke. He had enough to think about after a string of letters from Freya. Conditions near Dormshire were deteriorating, and Belkin had been desperate enough for council that he'd asked for the muscly Shay to join him in the strategy room with him and Tildimin.

His father's health was visibly deteriorating as well. Mesmal seemed weary, spending a significant amount of time with Dulanii at Gastel's bedside. He only managed to come to one meal a day in the dining hall and had suspended citizen hearings indefinitely. Belkin didn't know how to help him other than to continue to maintain what he'd been managing since Gastel had opened the first rift.

Belkin hid in his personal quarters. He needed a moment with Freya's latest letter. Her handwriting reminded him of her hair, with curls and loops weaving through each word. He could almost hear her voice in his head as he read. Or was it Raemian's? The two women seemed to blend together in his memory.

A knock at his door startled him. "Come."

It was Tildimin in his usual red leather armor and burnished black pauldrons. As the unofficial general of the guard, he was always battle-ready.

"Your father wished me to fetch you to his study."

"Errand boy now, Tildimin?" Belkin tsked as Tildimin let a sly grin break his otherwise emotionless countenance.

"Only for Mesmal."

They shared a smirk before Belkin set Freya's letter aside.

He found his father in his favorite leather chair, the one across from him woefully empty. How many times in the past couple of decades had he interrupted Gastel in that chair?

"Belkin!" Mesmal's voice was cheerful, yet he hunched over as though his thin shoulders were a challenge to hold up. "Please, sit."

"What troubles you, Father?" Belkin eased into his brother's chair.

"There doesn't always have to be something troubling me to sit and chat with my heir."

Belkin had not often been referred to as Mesmal's heir. It was assumed. He was the oldest; he'd accepted and excelled at all the responsibilities of the heir apparent. He'd received additional education in his elflinghood to help prepare him. But the way his father spoke now...

"My life wanes."

"You have centuries left yet, Father."

Mesmal shook his head, looking down at his hands folded in his lap. "It's time I stepped down for the good of our people."

Belkin was out of the chair in an instant. "This is a cruel joke to play while Gastel lies lifeless."

"This is not a joke, my son." Mesmal closed his eyes, taking a deep breath.

"No." A bolt of energy shattered through Belkin as he paced behind the chair he'd just occupied. "Not yet."

"My degrading health has been noticed."

"Only because you've allowed it to be."

"Please, Belkin, it's time. I'm not asking."

"This is ridiculous." Belkin glared at his father. "You truly can't be serious."

Mesmal sat with his signature stoic calm. Belkin could tell he was completely serious. Perhaps the most serious he'd been in months, and while it was refreshing to have his confident father back, what he'd said was absolutely preposterous.

"You're more than ready, Belkin."

Belkin shook his head, clenching his teeth to keep from showing all his frustration. "It has nothing to do with me being ready, Father. It has everything to do with whether the Bleck Larin people are ready. This isn't something to be decided on a whim."

Mesmal delivered a sugary-sweet smile that drove Belkin absolutely insane. It was the one that spoke of things his father knew but wouldn't share. Belkin had seen him give it to Gastel so many times. The fact that Mesmal was giving it to him now gripped him harder than the news that he wished to step down.

What was his father not telling him?

"Trust me, Belkin. It's time." His stare was not unfriendly, but it was unyielding. His father had been king for centuries. A beloved king—one who'd seen hundreds of years of peace. He'd made mistakes. But who hadn't?

Belkin shook his head with vehemence. It meant more changes when Rhend was already fragile. It threatened the already vulnerable peace between Bleck Larin and Shay. It would undermine the delicate attempts at maintaining the situation to keep it from degrading further. Tensions were nearly as high as they'd been when the warring had started, with poor Freya trying her best to hold the modicum of truce.

"Please, give this more time. Just a little more time." Belkin was suddenly very self-conscious of the pleading in his voice.

"I've already given it plenty of time and significant thought. This decision has consumed me for months, Belkin. I would rather step down now than be forced down later. And I would rather ensure *you* are crowned king with no question to your qualifications."

They both knew what he referred to. Reports of the man leading the band of black-clad Bleck Larin on targeted attacks toward the Shay had spread like wildfire over the wilds. There was little doubt between Belkin and Mesmal about who the man was, but without being able to definitively prove it, there was little they could do. Roulin would have to be caught, which they'd thus far failed to do, though this was partly because Belkin hadn't invested enough resources into the matter.

He closed his eyes, letting the frustration pass over him. He'd spent his entire life knowing this day would come, but 284 years was not long enough to adequately prepare to be king. Not when it would be for a thousand years or better.

"Belkin. My son. Not only are you ready, but you will make a far stronger ruler than I have ever been."

He wouldn't. He didn't have the patience, the calm demeanor, the grace. He was not Mesmal. He was Belkin. A warrior. A killer. Hardened by the lives he'd taken with his saber, the choices he'd made. He smoothed a hand over his hair.

He suddenly realized why Gastel was so important. Though young, he had his father's calm, kindness, and empathy. Gastel was not Mesmal's sounding board. Mesmal had been training him to be Belkin's. The man who couldn't plan had been planning something far greater all along by providing his heir with everything he could ever need to rule the Bleck Larin people.

"I've made my decision. You shall be crowned in two weeks on the first day of your 285th year." Mesmal stood and approached his eldest son, his gentle smile filling Belkin with a strange reassurance that seemed out of place. "No need to manage the preparations. I'll have them handled."

How was he so certain when Belkin had so many concerns, so many questions, so many doubts?

"We will need to select a new commanding general, and I will need your recommendations on this," his father said. "I had once hoped Roulin could fill this role for you."

He started to turn away but stopped, facing Belkin again and placing a gentle hand upon his shoulder—all the love of a father in those golden eyes.

"Don't doubt yourself, Belkin. You have been preparing your entire life to be king. I have every confidence in you." He glanced over his shoulder. "And call your brother back from Korthan for the coronation. Whatever bad blood remains, I insist, as my last request as your king, you provide him with amnesty while he's present."

Belkin bowed and was left standing alone in his father's study. "Your will is my deed."

Family First

Roulin rolled the last drops of wine around his glass, glaring at the crumpled paper on the table beside him. It was an invitation—or what was left of one. Mesmal was stepping down. Belkin would be crowned king.

He slammed the glass on the table, sending razor shards into his hand and across the room. It hurt, but not nearly as much as the coy note on the bottom of the invitation.

Blood pooled under his palm, but he didn't move, watching it ooze across the woodgrain. He pressed an index finger into the puddle and pulled it through.

You are required by your king to attend.
You may be accompanied by a retainer of two guards.
You shall be granted a twenty-four-hour amnesty.

Roulin had no king. He *was* the king. He had no intention of submitting so easily to Mesmal's or Belkin's wishes. Never again. He was the Wyvern King.

So why was he even troubling himself to be angry?

He drew a crude *R*, the lengths of the letter exaggerated and jagged. It was fitting. He would have to take what he deserved. The whore queen had destroyed any chance of the easy kingdom he might have had. Now his father had decided to step down, and he wasn't sure how to use this to his advantage.

He couldn't bring himself to regret the handful of times he'd accompanied the campaigns to the Eastern Pass, the delicious screams of Shay as his fighters slaughtered them. But he was out of time. Belkin was likely plotting how to smother him as he sat and drank his wine.

A servant flitted about, sopping up blood and wine with a dirty rag. Everything in this place was dirty. He was lucky he had any servants at all. What he wanted was the castle stronghold. He wanted luxury and opulence. He missed his personal quarters down the western slip of the castle. He missed the courtesans who would throw themselves in his bed.

He was the Wyvern King, but no one seemed to acknowledge it.

He would need to help them see.

"Send for Tace."

The servant scampered from the room, leaving the rag in a sticky heap on the corner of the table. He could smell it—musty and honey-sweet.

He had yet to hear from all of his allies and was growing frustrated. If things didn't start happening soon, he'd be forced to find others. Even though he'd heard the princeling was bedridden, the pet regent was still frantically trying to find all the pieces to the prophecy. The convoluted fairy tale was dangerous in the wrong hands. Not to mention if one of the original copies was found.

Roulin inspected his hand, pulling a chunk of gooey glass from his wound and whipping it at the wall. It embedded in the plaster, spraying a fine mist of blood across the peeling paint.

"Fucking Gemma." He'd write again. Perhaps she hadn't received his last missive. Or the one before that. It wasn't like her to go so long without sending some pithy response. Since abdicating her throne, she'd become increasingly harder to get in contact with.

Tace poured into the dining room, so drunk that Roulin could smell him from across the room. The sound of his haughty patent leather slippers on the stone made Roulin bite the inside of his cheek to keep from punching him.

"You called, Majesty?"

Roulin liked Tace, but he didn't care for his flamboyance or sarcasm. He still treated Roulin like he wasn't quite sure what to do with him. It was always that way. At first, Roulin had respected him for his ability to overlook rank. It made the tasks he assigned Tace less likely to come back to him. But now, it was irritating. He never knew if Tace was being serious.

"I need two loyal fighters."

"Of course! What game do we prepare for?"

"My brother is being crowned king."

"But *you* are the king."

"That news hasn't seemed to have filtered into Parth quite yet." Roulin brought his hand to his mouth and licked the blood from his palm. Salty. Metallic. It would be more delicious if it were Belkin's. "How long until we have the weapons ready?"

Tace made a show of turning his head to the side to think, tapping his index finger to his chin. "Two months, maybe longer."

"Fuck."

"Why, thank you, I do all the time, Majesty."

When Roulin's eyes found Tace, the man was grinning with lurid satisfaction.

"At least someone is enjoying themselves in this shithole."

Tace bowed deeply before he tried to right himself and failed, nearly falling face-first onto the floor. He finally managed to prop himself up.

"Where's Belkin's mistress?"

"She's been refusing food again, so we've locked her in one of the pantries." Tace beamed from ear to ear, pleased with the irony of his choice of prison.

Roulin shook his head. He'd allowed Venna a leniency that he didn't extend to others. She was here for a reason, and soon, he'd have to choose how to deliver her to Belkin with his final ultimatum. Before that time, he'd decided she could do as she liked.

"Bring her to my bedchamber."

Tace whistled. "Finally! I've been waiting for you to—"

"She shouldn't be locked in a pantry." Roulin glared at his second-in-command. Though not easily, Tace could be replaced.

"Of course, Majesty." The smile had slipped from Tace's lips, but the man couldn't wash away his drunkenness so easily. He stumbled from the room, leaving the door wide in his wake.

Roulin would speak with the woman privately so she understood her place before he left to attend Belkin's coronation. Perhaps he'd glean some important detail or information that would make all this worth it. That would prevent making the charade he was about to embark on, a massive waste of time and energy.

———

The coronation preparations were wasted on Belkin. He had no interest whatsoever in frills and fancy. At least his father had taken the lead in the planning. It was nice to see the man doing something other than sulking at Gastel's bedside.

Mesmal sat in his regal robes upon his throne for the first time in weeks. He was majestic—truly a king for the ages. Belkin tried to remain stone-faced at his side, listening as his father oversaw the proceedings of his final citizen hearing. It was late afternoon, the heat of summer wafting into the vaulted ceiling of the throne room.

Belkin's eyes snapped back to a soft pink face rounding the corner, and then another and another: Bowrhem, the guard Belkin learned was named Solena, and finally, Freya. The regent was radiant as she'd been the last time he'd seen her. She was modestly dressed in a green traveling tunic and soft brown leggings. No cloak, no finery, just flame-red hair pulled back into a loose braid that cascaded down her back.

His father was on his feet and moving before Belkin could introduce her, a strange youthfulness in his step that Mesmal hadn't had for months.

"Regent Freya, I presume."

Freya's eyes darted to Belkin before she curtsied before Mesmal.

"Your Majesty. I am beyond pleased to finally meet you." She didn't wait for him to address her before she righted herself and stepped forward, her hands coming up to grasp Mesmal's.

"I've heard nothing but wonderful things about you." Mesmal's voice was soft, for Freya only.

Belkin stood and joined his father, unable to take his eyes off the woman.

"Rae spoke so fondly of you as well."

"Belkin said his visit to Tremire was warm and welcoming. I apologize for not coming myself."

The warmth in her eyes shifted to humor. "It was my pleasure, though clearly, he sugarcoated the truth, Majesty. Tremire is just a fancy forest."

"A fancy, warm, and welcoming forest," Belkin said, unable to help himself from chiming in.

Freya glanced at him with that same warmth in her eyes, her cheeks blushing under his appraisal. He didn't spare her by looking away; instead, he let the smile on his face linger until she could no longer hold his gaze, dropping her eyes to the floor in front of Mesmal's feet.

"Let us retire to somewhere more comfortable." Mesmal nodded to Bowrhem and Solena. "Please, join us."

They were led rather unceremoniously into the dining hall, where Belkin and his father sat in their customary places. The Shay were seated across the table from Belkin. It gave him a chance to see both Bowrhem and Solena a little more clearly.

The girl was young, perhaps in her first century. Her white hair was pulled back into a high ponytail, plaited down her back, and hanging nearly to her waist. She was perhaps the epitome of female Shay strength, easily as muscular as Bowrhem. And with her white hair and casual plate mail, she could have been the man's daughter. They shared the same height, with broad shoulders and trim torsos.

"I trust your journey went well?" Mesmal's tone was kind but expectant, as though he wished for nothing to disrupt the growing excitement.

Dinners and festivities were planned for the coronation, and Belkin was already tired of it. He'd be sneaking away as soon as he could.

"Uneventful," Bowrhem chimed in. "Just the way I like it."

"Perfect!" Mesmal's eyes swept across the Shay.

Glasses of wine were set before them, dark liquid, stronger than the berry wines Shay usually drank. Mesmal reached first, raising his glass in front of his face.

"To peace, to love, and to my son Belkin." He raised the glass high, his eyes landing firmly on Belkin. "Cheers to the future."

A resounding "to the future" rippled across the table before they all brought the wine to their lips, Belkin's eyes meeting Freya's.

The future.

He took a long drink, letting the liquid slip down his throat and coat his concerns. He would be king tomorrow. Belkin swallowed. He would be king. His father continued to speak, drawing Freya's attention, but Belkin could only stare at her, lost in thought.

He would be king.

TWENTY-THREE

Taking

Other than a name, Raemian had no memory of her past. How was she supposed to recall?

Waving the falchion back and forth, she swallowed, unsure what to do or where to start. The world began to recede as fear boiled in her blood. How was she to defeat these hungry monsters if not with the blade that felt both familiar and foreign in her hand? She didn't have time to dwell on the question because the first lunged with a gaping maw toward her throat.

She dodged a taloned claw. It missed her by a hair's width. Another one swung at her legs, and she jumped over its hand. She had to do *something*. She stepped back and focused on her meditation breathing.

Time seemed to slow. Like shadows of the future, she could see each move the wraiths would make before they made them. Noe-eb had said she had to use all her skills. He knew her past and would know what talents she possessed, wouldn't he? Perhaps she could use instinct? She swallowed hard, then let go of her thoughts.

She swung, slicing through the nearest wraith with shocking accuracy, but the blade passed harmlessly through. This is what Noe-eb had meant. The falchion couldn't touch them.

She sidestepped another wraith's talons, again letting her body's instincts take the lead. Somewhere in her past, she'd fought with a sword. How else could she know how to move, where to strike, and when to step clear? Again, she sliced through a wraith, leaving a trail of black smoke.

There had to be another way. The air around her tightened as she took a deep breath, drawing in part of the world's essence. The beasts slowed further as if they moved through viscous liquid. Slower still, and she walked through them, ducking out of the way easily and ending up on their backside.

Lifting her blade, she held it in line with her nose, watching the wraiths turn in her direction. It was clear they could still see her and react to their environment. This didn't tell her how to kill them, though. It just slowed them down.

She realized Noe-eb hadn't actually told her to kill them. He'd only said they couldn't be killed with the falchion. She wondered if this was part of a test. Was there another way to defeat them? One that didn't require killing them at all? She glanced back at the stairs that led down into the monolith's core, wondering if Noe-eb stood there, just out of sight, waiting, listening. How was she to use Eishtala to defeat them? Had there been an answer in his words?

Eishtala was not for killing. It was for healing and growing. Noe-eb had shown her how to heal with it. He'd cut her hand deep and demonstrated, knitting her skin and sinews back together. The pain of healing had been equal, if not worse, than the pain of the cut itself. He'd cut his own hand and instructed her to do the same, but she'd failed.

How then? What did she have to do? How could she pass this test?

They approached again, and the forwardmost beast was nearly close enough to reach her. She passed back through them, evading their desperate swings and running to the monolith's opposite side. Sitting in the same place she'd always meditated, she closed her eyes and focused on her breathing, her heartbeat—the rhythm she could never forget because it was always with her.

Drawing her breath through her nose, she pushed her mind out, flowing across the top of the monolith and over the edge, falling like raindrops onto the white sands below. Tendrils of her consciousness met the sand, and she immediately drew it back within herself, pulling with all her strength, with all her might. Fast and hard and reckless. It plunged into her like wispy knives of steam, penetrating every inch of her flesh. It burned as she struggled to hold it.

The hair rose on the back of her neck. She stood, spinning in place as she came up to face the monsters that had come entirely too close. Lifting her blade parallel to the line of her nose again, she held the power tight in her chest, waiting. Waiting until what? She didn't know. But when she was satisfied the wraiths were close enough, she let it all out at once and into the falchion, igniting the blade in an eerie green glow.

She let her body take over, swinging through the wraiths, slicing extremities from their suddenly very solid bodies. Limbs dissipated into smoke and wafted harmlessly to the sky before she moved on to the next one. She ducked under talons and spun through them with ease. When she reached the other side, she turned. All five of the wraiths lay on the sandy surface of the monolith, struggling to rise in different states of dismemberment. One managed to turn and dragged itself toward her with its remaining claw.

They weren't defeated, only gravely injured. This wouldn't do. Even if they were evil and deserved death in its purest form, to cause suffering was never her intention. She closed her eyes again, and this time, rather than focusing on flowing out and over the side of the monolith, she focused on the wraiths themselves, tearing at their putrid magic with all her strength.

They did not come away easily, but she yanked ferociously, breathing them into her lungs. They pressed at the confines of her mind, leaving her dizzy and disoriented. She opened her eyes to find the wraiths gone. They'd vanished, with nothing but tufts of smoke floating away in the light breeze.

A moment of relief was followed by absolute despair as she realized all five of them were within her, fighting for some semblance of control. Noe-eb stepped from the opening with purpose, his face washed of any emotion.

"Let them go." He glared at her, a firm set to his jaw. "Let them return to my Sheol."

But she shook her head. Her eyes welled with tears from the effort. "Tell me his name first. Tell me who I am and why I see only him in my dreams." She shook with the effort it took to hold them within herself. "Tell me, please." She refused to back down. "I have passed your test. I have done everything you've asked."

Noe-eb nodded and glanced down at the sandy surface of the monolith. "Let them rest, and I shall share it all."

She let her shoulders sag as she released the energy in a sigh of some terrible, wonderful power that eased from every pore of her flesh. It burned as their essence left her body, with nothing to shape or wound to heal. They were gone, rolling over the edge of the monolith on the wind like everything else she'd held and let go, tumbling over and over until they reached the dunes.

A single tear rolled down her cheek before she glanced at her hand still holding the falchion. The green glow was fading with the magic.

"They're just like the others, aren't they? Souls. Like the sand."

Noe-eb nodded, a smile crossing his lips as he closed his eyes with knowing. He'd created them, as he'd created everything around them. The monolith. The winds. The world. The pink sky. It was all his.

He held out a hand, and she took it.

"Come, Raemian Starling. I have much to give you."

The Color of Blood

Belkin knelt before his father, eyes cast down. His hair was braided into an elaborate plait that stretched down his back. The moment was surreal—the silence in the great hall incongruous with the chaos roiling in Belkin's stomach.

Two formally robed Bleck Larin stepped past him toward the king. He knew his father wore the same calm expression he always did—built from the confidence of centuries of ruling. Mesmal's elaborate braid was carefully unwound from the cuff that usually held the mass of his topknot. Nearly two millennia of hair was carefully unwoven as their eyes met, and a kind smile crossed his father's face. Mesmal likely knew that for the first time in Belkin's life, he was truly nervous. Not entirely ready to accept the crown that would be placed upon his head, unprepared for the weight of the kingdom that would rest upon his shoulders. But he was out of time to prepare.

He had an urge to look back at Regent Freya, who sat beside Dulanii. The muscly Shay had actually donned a shirt and vest for the formal occasion.

Belkin wanted to see the expression on Roulin's face. So far, the traitor had made a show of being cordial. Belkin resisted and, instead, let his eyes follow the hands that pulled the last of his father's hair down.

Goosebumps rose across Belkin's arms, which were thankfully covered by an elaborate cloak of rich red velvet trimmed in the softest white fur. Red—the color of the Bleck Larin royal family. The color of blood.

Time moved too quickly. His father's cuff was placed upon the crown of Belkin's head, and he closed his eyes, swallowing hard. The weight of it was so much more than the one he'd worn for years. He shivered as his hair was drawn around it, secured with a curved pin, which was impractical for battle. The three feet of remaining braid was left to hang down his back as he was customed.

When he opened his eyes, he'd hoped to meet his father's comforting gaze, but the throne was empty. It waited for him. It was no longer his father's throne.

It was his.

He let himself be helped to his feet and numbly stepped up to the throne, turning to look over the crowd that filled the throne room to the point of bursting. Desperate to hold that perfect Bleck Larin stoicism on his face, Belkin clenched his teeth, hoping only the two Bleck Larin performing the crowning were close enough to notice. He'd don the mask his father was so good at wearing...or die trying.

Half a year ago, he never would have thought he'd see the bright pink faces of Shay among the people, only a sea of dark hair and dark skin. A current of pride flowed through him. He would rule in a Rhend that was finally coming back together.

It was quickly washed away by Roulin's menacing glare. There was still so much hate clouding the careful peace. If Roulin couldn't embrace it, how could Belkin expect the rest of the Bleck Larin territories to do so? Or any of the Shaylands?

But Freya? Her warm smile and gentle confidence were so similar to his father's. She gazed at him with a respect that was both genuine and endearing. She'd not overstated her status as regent over the Shaylands, having instead chosen a simple dark blue gown with a corseted bodice of the same color. No frills or decorations to identify her as a ruler in her own right. There was something immeasurably attractive about her humility, and his eyes lingered on her—perhaps longer than they should have.

"All rise for the King of the Bleck Larin."

As one, the people stood, and Belkin resisted the urge to stand. He still didn't see himself as the king. His father was the king. He glanced to his right and nearly choked to see Mesmal standing, a proud grin across his face, his long plaits tied back with a simple cuff that looked much like the one Gastel had worn before his hair had been sheared away.

"Long may you live, King Belkin. Long may you reign."

A sea of Bleck Larin and Shay alike sank to one knee before him, rippling back through the throne room. Heads bowed. Eyes dropped to the floor before them. In unison, the crowd responded, "Long may you reign, King Belkin."

And for the first time in his life, Belkin wanted to run in terror.

Roulin was guarded like a common criminal. Tildimin watched his every step. There had been a time when Roulin and Tildimin were friendly. Perhaps *friendly* wasn't the word. Roulin wasn't particularly friendly with anyone. *Hospitable* was more accurate. Tildimin was

Belkin's companion. They'd been close since elflinghood. Roulin had no one. The closest thing he had to a friend had been killed in the Culling because the idiot had refused to leave his Shay bondmate. And even with that man, he'd been careful not to get too close. Secrets were powerful. Roulin refused to give anyone such power over him.

As the crowd was herded into the ballroom, Roulin was last to be announced. He was seated at an out-of-the-way table with a few dignitaries from Raggethan that Roulin remembered meeting once or twice at other royal functions. The younger of the two women stared openly at him in a way that made his skin crawl. One was the councilman's daughter, perhaps looking for a faster track to a royal bonding.

There were speeches, toasts, and pointless drivel. Belkin was seated where Mesmal would have been at such events, dressed in a formal white doublet with gold trim rather than his usual red and black. He was king now. The color of blood was no longer suitable for him, and yet Roulin knew better. Just because you wore a crown didn't mean you weren't a killer.

Roulin's eyes were drawn more than once to the dragon wing cuff that held Belkin's topknot. Mesmal's cuff. The crown of his people. It looked bulky on Belkin's head. Pompous. Roulin wondered if it was as heavy as it looked.

As he stared at his eldest brother, he didn't notice that Belkin stared back with empty eyes, his dark eyebrows arched in the customary Bleck Larin stoicism. A mask of lies. One that Roulin had never been good at wearing.

"I've heard there are no prospects for a bondmate for our new king." It was the councilman. He was speaking to his daughter, but loudly enough that Roulin was certain it was meant for him. "Perhaps he'll consider you?"

The councilman's tone was teasing, but the derisive sneer she returned proved that his jeering was in poor taste.

"Perhaps he'll consider making you his footstool," she said.

The councilman laughed, and she met Roulin's curious gaze, her eyes pleading for him to intervene.

"Belkin has a whore he beds when he needs company. Why would he consider a bondmate at his age?" Roulin's voice was as tight as his temper. "There's no reason for him to bother with the hassle of pleasing some worthless partner when he can pay for what he desires."

The councilman's eyes grew large, but his daughter smiled.

"And what about you?" Her voice splashed over him like a cool glass of wine.

"I take what I want."

"Yes, but what do you want?"

She was fishing for an answer she would never get. Roulin didn't have time to think about trysts and bondmates. Not when he had bigger plans.

He stood, his fingers lingering on the tabletop as his eyes washed across the ballroom bedecked with tables dressed with tall candelabras and black silk tablecloths. This is what he wanted. Elegance, royalty, and servants at his beck and call. He glared down at the councilman's daughter.

"I want a crown."

The room had drawn deathly quiet, eyes turning in his direction as the last word left his lips. When he realized his error, that in standing, everyone in the hall had assumed he had some flamboyant speech to give, it was far too late.

"Speak up, Brother. We can't hear you in the back of the hall."

Belkin's condescending tone was the last thing Roulin needed. He'd lived his entire life in the shadow of this man, constantly being told he would never be as good or as smart or as powerful. But what did these people know?

"Congratulations, *Your Majesty*." He did little to hide the mocking tone from his voice. "I was commenting on how well you wear the crown." Roulin slid away from the table slowly, deliberately, his hand falling to the empty place on his belt where his sword hilt should have been. "It suits you. All of this." Roulin gestured to the room, the finery, the food.

Belkin's jaw tightened. He knew exactly what Roulin was saying. Roulin was calling him weak. And Roulin would call him that again and again until he came to his senses—or met him on the battlefield. Whichever came first.

Roulin's gaze fell to the pink-fleshed faces. A handful of Shay were present for the coronation. One of them was Regent Freya, the woman who had taken the whore queen's place. Bowrhem, general of the Shay army, sat stiffly at her side with a younger Shay woman. The usually shirtless, empty-headed Shay that had loitered around the castle stronghold when the Starling girl had been alive was with them as well.

He burned with hatred for these people. With their dead blue eyes and shaymarks that reminded him so much of blood.

"For three decades, we kept these monsters from our lands, and here you invite them as honored guests. *As friends*." Roulin let his gaze slip back to Belkin, who was practically out of his seat with rage. "Sit on your throne, Brother. Rule your worthless kingdom. Invite these savages into your home."

He took a deep breath, his eyes flowing over the whole hall. The vast majority of the faces glaring back at him were twisted with thinly disguised fury, but there were a handful that seemed overly stoic. Some, he recognized from his meeting in Raggethan. Others, he did not. These would be Roulin's next targets. He needed allies, and he would recruit anyone and everyone he could to help put him on the throne.

"When they destroy you, I'll be waiting to pick up your bloody crown."

Roulin turned. Without looking back, he snapped his fingers as he passed his two guards. The only sound as they left the banquet was their boots on the stone floor.

Terrible light slashed at her eyes, sending Neith into a panic as she woke. It was a sharp reminder that she was no longer in Dakarai, not in Kekk, not in the earth at all, but somewhere in the company of a stranger. *A Shay.*

She curled into a protective ball, knees to her chest, hands trying to block out the light. Even with cloth covering her eyes, it wasn't enough. The world of Noor Above was...*painful.*

"You're awake!" It was the same Shay. His voice was laced with youthful excitement.

Neith eased back a little as her consciousness touched his. His aura emitted only friendly intentions. She could feel it radiating from him like a beacon with a brilliant orange hue.

"Are you Aequus?" The word sounded strange. The sound of the *S* lengthened unintentionally as it slipped from her lips. She squeezed her legs tighter against her chest as if they could protect her, but it only caused the pain in her leg to radiate up into her hip.

She heard him shift his weight. Nervousness?

"In a way, yes. The Aequus seek many things. I just seek peaceful exchange between our people."

Neith pulled the words apart in her mind as quickly as she could, but her thoughts were heavy, thick with the remains of whatever toxin had been coursing through her veins. What else could the Aequus seek?

"How does your leg feel?"

Even without the use of her eyes, she could tell he moved closer. She was surprised at how well she could feel motion with just the displacement of the atmosphere around her. It hadn't been so easy in Dakarai. She took a deep breath; the smell of soil was strong. So fresh and warm and *clean*. The acrid scent of the reflecting pools in the Netherfields—the stale, cool air of Dakarai itself—was gone.

"It hurts."

She tried to fold into herself again, self-conscious of the way she looked to others. She'd been taught the Shay and Bleck Larin found Trove elves repulsive, with their white flesh and diminutive stature.

"May I see it? I worry you may have an infection. It was a nasty bite, and I did my best to stitch you up, but I'm not an Eishtala healer."

Eishtala. The magic of the Shay. It was healing and growing. Pure and beautiful. She'd been obsessed with learning about it when she'd been young enough to dream. She shook her head and pushed away from him. Even though he'd not moved any closer, he was entirely too near.

"I won't hurt you. I know this is probably strange to you. I just want to check..." He reached and lifted the blanket from her legs.

It was like a red-hot, angry wind. Rage built and exploded from her mind. She threw her consciousness at him, no caution, no softness, just self-preservation. Invisible to the eye, it slammed into him as hard as a rock tumbling from a cave cliff and flung him back against the wall. A grunt ripped from his lips, then a thump as he fell to the floor, limp and unconscious.

She cowered in on herself. What had she done? She'd hurt him. She'd more than hurt him. She'd thrown him hard like her father had done to her, but with her mind instead of her hands. If there hadn't been a wall, how far would his strong Shay body have traveled? A sob escaped her throat. She was no better than her angry father. All this

Shay had shown her was kindness, and she'd rewarded it with evil, filthy, cursed magic.

"I'm sorry. I'm so sorry." Her lower lip quivered as the words flooded out. "I'm so sorry!" When she reached with her mind again, she found his still form on the ground beside her, but she could do nothing. She was too terrified of him, of herself, of this world to move or do anything. "I'm so sorry."

She threw her arms up over her eyes. Gods, the light was too harsh. It felt like a million needles puncturing the softness around her eyes. This world was all wrong. There was a beautiful simplicity to the darkness. She pulled the blanket over her head and tried to sink into the ground beneath her. Perhaps she could dissolve back into the blackness of the deep below where she belonged.

TWENTY-FIVE

Never Apologize

Belkin glared at an elaborate door down the guest hall where the majority of the dignitaries visiting for his coronation had been housed. It was late. Most were likely sleeping, but a promising light bled from under this particular door.

His knuckles hovered above the surface of the wood. What was with this day? He'd never been so nervous or doubted himself as many times as he had today. He knocked, secretly hoping she wouldn't answer. He hadn't considered what he'd say if she did or prepared himself for the fresh, powder-pink face on the other side.

Freya was dressed in a silk nightgown, which draped over her curves in a way that accentuated her figure rather than hid it. She carried an open book pressed against her chest.

"Majesty." She pulled the door wide, bowing. "I wasn't expecting you."

Belkin summoned his confidence and stepped into her room, taking a direct route to a sofa in the generous seating area.

"Prince or king, you may always call me Belkin."

His eyes followed her as she crossed to place the book on a night-stand and retrieve a robe.

"Forgive me for intruding at such an hour," he said.

"You aren't intruding." Her smile warmed her face as she sat across from him. "You're always a welcome guest." She glanced to the side before meeting his gaze again. "Though, I am curious how we keep finding ourselves in this exact situation."

Belkin tipped his head. "Situation?"

"Late nights, alone."

The way her eyes never wavered from his, the slice of pink flesh against creamy silk peeking from below her robe. He pushed away the errant thoughts of attraction.

"It was a strange day, and I find myself in need of..."

"The company of someone else who's taken on a role they don't feel remotely qualified for?"

Belkin hummed his acknowledgement with a nod.

"I understand and would go so far as to ask where you were the evening I made my own oath." She winked before giving him all her attention. "What plagues your thoughts this evening, Belkin?"

"I guess I should first apologize for our last meeting."

"I thought we established there was nothing to apologize for," Freya said with a soft upturn of her lips.

"So, we did." He took a deep breath, rubbing his hands on his knees as he put the pieces together. "My brother, the troublemaking one—"

"Gastel isn't such a troublemaker in his current state." She grinned, and Belkin couldn't help but join her.

"You are more wrong than you realize, but no, I refer to Roulin this time."

She shifted a little, the smile fading from her face. Roulin hadn't made a good impression on anyone during the banquet, delivering a handful of dark words before he'd turned and left.

"He was given amnesty for today."

Her eyes darted back to his, a pensive understanding crossing her face.

"I hope you understand. It was one of my father's final requests as king."

She nodded. Of course, she understood. How could he have doubted her?

"I was surprised at first, but Dulanii explained." A spark of memory crossed her expression. "Speaking of Dulanii, I have need of him if you can spare him."

"Of course. He's doing nothing but entertaining my father and growing mold at Gastel's bedside."

She shifted a little, sadness crossing her eyes before she met Belkin's gaze again. "Has there been any change in his condition?"

Belkin took a deep breath before letting it out slowly. He wished he had better news. "No, though his body seems to be sustaining itself somehow. The healers say he's of suitable health at least. No signs of the usual ailments that come with long periods of inactivity."

She nodded. "And how have you been holding up?"

He leaned back in his chair, bringing a hand to his face. How had he been holding up? He couldn't maintain her eye contact.

"I need his guidance, his empathy. He's spent his entire young life at my father's side, learning the daily ins and outs of running a kingdom. The things I've not been involved with over the last three decades." He glanced up at her. "For obvious reasons."

"To have that kind of guidance would be invaluable."

"Exactly. As it stands, I've ..." He wasn't sure he could continue, then he realized how much he'd already shared. She made conversation easy. "As it stands, I've been bored."

"Bored?"

"Bored." He folded his arms, smirking at her shocked expression. "You forget that for the past thirty years, I've spent most of my time hunting down my enemies. Now I find myself without anyone to hunt."

She pursed her lips. "Are you so sure there's no one to hunt? I would think it depends on your definition." A sultry smile flitted across her lips before it fell. "I forget about your reputation sometimes. You don't act like a bloodthirsty warlord."

He let his hands fall to the arms of the chair as he took in the shape of Freya's soft face. He wondered if she knew how beautiful she was. His chest tightened. Part of him had originally wanted to come to explain himself. Their last private visit hadn't concluded quite the way he might have liked. But this part of the conversation was hard. He hadn't been sure he was planning to tell her why he'd hesitated. It was hard for him to fully understand it himself.

"I'm sorry you've been given the wrong impression of me, and my actions at our last visit didn't help, I'm sure."

"Any impression I'd had of you was destroyed when you kindly let the miscreants at the banquet live." A playful smile brightened her face. "But I will admit, I hadn't anticipated a man so much as a monster."

He nodded. "I don't blame you. Is there nothing I can do to maintain my heartless reputation?" he teased.

She chuckled. "I'm sure we can find *something*."

But his smile fell. Their flirting only made it harder for him to explain. In a moment of honesty, he rallied his courage. "I've had to force myself to push you away."

She let her own smile slip, gazing down at her hands. "I could never fault you for that."

"Couldn't you?"

Her eyes snapped to his, confusion wafting across her brow as her cheeks grew violently pink.

"We're clearly attracted to each other." He paused. It was now or never. "I need you to know why I pushed you away."

She held his eyes, unwavering, waiting.

"I..." But the words were stuck in his throat.

"I think I already know. Because I fear I have the same problem," Freya said as she glanced away. "We remind each other of people we've lost. Ones we loved, ones we wanted."

But that wasn't the entire reason. He was drawn to her. His eyes were like magnets to her location. And yet he constantly compared her to Raemian in a way that wasn't fair or right. Before he could form these thoughts into words, she continued.

"And maybe you're afraid that's the only reason we're drawn to each other. That once the newness fades, you'll be left with only lost memories and regrets. Empty comparisons, unfair judgments."

Belkin met her eyes. Pure blue, the color of the summer sky. They glittered at the corners with unshed tears. Framed by brilliant shaymarks that only accentuated her burning cheeks as she continued to blush. Something about her vulnerability was gorgeous.

He stood, taking the few steps to stand in front of her. She looked up at him, tipping her head back, a tear slipping from the corner of her eye.

"I'm sorry," she whispered.

He tucked a finger under her chin, drawing a line down her neck to the collar of the robe.

"Never apologize." He pushed her robe aside as he followed her collarbone with his index finger. "Not to me."

Her eyes fluttered closed as his fingers wandered over the impossibly soft skin of her shoulder, dropping the robe behind her onto the chair she occupied. With her eyes shut, she looked less like Raemian. She had a delicate fullness to her cheeks, no hard lines. A softness that ignited a dangerous fire in Belkin's core. He took a tight breath when she opened her eyes, those inquisitive eyes that saw all of him.

"I think you may understand me better than I understand myself," Belkin said, letting his hand slip from her arm but refusing to step back.

"No one understands themself. Not truly." She reached for his hand, entwining her fingers with his. "Stay tonight."

A younger Belkin would have had her against the wall. He wouldn't have given her a chance to reconsider what she'd just offered. How many countless courtesans had paraded themselves through the castle stronghold? A younger Belkin had enjoyed himself, allowing willing women and men to entertain him late into the night. But that wasn't who he was anymore. Now, he was calculated with his lovers. Venna was one thing. A tryst with a dignitary was another entirely. Today, he'd become a king, and with that came a level of caution that he couldn't ignore.

But her fingers running up his arm kindled a longing he hadn't felt in years. She stood as her hands found his chest and roamed to his waist.

"I..." He lost his train of thought at her closeness.

"I know—you can't stay." She reached her arms around him, pressing the side of her face to his chest. "Thank you for this. For your visit. For your honesty."

He eased into her embrace, enjoying the feel of her body pressed against his. Leaning his head down, he could smell the bright lemon scent of her hair as he wrapped his arms around her.

"I can't stay...*long*." This last word drew her eyes and her hands as she reached to kiss him, and he let her, holding her firmly in place, his fingers tangled in her hair. Maybe it wasn't appropriate. Who was to say? He was a king. If he wished for an evening with a beautiful, intelligent woman whom he felt drawn to, who was to stop him?

Her lips found his neck as her fingers untucked his shirt from his pants. A bolt of desire burned through him as she pulled it the rest of the way over his head without hesitation.

She stood back, her eyes following the paths of his muscles, taut to keep himself from dragging her to the bed behind him.

"Gods," she whispered.

"The Gods have nothing to do with *this*." He gestured to himself before closing the distance, running his hands down the length of her back. He kissed her with gentle intention. She tasted like honey cake and wine.

Her fingers found his topknot, and he froze. Letting down a Bleck Larin's hair was such an intimate gesture. Not even Venna was willing to assist him. The act was for bondmates to share. Something about the way Freya knew exactly how to unravel it from the cuff that held it caused gooseflesh to bloom over his arms. It should not have come as a surprise. She'd been bonded to a Bleck Larin, but he couldn't recall ever having a lover assist him.

After slowly lowering his braid behind him, she held the cuff out to the side and stepped back. Her eyes were wide with fear.

"I...I should've asked..." The quiver in her voice was soft and endearing.

"I'll forgive you."

"When I saw your hair today...You're younger than I thought."

His eyes lingered on the cuff in her hand. Not *his* cuff, his father's— the king's. A crisp moment of clarity. He *was* the king.

He closed his eyes and took a deep breath before finding Freya again, his gaze falling to the way her silk nightgown poured over her perfectly delectable breasts.

He stepped forward, savoring the way her breath hitched as she backed up until she hit the dressing table. He followed her, knowing full well that he wore his hunger in his eyes. He lifted her up, her nightgown gathering at her hips. Fitting himself between her legs, he brought her tightly against him, his hands ravenous for every inch of her full figure.

Her head tipped back as he kissed her neck, nipping her earlobe and drawing a delicious gasp from her lips. She'd abandoned his cuff, both of her hands exploring the planes of his chest to his abs. She tucked her thumbs below the waist of his pants to follow the line of muscle at his hips. Those fingers. They were almost unbearable, sending a shiver down his spine.

"What magic do you wield, My Regent?" he asked with a whisper before he nibbled at her lower lip.

She grinned, pushing him away just enough to pull her nightgown over her head and lean back to let him admire all of her. "Magic has nothing to do with *this*, My King."

Gods, he would savor every moan he drew from her lips.

TWENTY-SIX

Knowing

They'd been walking since before the sky began to warm with light. Raemian's mind churned through the information Noe-eb had given her the evening before. She could finally fit pieces of her past and present where they belonged.

Her blood was the reason Eishtala worked so strangely for her. Two races of elves lived within her. While mixed blood wasn't unusual, Eishtala was the magic of Shay. Her Bleck Larin heritage grated against it, making it harder for her to channel, but it also gave her the ability to use it differently.

She trudged along behind him, sorting out the details. There was a sudden urgency in her soul to return to the place she'd come from. He said everything would be so much clearer once her feet were firmly back in the realm of the elves. But right now, she wanted to know why she was able to use Eishtala at all. If Noe-eb had given her the gift, why hadn't he anticipated her unusual abilities?

He hadn't given her all the information she wanted. Only what she needed. Just enough to answer her questions and feed the urgent fire building in her heart. He refused to give her the name she wanted. The name of the one whose eyes burned in her dreams. Only that it was imperative that she find him—and another.

So, she followed without verbal complaint, but her exhausted body language and short words were more than enough to voice her frustrations. Plus, Noe-eb wasn't shy about entering her mind whenever he pleased.

The monolith loomed against the horizon behind them as a misty reminder of the distance they'd traveled. Like most days, there would be no food or water until her training was done, and her throat felt charred by the hot sand she waded through. Noe-eb seemed to float upon the surface with frustrating grace. Perhaps he was a wraith himself.

After what seemed like the better half of a day, Noe-eb stopped at the crest of a massive dune and waited. She caught up quickly, sensing they'd finally come to what he wished to show her. When she reached the top of the dune and looked out, her breath caught.

It was as empty as the night sky. Bottomless. Jagged. A massive fissure that seemed to swallow the sand into blackness.

"This is the end of existence. The Sundering."

This word was viscous. It worked its way through her, sending a chill up her spine. She knew this word like some deeply lost history, buried in the clouds that hid her memories. It sifted to the surface of the dunes that now filled every inch of her mind and gave her the name she'd longed for.

"Good. You remember." Noe-eb turned toward the gaping emptiness and let his eyes rest there for a moment while she continued to turn the name over in her mind. "It has been growing since you came here. It will continue to grow until it swallows my Sheol of Living Souls."

Sheol of Living Souls? The sand...

She needed a moment, taking a deep breath as she looked down at her feet, sunken into the white dune they perched atop. The sand pooled around her boots, drawing her eyes to the footprints she'd left as they walked.

"Living Souls?"

Noe-eb didn't answer right away, not until she'd pinned him with wide eyes.

"The granules of sand represent all the lives in my world, your world, and all the worlds."

More questions flooded through her as she continued to digest his words, but the face of the man from her dreams kept floating to the top of her thoughts. The shape of it was more comforting than she'd anticipated.

"I need you to find him and another and repair the gate that was created by the Elder Gods."

She swallowed, her throat tight and dry. "Who is the other?" More questions. They came fast and heavy now, making it hard for her to focus.

"I cannot see the name. Only a face as white as the sand. A soul as broken as the magic."

"What broke the magic in the first place?"

He glanced across the strange nothingness. "Imbalance. The rifts to this dimension and the others of Anam and Svet were closed out of fear. Histories were tampered with. Power over your people changed hands, and in that confusion, things were undone. The Elder Gods had warned of such things, but—"

"Power of my people?"

He smiled softly. "Suffice to say, crowns and kingdoms cause elves to do terrible things."

This wasn't an answer, but it caused Raemian to think harder about her next question rather than blurting out the first thing that came to her mind.

"If the Elder Gods warned of such things, why would my people ignore this?"

"Words are powerful, Raemian. Your life only lasts so long, and with you die all your memories. But the written word can be dangerous, tampered with. Destroyed." He glanced out over the nothingness. "But not all of the copies."

She let this sink into her soul—it was important. Something she might need to do or find.

Noe-eb turned to her, sadness growing in his expression. "Long ago, when we Elder Gods gave our magic to create the barrier between Rhend and Toul, we also gave our ability to leave our realms. I cannot fix this myself."

More new words flooded the space between them. "Rhend and Toul?"

"Rhend is your home, the world of the elves. Toul is the world of the humans."

"Why must they be separated?"

He shook his head. "That's not important now. What *is* important is how the barrier was made. We knew the consequences should someone choose to break the balance...*when* someone would choose to break the balance."

"Balance," Raemian said, giving herself a moment to slip the pieces into place. More memories were returning, but they seemed insubstantial and thin. She squeezed her lips together to keep from asking more questions.

"I have every confidence you will know what needs to be done."

"Why me? Why now?"

He smiled. "You gave yourself without hesitation."

"I don't understand."

"You will. I promise."

TWENTY-SEVEN

Zennor

Neith could feel his eyes every time they touched her. It wasn't an entirely uncomfortable feeling, but having her own eyes covered made it seem awkward. The painfully bright ball of light had finally left to rest, yet she still found it too painful to remove the cloth from her eyes with the small lightsource he kept.

"Are you hungry?" His voice was calm but laced with concern. "It's been days since you've eaten."

She'd come to know his tones of voice. After she'd somehow managed to throw him with her filthy magic, he'd woken confused and angry, but he never hurt her. Never touched her other than to check on her health.

He'd been scared when she woke with a raging fever, his questions framed with a low softness. He'd sat close, checking her forehead with his warm hand, the heat from his body radiating into her in waves. She'd smelled his fear, a strange, woody scent akin to the foliage of the

Netherfields. He'd made sure she drank water, which had a sweetness to it. His voice was always gentle as he explained what he was doing and what she was drinking. She thought at one point she'd woken from a fever dream to the sound of a soft song, but once she stirred, he stopped singing, and she never heard it again.

"Will you tell me your name? I hate not knowing it."

She drew her thin legs to her chest and wrapped her arms around them. Maybe one of these times she could disappear entirely. Instead, the pain and heat from her poorly healing wound radiated into her hip, reminding her she was an elfling, not a stalagmite.

She wasn't sure she wanted to tell anyone her name ever again. It had brought her nothing but misery. The nasty way her father had spoken it, spittle flying from his enraged lips. She shook her head, and she could hear the distinct thump of a head hitting a wall in defeated.

"Mine is Zennor," he said. The smell of something salty and meaty met her nostrils. "Are you sure you aren't hungry?"

Her traitorous stomach chose that very moment to gurgle loudly, and to her surprise, Zennor chuckled, a warm sound that pulled at her heart in a way she didn't understand. She wanted to curl up next to him. To bury herself in his safety. This Zennor had never hurt her. He'd only helped her and had been nothing but kind. Had her father ever laughed? Her mother? If they had, it hadn't been in her presence. The sound was pure and wonderful, and she wanted to hear it again.

"My name is Neith," she said so softly she wasn't sure he'd heard it.

"Well, Neith, would you like to try a piece of jerky? I don't know what Trove eat. Perhaps if you told me, I could try to find you something more to your liking?"

She could tell by his voice that he was smiling. Smiling! She knew she'd never seen her parents smile, and she felt a need to remove the binding around her eyes to see this Shay's face, to experience that smile with her eyes. But she knew he'd keep his strange lightsource lit until she slept. Shay eyes were useless in the dark.

The scent of the rich food he called jerky tempted her again. What harm would there be in trying it? It *had* been days since she'd eaten. Surely, her lack of food was contributing to the slowness of her healing.

With considerable hesitation, she reached a hand toward him. The air moved as he came closer and deposited a single piece of something rough and cool into her palm. She brought it to her face, smelling it. Not sure why since she smelled it well enough from a distance. Finally, she took the smallest nibble, tasting the salty sweetness of it as she chewed.

It was delicious. Not like anything she'd eaten before. She immediately popped the rest of the jerky in her mouth.

"Do you like it?" His voice held a current of concern, as though he needed her approval, required it.

Again, the feeling that this man was so much kinder than her father overwhelmed her. When had her father cared for anything she thought? She nodded, her lips turning up slightly in her own withered smile. Something that only Adott had been able to pull from her.

"I have more."

She knew he watched her as she ate, his curious soul burning in the shadows of her mind. Having no interest in being self-conscious of how she must look to him, her sudden ravenous hunger took over. She finished the piece of jerky and felt the air touch her skin like gentle petals of flowers from the Netherfields as he extended his hand again. That longing to see him, to curl up closer to him, to feel his warm hands on her forehead again was unruly.

She heard him chuckle. Gods, it was a wonderfully welcoming sound. Something so foreign. Adott's laugh was bright and trill—the laugh of an elfling girl.

"Forgive me, Neith, but you look so young."

She shuddered. She *was* young. Too young to be alone in the world. Much too young to be a Trove in the world of Noor Above.

"How old are you exactly?" Zennor asked.

"I'm in my fourteenth year," she said softly and felt him shift a little across from her.

"And your parents?"

She leaned her head against the wall behind her. She didn't want to think of them. She never wanted to see them again. Not ever.

"They must be worried," he continued. "They must be searching for you."

She drew into herself, not wanting to tell Zennor her parents would never worry about her. They were probably celebrating that she'd finally left. That they were finally rid of her. The only person in Dakarai that would miss her was Adott.

"They would never look for me. My father hates me, and my mother loves my father too much to ever go against him."

He drew a sharp breath across his teeth, and she squeezed her legs tighter, trying to make herself as small as possible. Would Zennor wonder why? Would he think perhaps she was evil if her father hadn't even wanted her? If her father could hate her so much, what was wrong with her?

"I'm so sorry."

"I'm not," she blurted out, then sank back into herself. How could she be so callous? Zennor would think she was truly a monster.

"You're probably better off having run from him, then." His voice held an encouraging quality that was unexpected.

Neith found herself gravitating toward him just a little more.

"Being alone must have been terrifying, though."

"Only when I knew I was going to die."

He hummed his understanding, a rich sound that filled her with a calm she hadn't felt in days. When he spoke again, his voice held a solemn tone. "My father was killed. He was always good to me."

The sadness in his voice flooded Neith with sorrow. She relaxed her arms from around her legs and leaned closer to him, feeling a strong desire to comfort him.

"How old are you, Zennor?" The sound of his name on her lips was so smooth and natural. She liked saying it. Such a wonderful name, Zennor.

"Young for a Shay. I am only in my sixteenth year. Still an elfling, but I made a promise to my father that I'd continue his work."

"What was his work?" Her curiosity grew the more she learned of him. A Shay who'd been at the right place, at the right time, to pull her from the death she would surely have succumbed to.

"He was trying to establish some kind of relationship with your people. He'd been to Dakarai and Kekk but was turned away." He paused and must have noticed the concern that clutched Neith's heart. "Are you okay?"

"Your father has been to Dakarai? Recently?"

"Within the last year, yes. He said the Ethnarch saw his presence as an omen. That one of his people foretold his coming. My father said it was likely a Trove with Svet abilities."

Goosebumps bloomed on her arms. A shiver of knowing. There had been no Svet Priests in Dakarai. She was the only Trove who'd known the Shay was coming.

"Are you from Dakarai?"

But her mind couldn't leave that word: Svet. Like a dirty secret buried under layers of rock and hatred. The Svet curse had not been bestowed on anyone in many decades. For so long that the last of the Svet Priests either left or died. They'd always been ostracized and driven away. It had been said they were shunned even more by the Shay and Bleck Larin. A useless, evil magic. The reason her father hated her.

She was lost within herself and hadn't noticed that Zennor had drawn closer. His hand on her forehead yanked her from her thoughts.

She jumped, and he pulled back quickly, most likely remembering how she'd managed to throw him against a wall without the use of her hands.

"It's okay; I won't hurt you. I just needed to check your head. Your fever has—"

"Do you fear Svet magic?" She had to know. She needed to know if Zennor would hate her if he learned she possessed the curse. She'd keep the secret forever if this Shay, who was quickly becoming the only friend she had, would shun her for her strangeness as well.

"Svet is rare and powerful. It's not to be feared. It's to be protected. Svet Priests are coveted here. But they're also taken and held captive by those in power because their magic can be used to resurrect the dead." She thought she sensed some knowing in his voice. Some strange overtone of caution.

"Taken?"

"No one will take you, Neith. I'll protect you."

Every muscle in her body tensed. Fear as thick as the vines that covered the stalagmites of the Netherfields crept in around her heart and squeezed, chilling her to the bone. She shivered and drew her arms back around her legs.

"No one will hurt you, Neith. I promise."

He pulled himself closer to her, so close she could feel the heat from his body. She was so cold; she wanted to curl up into that warmth and sleep. He placed his hand on her forehead again before she felt him move closer, an arm wrapping around her shoulder, and she leaned against his firm chest.

"I need to find some wormwood so I can steep you some tea. It will help with your fever, but finding it may take me a while." He squeezed her shoulders. "Will you be okay here alone?"

Panic, so much panic. She didn't want to be away from him. She drew herself against him, fisting his shirt. So warm, like how her mother had felt when she was a tiny elfling. Before the beatings and the nasty words and the lockups in the lavatory.

"No. Please stay, Zennor."

He chuckled, the sound vibrating through her. She'd been right. It was so much more soothing when she was pressed against him.

"I'll only be gone a half an hour at most."

She eased away, remembering that a few moments ago, she never would have dreamed of being so close to a Shay. How could she have allowed herself to be so familiar with this stranger? A man who could beat her like her father had beaten her. He pulled away and rose to his feet. She cringed and drew her arms over her head, curling into herself, trying to be as far away from him as possible.

"Neith. You're safe. I won't hurt you. No one will. I promise."

She tried to calm her racing heart, her frantic breaths. This was Zennor. He'd done nothing but help her. He was kind. He was not her father. He would never be anything like her father.

She nodded. Without another word, he left, his footsteps fading into the distance. He'd taken the lantern with him, leaving her in darkness deep enough that she finally felt she could remove the cloth from her eyes.

TWENTY-EIGHT

Leaving

Raemian woke in the dark chamber like all the other mornings, seven marks for seven days in the sand beside her bed. She pulled the bracelet from under her pillow and slipped it on. She took the sleek falchion Noe-eb had gifted her and tied the scabbard at her side. Its familiar weight no longer surprised her. She stood, staring down at the hash marks in the sand before she stooped and swept them away.

She was leaving today.

She pinched some sand between her fingertips and stood, watching as the granules drifted in the stale air to her feet. She would be done with sand today. So much sand.

Noe-eb waited outside, perfectly straight-backed. His curious, light-blue eyes watched her as she slipped through the eerie darkness toward him. She didn't have to tell him what she felt. He could pull those thoughts from her mind. And he did, smiling warmly.

"Before you go, I wish to give you something of myself." He flipped his hair into his hand and ran his fingers through the silver strands, pulling away a few threads.

With nimble fingers, he wove them until he'd made a plaited loop. From his pocket, he pulled a minuscule acorn charm made of rose gold and fastened it to one side.

"It has been a very long time since I've had a fosterling. And I have never before taught someone such as yourself. A fighter. Both Shay and Bleck Larin. You have questioned me every step of the way. But you are better for it. Stronger than any other I have had the pleasure of instructing." He slipped the bracelet onto her wrist, pulling the tiny acorn through a loop to fasten it, then held her hand in his. "I have never had offspring of my own." He met her eyes, a warmth so deep it softened the features of his face.

He could see her thoughts, but she had never seen his. Only now, it seemed there was something there. Something she'd felt the entire time. Faint at first, but it grew as he watched her. Strong and powerful and building into the essence of purest fondness. Tears welled in her eyes. So much love she wasn't sure she deserved.

"You are the first Eishtala Knight, Raemian Starling of the Shay *and* Bleck Larin." As she tried to form the words to thank him, he seemed to grow less corporeal. He let her hand go as his form began to shimmer. But it wasn't just him; it was all around him. The dark stone walls of the interior of the monolith. The sand at her feet. It was fading, like the dreams that had plagued her.

"Wait." She reached for him, but her hand passed through. "Wait, Noe-eb!"

"Find them."

Rae sat up with a start. *Gastel.* She looked around frantically, but there was no one. Just herself, the trees, and the rift, its white flames twisting and turning—dancing in slow-motion. She was a mere inches away from the flames, yet there was no heat. She stretched her hand over it and watched the white fire twist harmlessly around her fingers.

She pushed herself to her feet. Had it all been a dream? But it didn't fade. It was all there, plain as the bracelet Noe-eb had given her on her left wrist. She placed her hand over it and looked into the rift again. She'd been to the Eishtala realm. She'd trained atop a massive monolith and had stood looking out at a sea of pure white sand.

The sand—she'd been to the Sheol of Living Souls—the Sheol of Life.

She'd forged with the power of Eishtala but not as the masters in Tremire manipulated it. Hers was different in confusing ways.

Rae looked down at her hands. Was it just in the Eishtala realm she had such magic? She closed her eyes, taking a deep breath, feeling the trees around her. So much life here. It was almost too much. She found she had to sift through the trees, find the right ones, and draw the life force carefully. It was easier here—frighteningly easy.

She yanked at the life forces and peeled her eyes open in time to watch the last few leaves of a nearby sapling drop away.

Gastel had opened this rift. The last thing she'd seen had been his anguished face as she'd plunged into it after losing her footing. She looked around the clearing. The leaves on most of the trees were stained with beautiful shades of auburn and rust. Autumn? But that didn't make sense. It had been early summer.

She shivered and tucked the strangeness away for later. She needed to get to Parth. Rae peeked up through the canopy to orient herself, but she worried she was turned around. She closed her eyes and tried to calm her racing heart. She'd always been able to find her way; she just needed a moment of clarity.

The Middlelend Forest felt different somehow; the trees leaned closer with curiosity, and their life forces crowded around her. Rae wondered if this was how all Eishtala Masters experienced the forest. The air was full of voices too quiet to be heard. She curled her fingers around a low branch as she focused on the energy, the silent pieces of life.

"Perhaps you can help me find the fastest route," she said aloud.

Why exactly was she talking with trees?

A few moments passed as she listened to the birdsong high overhead, the scurrying of a small animal through the fallen leaves. Like a whisper, a breeze touched the bare skin of her forearms where she'd rolled her shirt sleeves up. When she opened her eyes, an almost indiscernible path meandered between the tree trunks, golden sun streaming through the canopy to light the way.

"Ah." She hoped the forest could sense her appreciation, then decided it was best to make sure it knew. "Thank you."

In truth, she had no idea how far from Parth she was, but she refused to stop until she reached the castle stronghold. Time was tricky. When she'd passed through here with Gastel, it had seemed like they'd hiked forever. Part of that could have been the underlying fear of being caught that had followed them, another that she didn't have the forest to guide her.

After several hours passed and the trees started to thin, the path became less visible. She slowed on instinct, realizing she was likely nearing the edge of the forest and was unsure of how the peace process was going. Obviously, at this point, King Mesmal had to be aware of all that had happened and was surely making efforts to maintain what he'd seemed eager to establish. Without knowing for sure, Rae felt discretion was probably in order. Discretion and caution.

The thinner the trees became, the fewer birds and small animals she disturbed. The patches of tall grass grew larger and more prominent as the moors outside Parth crept into the forest. Tiny snippets of the city wall peeked around the last few trunks of trees as she reached the edge of the Middlelend Forest.

She stopped beside a particularly large tree, resting her hand on its trunk. Its age pressed on her mind, and she yanked her hand away, startled that it had spoken to her with ancient words she couldn't understand. After several moments of staring at the moss-covered bark of the tree, she surveyed the expanse of grass and heather that spread itself out before Parth. She stood perfectly still as though her bones hesitated. Something was different.

She was different.

Tucking her chilled hands under her arms, she stepped onto the moors.

TWENTY-NINE

Different Times

Nothing noteworthy had been brought before Belkin at the citizen hearings. These people were either scared to speak with him regarding their domestic matters or had learned from the ones who had been brave enough that King Belkin was not King Mesmal.

It was the end of another eventless day. These were the kind Belkin appreciated. It had been a couple of weeks since the coronation. He found the proverbial crown tiresome.

What he wouldn't give to have Gastel at his side. It was a thought he'd never entertained so fervently before, but his brother had spent more time at citizen hearings. Instead, Belkin was left to wait for him to wake. The boy was so much more trouble than he was worth. And yet Belkin surprised himself at how often he fretted over his youngest brother.

Belkin sat with his thoughts. Perhaps there was something they'd missed, something that could wake Gastel that the healers hadn't thought of. He pressed his index finger against his lips in thought. Just one more problem to deal with, and he might crack. The old Belkin—the high general—would return.

He clenched his teeth. He still needed to select someone as high general. Where once Belkin would have chosen Roulin, he now needed to decide what to do with his treasonous brother. He'd avoided the problem so long that it had become a serious concern. One he was still avoiding, if he were to be honest.

The last of the Bleck Larin shuffled out, and Belkin remained, leaning forward, back straight. His eyes rested on the stone floor a few feet in front of the throne, lost entirely in his thoughts. He didn't see her enter on silent feet. He didn't notice her until she stopped at the edge of his vision. His eyes traveled from soft leather boots to a Shay-blue tunic and soft pink face. Familiar shaymarks hugged along the edges of her high cheekbones. Hard lines for a Shay. Flaming red hair tied back in a loose braid down her back. Eyes as blue as the Rahven Sea.

Belkin was on his feet in an instant, unsure of what magic was at work. Who in Rhend could conjure such a perfect vision of her? She'd been dead for months! Yet here she was. He felt his stomach tighten. She was Gastel's, yet he longed to take her into his arms—a foreign feeling he'd never experienced. An urge to protect her. To keep her.

"Raemian?" He took the steps down from the throne and stood before her. She didn't look like a specter; she looked solid, real. Out of instinct, his right hand extended toward her shoulder. "How is this...possible?"

She curtsied with a grace that seemed entirely unnatural. Her eyebrows pinched together in some strange mixture of confusion and anguish. "Your Majesty." She righted herself and poured all her soul into the directness with which she looked at him. "Forgive me. I returned as soon as I was able."

"But you're...dead." He let his hand touch her shoulder, the warmth of her, the softness of her hair. She was real. She was here. "How are you...How are you here? You fell into the rift. Gastel nearly lost his hands trying to save you."

The anguish in her expression intensified. Of course, she didn't know. She'd been dead.

"And King Mes—your father? Is he well?"

Belkin closed his eyes and took a deep breath. How was this possible?

"He lives, but his health is..." Belkin shook his head. "How are you here?"

She swallowed and seemed to search the front of Belkin's doublet for answers. "I fell into the rift, where I had no knowledge of who or where I was."

Belkin squeezed his eyes closed, rubbing his temples. He shook his head. "How would it be possible for you to live but for Gastel's hands to—"

"May I see him? Is he here?" Desperation laced her voice—so much longing it hurt Belkin to even tell her. His stupid brother was alive but imprisoned within himself.

"He's..." He looked at the strange blade strapped to her side; around her right wrist was a familiar silver band decorated much like her father's Starling cuff that Gastel always wore. Upon her left, a delicate, braided bracelet adorned with a rose-gold acorn. "He's been unconscious since he opened the second rift."

Raemian's eyes fell to his feet, and he helplessly watched as they filled with tears. He wasn't good at this. He'd never been the one to comfort others. Yet the urge to take her into his arms was there again, and this time, he gave in. He reached and pulled her toward him, holding her to his chest.

She was warm and smelled like a fresh morning in the forest, loam and honeysuckle. With her head tucked under his chin, she fit so perfectly to the shape of him. He could feel her body shake as she cried. Rather than pull away, as he would have been inclined, he let his arms wrap around her and closed his eyes, living for a moment in a different world. One where he wasn't Belkin, and she wasn't Raemian Starling. He resisted the urge to run his hand along the length of her hair, so impossibly soft where it touched his chin.

There was something primal in that moment—a hunger that built deep inside him. This was not something he knew. He'd satisfied the fires of lust before. This was different. This was raw and rigid. Something deeper, built on emotions and tenderness. Definitely not something he was good at, and he instantly felt a heavy regret fill the pit of his stomach.

After several moments, she pulled away, leaving his skin cold where her hands had wrapped around his back.

"I'm sorry." Her cheeks burned an adorable shade darker than the rest of her face. Perhaps she'd sensed his thoughts? Or perhaps they were her own thoughts that colored her cheeks. "So much has changed so quickly."

But it hadn't been quickly. It had been months.

Raemian must have noticed Belkin's confused expression because she shook her head in disbelief, her eyes searching his in that familiar way. The one that confirmed she missed nothing. Saw everything. Remembered everything.

"It's only been seven days. How could so much have happened in only seven days?"

He raised his eyebrows in shock. Days?

"It's been nearly six months." He could see the moment her world fractured. Her eyes squeezed closed, lips pressing together in absolute despair.

"Six months?" Her voice shook. "But it's only been days in the Eishtala realm." She held his eyes for several seconds as if there were irrefutable confirmation there.

"Eishtala realm?"

She took a breath, and as she did, the air changed. The smell of grass and trees and the tepid warmth of an autumn afternoon encased them. With her eyes closed, she exhaled slowly, letting whatever strange magic was at work flow out and around them. When she opened her eyes, they were the color of emerald leaves, glowing with soft light.

"Noe-eb taught me how to harness Eishtala."

Belkin took a cautious step back. He'd seen Eishtala Masters perform their craft, but it didn't make it any less foreign. His hesitation didn't go unnoticed. Raemian's expression softened, a sweet smile turning up the corners of her lips.

"The Sundering threatens all of us. It threatens all that has been and ever will be." The words rushed from her as she let the Eishtala magic dissipate, the warmth of it filling the air around Belkin like a summer's day. "I need to help Gastel restore the rifts. It's the only way to reestablish balance to the magic so we can repair the damage that's already been done."

Belkin swallowed hard. If Gastel never woke, they could already be lost.

Rae hadn't been sure what to expect. Not this. Anything but this. When Belkin brought her to Gastel's room, the healers were placing him back in his bed, his limp body dead weight in the servants' arms.

Lifeless. Completely and utterly lifeless.

Rae's eyes filled with tears, unable to hold them back at the sight of him. His strange hands, how his flesh faded from gray to pale white. It only added to her confusion and sorrow.

"We've kept him as comfortable as possible." Belkin's voice seemed intentionally quiet. "The healers are doing everything they can. He is lost within his own mind and must find his way out."

Belkin's presence behind her was more comforting than she'd expected. Since being crowned king, he carried himself differently. An air of calm, whether forced or a symptom of the added weight of a kingdom, Rae wasn't entirely sure. And she wasn't sure she liked this new Belkin any more than the old one.

"How long has he been..." She choked on her words, desperate to finish the question but completely unable. Did it matter? The muscles in her neck strained as she tried to keep herself from smothering her eyes with the heels of her hands to wash away this image of Gastel's helpless form.

"Two months." Rae felt Belkin's voice grow strained with concern. "By the grace of the Elder Gods, his body has somehow sustained itself without food or drink. As if the Anam keeps him alive."

She shuddered. What magic could both hold his mind captive yet sustain him for two months?

Anam.

In all its terrible, fiery power, it was entirely dependent on the Wielder's life force. While it was obvious that Gastel was immensely powerful, he was not immortal.

"Can I stay with him?" She wished her voice hadn't been so unsteady.

There was still a strange current of uncertainty that rippled between herself and Belkin. She wished so much to hide her vulnerable side from him. Not that it mattered. Nothing mattered if they didn't have Gastel to open the last rift and help her fix the magic of the Wastelands.

After a moment, Rae turned and met Belkin's stoic expression. He watched her, his amber eyes crossing between hers, searching for something. Whether he found his answer or not, she wasn't sure, but he nodded and turned away without another word, motioning to the healers to leave with him.

The silence was deafening. The Gastel she'd spoken with last would have had a witty response, a confident tone to his voice. A forcefulness in his words that would have reassured her. But this? A sob escaped her lips, and she pulled herself onto the bed beside him.

There'd been a moment of hope when she'd sat up next to the rift, remembering all of who she was and what she had to do. But that was gone, washed away by the tide of the Sundering as it raged ever closer. Without Gastel, would there be a Wielder strong enough to open a rift? And even if there was, did Rae want to live in a Rhend without him?

Rae watched his chest rise and fall with even breaths, his eyes refusing to move beneath his eyelids—a dreamless slumber. She reached a hand to trace the lines of his face, across his cheek, along his jaw. She'd never have been so forward if he'd been awake. But there was no one to see her, no one to know how much her heart was breaking into a million pieces and spreading themselves out around him.

"I'm so sorry, Gastel." She let her hand glide down his exposed shoulder and along his arm, still deceivingly strong, as if his muscles had not atrophied from disuse. Her fingers traced the length of his forearm, where his gray skin began to fade to white, so warm under her fingertips. She wished to curl herself up in his strong arms. Instead, she closed her eyes and let her mind fall over the edge of his bed, flowing across the floor and out the window to the grass and shrubs in the gardens. She could pull the life force in and try to heal him with Eishtala, but she had failed to heal Noe-eb. She would only succeed in killing the nearest plants that would succumb to her coaxing.

Still, she refused to dismiss the opportunity and pulled the power into herself, feeling the sun's warmth on the leaves of the nearest shrubs, which now withered in their sacrifice. Rae held the magic within herself for a moment, silently asking for a miracle, some blessing from the Elder Gods, before she pushed the Eishtala through her fingers and into Gastel's body.

He didn't move, not a flinch, not a single jerk. Nothing. Motionless and empty. And she felt that emptiness like cold rain on her face. Thick tears ran across her temple and soaked into the blanket below her. He was lost, and she had no idea how to guide him. She curled into a ball beside him, refusing to let go of his hand, not yet. She needed to stay, to touch him. To see his amber eyes, even if only in her memory.

Just a little longer.

THIRTY

Vulnerability

Belkin was lost in his own thoughts, turning over the reality that Raemian was alive and possessing at least some proficiency in Eishtala, which she'd not had before. He'd wandered along the dark halls of the castle stronghold after leaving her with Gastel and her heart-wrenching sorrow. There was nothing that could be done, but she'd wished to stay with him, and Belkin could not bear to sit and watch her as she gazed longingly at Gastel while he slowly died.

It was nearly the evening meal, and Belkin thought it only proper to at least invite the Shay to dine with him and his father. He knew Mesmal would welcome the girl with genuine warmth. After all, it had been his father who'd spared her life all those months ago when she'd been captured in the Middlelend Forest.

He pushed the door to Gastel's chambers open, knowing full well that his brother's library would be dark and empty. The books that lined the shelves hadn't been touched in months, but the smell of the leather bindings still assaulted him. He crossed to the open door that led into Gastel's bedchamber. The soft glow of the remaining afternoon light danced across the stone floor at his feet.

She was curled into a tight ball on the bed, fast asleep, her face turned in Gastel's direction, her hand covering his. The warm light illuminated her hair, turning the strands a brilliant copper. Belkin moved closer, mesmerized by her closed eyes, the relaxed serenity of her expression, and her slightly parted lips.

His thoughts grew dark. What if Gastel never woke? She'd been here for half a day, yet Belkin dreaded what such sadness would look like on her face. He could see the memory of Gastel's anguished expression when he'd returned from opening the first rift. For some reason, it was easier for him to accept his brother's sorrow than hers.

Raemian's eyes peeled open slowly, so slowly, held together by threads of red lashes. Belkin couldn't pull his attention from her face as she looked from Gastel to the afternoon light flickering across the surface of the blankets, then finally to Belkin. Her lips tugged up at the corners as she pushed herself up to sit cross-legged.

"I…" She stumbled on her words with a gentle voice, one he'd not heard from her lips before. Smooth, honeyed with drowsiness. "I didn't mean to fall asleep."

Belkin stepped closer, standing at the end of the bed, his hands reaching to rest on one of the heavy posts. He looked from her to Gastel's empty expression. Some part of his brother was still in there—he had to be—rebuilding his Anam after sharing so much of himself with the rift he'd opened.

"I was curious if you wished to dine with me and my father." He spoke with more confidence than he'd intended, but she didn't seem to mind. Instead, her smile brightened, and she pulled herself to the edge of the bed, letting her legs dangle over.

Belkin was thrust back to the memory of her as she'd sat on the rickety cot in the north tower when he'd informed her he'd be returning her to her queen. Months. It had been months since then. The Shay he saw before him was so very much the same and so very, very different at once.

She'd been a scared lamb, a terrified girl at the mercy of her enemies then. She'd tried to hide behind a stoic mask, but he'd seen through her, seeing the small and helpless woman before him. It had startled him to see her that way, when the night before, she'd defeated and spared his life in the most maddeningly glorious duel he'd ever fought. Raemian Starling, one of the Shay's most decorated warriors. Swift, calculated, deadly. And yet...vulnerable, terrified, and fragile.

And now? She was still a vulnerable Shay woman, but there was a strangeness to the way she held herself. A determination had seeped into her bones. It resonated louder than the soft helplessness that clung to the edges of her slender frame. A strength that emanated from her more confidently than it had before.

"I should like that very much, Your Majesty."

Belkin smiled. She was always so formal with him, even before, when she'd had no reason to be. They'd been enemies. He, the high general of the Bleck Larin army. She, the renowned warrior of the Shay.

"It's Belkin."

Her face flushed, that gorgeous pink burning brighter in her cheeks as she jumped down and approached him on silent feet. The same feet that had tracked through forests, snuck up on her enemies, and soundlessly moved through the world. She was still a Shay and a dangerous warrior, but for the first time, Belkin knew that he'd never have to fear her blade again.

"Well then, *Belkin*, I should very much like to dine with you and your father."

Neith's leg throbbed. The wound hadn't closed properly. Zennor had tried his best, but he was not a healer, and Neith knew even less about tending to injuries.

It smelled horrible, putrid like the refuse heaps in Dakarai—dying and diseased. Thankfully, the fever came less. Still, Zennor checked on her throughout the cycles of light with vigilance, calm, and insistence on changing the dressing on the wound each day.

He'd been away most of this cycle of light for supplies. He'd promised he'd find her more wormwood and hunt so he could make more of the delicious jerky he'd shared with her. So, she sat alone, two pieces of cloth over her eyes, the light still bleeding through and causing a wretched headache. Would her eyes ever adjust to the light of the world of Noor Above?

The ball of light Zennor called the sun was sinking in the sky, its warmth fading. He'd described the trees, the hills, everything around them, but she longed to see them with her own eyes—to see what he saw. If her eyes never became accustomed to the light, that wouldn't be possible.

Someone approached outside, and she pushed herself up from her bed and back against the wall behind her. She sent her mind out and touched the edges of Zennor's consciousness. It was warm, like always. With heavy steps, he trudged in and crouched beside her before he lifted his hand to her forehead.

"Your fever is back." His voice was strained.

"What's wrong, Zennor?" She could smell his sweat, pain...blood? He sat back hard as if he could no longer hold himself up.

"It's nothing." He slid down so that he lay beside her makeshift bed on the dirt floor. "I'm just exhausted."

She knew he was lying. She could feel it. Why would he lie? She reached and touched his consciousness, feeling his discomfort radiating out.

"You're hurt." She pulled herself closer to him, feeling for him with timid hands, and found him lying on his back. She let her fingers travel along his torso to his arm and followed that to his face. He let her hands wander without moving, without flinching. She touched the soft skin of his cheek and traced the line of his jaw without realizing how intimate her touch seemed until he took in a sharp breath through his teeth.

"I'll be okay. I fell down a ravine and...hurt my knees."

For a moment, they remained in silence until her nerves settled. She pushed fear and apprehension away, pulling herself closer, ignoring the pulling of the flesh around her wound. Ignoring the way his breath caught for a moment before it evened out again. She tucked herself against him, soaking in his warmth. He was always hot. Her skin burned where she touched him. But she drew herself closer, wrapping her arm around his solid chest.

He was still for a long time. Too long. She rested her hand on his sternum so she could feel his breathing. It had evened out and was slow and steady, as though he'd fallen fast asleep. So, she waited, listening to the sound his breath made as it passed through his nose. His warmth enveloped her and filled her stomach with a strange longing to stay like this forever. She did her best to ignore the pain in her leg as it throbbed, and she slipped to sleep, tucked under his arm.

Burning Blood

Neith woke in the depths of the cycle of dark—what Zennor called night. Strange chirping sounds filtered in from outside, in the world of Noor Above. It was almost as soothing as the feeling of his body next to hers. She reluctantly pulled away from him, and thankfully, he didn't stir. She hadn't wanted to wake him. He'd been so exhausted when he'd returned.

Neith reached for the strips of fabric protecting her eyes and pulled them over her head, a sudden urge to see him.

She'd never seen a Shay or a more beautiful being in all her life. His face was like a dream: pale pink flesh, full cheeks, strong, sharp jawline. His shaggy white hair was splayed out behind his head. His lips were full, not like Trove elf lips, which were usually thin, pale lavender lines. Strange red markings stained the sides of his face and down his neck until they slipped beneath his shirt. And the shape of his chest beneath was certainly nothing like a Trove. He was perhaps three times the size of most grown Trove males. Easily that much larger than her own father.

He took a deep breath, and she watched that powerful chest rise and fall, the muscles in his abdomen tighten, drawing her eyes down the length of him. Even his legs were powerful. The material of his leather pants pulled tightly across his thighs. The knees were torn and bloody. He'd not been lying when he'd said he'd hurt himself.

For a moment, she wished she hadn't looked. Now she'd have this image of perfection in her mind every time Zennor talked. She would long to see him again, but the light would prevent it. She was about to pull the cloth back over her eyes when he opened his own, staring up at the ceiling. Clear, glorious blue eyes framed by white lashes. She was lost in those eyes as he took an extra deep breath, then looked around, likely noticing that she wasn't tucked against him.

"Neith?" He sat up, his eyes searching the darkness, but she knew he couldn't see her. Still, he reached one strong arm in her direction. She didn't move, letting his hand find her shoulder and travel to her face. "Are you all right?"

"I was worried about you." Her voice was softer than she'd intended it to be, whispering as though there were others sleeping around them.

His fingers found her temple, and he drew his hand back.

"You don't have your eyes covered." His voice matched the furrowing of his brow. She reached for his hands and took them with her own. They were so much larger than hers.

"I wanted to see you. I've never seen a Shay."

He smiled. Gods, if he was beautiful before, the smile lit his face up in ways that gave Neith a strange warmth in her abdomen.

"I'd never seen a Trove until I found you."

"Shay are more beautiful"

His smile grew larger, and he chuckled, warm and rich. "I don't know if I entirely agree." His voice was thick with something she couldn't quite understand. After a moment more of staring in her direction, unable to see her in the dark, he slipped back down onto his back and put his arms behind his head. His brilliant blue eyes closed, but Neith watched him for another moment.

"Wait till you see a Bleck Larin. Now, *they* are beautiful."

She shivered. Bleck Larin? She'd heard of them. Tall, dark creatures. The opposite of Trove appearance in almost every way.

"Perhaps I'd rather not." She pulled the cloth back over her eyes and lay down on her bed, turning in Zennor's direction. As much as she wished to tuck herself against him again, she thought it best not to get too used to such closeness.

＋———　———＋

Rae had to keep collecting the pieces of her broken heart. Sitting in the dining room with Mesmal, she couldn't help but notice how thin he'd become. The lines of his face were deep with sorrow. He no longer carried the air of youth as he had when she'd first faced him in his throne room months back, and it destroyed her. Why had he seemed to age so quickly?

"Still no change in Gastel?" Mesmal's voice held hope and hurt at the same time, as though they were two threads holding the same hem of his sanity.

Belkin shook his head, clearly reluctant to admit that even with Rae's presence, Gastel didn't wake.

She swallowed her words and glanced at the plate in front of her, realizing that she sat in Gastel's seat at the table.

What had she done? Could she have saved him if she hadn't fallen into the rift?

Rae immediately answered her own questions. This was not her fault. She'd been desperate to save Gastel's life and slipped. Accidents happened, and she'd spent enough of her life consumed by guilt for things she had no control over.

If she hadn't fallen into the first rift, she might have been able to help him open the second one, but she wouldn't have acquired the power of Eishtala, and what she could do with this new magic was yet to be seen. Noe-eb had been clear. Her power was needed to help stop the Sundering as much as Gastel's.

"Raemian, tell me again about the rift." Mesmal's eyes glittered with curiosity. She'd explained much of this to him as the three of them had walked together to the dining hall, but she would indulge him. She would *always* indulge him.

"What do you wish to know?" She matched his warm smile, resting her hand over his.

Belkin leaned back in his chair as if preparing for a long story he hadn't heard. His calm expression was so much like his father's. The longer she spent with this new Belkin, the more she felt comfortable with him, though some part of her knew a man couldn't just change his soul with his clothes.

"Tell me of Noe-eb and Eishtala."

She cast her thoughts back, but the memories had blurred some as if viewed through the surface of water, ripples distorting the time and space into a disjointed painting. An air of knowing in Mesmal's face stopped her before she could speak.

"You've met Noe-eb?"

Mesmal glanced down at her hand still resting over his, a wry smile turning up his lips. "I know *of* him. Many years back, when I was a spry elfling, and the legends of the Elder Gods were fresh in the history books, he was known as the patron of Eishtala—the bestower of the gift of growth and healing. Guardian of the Sheol of Life." He met her eyes again, that same twinkle lighting up his face. "I thought him lost to the ages, but he has dwelled in solitude in the Eishtala realm. It seems fitting."

Goosebumps flowered across Rae's arms as she was reminded that Noe-eb was an Elder God. One of the very beings responsible for the creation of the elves themselves, the shaping of Rhend and givers of magic.

He took a long sip from his glass of wine before glancing over at his son. "What we wouldn't all give to meet an Elder God ourselves."

Something passed between father and son, and for a moment, Rae felt as though she didn't belong. Finally, Belkin turned to her, calm interest mapped across the sharp angles of his face.

"That he should feel so inclined to bestow the gift of Eishtala upon one whose blood is stained with Bleck Larin heritage intrigues me," Belkin said. The cool repose of his bearing was jarring. How could a crown draw the anger from a man? "But explain further the rifts. My inclination has thus far been to assume that this Sundering is nothing more than youngling stories."

Rae braced herself for what she needed to explain. It was hard for her to understand, and she had the added benefit of hours to think it through. Broken balance aside, the concept of opening tears in the reality of the world to allow for magic to bleed into their realm seemed fanciful. And yet, the fact that there had been Wielders capable of repairing those tears in the first place seemed all the more impossible.

"Gastel spoke of repairing balance, something Freya mentioned as well, but I don't see how that alone will restore the barrier across the Wastelands," he continued.

Rae shivered. So, it was true, then. The magic of the Wastelands, which was put in place after the Hundred Years' War to keep the humans from Rhend, was damaged. Just as Noe-eb had shown her.

Mesmal watched and waited with rapt attention. He either had little to interject or wished to wait until he'd heard what she had to say.

"I only know what Noe-eb instructed me to do." She tried to keep her words collected even though her heart was racing. "He said the rifts needed to be opened to restore the balance of magic and that the barrier between Rhend and Toul needed repair. He said I would know what needed to be done when I returned to this realm, but I'm struggling to understand my role." She folded her hands in front of her as both Mesmal and Belkin's eyes burned into her. "I feel like I'm still missing something. He told me that I would need the help of Gastel and a Trove gifted with the power of Svet to repair the magic, but nothing on how."

She let this sink in, preparing herself for the first thing she needed to do. It was the last thing she wanted. If she could choose, she'd rather spend her days at Gastel's side until he woke, holding his strangely healed hand.

"I need to find a Trove who can help us. The sooner, the better."

Belkin glanced at Mesmal, perhaps expecting him to object, but he only watched her with his same emotionless mask, a knowing raise of the eyebrows as he glanced at the food that was being placed in front of them. The awkward pause seemed to drag until Belkin cleared his throat.

"Whatever assistance you require, you have but to ask," the king said.

The new king!

Rae was still trying to get used to Belkin as the king of the Bleck Larin, and here he was, graciously offering assistance. A genial smile crossed his face as he gazed at her from across the table. She held his amber eyes for another moment, trying to discern if there was some hidden meaning in his kindness, but she eventually settled on doing something she never thought she could do—not with Belkin.

"Thank you, Belkin."

She would trust him. She would rely on him.

But before she did anything else, she needed time. She'd spend a few days at Gastel's side to ease the ache in her heart before she left.

"I'll leave in a few days, if you'll allow me to stay." She looked down at her hands. "I just need a little time..."

"Of course," Belkin said. "You are always welcome. Stay as long as you need."

As long as she needed. That's what it was. It was need. She *needed* to be with Gastel for a little longer. The beautiful friendship they'd shared had been blossoming into something much more significant than she'd anticipated—new and scary in a wonderful way. She craved it. She craved him, a hope so deep within her that she wasn't sure she'd survive if he never woke.

But then again, would any of them?

THIRTY-TWO

Our Miserable Fate

Rae had been given her room from before along the guest quarters. She'd slept, but terribly so. When the morning meal was brought in to her, she was provided with a gown so her clothing could be laundered. The feel of silk against her skin felt unnatural. She was used to cotton and tight leather. She pulled the laces, cinching the red brocade around her ribs before glancing in the mirror.

The neckline was lower than she liked, showing her prominent collarbones and the swell of her breasts. The color made her hair look brassy, with unruly waves flowing over her shoulders. She pulled it into a braid, then ran her hands down the bodice, trying to ignore how exposed it made her feel.

Ducking into the hall, she nodded at the handful of servants who bowed as she passed on her route to Mesmal's study. She wanted to speak with him before she visited Gastel again.

She knocked, stepping back and clasping her hands behind her. Perhaps Mesmal wasn't there. A warm glow spilled from the crack below the door, and after a thick moment, the shadow of feet shifted across the light.

Belkin greeted her on the other side of the door. His stern expression eased as his eyes raked from her toes to her face. So immensely strange to see him wearing the same calm kindness Gastel always offered her. His cream tunic, trimmed with tiny gold embroidered dragons, made him look thinner and less dangerous. He stepped to the side, sweeping a hand across the space to welcome her.

"Raemian!" Mesmal's weary voice met her from across the room. "Please, join us."

"Actually, Father, I was just leaving," Belkin said as his eyes followed Rae. The way he looked at her was...different.

"Forgive me for interrupting," she said, noticing that the cases of correspondence that had littered the room the last time she'd been there were gone. The study was tidy, the massive hearth bursting with a warm fire, pouring golden light across the otherwise cold stone floors.

"You could never interrupt," Belkin said as he stepped into the hall. "Good day, Father, Raemian." He pulled the door closed behind him.

Mesmal nodded at his son before reaching for something on his side table. Rae was left standing. The chair that sat across from him looked beyond comfortable, but she couldn't bring herself to sit without permission.

Mesmal's glance was expectant. "Please, sit. We have much to discuss."

And they did. She'd been making a mental tally of all the things she wanted to ask him. Questions about the houses, the royal families, and whether Mesmal had spent any time studying the prophecy. Rae eased into the leather chair, the cushions cradling her. Perhaps she'd manage to bring herself to ask Mesmal about her father and mother. She had so many things drifting through her mind at once that it was hard to focus on where to start.

"I found something in my correspondence that I wanted to show you." He handed her a letter, his eager eyes glittering in the firelight.

The written words drew goosebumps across her arms as she read, a hastily scrawled *Starling elfling* standing off the page. Bowrhem's words were vague but enough for her to understand their meaning. Rae had always admired her legion for his un-Shaylike calm and contemplativeness, but she hadn't realized that he'd admired her as well.

"The first battle was…" Mesmal struggled to continue. So much history in his eyes. He took a deep breath and started again: "Bowrhem knew what Gemma was trying to do and felt helpless to stop it. He worked from the start to find some way to calm the storm. In the end, he knew she would take what she felt was deserved, and there was no one in Rhend that could stop her." He paused; his eyes held hers for a long moment. "No one but perhaps your father or you."

Rae had been a tiny elfling when the war had started—her mother taken from her in the Culling. To think, there were those who'd known all along what her role might be in the changing of the tide of Rhend made her self-conscious.

"Your skills as a fighter were a blessed gift from the Gods after Gemma sent you to train. Bowrhem tried to pair you with his brightest fighter, but you bonded so quickly to young Dulanii." Mesmal smiled to himself. "He turned out to be a perfect partner for you, though, I should think."

"You knew all of this—what I would someday do—when you saw me in your throne room? When I was brought here?"

Mesmal glanced at the fire, his usual stoic calm settling over his features. "I did. At least, I hoped. Dare I say, I was elated that things might finally be changing after years of our people suffering in needless war over Gemma's petty grievances and my rash mistakes." He met her eyes. "You were not at all as I thought you'd be. Part of me worried that Belkin and Roulin would break you."

She glanced down at her feet. A part of her had thought perhaps they would as well. The memory of Belkin's glare, Roulin's hateful words. But it all melted away when she thought of Gastel's smile and gentle confidence.

"You seemed so small, hiding your terror behind an unfaltering reputation. I'd assumed when Bowrhem sent me this a few years ago"—Mesmal handed Rae another letter—"that you'd be significantly more formidable-looking at least."

Bowrhem's words were more urgent in this letter. It was short and significantly more cryptic. He spoke of plans, within plans, and Gemma's treatment of family. And the elfling that had become an unparalleled fighter, but Gemma tried desperately to be rid of them.

It seems only a matter of time until I fear there shall be nothing we can do but endure until the Elder Gods, themselves, determine our miserable fate.

"And then he sent me nothing." Mesmal looked toward the fireplace. "Time is such a strange state of being. I've squandered so very much of it."

Rae leaned forward, reaching a hand to Mesmal's knee. "There's still some left."

He smiled without looking at her, sadness sinking into the lines on his face. "For you, yes."

She sat back, trying to process everything he'd shared about Bowrhem, the other tidbits he'd managed to rediscover in his correspondence, the melancholy in his voice, the bone-tired way he hunched his shoulders. Rae had so many other questions, but seeing Mesmal now washed them all away. He was spent, and she'd need to be pleased with the information he'd already shared.

"I shall leave you to rest." She grasped the arms of the chair to rise, but he turned to her swiftly.

"No, no, you have questions. I can see them in your eyes."

"Another time, Mesmal. I hate to tire you more."

"I am always tired these days. I can rest when I'm dead."

She pinched her lips together, unhappy with discussing death with a man she admired more than he'd ever know. "The split from the houses…"

He nodded, his eyes finding the rafters of his study. "Ah. Strange times, those."

"When I tried to find information in Dormshire, I found many of the books tampered with."

"It's hard to know exactly who it was that altered the histories, but I think we both have our suspicions," he said with a sly smile.

Rae recalled what the librarian in Dormshire had said: Gemma had collected various documents. She wished she'd had the forethought to ask more. "Gemma?"

He nodded. "Though I wouldn't put it past her father to have planted the seed." He smoothed his hands over the knees of his robes. "I was still a fairly new king with much to prove. And Clore Tremire was ruthless. I sought to keep things peaceful between us, but it meant changes I wasn't always excited to make."

"Did my grandfather relinquish his crown to Clore peacefully?"

"It was made to look that way. Mostly that Somsunder refused to give up the Starling House name so easily. I, for one, had hoped to build better relations with the Shay and found the houses and their strangleholds to be tiresome. It was easy for me to step away from the House of Raggethan."

"But why would anyone wish for the royal families to relinquish their house names in the first place?" she asked, more to herself than to Mesmal.

"Because it's easier to hide history when there's anonymity. No house names, no complicated arguments regarding the royal lineage." Mesmal sighed. "Clore was truly conniving. He'd wormed his way into Somsunder's life, perhaps to steal a crown all along. He took his intentions with him to the Great Sheol."

Rae nodded, trying to put the pieces to the puzzle in place. "What is your knowledge of the guilds?"

He shook his head slowly. "You dug deep in your quest for information."

Her cheeks heated under his gentle smile. "If only you knew."

Mesmal's smile faded. "If I'd known who Niminea Amfithere was when I met her, I might have been more cautious with my heart." He closed his eyes and took a deep breath. "The Anam Guild seemed so single-minded in their quest. There was no one who could talk them out of it. She was a pawn in their games, I fear. I never learned if there was some deeper reason other than to keep the magic out of the wrong hands, but they were resistant to anything other than closing the rifts entirely."

Rae reached across the space and laid a hand on Mesmal's knee again, his downturned face instantly brightening. "If you hadn't fallen in love with Niminea, we wouldn't have Gastel," she said.

He grinned and nodded. "She was my muse. After Dalkin, my bond-mate and queen, passed, I never thought I'd love again. Being a king and finding love is so rare, to have found it twice?" He shook his head. "Between Gemma's unwavering lust to solidify her claim to the throne and my sorrow at losing Niminea, we left Rhend in a wretched state."

The crackling fire filled the quiet between them as they sat with their thoughts. Rae had more questions, but she could see the conversation wearing on Mesmal's shoulders. He was slumped over even further than he'd been when she'd come to his study.

"Thank you for your words, Mesmal, but I truly think you should rest." She stood, but he reached a hand in her direction to stop her.

"The prophecy."

The hair rose on the back of her neck.

"I have a copy. It was my father's and my father's father before him. Only the Elder Gods know whose it was before that." He rose, a gentle hand taking Rae with him. "It's been locked away for years." He seemed suddenly energized and pulled Rae along behind him. "Let's fetch it. I haven't read it since..." He paused in thought. "I was an elfling. Gods, that was...a world ago."

A world, indeed. Rae wasn't certain how old Mesmal was, but she knew he was well into his second millennium.

"I remember very little of it at any rate."

"I think we can forgive you for that," Rae said with a smile.

Mesmal chuckled as he led her through the castle stronghold to a set of heavy doors on the opposite side of the throne room. She knew Gastel had his own library, but she hadn't realized how extensive Mesmal's would be.

Shelves stacked upon shelves soared to the ceiling, all filled from edge to edge with books. It was nearly twice the size of the library Rae had visited in Dormshire. Mesmal left her stunned at the entrance and walked directly to a cabinet at the back. Rae could only stop and stare. She'd need a thousand years to read all these books. Her eyes widened as she realized...

"Have you read all of these?" She might have been embarrassed by the awe in her voice, but Mesmal hadn't seemed to have heard her. Instead, he continued to rummage through the cabinet.

Rae was drawn to a long desk scattered with bits and bobs and more books. A round disk of glass that seemed to magnify the text below it, a letter opener in the shape of a dagger, a falcon's claw with the talons curled in on themselves. She trailed a finger across the wood surface until it stopped in front of a cuff that looked much like the one Gastel had worn before his topknot had been sheared away.

"It was Niminea's." Rae jumped at Mesmal's voice so close behind her. "It reminds me that even at my age, I am still capable of tremendous love."

He gave her a warm, fatherly smile with so much adoration and trust she didn't deserve.

"And this"—he extended a small, unassuming manuscript forward—"is my grandfather's copy of the prophecy."

Rae hesitated before taking it from his hands. It was lighter than she'd anticipated, the pages brown with the patina of time. She ran her fingers over the unadorned, brown leather, then flipped the cover open to see elegant ligatures of a name. *Morisal Raggethan*, further proof that Mesmal and his sons were indeed the descendants of the House of Raggethan.

"I don't know if it will help you in your curiosity. There are so many different translations, it's hard to know which is the most accurate." He sighed. "I wonder how many of them have been tampered with like the histories or if the Elder Gods had hoped to confuse us for their own amusement."

The Elder Gods—now that Rae had met one, she wished she could return to Noe-eb and ask him herself. How many more Elder Gods still existed, and were they all trapped in alternate realms as Noe-eb was?

So many more questions. Rae worried she'd spend the rest of her life searching for answers.

"Thank you, Mesmal." She clutched the book to her chest. If Gastel never woke and she failed in her quest to find a Svet priest...If the Sundering destroyed all of Rhend, the world, and every world that ever existed, she'd at least cherish the friendship she'd built with Mesmal for the rest of her life, however long that might be.

Of Loneliness and Wine

It was heart-wrenching sitting at Gastel's bedside, and yet Rae would rather do nothing else. She'd lost track of how many days she'd spent this way, unable to pry herself from his side or to wander from Mesmal's study to the library and back again.

Late afternoon light streamed through open curtains, leaving stains of gold across his legs, tucked tightly beneath bedcovers. His lips were parted. Had they been parted before? She wondered if he'd stirred, if this was the first sign of consciousness.

She'd put off leaving more than once, thinking perhaps it would be the day he'd wake, but she couldn't any longer. With a heavy heart, she'd informed Mesmal and Belkin of her intentions at the evening meal over a carafe of wine. She had needed every drop of it to calm her nerves. While they both seemed saddened for her to leave, Belkin's mood changed. She caught him staring at her more than once, his expression tortured.

When Mesmal had pried, she'd shared her plans. She intended to head to Tremire but would go west and work her way along the Hill of Tombs rather than through the Middlelend Forest, hoping to stumble upon an easy route to one of the Trove Holds. She didn't think she'd find anything, but the extra few days of travel it added was worth the opportunity.

Otherwise, she needed to see Freck. Dulanii was her truest friend. He would be upset to know she was back and hadn't called on him sooner. Not to mention, Regent Freya was the one elf in Rhend who she knew could help her find a Svet Priest. As the former leader of the Aequus, there was sure to be a connection Rae could explore.

She took a sip of wine she'd brought with her to Gastel's bedchamber. She'd been drinking more of it than usual; the headiness of Bleck Larin wine was so much stronger than anything she'd previously consumed, but she needed the layer of distance it gave her from her fear that he'd wake as soon as she left—or that he'd never wake at all.

She eased down beside him, her fingers falling to his arm, tracing the lines of his muscles. He still looked like the same man who'd stood in the stream on the edge of the Middlelend Forest; his dark, ethereal strength couldn't be tamed by whatever held him.

"I wish you'd wake."

She watched his chest's gentle rise and fall, rhythmic and soothing. After a few moments, she sat up, her head swimming from the change in position. Too much wine and yet not nearly enough. Opening the book she'd brought, she read to herself. It was the convoluted translation of the prophecy that Mesmal had given her. It was by far the oldest manuscript Rae had ever held in her hands.

Setting the book down beside Gastel, she frowned, her gaze falling on his closed eyes. She reached for his hair, her fingers brushing over the soft locks splayed across his forehead. If he'd been awake, he would have pushed it out of his face, leaving it messy and perfect.

If he'd been awake…

"Perhaps if I read to you." She cleared her throat, leaning to see the page. "'But time doth a tricky mistress be. For thy shall hold love in crystal hands cut of sorrow. The work of many undone by the work of one.'"

She gazed over at him again before she reached, her index finger trailing along the side of his face to his chin and over the sharp line of his jaw.

Over the last few days, she'd become more comfortable touching him. Little touches, soft, intentional. Maybe he could feel her somehow, her wanting bleeding through her skin and into his. Anything was possible, she told herself. She'd managed to fall through a rift and live, learning to control Eishtala from an Elder God—surely Gastel could pull himself from whatever held him captive.

She picked the book up and laid it across her legs, turning the page, trying to find a better place to read from. Flipping through a couple more, her attention snagged on a new area.

"'With dust of an old world at thy feet, ye shall behold the Sheol anew. Bright like stars within a new mooned sky. Hold souls in thy palm and breathe the life of Gods.'"

She set the book back down. Reading aloud felt strange. She flipped through more pages, reading to herself for a while, the minutes thick as the last blades of light from the window bled onto the far wall.

The words were flowery and hard to connect, especially with her wine-doused mind. There were double meanings in all of it. Plus, the understanding that the elf who had recorded this particular copy may have translated it incorrectly.

Rae glanced over at Gastel's slumbering face again. He didn't look as though he'd been lying in this bed for weeks; the color of his face and lips were still their usual stony gray. Gods, she wanted to kiss those lips. Instead, she let her eyes wander down his neck and collarbones, an unfortunate longing coursing through her before she cleared her throat and looked over to the side table, where her wineglass sat empty beside a half-full carafe.

She slid closer and filled the glass, red facets of light filtering through and splaying across the palm of her hand. She took several long drinks. It was refreshing in a way she wasn't used to, leaving her chest lighter, her mind free, so she had more before looking back down at the book.

"'A score shall be settled. Only the Reborn, the Restored, and the Returned shall play the game of Gods.'" She swallowed more wine. Something in those words resonated in her stomach, rich and full. "'When the worlds are at their thinnest. When the sacrifice of the Elders dissolves into beautiful remembrance. When the day cracks into three. When a heart is broken by another's choice, a heart is forged in family, and a heart is gilded of purest silver.'"

She held her breath for a moment. Three pieces, three hearts. The Reborn, the Restored, the Returned were also three. Three races. Three types of magic. So simple, yet how did all these things fit together? And what held them as one? Noe-eb had said Rae needed the help of Gastel and a Svet Priest. The three of them likely represented the magic and the three races, but what about the other things? What was the sacrifice of the Elders? How did a day crack into three?

Rae lay back with the book still in her lap, the room spinning. She glanced over at the glass on the side table. It was empty. Some sultry part of her wanted just a little more, even though she knew she'd already consumed entirely too much. Closing the book, Rae pushed it away before pouring another glass, emptying the carafe.

The light was fading, frayed as it glittered on the wall. She took a drink, then another. Long sips, the crimson liquid coating her thoughts with calmness. She'd spent the better part of a day at Gastel's bedside. *Again.* Still, he hadn't woken. She set the glass back down and lay on her side facing him, tracing the profile of his perfect nose with her eyes back to those lips.

"I wish you'd wake." She knew she'd said it already. She'd say it again, over and over, until his eyes opened. "I wish I could tell you everything that's happened. I wish so many things, Gastel."

The world grew blurry around her as her eyes filled with tears.

"Please wake."

She curled into herself, reaching a single hand to rest on his, the space between them growing thinner yet so far. So very, very far. Perhaps the wine was the secret to her sleepless nights all along because before she could take another sip, she closed her eyes to blessed darkness.

The silence of night held the castle stronghold in a greedy fist. There was no one to disturb Belkin as he paced the halls. He'd spent the day reviewing paperwork and trying his best to understand all the things his father had managed flawlessly for centuries. These were not things he was good at, and he wished more than anything he had better counsel.

He stopped in front of Gastel's door. This part of the castle was entirely too quiet these days. After glaring at the woodgrain for another moment, Belkin pushed the door open, wondering if Raemian was still at his bedside. He was drawn to her more than he was comfortable admitting. At least, this time, he had an excuse. He hoped he could ask for her thoughts on how she'd handle the situation with Roulin if she were in his position. If he didn't do something about his troublesome brother, he worried there'd be dire consequences.

The sun had set hours ago. Usually, he'd have seen her sneaking into his father's study or find her in the library poring over manuscripts, feeding some hunger for knowledge that never seemed satiated. She'd announced her intention to finally be on her way—to face the same lingering fairy tales Gastel and Freya had been so bent on seeing through, and he'd hoped to speak with her one more time.

A single candle burned on a dressing table, likely lit by a servant who came with the attending healer to evaluate Gastel's condition every evening. The flickering light glazed Gastel's still form with gold, his stark-white hands glowing against the dark bedcovers. Beside him, curled into herself as before, was Raemian. Her hair splayed out behind her in a mess of fiery curls. An empty carafe of wine and a half-full glass sat on the side table.

"Raemian." She didn't stir when Belkin approached.

He raised his hand to touch her shoulder but waited, worried he'd startle her, unsure of how she'd respond. If she was anything like him, a knife would be at his throat in an instant.

He watched her sleep for a moment more, the gentle rise and fall of her shoulder, the way her eyes moved beneath her eyelids. If she'd consumed an entire carafe of wine, it was possible she was too inebriated to be roused with words alone. He clutched her shoulder.

"Raemian, it's late." He gently shook her. "Raemian."

She rolled to her back, her brow furrowing. An annoyed moan escaped her parted lips. Reluctantly, her eyes peeled open just enough to find him.

"Hmmm?" She squeezed her eyes closed before opening them a little wider, desperately trying to focus on Belkin. "Gods, I've...much too much ...too much wine."

"So, it seems."

She tried to sit up but failed, and Belkin reached an arm behind to help her.

"I...should find some water." She tried again to focus on Belkin's face. "I'm sorry...I ...can you..." She stumbled over slurred words, her eyes glittering gems of partial consciousness in the candlelight.

"Are you asking for my help, Raemian?" He smirked. It wasn't like her to request assistance from him. She'd maintained an impenetrable barrier since she'd returned from death, never letting him in closer than small talk.

"Please." Her eyes fell to his lips. "Can you help me?"

He swallowed hard at the way she looked at him. Those were hungry eyes. He'd walk her to her room and leave her at the door. Nothing good would come of doing anything more.

Belkin helped her slide to the end of the bed and onto her feet, her hand clutching his forearm. He stepped back to lead her, but she lost her footing and slumped against his side, throwing her arms around his waist in a clumsy effort to keep upright.

"You're in no shape to walk." He stiffly grasped both her shoulders, holding her at arm's length.

"I can..." She pushed away from him, adorable stubbornness scrunching her nose. "I *can* walk." But when she tried again, she stumbled.

"Nonsense." He swept her from her feet. "You've nearly fallen twice."

Belkin was startled at how light she was as he hauled her from Gastel's room. How had a wisp of an elf caused so much trouble on the battlefield? He tried to push past the simmering warmth building in his stomach. He'd carry her to her room and nothing more. He'd place her at the door and call for a servant to help her to bed.

Nothing more.

Her head fell against his chest, and Belkin bit his lip—the caress of her breath brushed over his skin. Her face tucked so perfectly against his neck.

"I miss him," she whispered as she fisted the front of Belkin's shirt with one hand, her other splayed across his chest, the heat of it soaking through.

"I know."

When he got to her room, he realized he'd likely need to place her directly in her bed. She was in no condition to stand, even for the few moments it would take to fetch someone to help her.

The curtains were drawn, and not a scrap of light filtered through. Thankfully, most of the rooms in the castle stronghold were of a similar layout, and he was able to navigate with only the pale slice of illumination from the hall.

Belkin tried to set her down, but she refused to release his shirt.

"Raemian." She only held tighter, nuzzling against him. Hot longing rippled through him, molten and delicious. He swallowed it, desperate to push away the errant thoughts filling his chest with butterflies. "Raemian, let me get you some water."

"Please don't leave me, Gastel."

He stiffened, letting the name she'd used wash over him like a carafe of cold wine to the face. He shouldn't be with her like this. He needed to extract himself from her grasp, and he feared it would require both his hands to do so.

He sat on the edge of the bed with her in his lap as she pulled herself against him tighter.

"Raemian, please let go." He needed to leave. "I need to get you some water."

"Another moment, Gastel. Please. Just another moment." She spoke against the crook of his neck, her lips brushing over his skin. So close, so dangerously close. "Please," she whispered again. "Please."

It broke him, like the moment in the throne room when she'd learned of Gastel's fate. He wrapped his arms around her, savoring how she melted into him, curving to fit against his torso. That nagging part of him screeched to pry himself from her. But a louder part wanted to hold her, to drag her further onto the bed. To find the rhythm of their bodies until she screamed his name. But he knew it wouldn't be his name she'd scream. She didn't want him.

She wanted Gastel.

She sobbed against him, all the heart-wrenching time she'd spent at his brother's bedside in those tears. Belkin cradled the back of her head, his fingers tangling in her hair.

"Only a moment," he whispered before he pressed his lips to the top of her head, the scent of sweet wine filling his lungs.

One of her hands yanked at the bottom of his shirt, pulling it loose from his pants, meandering fingers branding his stomach with tantalizing fire. His breath hitched at her touch. She pulled herself up, bringing her face within inches of his. He froze as she straddled him and remained firmly in place as she took his face in her hands. She gazed at him for a long moment, her expression concealed in the darkness.

Who did she see? Did she see him? Or did she see Gastel?

He took a breath to speak, but she closed the distance, their lips crashing together with urgency and teeth.

Somewhere, lost in the back of Belkin's mind, was the voice of reason, hopelessly fighting its way through the thick fog of his own desire.

This was wrong.

She was drunk.

He was not Gastel.

But the ache, Gods, the yearning in every fiber of his being. He'd dreamt of this over and over again—fucked Freya when Raemian was whom he truly wanted. His hands found her hips and yanked her onto him as he slid them both farther onto the bed. She kissed him harder, her tongue hungry as she forced it between his teeth.

He desperately tried to remember what had held him back a moment ago. Every nerve in his body was alive. Every touch of her fingertips left trails of fiery wanting on his skin. She pulled his shirt up, her hands tracing the lines of his muscles. The heat of her skin against his was maddening. She tasted exactly as he'd feared—delectable—rich, ripe berries dipped in the sweetest honey. So good. So very, very…

"Fuck, I want you." The words escaped him before he could temper them, gilded in months of dreaming of this—of her.

His fingers ran the length of her firm, toned muscles with softness in the perfect places. He cupped her ass with one hand as his other snuck beneath the front of her shirt, rucked up around her ribcage, his fingertips grazing the lower curve of her breast.

"Please," she mewled against him, an anguished need in that word so powerful it turned his insides to liquid. She dragged her nose along his jaw, nipping his earlobe. "Please…" Her whispered breath on his ear was more than he could bear. One of her hands traced the length of his chest to his neck; her other found the front of his pants and traveled lower, grasping him.

He gasped. This was wrong.

"Rae …"

This was very wrong. She was drunk.

She didn't want him.

"Raemian, stop."

He forgot how strong she was. Strong enough that it took significant force to take her by the wrists and pull her hands away from his body. His entire being burned for nothing more than to let her explore every inch of him if she so desired, knowing full well he couldn't hide his own desire, hard between his legs.

"Raemian." He forced sternness into his voice, and she paused, leaning away from him, swaying a little. He could see her outline, perfectly framed in the light from the hall, her face left in shadow. "Rae, I'm not Gastel. I'm Belkin."

"Belkin." Her voice was small, tainted with the slur of drunkenness. "Belkin?"

"Yes. Belkin." Every muscle in his body tensed as he fought against himself to hold her aloft.

She let out a heavy, pained sob, yanking her hands from his grasp and covering her face.

"It's fine. You've done nothing wrong. You thought I was..."

His hands hovered in front of her arms, too scared to touch her again for fear of what she would do—of what *he* would do—when they'd already done too much. He knew he would never be able to forget the weight of her body on his, her taste. Her soft, pleading whispers.

"It's fine, truly, but you need to get off me." He only had so much self-control left. Gods help him, if he'd been able to see her face, her pouty lips, the gorgeous shade of magenta she turned when she was embarrassed. "Please, Raemian, I need you to move. *Now*."

She slid off him, dragging herself to the head of the bed, where she buried her face in a pillow, her shoulders shaking as she wept.

He lay back, staring up at the ceiling, hands frozen in the air above him. He forced long, slow breaths into his lungs before he sat up, glancing over at her still form. Had she already fallen asleep?

Exactly how drunk was she?

He already knew the answer. Drunk enough that she'd kissed him—forcefully. Thought he was his brother. Straddled him, pinned him down. Might have done more things with him she'd have gravely regretted.

He stood, slowly—reluctantly—glancing back at Raemian. He feared the guilt of this would be unbearable in the morning, but at the moment, his only regret was not having appeased what she so painfully craved—a physical need that would croon within her until satiated.

Belkin closed the door to Raemian's room behind him, finding a servant as he fled and requesting that they deliver water to her as soon as possible. Whether they noticed his frazzled state or rumpled clothes, he didn't care. He needed to put distance between himself and Raemian.

A lot of distance.

When he was safely locked in his own room, he pressed his back against the door, chest heaving, eyes wide. He'd nearly made the worst mistake he'd ever made. He'd never taken advantage of a drunk lover, much less a woman who thought he was someone else. Yet part of him begged to return to her room. Now, with enough to occupy his mind into the wee hours of the night, he'd be forced to relive her hands, her scent, her whimpers. He needed to do something about this burning desire festering under his skin, or it would consume him entirely.

⊹ —— —— ⊹

A splintering stream of agony lanced through solid darkness, sending shards of colors and light ripping through Gastel's mind. Hopeless, he couldn't move, couldn't see, couldn't hear.

He could only wait. For something. Anything.

Wait in the crystal clarity of deafening silence and nothingness.

Until he opened his eyes and found himself staring up at the ceiling of his bedchamber, stained with the flicker of candlelight, the smell of leather book bindings and medicinal herbs sharp in the air. Another scent: fresh morning dew and wine. Perhaps it was a latent memory as he struggled to wake.

He tried to sit up but seemed paralyzed, as if he hadn't moved in days, weeks, perhaps longer. With terrifying lucidity, he could feel every inch of his body as it was frozen in place, off limits to him entirely.

He'd finally broken free from the void of his own mind only to be trapped in a paralyzed body. He reached through himself down to his fingertips and toes. If he could move one finger, he could slowly work the strength back into the others and into the rest of his body—or so he hoped.

He focused on the blood pumping through his veins, the breath passing his parted lips. He pulled at the strings that seemed to hold his extremities firmly in place, yanking with all his strength.

Until his finger moved.

Only a tiny bit, but it moved.

He lifted his index finger a mere inch off the surface of the bed, but it was something.

Exhaustion flooded through him, and his eyes slipped closed, his eyelids too heavy to hold open. Gods, he didn't wish to return to that dark place where he felt he'd already spent entirely too long. He grasped at the edges of his consciousness with all his remaining strength, but it was no use. He slipped down, further and further, until there was nothing.

The Color of Souls

Rae left without saying goodbye. She knew Mesmal would understand. Belkin, on the other hand, she feared he might hunt her down and confront her, and she didn't need any additional confirmation of the events between them.

She'd hoped it had been a dream. That her alcohol-addled brain had concocted some horrible torture for her to endure. But she knew it wasn't. The memory of his hands on her body was too real. Of *her* hands on *his* body, firm muscles shifting below her fingertips, hot silky flesh beneath her hands. She'd kissed him, and he'd reciprocated with haunting strength. She couldn't stop dwelling over her stupidity, reliving every...single...devastating moment.

Fuck, I want you.

His words were branded across her flesh, flowing down her spine, igniting her stomach. Over and over and...

Fuck, I want you.

The thickness of his voice had stripped her bare, leaving her raw and exposed—ripping everything she knew from her mind in that terrible moment. All of it coated in a veneer of wine-drunk haze and loneliness.

And she needed to rid herself of the memory of it, or she feared she'd lose herself, guilt drawing tears from her even as she stalked through the northernmost edge of the Middlelend Forest. She'd hoped the trees would swallow her whole. This forest had a way of cleansing her of dark thoughts, forcing her to concentrate on moving through undetected. The last thing she wanted was for Belkin to track her down. Now that he was a king, perhaps he wouldn't venture out on such lowly tasks.

A king. Belkin was her king! She'd drunkenly thrown herself at her king! Her cheeks burned, but she only increased her pace, putting more distance between herself and the castle stronghold. She would smother these memories with this new task at hand—and by conjuring the perfect mental image of Gastel's sleeping face.

It seemed like days had passed since Gastel opened his eyes to the ceiling of his personal chambers. He was slowly starting to move his extremities. First his fingers, then toes, then slowly his arms and legs. Each time he'd forced himself through the motions, he was rewarded with intense exhaustion. It felt like days, but it might have only been hours for all he knew.

He pried his eyes open and lay as he always seemed to in the dim light of his bedchamber. Alone. Always alone. He wasn't sure if anyone bothered with him or how long he'd been like this, but whatever the answer when he woke, there was no one.

Gastel steeled himself against the strain it would take to finally sit up. It was time. Certainly, someone had noticed that the blankets around his arms were rumpled a little differently than they'd been before.

He clenched his teeth and brought his knees up and then his chest to his knees. It was harder than he thought it would be, but he was sitting, head spinning, vision blurry.

Gods, how long had he been lying in this bed?

Shoulders slumping over, he sagged forward with the effort it'd taken, but he managed to remain in a mostly upright position, letting his eyes travel around his familiar room. Everything was as it had been before he'd left for the Vail. His cuff rested upon his dressing table. His formal longsword with its gem-encrusted hilt was cradled in its stand on the top of his wardrobe.

There were some things different. The Starling bracelet he'd worn rested on the nightstand beside him. His mother's soul stone lay flat on the top of his dressing table. The door to his library was left open, which he so rarely did when he slept. The curtains on the window beside his bed were pulled open, letting light pour in across the floor, the angles shifting where it touched the edges of the soft rug in his sitting area.

A murmur from the hall met his ears, and he perked up. It could have been his father's voice. It held a resonance that he and his brothers shared with Mesmal. But there was an authority there that seemed incongruous with his father.

The door opened, and Gastel met Belkin's eyes. His eldest brother's expression shifted from concern to sheer joy as the man walked with a measured stride through the library and into his bedchamber.

"Brother." Belkin stopped at the foot of his bed, resting both his hands on the elaborately carved footboard with a grin that was entirely out of place for his character. "You've finally decided to join us."

Gastel didn't have the heart in that moment to share that he'd been awake for quite some time, unable to move. Even now, he wasn't sure he could speak.

"I feared the price you'd paid to open the second rift was your consciousness."

How correct Belkin was.

"How..." He cleared his throat. "How long?"

"You've been unconscious for two months."

There was something strange about Belkin. It wasn't just the kind words and soft tone he used. There was a gentleness that didn't belong. Gastel's eyes glossed over the cream doublet he wore instead of his customary blood red and black before his eyes landed on the dragon wing cuff holding his topknot in place. It wasn't the same one he'd worn for years, yet it was familiar in a way that made Gastel feel he'd missed something very important.

Fear flooded through him. Fear that his father had befallen some tragedy while he'd been slumbering away. Belkin must have noticed how his face tightened with anguish, and he moved around the bed so that he could step closer.

"All is well, Brother, but much has changed." The slightest smile turned up the corners of Belkin's lips.

"Is Father..." Gastel closed his eyes as he struggled to speak, his breaths coming short and harsh as his body struggled to keep him upright. "Is he..."

Belkin's smile deepened, and he glanced down at his hands, which rested on the bed coverings. "He's well." With eyes full of knowing, Belkin met Gastel's questioning gaze. "He stepped down to ensure that I could take the throne without contention. There is much we must speak about when you are well enough."

It took a moment for his words to sink in and for Gastel to realize that he was speaking to his king. Heat rose in his face, and he squeezed his eyes closed. He'd missed so much. Two months? He had so many questions and no time to ask them because he felt his energy waning and his vision clouding over.

"My King..."

"There will be time enough for that nonsense later." With firm hands, Belkin eased him back down to the bed where he could do little more than lie there with his eyes closed, watching the shadows of the last two months of being lost within his own mind dance across the inside of his eyelids.

"Rest now, Gastel. I shall send Father to you."

Gastel's eyes popped open, urgency blooming in his stomach. "Dulanii. Is he..." He felt his chest tightening with fear at the thought of the Shay who had stayed by his side through everything.

"Dulanii returned with Regent Freya to Tremire after my coronation. I wouldn't let him waste away at your bedside, and Freya had need of him."

Gastel squeezed his eyes closed, tears brimming along the edges. Too long. He'd slept for too long.

"Kal and Inara?"

"The Effrin insisted on taking Inara home to her family."

"And the rift?"

A warm chuckle, so strange from his battle-hardened brother. "I am told it roars with the white fires of Anam."

Even as Belkin was finishing his words, Gastel was slipping away, the room growing unnaturally dark around him. He tried to speak again, but the words were no longer there. He'd run out of time and drifted into unconsciousness.

He'd been gone three cycles of the light. Neith was beginning to fret. Without a beast he called a horse, he said it would take him a few days to travel to the nearest Shay settlement and back. Her leg had still not healed, and her fevers were coming more often, even with the wormwood. They needed more supplies, he'd said.

So, she waited, fretting, lying in bed with her eyes wrapped, listening for the sound of his footfalls. She sent her mind out every so often, but she only found the tiny creatures that lived around the dwelling. Something called rabbits. Squirrels, mice, snakes, insects. All new things that Zennor had described to her as they'd sat and talked in the waning light.

They'd exchanged stories of their homes. He'd told her of the great trees that the Shay preferred to make their dwellings from. That his home, where he and his father had lived when he was much, much younger, was the greatest of all the Shay cities, the tree city of Tremire. It sounded like a fantasy to her when he described it, and she wished more than anything to travel there with him and see for herself.

He'd been under a strange spell, paralyzed with rapt attention, the evening she'd told him of Dakarai, of the Netherfields, of the long tunnel to Kekk that she'd traveled alone. The terror of the monster that had chased her—the one Zennor called a cave tendron.

But now, she was alone again. She'd never thought she'd meet a Shay, and now she couldn't see herself being without him.

She sent her mind out again, farther, pushing out until it grew uncomfortable. The farther she went, the stranger it felt, like something kept her from seeing things as they truly were. There was nothing but the animals with fluffy tufts of fur and tiny insects scurrying about.

Neith adjusted her leg, causing the pain to radiate into her hip. She felt with her fingers; it was hot and angry. She was sticky-warm yet cold. The fever burned in her veins and sent shivers along her spine so deep her entire body trembled. She longed for Zennor's hand on her forehead as her teeth chattered.

She sent her mind out again, restlessly searching, finding the rabbit, the family of mice, the…

A woman. A Shay? She moved deftly through the trees as though she'd passed through this way before. Her aura was strange, radiating some essence of pure green that caught in Neith's throat.

She struggled to sit up, ignoring the pain in her leg. The Shay would see the dwelling. Neith reached with her mind again to find the Shay was there, just outside, calm and quiet.

"Hello?" Her voice was like a song. Like Zennor's but much higher in pitch. Smooth, not like she'd just been bounding through the forest. She was close enough now that Neith could hear her nearly silent footfalls. "Is anyone there?"

She stepped into the dwelling and stopped. All Neith could do was sit there, as still as possible, back against the wall. She stared with her wrapped eyes in the direction of this new Shay, waiting for her to say something, anything. She feared her heart might beat out of her chest, and yet she knew this woman was not dangerous. Her consciousness held a refined peacefulness.

"Hello," she said, her voice soft, nearly a whisper. "Are you hurt?" She could likely smell the same things Neith could smell—disease and blood and infection. Fever and sweat on the blankets she'd been lying on for so long she could no longer say.

But Neith only shook her head no and wrapped her arms around herself.

"I won't hurt you." She took a few steps closer, and Neith pulled away as far as she could but was met with another wall. Pinned in the corner, she felt the woman's hand on her forehead. "You have a high fever." She let her hand fall away, and Neith felt her rummaging along the blankets, trying to pull them away.

The Shay woman would see Neith's leg—see the infection. Neith was certain it was as disgusting to see as it was to smell. But when she tried to push the woman's hands away, she realized how weak she'd become. She did little more than rumple the blankets around the Shay's hands.

"I can help you. I have Eishtala magic."

Neith paused. Zennor had mentioned more than once that she needed an Eishtala healer to help her.

"Who are you? Do you know Zennor?"

"I'm sorry, I don't know Zennor. My name is Rae. I promise I can help you at least a little. Can I see your injury?"

"Zennor will be back soon." She pushed away again with feeble fingers. It did nothing. She was too weak and too tired.

The blankets were pulled away from her leg, and the Shay woman sucked breath across her teeth.

"This is...How long have you been injured?"

"Zennor would know. He'll be back soon."

But Rae was pulling the blankets farther away, most likely looking at the blue lines that traced up her leg. Her fingers were hot like Zennor's. Too hot.

"Please. Zennor will be back. He promised he would be back."

"How long has he been gone?"

Neith felt a strange tickling on the edge of her consciousness and drew herself in tightly, pulling her mind as far away from Rae as possible. This was magic. It seemed to tug at her soul, lengthening it into wispy threads.

"What are you doing?" Neith's voice quivered. She was effectively blind, but for the first time since Zennor had brought her to this place, she was willing to risk the blades of searing, bright light to see what this Shay woman was doing.

She went to pull the cloth from around her eyes when it stopped. Rae moved away and stood. From outside, the sound of heavy footsteps.

Rae moved away as she stepped out of the dwelling. The sound of metal scraping across metal sent a shiver raking up Neith's spine.

"Who are you?" It was Zennor's voice from across the clearing. Strong, deliberate, unyielding. Neith let out a sigh of relief. "Have you hurt Neith?"

"She needs a healer."

The woman didn't move, but she could hear Zennor's confident steps as he hurried closer.

Neith let out a pathetic whimper in fear, trying to press herself farther into the corner of the dwelling.

"You've hurt her." A primal growl ripped from Zennor, and before he'd finished uttering those three words, he was running, his haggard footsteps almost too loud.

"I've not hurt her. I'm a healer. I can help her."

Steel on steel rang out, and Neith let herself slip down the wall and back under the bed coverings. She risked sending her mind out and touched them both. Zennor's aura was red with rage.

"If you've hurt her, I swear I'll kill you." He moved back, seeming to rethink this strategy, which was good because Neith could see how calm Rae's soul was. Even the sight of Zennor's massive solid muscles had not intimidated her. Her aura was still a vibrant green, a peacefulness so deeply rooted.

"I've not come to hurt anyone."

They were quiet for a moment. Neith wondered if they were sizing each other up, staring at each other before she heard Zennor's sword slide back into its sheath.

"Are you an Eishtala Master?" Zennor's voice had changed. There was a softness to it. A strange quality that she'd heard only a handful of times. Always when he talked about her health and how it seemed to fade away before him.

"Not a Master, but I do possess some level of healing. Enough to help. I don't know if I can completely heal her leg, but I will do what I can."

Zennor must have walked past Rae because before Neith could do so much as say his name, he was falling to his knees beside her and scooping her up. He was hot where he gathered her against him. She could do little more than place a hand on his chest, his body trembling with terror.

"Gods, if you'd been hurt..." His voice was soft and low, and it rumbled through her as she nuzzled against him, instantly soothing her fear. He turned back to Rae. "Please, if you can heal her...I've done all I can. I've tried everything I could think of." He laid her back down on the blankets and swept a lock of hair from her face with careful fingers. "She was bitten by a tendron. I was able to give her the antidote and stitch the wound, but it's slowly gotten worse."

Neith felt the pulling again on the edge of her mind, stronger this time as if it yanked her consciousness away in long strings. She struggled against the magic and curled her fingers into Zennor's shirt.

"I'm sorry, but this will likely hurt."

Whatever power this was, it was painful. A stifled cry ripped from her lips, cut short by blinding agony. Zennor tucked himself around her, his hands cradling her face against his chest, but it was no use. Her voice caught in her throat as the pain ripped away her consciousness.

It was dark when she opened her eyes again. Neith could always tell when the cycle of light had passed, even with her eyes covered. She sat up, and for the first time in a very long time, her leg didn't hurt. She pushed herself against the wall of the dwelling and pulled the blankets back.

It couldn't have been so easy.

She remembered the magic, the Eishtala, as it had flowed around her, tugging at her mind, yanking at her very soul. Blinding pain had shredded down her leg in waves of heat and prickly needles. The strange Shay woman who called herself Rae had told her she could help, but had she?

Neith's fingers gently probed along the side of her leg, slowly making their way down to where the tendron had sunk its wretched fang deep into her muscle. But there was no pain at all, only numbness around a puckered scar that ran the length of the bite.

She pulled the wrappings from her eyes, glancing down at her injury. Sure enough, there was nothing but a violet scar. No infected flesh. The smell of rotting was completely gone. Even the blue lines that had snaked up to her abdomen had disappeared. She ran her fingers over the puffy skin with wonder.

"Neith?" It was Zennor's gentle voice.

Neith found his concerned face in the blackness, his throat bobbing with fear.

"Forgive me for waking you, Zennor." She kept her voice at little more than a whisper as another lump of a sleeping elf was in the far corner of the dwelling. She didn't want to wake Rae as well.

"Are you okay?" He pulled himself closer, his helpless Shay eyes requiring so much light to work properly.

"I am." She moved nearer, yearning to tuck herself into his arms. He'd been gone for three days, and she hadn't had an opportunity to speak with him. "My leg feels...fine."

Genuine relief showed in his expression.

"I thought..." He hesitated, which gave Neith time to inch a little closer. Close enough that she could feel his breath, smell the fresh forest on his skin. "When you lost consciousness, I thought..."

"I'm fine. I'm better than fine. My leg feels completely healed." She reached for his hand. "Here." She placed his fingers upon the puckered scar; the fire of his fingertips traced across its surface, that strange numbness still there. "She healed me completely."

He drew himself closer and lifted his hand to her face. She leaned forward to close the distance, letting his fingers touch her cheek and trace along her temple to her forehead to feel for fever.

"You've uncovered your eyes again."

"I wanted to see."

"Can you see me?" His hand trailed back down her temple to her jaw before he dropped it to his side. "Even in this darkness?"

Such a soft touch, something she was still not so certain of. It gave her a moment of pause before she answered.

"I can."

He smiled, but it was fleeting.

"I wish I could see all of your face without your eyes covered, just once."

The corners of her lips tugged up at his curious words. So endearing. As much as she wished to move closer, to wrap her arms around his shoulders, to tuck herself against him as she had before, she remained still, watching his eyes as they struggled to see anything in the dark. Instead, she slipped down to her bed, pulling the wrapping back over her eyes.

"Maybe someday my eyes will be used to the light."

He must have heard that she'd moved away because he lay back down on his back with his arms behind his head, as he usually slept, and gazed up at the ceiling with his crystal-blue eyes.

"Or maybe someday I'll figure out how to see the way you see," he said.

She shivered. Why would anyone want to see as she could see, with searing pain at the slightest bit of light? The light that made the world of Noor Above the amazing place it was. But she didn't say this; instead, she took a deep breath, let it out long and slow, and waited, listening for the telltale sounds of Zennor's deep breaths as he slipped away to sleep.

Tender Elflings

Rae had always been one to wake late, but under the current circumstances, she woke with the sun streaming through the cracks in the door of the hut she shared with Zennor and the Trove. She stretched as she sat up to find the girl awake, back against the far wall, covered eyes pointed in Rae's direction.

Her name was Neith. Zennor had given her backstory after Rae had managed to heal her leg. Rae didn't hide that she stared at her. Neith was the first Trove she'd ever seen, other than in art depictions and the stained-glass window that hung high in the tower at the castle stronghold. Her flesh was so pale it seemed to glow with every drop of light available. Her hair reminded Rae of Noe-eb's. Straight and so white it appeared silver. It glittered when she moved in a way that caused Rae's fingers to itch with a yearning to touch it. Her lips were two plump, violet petals resting above a delicate, pointed chin. In proportion, she looked like an elfling. Heart-shaped face, thin neck, dainty extremities. Her arms and legs were longer than they should have been for her height, but perhaps their slenderness made them appear this way. She was petite and graceful, beautiful in an uncanny way.

"You're not like Zennor."

Rae jumped, not expecting Neith's soft, emotionless voice to cut the morning silence. How the girl knew Rae was awake and watching her was interesting.

"I'm not?" Rae asked, curious if the girl would elaborate.

"You look...You're different."

It was in the words she didn't say that Rae found meaning.

"How can you see me?"

Neith seemed to sink into herself as though she could melt into the wall of the hut.

"I..." She glanced in Zennor's direction, who still slept soundly beside her bed. Could she see him? Neith swallowed, took a deep breath, and then sat up straighter as though she needed a moment to build up the courage to speak. "I can see your soul. It's not like Zennor's."

Goosebumps bloomed across Rae's arms. If the girl could see her soul, did she have the gift of Svet?

"Is this something all Trove can see?" Rae tried to keep the excitement from her voice and school her heart, which was beginning to race. If she'd found whom she was looking for in the first place she searched...

"No." Again, Neith sank into herself, scared of something. Of Rae, perhaps? Zennor had mentioned he'd thought she'd been abused by her parents or someone close to her. When he'd found her, she'd had old bruises across her face. They were several days old already, so it didn't occur from her tendron encounter.

"Zennor said your name is Neith?" Rae asked, hoping she could establish trust. "That's a beautiful name."

Neith folded her arms around her knees and drew them to her chest. "It was my dama's name."

"Dama?"

"My mother's mother."

Rae nodded, not sure if Neith could see the motion through the cotton covering her eyes. "He said he found you hurt."

She eased a little, letting her legs slide back down, opening up a tiny bit. "He said it was a tendron. It chased me and bit my leg."

"And your parents? Were they not with you?"

Neith closed down again, her shoulders arching in on themselves. Her body language alone proved that someone had hurt her.

"I was alone. I was traveling to Kekk."

Rae was vaguely familiar with Kekk, the center of power for the Trove, but how to get there was still a mystery to most Shay and Bleck Larin. Countless tunnels dotted the western borders along the Hill of Tombs, but most dared not enter for fear of exactly what had befallen Neith—the monsters of the deep.

"Were you coming from Dakarai?" Rae had taken a guess based on how far north they were, and the way Neith's posture changed made her assume she'd guessed correctly, but the girl didn't answer. Instead, she turned her head toward Zennor as he stirred. She seemed to watch him as he rolled to his back, throwing an arm over his eyes.

Zennor was young. Perhaps still an elfling. He was both confident and clumsy. It reminded Rae of how Freck had been when they'd first met. It was obvious from her first encounter with him that Zennor had not been through any type of battle training; perhaps all his knowledge of how to wield a sword had been self-taught.

He sat up suddenly, glancing first in Neith's direction and then toward Rae, his eyes more alert than hers would ever be immediately after waking. He stared at Rae for longer than he should have.

"I thought you said you weren't an Eishtala healer." He glanced over at Neith.

"I'm not. Not yet, anyway." Rae stood, her stomach grumbling.

"Who are you, if you aren't an Eishtala healer?"

She paused, her eyes finding Neith from across the hut and holding on the girl's bound eyes. Rae wondered if Neith could see all of her, the parts that were Shay and Bleck Larin. A burning curiosity of what made each soul different lanced through her. Was it a person's race? Their morality? Could Neith see her past? All the lives she'd taken in the name of a forsaken queen?

"Just a Shay who can channel Eishtala."

There was silence. Zennor glanced at Neith before shaking his head and running his fingers through his shoulder-length hair.

"Well, whatever you call yourself, thank you," he said. "I..." His eyes dropped to his hands in his lap. "I had tried everything, and I thought..."

Rae couldn't help but smile at Zennor's tenderness. Her stomach interrupted her thoughts again. "Are you two hungry?"

Rae kept moving; the antsy feeling that clutched her heart over the last few days took hold in her fingers as she prepared a meal for the three of them. The trees here were young and spindly. They grew in clumps with low branches, casting speckled shadows that shifted as the breeze danced through them. Squirrels flicked fluffy tails as they scented the air and scurried about, busy hiding their treasures for the impending winter. Late mornings were Rae's favorite. The world was awake, warmed by a friendly sun, oblivious to the chill of autumn.

Zennor fretted over Neith after finding her a comfortable spot in the clearing outside the hut. It was endearing, the way he ensured she had everything she could ever need. Rae sat across from them, placing a crude bowl between them filled with the morning's foraged fare—wild berries, walnuts, and a handful of radishes, cleaned and sliced. She had a single round of flatbread that she tore into equal parts and gave to each of them.

Neith had wrapped her sensitive eyes a second time. It left all sorts of questions in the pit of Rae's stomach. She didn't want to overwhelm the girl with her curiosity, but she burned to know more about the conditions in which she lived.

"How long have you been living here?" Rae eventually asked Zennor.

He hesitated, glancing quickly at Rae's side, where she'd already strapped her blade.

"My father had been attempting to establish some measure of contact with the Trove for years before his passing. I came about a year ago to help him."

Vague as his answer was, it satisfied what Rae needed to know. Zennor could most likely help her understand the dangers of the caves. She'd been taking her time meandering along the base of the Hill of Tombs, hoping she'd stumble upon an entrance to Kekk, knowing full well that many of the caves were decoys and led to dead ends or worse.

If there was one thing Rae hated, it was caves. Part of her had been avoiding plunging into the darkness, but another part of her desperately wanted to get to Tremire so she could return to Parth in case Gastel had awakened.

"I may need your guidance. I need to find a Trove with the gift of Svet," Rae said.

Neith shifted, drawing Rae's attention. With the girl's eyes covered, she shouldn't have seen Rae's reaction, but Zennor did. He turned in Neith's direction as well.

"I'm not sure I can help you," he said softly.

"I only need to know which tunnel leads to Kekk. Unfortunately, I don't know enough of the entrances to be certain I'm taking the correct one." Rae popped the last bite of bread into her mouth, chewing slowly as Zennor stared at a patch of grass in front of him, deep in thought. "I would never want to put you in danger."

Zennor's eyebrows knit together. "It's not myself I worry about."

Rae nodded. She understood more than he could know.

"You won't find the curse of the Trove easily." Neith's voice held an air of authority compared to how she usually spoke. "It is shunned. Hidden away. A dirty secret." She clasped and unclasped her hands as she continued. "Those who possess it are usually driven away or treated like tainted monsters."

"Svet is said to be a gift," Rae said as she leaned forward. "Together with Eishtala and Anam, it can save our world from the Sundering."

Zennor perked up at these last words. "The Sundering?"

Rae nodded, then realized Neith would not have seen the gesture. "There's a prophecy that speaks to an event that will destroy all that exists."

Again, Neith perked up. Whether she'd heard the stories or was just genuinely curious, Rae couldn't be sure.

"I know of a very powerful Anam Wielder. He..." She didn't know how to continue. There was no way of knowing if Gastel would ever wake. Without him, the plans Noe-eb had laid at Rae's feet would be difficult at best. "He sleeps, his soul lost within his mind."

"Lost within his mind?" Neith sounded less confident again.

"He opened one of the rifts to the magic realms and has been unconscious since."

They sat in silence again, Neith nibbling on the last of her bread.

"What is it that you can do with this Anam Wielder and a Svet Priest?" Zennor asked.

Rae pressed her lips together as she tried to craft a reasonable response. In truth, she wasn't completely sure. "I assume the use of all three types of magic is needed to mend the barrier of the Wastelands. It's been damaged by an imbalance of magic, and unfortunately, the Elder Gods can't remake it themselves."

A thought popped into Rae's mind, and before she thought better of it, she asked: "Did your father know Freya of the Aequus?"

It was Zennor's turn to hesitate. He gnawed on the side of his lower lip as he considered his words. "He communicated with her before his passing, but he didn't always agree with her obsession with the old texts like the prophecy."

Rae held in her momentary elation at being right. A part of her still loved it when pieces came together.

"Have you ever met her?"

Again, hesitation, but this time it lingered.

"Once. Before my mother passed."

"I'm sorry about your mother."

"Thank you, but in a way, it was a blessing. She wasn't exactly a caring parent." Zennor side-eyed Neith before continuing. "She left me alone a lot when I was very young until my father took me away. I lived with my father's siblings in the small settlement west of the Forest of Tremire for the better part of my life...until coming here."

This history about the boy was enlightening but only opened up more questions.

"How old are you?"

Zennor smiled. "How old are you? You look young for a Shay but sound so much older."

Rae met his smile. "I'll be thirty-six soon."

Zennor glanced down at their breakfast remains. "Not as old as you sound, I guess. I'm in my sixteenth year."

"Still a tender elfling for a bit longer." She smiled.

His eyes darted to hers with a hint of annoyance that washed away quickly. "It's all in your perspective, I guess. I've been living on my own for a while."

Rae realized Neith was no longer paying them any attention. She'd turned her head toward the north, her covered eyes searching for something that could not be seen.

"What do you sense, Neith?" Rae asked.

The girl sank into herself at the acknowledgement. "Only an animal. I think Zennor calls them rabbits."

Rae stood, her fingers itching for meat. Perhaps the girl's strange sense could help her in more ways than one.

***

Roulin hadn't had favorable news in weeks. After all the careful planning, waiting, and enduring his brother's coronation, it was time he made some.

The sun was high, washing away the shadows, making it hard for him and his black-clad fighters to blend in. So, they didn't bother trying. Instead, they ran in the open across the Eastern Pass, racing across the fields to the north of Dormshire with blades drawn. Autumn meant the fields were ready to come off, which meant the Shay were out to harvest them.

And they would be harvesting Shay.

The first pathetic group was mowed down with shocking speed. Their wretched screams were delicious to Roulin's ears. He paused to savor the view of bloodied, pink hunks of flesh littering the ripe earth. Melons and squash stained with gore.

He pointed with his sword to one mound that was still moving, and the nearest fighter swooped in.

Ah, yes, the power he wielded was as wonderful as he'd thought it would be. After decades in his brother's shadow, to have his own orders followed without little more than a wave of his hand was better than a morning orgasm.

The next field was empty. A shame. Roulin's blade was thirsty. They stalked closer to Dormshire proper, savoring the shrieks of fear as mothers grabbed hold of elflings and fled toward the city.

His lips curved up as his fighters rushed ahead. He was keenly reminded of how much he enjoyed the chorus of screams from the terrified Shay. The sounds of war were so different. This was pure anni-hilation mixed with a dash of retribution.

A cold memory washed over him, and he stopped in his tracks.

He had been in his father's throne room. A letter was presented to the king by a pageant of pretentiously decorated Shay. There were six of them glittering and jingling with all manner of useless beads and bells. They were too pompous to hand the letter to his father themselves. Instead, the woman in the lead handed the overdressed parchment to one of the servants who stood at the king's attendance.

Roulin recognized the seal. He'd seen it a number of times during his correspondence with Gemma over the years. A shiver of understanding caused him to stand a little straighter.

A promise of bonding, but not with Roulin. No, the bitch had chosen Mesmal. She was already a queen; she didn't need to solidify her crown. She had no need for land. Her wealth was abundant enough to send six worthless attendants to deliver her mail rather than presenting herself.

After all the words they'd exchanged, the promises the two of them had made to each other, and the whore had wanted more? Greedy, righ-teous fucks. Every. Last. One of them.

His blood boiled in his veins. How long had Roulin been trying to establish this bonding? He wanted out from under his father and brother.

He wanted his own kingdom. His own servants. His own stronghold. That which a Bleck Larin prince, descendant of the House of Raggethan, truly deserved. And he would have it all, everything he wanted.

Or so he'd thought.

His fighters hadn't noticed he'd stopped, and he was left standing in a field with the overripe fruit of his disgust. Snapping back to the moment, he swallowed the bitter taste of hatred. The whore would pay. A sweet tingle of happiness lifted one side of his lips. He'd heard the Starling wench had slashed Gemma's eye before the girl had met her deserved death. Delightful. Even Eishtala couldn't heal everything.

Roulin wished he could spit in Gemma's flawed face.

Correction: he would spit in Gemma's face, but not until after he'd slaughtered as many Shay as he could get his hands on—and had taken what was rightfully his.

Roulin strolled to join his fighters, glancing down at the broken and mangled corpses of men, women, and elflings. His fighters had a handful of them and were dragging them back toward the Eastern Pass as crucifixes were being erected in the fertile earth. Think of the food they could grow, nourished by the blood of these worthless, lazy fucks.

Laughter broke free from his lips. Wild, rapturous laughter. He leaned forward onto his knees, unable to contain his mirth.

This was the price of lies and broken promises.

This was the price of peace.

THIRTY-SIX

Kingly Work

Gastel plopped down onto a bench in the practice arena as his brother snatched the practice sword from his hand. The sly smile on Belkin's face was enough to ease Gastel's frustrations, but he was still disappointed in himself. It'd been three days since he'd managed to drag himself from his bed, and he still felt terribly weak.

"I'll just pretend you're an elfling." Belkin stood before him, feet shoulder width apart, each hand holding a wooden practice sword. "I'll enjoy these victories while they last. You'll be destroying me again soon enough."

But Gastel wasn't so sure. After his hands had been desecrated in the fires of the Eishtala rift, he'd felt the same humbling frustration at his helpless state. Now, it was less about the condition of his hands and more about his stamina. He had no energy. Three, maybe four maneuvers and his strength waned.

He hung his head, wishing Belkin would leave him to his sulking, but he knew he wouldn't. That wasn't Belkin's way. He'd push Gastel until he was satisfied that he'd gotten the very best out of him. It was far worse than Dulanii teasing him until he'd come to the training arena.

"Take another moment, then we spar again."

Gastel looked up and met Belkin's cheerful expression with his disheartened glare.

"Don't you have a citizen hearing or a council meeting or some other kingly duty to attend to? I would think there wouldn't be enough time in your busy day to help your feeble brother."

"You're not feeble. Frustrating, angry, maybe a little insufferable, but not feeble." He stepped away, running through a weapon form for dual wielding, crisscrossing the practice swords with flawless precision as he turned back to face Gastel. "Again."

He handed Gastel a stick and stepped back. How many moves would it take for Belkin to beat him this time? His arms were beginning to feel weighed down by layers of wet clothes.

Gastel rolled his shoulders, then his head, trying to procrastinate another few seconds, but Belkin lunged into a mind-numbing attack. One Gastel had no hope of fending off. He blocked the first three strikes to his chest but took the fourth hard in his ribs and a fifth to the side of the head, sending him sprawling on his back. Stars swam across his vision as Belkin stood over him, a wicked grin across his face.

"I forget how fun it is to beat you."

That could have been taken more than one way, besting him at a duel or pummeling him. Either way, Gastel closed his eyes, letting the pain numb his thoughts.

"Come now, Brother, I didn't hit you *that* hard—"

Belkin was interrupted by a soldier in battle armor, his horse galloping at full speed across the gardens, leaving scars on the turf. Gastel's brother yanked him to his feet as the horse came to a halt a few feet from them.

"Majesty, Regent Freya has sent an urgent missive."

Belkin snatched the letter and cracked the wax seal as he tore the top layer of crisp parchment. Gastel didn't want to hover, but he couldn't help but focus on how his brother's eyes tracked across the letter, eyebrows drawing together as he read.

Without looking up from the parchment, Belkin dismissed the soldier with a wave, then turned to Gastel with cold, angry eyes. Eyes that could never hide their emotions no matter how well the rest of his face could.

"I need your guidance."

Gastel had given his father his opinion on more occasions than he could count. He was no stranger to providing his thoughts. But Belkin hadn't always been the type to respect his opinions. It felt strange yet somehow appropriate. As if perhaps his father had been grooming him for this role.

"There's been an unprovoked attack just south of the Eastern Pass. A large force of Bleck Larin in black armor."

A tug at Gastel's memory left him disoriented. He was no longer standing with Belkin in the practice arena. He was thrust back to before he'd opened the Anam rift—an altercation...but the details were difficult to discern.

Gastel took a step back, shaking his head in frustration. There was something important in this memory. Something he needed to recall. He squeezed his eyes closed. Four mercenaries in the forest outside of Thandor. Something about a Wyvern King.

The echo of a voice solidified in his mind.

He said you were soft. That you couldn't kill a soul.

"Roulin."

"How would you know this?" Belkin asked.

"The time leading up to the last rift I opened is still hazy, but I get glimpses. Bleck Larin mercenaries attacked us. One of them mentioned a Wyvern King. Something she said leads me to believe that this Wyvern King is Roulin." He paused, letting his words sink in. "I could be wrong."

"Unfortunately, I don't believe you are." Belkin looked out across the moors as he handed Gastel the missive to read for himself.

Sure enough, Freya spoke of both soldiers and civilians being massacred on the northside of Dormshire by a group saying they were loyal to the Wyvern King. Gastel focused on Freya's scrolling handwriting for a moment longer, letting the words on the page drip across his consciousness like warm honey. He wished he had Raemian's keen eye to see all the puzzle pieces in play.

He took a sharp breath. It had been a while since he'd thought of her. Not terribly long, but long enough that as the memories flooded back, he was left with an empty pit in his stomach and a tightness in his chest.

Thankfully, Belkin was still distracted, staring down at his feet, his eyebrows drawn together in frustration. The classic Belkin expression—stern, battle-weathered anger under the surface of his fragile, calm façade.

"We'll have to deal with him sooner rather than later."

A hot shiver writhed up Gastel's spine. Deal with him? What possible way was there to deal with him other than the obvious? What a way to start one's rule. Putting your own brother to death for treason. The brother who stood with you for centuries and fought at your side during great unrest between the races.

Belkin took the practice sword from Gastel's hand and chucked it across the arena before turning toward the castle stronghold.

"Time to do some kingly work."

Belkin had warned Roulin. Had told him what he would do, and still, the idiot had pushed and pushed. Now, he was calling himself the Wyvern King? He was more than an idiot. He was a dangerous idiot who had other idiots following him.

How large of a force had Roulin amassed that made him brazen enough to attack so openly outside of Dormshire? If Freya weren't so levelheaded, an act like that would be considered a declaration of war. And then another thought—how many followers before Roulin would feel confident enough to challenge Belkin?

He'd waited long enough. He needed to address the situation. And he didn't like it.

In fact, he hated it. He hated everything about it. This was not how it was supposed to be. He was supposed to be a king with Roulin at his side, ruling essentially as equals in all but name—king and advisor.

As he and Gastel walked with purpose through the main hall of the castle stronghold, Belkin couldn't ignore how his youngest brother kept himself a few steps behind. Had Belkin never noticed how Gastel positioned himself? Always behind. Always less than. But Roulin? He had walked beside him as an equal. Bleck Larin princes, raised by the same calm and tender father, growing up in peaceful times and tempered in the fires of war in the most recent of times.

What had caused Roulin to turn so savagely against him? Against everything they'd ever come to know and love? It couldn't be the Shay, and yet that was the only thing that loomed over them like a vulture, circling and watching for a place to land and pick at the carrion lying at Belkin's feet. There was a war that had not been resolved in battle but through politics. One that had been brought to a screeching halt by a single Shay warrior whom everyone thought was dead but who was very much alive.

Belkin glanced at Gastel out of the corner of his eye. His brother wore their father's face, a soft stoicism that hid anything he was thinking. He couldn't speak with Gastel about Raemian. He'd made the potentially disastrous decision not to tell his youngest brother that she was alive. He feared if Gastel knew he would leave to find her, and in his weakened state, Belkin feared he wouldn't fare well. Not to mention, Belkin needed him. He needed his empathy more now than ever.

If Gastel knew Raemian was wandering around Rhend, chasing the same fairy tales he'd been chasing...

Belkin led Gastel to the strategy room, walking to stand in front of the map. He squeezed his eyes closed, rubbing his temples. If Raemian took much longer to return, he'd have to tell Gastel, and when he did, Gods help him. Gastel reminded him of his father after Niminea had died. Simmering with hidden thoughts and dark moments of reflection.

Gastel's temper was another issue. It had never been a problem before, but since returning from Tremire after learning of his power, the youngest son of Mesmal had finally grown into his anger, like Belkin and Roulin before him.

Belkin already knew there would be fury. Correction: There would be absolute rage that he'd not told Gastel sooner about Raemian, and he'd sworn the entire castle stronghold to secrecy. Mesmal had given him such a derisive glare but could say nothing because their father had hidden so very much from Gastel for far longer.

No, in the end, Belkin would pay for withholding the news of her. He prayed to the Elder Gods that his reasons weren't as selfish as they seemed.

"I don't know if I can be of much help." Gastel's voice was withered with defeat.

"I'm sure you'll be more help than you realize." Belkin glanced at him, trying his best to ignore the dark circles under the boy's eyes. He looked haggard. Perhaps Belkin had pushed him too hard in the training arena. "I'll start by informing Freya that I intend to handle the situation as swiftly and professionally as possible."

"But you don't know exactly how yet, I take it?"

Belkin looked away for a second before nailing Gastel to the wall with his glare. "It's not exactly something I had on my list of things I wished to do when I'd be king. How would you handle this?"

"I'd have him publicly executed for treason."

Belkin stood straight. The lack of hesitation in Gastel's cool voice wasn't what he'd expected. "Excuse me, what have you done with my youngest brother?"

Gastel smirked, taking a few steps toward Belkin. "I told you I didn't think I'd be much help." His smile fell, a dangerous anger left in its place. "Would Roulin do any different if he were you?"

Whether Gastel realized it or not, his words were exactly what Belkin needed to hear. But they also reinforced one little problem. There was a darkness growing in Gastel, and Belkin had placed himself in a precarious predicament by not being forthcoming about Raemian.

He yanked a sheet of paper from the writing desk and leaned over it, scrawling a reply to Freya. Each scratch of his pen nib across the paper seemed to scrape across his flesh. If he wasn't careful, his reign would be far shorter than anticipated. If Roulin didn't end him, Gastel very well might.

Tildimin interrupted before he could finish, wearing a mask of grim uncertainty. "From Raggethan."

He passed Belkin a folded slip of paper held between two fingers. Not an official correspondence and likely far more concerning.

The council of Raggethan maintains loyalty to the monarchy, but there are those who would seek to establish otherwise.

—T

Belkin glared at Treina's words. She was the general of the western division. She'd trained with Belkin and Tildimin as elflings, and her loyalty had made her one of Belkin's most trusted. If she was concerned enough to send a note, it was for good reason. Raggethan was a massive city with more resources than Parth. Perched in the northwest corner of Rhend, it felt like a world away. If Roulin had found supporters there, Belkin would have much bigger problems than disturbances outside Dormshire.

THIRTY-SEVEN

Svet

She couldn't see where they were going but could feel it through Rae and Zennor's souls. It was foreboding and dark. Neith had lived her entire life underground. She'd never seen the sunny sky during the cycle of light or the soft grass she'd sat on with Rae and Zennor. The world of Noor Above was scary. Still, the thought of diving back below the earth was far more terrifying.

Flashes of the tendron, the wretched sounds its legs had made as it had raced through the tunnel toward her. The searing pain as it had sank a fang into her leg. Her father's sneering face.

Neith shuddered in the makeshift harness Rae had constructed to strap her more comfortably to Zennor's back. With her eyes bound, walking was slow, and trying to cling to Zennor's shoulders for hours didn't seem practical. Rae had made a sling from one of the blankets and helped Zennor position it so Neith could be carried.

"Neith?" His voice vibrated into her cheek, which rested against his shoulder blade.

"Just remembering." She nuzzled closer, tucking her hands against the warmth of his back. He didn't seem to mind, continuing with Rae at his side toward the entrance where he'd found Neith. The one he thought might lead to a tunnel to Kekk.

Rae had told them what she knew, all that she'd been through. The story of the Eishtala realm was mysterious and intriguing. Some part of Neith was drawn to Rae like she was drawn to Zennor. Perhaps it was her calm soul, the strange color it emanated, or the soft way she spoke, weaving in and out of words like a magic all its own.

Rae didn't see a monster in white flesh when she looked at Neith. It was fairly obvious that Rae knew she possessed at least some strength in Svet but refused to insist on stealing Neith away. There was, instead, an unspoken understanding that Rae would never put her in a dangerous situation, not unless Neith consented.

The three of them grew silent once again, and Neith concentrated on Zennor's heartbeat, the occasional crunching of feet. Her eyes had been bound a third time to protect them from the intense light of the sun, but it kissed her skin, leaving stains of heat as it moved across.

The motion of Zennor's stride was lulling her to sleep, and while she might have forced herself awake, there was something entirely too comforting about being in the presence of these two. They were gentle, kind people, and she couldn't help but thank the Elder Gods for her luck in finding them.

"We should be close now." Zennor's voice pulled Neith forward for a moment; she tried to envision his face as he spoke to keep herself awake, but her thoughts were too heavy.

"Perhaps we find the entrance and then make camp? I can start out on my own tomorrow."

Zennor hummed his approval, the soft rumbling finally lulling Neith to sleep.

They made camp early, but the sun was fading faster than it should have until Rae reminded herself that they were well into autumn. They were pressed hard against the Hill of Tombs, the stone of the ancient ridge jutting out over them, providing a canopy should the growing overcast sky turn to rain. Rae helped Neith down from Zennor's back, and once the girl was comfortable, she drifted deeper into a thicket, where she could hopefully find some wild game for an evening meal.

The smell of meadow garlic was alluring. If only they had a way of boiling water, Rae could make a soup. Instead, she found some mushrooms and berries and resigned herself to a cold dinner after several minutes of no luck finding anything large enough to cook.

When she finally turned to wander back to camp, an unusual shadow moved across her peripheral. The hair on the back of her neck stood on end.

"You're a long way from home, Shay." The smooth Bleck Larin lilt froze Rae in her steps.

"Not so far away, considering the peace our people share." She raised her hands in a show of truce, but her mind was calculating the man's distance behind her at a sprinting stride.

He stepped closer until Rae could see all of him with a slight turn of her head. He was in all black, his face covered by a mask that only allowed his eyes to peek out. A memory of the same uniform, only this man didn't have a hood drawn over his head. Instead, he wore the simple cuff that held his uncut hair proudly. He was younger, perhaps a little older than Rae, his hair only about as long as Gastel's before Gemma had cut it.

"There is no such thing as peace between our people." He took a couple more steps to stand in front of Rae, his angry eyebrows drawn tight against his eyes. "Mesmal was so far out of touch with the Bleck Larin people, and Belkin is worse."

The man drew his sword, the sound straightening Rae's posture. She would wait until the last possible moment to draw her own, to give peace a chance. So many parts of this world were still broken, but she would do her best not to take a life unless she absolutely had to.

Rae flinched as a shriek tore through the growing twilight from the direction of the Hill of Tombs. Unless Rae was mistaken, that scream was Neith's. Urgency bloomed in Rae's chest. She didn't have time to be nice, to spare a life. Not if Neith and Zennor were in trouble.

She drew her sword as the lines around the man's eyes scrunched with a smile. The world around Rae slowed, particles wafting on the late afternoon breeze seeming to stand still in the air, which had turned as thick as water.

After four large steps, Rae twisted to the man's left, avoiding his sword by rolling along its length. With Rae's back against the man's chest, she elbowed him in the stomach. He stumbled back as Rae spun, cleaving her falchion up with both hands to meet the man's offhand dagger. She was nose to nose with him, glaring up into his amber eyes as he sneered under his mask, crossing her blade between his sword and dagger.

She reached for the man's wrist, cranking his hand back until he yelped and dropped his sword. He pushed Rae back, swinging wildly to keep her from moving in close again. Instead, she ducked under and spun through his flailing swipes, the tip of her sword slicing across his abdomen. He grunted as he fell to his knees, looking down at his bloody hands as he held his insides, keeping them from falling out.

Rae didn't waste time waiting for him to die. She sprinted back through the thicket toward their camp, her heart in her throat. If anything had happened to Neith or Zennor, she would never forgive herself.

Her feet couldn't move her through the rocky wash fast enough. Seconds felt like minutes. Her eyes welled with tears, whether from the sting of the growing chill in the air as she moved or the very real fear that her new friends had been killed or taken captive.

She rounded a small copse of trees and slid into the clearing behind another black-clad Bleck Larin. A Bleck Larin who clutched Neith in his arms, a knife pressed to the girl's throat.

"Leave her, please. She's an elfling." Zennor's voice broke with fear. "Please. Please, don't hurt her."

Time slowed before it stood still as Rae tried to figure out how she would get Neith safely from this man's arms.

"Not sure I could bring myself to kill a Trove," the Bleck Larin said as he tipped his head toward her hair and sniffed deeply. "Such a rare beauty."

The anguish on Zennor's face was real and terrible. Rae made a snap decision she prayed to the Elder Gods she wouldn't regret. She crossed the clearing in six long strides, sword high. The Bleck Larin must have heard her because he started to turn as she cleaved across his back, her blade biting into his left arm. Neith squealed in what Rae hoped was fear rather than pain as the man dropped her and the dagger before reaching for his now-decimated arm. Neith stumbled to her knees, then crawled toward Zennor, who crouched toward her, his eyes electric with fear.

Rae wasn't finished with the man. She nearly wrenched him from the ground by his neck, pulling him toward her. "Who sent you? Why would you hunt Shay in times of peace?"

He squirmed in her grip, gasping for air, but she didn't yield.

"Tell me, or I'll make your death as painful as I possibly can." She brought her sword up, blade level with his eye.

It was hard to see his expression with his face covered in a mask, but his eyes grew wide. For a tense moment, Rae thought she would have to torture him, which she didn't want to do in front of the elflings. They shouldn't lose their innocence this way, especially Neith. She didn't deserve for her dreams to be haunted by the anguished wails of an elf in the throes of a painful death.

"I've seen your black armor before, your faces covered. Part of a sect of trackers. Why the violence in this time of peace? Who has ordered this?"

She loosened her grip enough to allow the man to breathe. His amber eyes held hers with a conviction that made her blood run cold.

"The Wyvern King," the Bleck Larin gasped, squeezing his eyes closed, knowing that these were likely his last few breaths, his last words. "He will rule over all of Rhend, enslave you worthless people, and right the wrongs of the last thirty years."

Somewhere in the depth of her mind, Rae registered his words, but anger so hot and real seared through her. She tightened her grip on his throat until he choked. Some part of her broke as she squeezed tighter and tighter, his hands coming up to her wrist, trying desperately to pry her fingers away. She whipped her sword around, bashing the backs of his legs, then pressed him to his knees. A dark part of her took over as she stepped around him. With one smooth swing, both hands clutching the handle of her blade, she cleaved his head from his shoulders.

Neith whimpered when the head hit the soft earth, a hollow thump followed by the wet rumbling as it rolled until it stopped at Zennor's feet.

⊦——— ———⊦

Neith tried to rid the sounds of death from her memory, but it was hard. Zennor fretted over her, cleaning dirt from her face and neck and then carrying her back to the small pallet bed he'd made for her against the stone wall of the cliffs they followed. Neith struggled to calm her heart as she watched the souls of the two dead Bleck Larin lingering around their camp. They were angry souls. Bitter and fragmented.

"Are you sure you aren't hurt?" It was the tenth or eleventh time Zennor had asked, and for the first time, Neith started to be annoyed by the attention he showed her.

"I'm more than fine, thanks to you and Rae."

He took a deep breath through his nose and let it out long and slow. "Thanks to Rae, you mean. All I did was panic."

Rae had been pacing the outskirts of their camp since the attack, but she approached and sat near them, setting her sword beside her.

"You were fine, Zennor. You distracted him long enough for me to get back to you." She was calm, perhaps too calm, after having killed two elves.

Neith could see the soft green of her soul, as it had always been. For a moment, she'd glimpsed a change, a strange whiteness that tinted the edges of her life force that gave Neith a certainty of one thing: Rae was far more righteous than anyone she'd ever met. Even though she'd taken the lives of two Bleck Larin and perhaps countless other elves, she'd done so with justice in her intentions.

Neith turned to Rae. "Will you go to Kekk tomorrow?"

Zennor shifted beside her.

"I plan to," Rae said.

Neith could tell Rae was watching her, even with her eyes covered. Rae stared at her a lot. It might have made her uncomfortable, but with Rae, it didn't seem so bothersome.

"Though the threat of Bleck Larin trackers to you and Zennor weighs on my mind. I may need to take you both to safety before I venture into the tunnels."

"Must you go to Kekk?" Perhaps if Neith could see Rae's eyes, she would have been more nervous to ask.

"I need to find a Trove blessed with the gift of Svet." She took a deep breath. "I've spent so much of my life contributing to the chaos of our world. If this is something I can do to save it from the Sundering, I will."

"How do you know the Sundering will even happen?" Zennor didn't hide his skepticism.

"Because I trust the words of my teacher, Noe-eb. The things he showed me... Something is happening. Whether it's the Sundering the prophecy speaks of or something else, I don't care to leave it to chance."

For a long moment, they were quiet, with no sound except the popping of the fire which bathed Neith with warmth and took the edge off the growing chill as the cycle of light came to a close.

"What's to say the prophecy isn't wrong?"

"Would it be the prophecy that's wrong? Or the elves who translated it?" Rae asked, but she didn't wait long enough for an answer. "We all see things through a lens of our own creation. The real difference between good and evil. Friend or foe. I have spent so much of my life not realizing what side I was truly on."

Rae's words were like a balm coating the sharp edges of Neith's fears. So much of her own life, she'd seen herself as a monster, a thing that held a dirty secret in the depths of her being. Neith was able to see the souls of others but not her own. Who was to say the color of her own soul was any more or less righteous?

"What if you'd already found someone blessed with the gift of Svet? What if you didn't need to go to Kekk?" She heard them both turn to look at her. At that moment, she wished she could rip the coverings from her eyes to see their surprised expressions.

"I would never wish to put you in danger, Neith." Rae's voice held a hesitation that bled over the softness of her life force. "I could never—"

"Wait." Zennor stood, and Neith tipped her face in his direction. "Are you...are you saying..."

Neith smiled at the fact that he hadn't realized after all this time.

"It is a curse that my parents never wished for. Those tainted are shunned. They are dirty and forsaken." She wrapped her arms around her shoulders and sank into herself. "Does this make you hate me? To see the filth that I am?"

He crouched, taking her hands in his, the warmth of them radiating up her arms.

"Never. You are Neith. Svet gift or not, you are still my friend."

She felt his eyes burning into her and again wished she could pull the coverings from her own. To see his beautiful face as it saw her for who she truly was.

After a few moments, he let her hands slip from his and sat beside her, closer this time, the heat from his body wicking through the blanket that Neith had wrapped around herself.

"I don't know what must be done—or how." Rae seemed to work through the puzzle of information she'd been given by her mysterious teacher. "I worry..."

"That I won't be powerful enough?"

Perhaps Rae shook her head; perhaps she simply didn't know how to respond, but she grew silent again, letting the chirps of insects creep in around them as the cycle of dark closed in.

"And I don't know how to teach you."

Again, Neith smiled. Did Rae have so little confidence in herself? She'd already taught Neith some of the most important lessons she'd ever learned That trust could be found. That the righteous existed. That family was more than blood. That maybe, somewhere in this world, Svet was, in fact, a gift.

THIRTY-EIGHT

A Trove in Tremire

The last time Rae had been to Tremire, circumstances had been wildly different. She'd left a disparate city to attempt to open a rift with Gastel and Freck. She'd been with Gastel when he'd been bound and brought to Tremire; now, she garnered ample stares as she was accompanied by Zennor, who carried a very shy Neith in a sling across his back. How many Shay had seen a Trove in their lifetime? Rae always seemed to be bringing the strangest elves home with her.

As they approached the court, Rae was hesitant, unsure of what she would find. If Belkin had thought her dead, he couldn't be the only person. Rae blushed thinking of her new king and how she'd left things in Parth. With Gastel still unconscious, Mesmal's life waning, and... Belkin.

"Raemian Starling?"

She was yanked from her thoughts at the sound of her name.

"Rae!"

Rae turned toward the familiar face of a woman in royal armor barreling toward her from the entrance of the court.

"Solena!"

"Gods, Raemian!" Solena didn't wear a helm; instead, she left her long white hair pulled into a high ponytail, pouring over her shoulders like snowy dunes. "Where have you been? We thought you were dead!"

She took Rae's hands in hers in a way that was entirely too casual for a guard on duty.

"Freya will be ecstatic!" She looked Rae over from head to toe, squeezing her hands with excitement. "Come, she's just finishing a council session."

Solena refused to release Rae's hand, pulling her through the crowd in a very un-royal-guard-like manner. The last time Rae had seen her, she'd been dutifully formal, guarding the Court of Tremire as though nothing had changed.

Rae turned toward Zennor and Neith and motioned for them to follow. She would have a lot of explaining to do, but the last thing she wanted was to lose her two newest friends in the crowd.

At the steps of the court, the Shay parted, allowing them to pass, murmurs following them in.

"Rae!"

The sound of Freya's voice was a balm to her ears. She hadn't realized how much she'd missed the woman. They crashed together in an embrace longer and more intense than the one Rae had shared with her the day she'd returned to Tremire after Gemma's abdication. Freya pushed Rae back, taking her cheeks in her hands.

"Raemian Starling. I should have known you'd find some way to make it back to us, even in death." Freya kissed her on the cheeks as though Rae were her long-lost elfling, who'd finally returned.

It took Rae a moment to center herself as whispers echoed around the court. The council members had been slowly filing out when Solena had dragged them in. Unable to determine where to start on what had happened, Rae instead turned toward Zennor and Neith.

"This is Zennor," Rae said, and as though he were already aware of what he needed to do, Zennor knelt and helped Neith from his back. Ever the protector, he took her by the shoulders and pulled her back to him, his face a calm mask of concentration as he hovered.

"And this is Neith."

Rae was just as protective of her, feeling a ripple of fear at the way others stared so brazenly at the girl. She reached for Neith's hand, and the girl entwined her fingers with Rae's. To her credit, Neith seemed not to be bothered by her circumstances and instead calmly stepped from Zennor's grasp to stand beside Rae.

Freya was silent, her eyes unable to move from Neith's beautiful white face, her eyes tightly bound with no fewer than three strips of cotton. Though Neith couldn't see Freya with her eyes, Rae was confident Neith could see her soul perfectly well.

"It appears we have much to discuss," Freya finally said.

"More than you know."

"Come," Freya said warmly. "We can talk over lunch. All of us."

***

The world of Noor Above had always been strange to Neith, but the City of Tremire was an entirely different place. She'd become acquainted with the smells and sounds of forests, bugs, animals, and the scent of soil and grass. Here in Tremire, the sound alone was jarring. So many people were all talking and moving at once. To her sensitive ears, it was like a roar of chaos. It was nearly impossible to isolate specific sounds, and she found herself asking more than once for Zennor to repeat himself as he helped her get comfortable at a table for a meal.

In her family home, sitting on a chair at an actual table was unheard of. They sat on cushions on the floor and held plates in their laps—when she was even permitted to eat with her parents. She was usually on the hard floor, tearing bits off of whatever she could hold in her hand.

At least the room they'd been led to was fairly quiet, and Neith could finally hear Rae's gentle voice, the softness of the woman named Freya, another man whose rumbly voice seemed to settle in Neith's stomach, and the vibrant, almost brassy timbre of the woman who had greeted them.

More people joined them, and Neith stiffened. These souls were different. One was a shocking shade of blue, so dark it was almost black. The other, a warm gold that seemed to ripple with cheerful friendliness.

"Geri!" Rae's voice held more emotion than Neith had heard from her thus far as her soul shared space with the golden-souled elf. "You've pulled your hair up."

"My father felt it was time."

This girl's voice was airy with a singsong quality. There was a long pause, and Neith assumed they were looking at the two unknown elves at the table.

"Zennor, Neith, this is Tor and his daughter, Geri," Rae said with hesitation.

"You've probably never met a Bleck Larin, have you, Zennor?" Freya asked.

"I...I've..." Zennor stumbled over his words before Neith felt his hand take hers. "Only the ones that attacked us on the way here."

There was a strong silence in the room, and Neith longed to see their faces, especially Tor and Geri's. She'd never seen a Bleck Larin, and after meeting the two that had tried to take her, she had decided she never wanted to. But the aura of this girl was so...friendly.

"Well, I'd never be able to attack anyone," Geri said with a matter-of-fact quality that caused chuckles around the table.

The sound of feet and shuffling was followed by a rich, salty scent like the jerky Zennor had shared with her, but stronger. Then, the smell of bread and overripe sweetness as platters were set on the table in front of her. Neith stretched her fingers across the wood surface, touching the smooth rim of a plate.

Zennor must have noticed her wandering hands because she felt his warm breath on her ear before he spoke.

"Would you like a slice of meat? It's the same as the jerky, only warm and juicy." He waited patiently, always so patiently. "There's bread as well, and fruit tarts and soup." His voice was low, meant for her alone. "Have you ever had soup before?"

She shook her head, unsure of what he meant by *soup*.

"Would Neith like anything specific?" It was the woman's voice from Neith's left. She turned her head in the direction of Freya's warm, white soul. "It's been a long time since I've had a Trove at my table; I unfortunately don't recall what types of foods you might prefer."

"I'm sure whatever you have provided will be perfect," Neith said as she tucked her hands back into her lap.

There was more shuffling, the clang of metal on glass, and the vague sounds of various foods being placed upon plates. The scent of the meat grew stronger before she felt Zennor's hand reach for hers beneath the table again.

"I can help you."

She smiled and let him guide her hand to a metal utensil. This would be difficult. She'd seen flatware a handful of times in her life but had never used it. And other than the jerky, bread, and berries, she hadn't eaten much else here in the world of Noor Above. All things that she could pluck from a plate with her fingers.

"There's soup as well." It was Rae's voice across from her; the warmth it resonated was reassuring. "Leek and mushrooms. I think you'd like it."

This soup must have been a delicious sort of food for both Zennor and Rae to suggest it. Liquid was ladled into a bowl near her. It was overwhelming. The smells. The sounds. Her distinct lack of vision in such strong light. She squeezed her eyes closed beneath the bindings.

"Just some bread, please," she whispered, and a slice was placed in her hand, whether by Zennor or someone else at the table she couldn't be certain. She would be content to rip it and thrust tiny bits of it between her lips.

"Open your mouth. I can give you a bite of meat."

She did as Zennor requested, but it felt strange to have someone feed her, though the meat was indeed delicious, heavy, and rounded out with the most delightful richness that melted into a spicy earthiness. The next time he offered her a bite, she refused and instead focused on Rae's words as she recounted her adventures within the Eishtala realm.

"And you've been to Parth?" Freya asked.

"I have. I went there first, not realizing how much had already happened. For me, it was only a week." Rae paused, and Neith wished she could see her expression because her aura seemed to shift and pulse. "I didn't know he'd…" Her voice wavered with emotion, further piquing Neith's curiosity. There was something about the man Rae spoke of—a weight to her emotions that pressed on Neith's chest.

"When I was in Parth for Belkin's coronation, I visited him. It was devastating to see him that way. I stole poor Dulanii away from his bedside."

A flare of life to Rae's soul caused Neith to sit up a little straighter.

"Is Freck here? Dulanii, I mean."

"He's somewhere between Dormshire and Parth, I'm afraid." Freya paused, perhaps to take a sip of the fruit-thick beverage that had been poured into all their glasses. "He's been helping me with running correspondence."

There were more strange names, and Neith listened intently, continuing to nibble on the crust of bread, forgetting that Zennor still sat beside her until she felt his hand on her shoulder.

"Do you need anything else to eat? A drink of wine?"

Neith shook her head, trying not to be rude but also desperately curious about these new people Rae spoke of—the life the Shay had before she'd stumbled upon Neith with her withered leg and raging fever.

"Did King Belkin mention anything about the magic of the Wastelands to you before you left?" Freya asked after a pause, likely to take a few bites of food.

"Noe-eb did." Rae took a deep breath.

"We have some unsubstantiated reports of wraiths along Rhend's western border. Only at night, which would lead me to believe it has to do with the ancient magic the Elder Gods put in place."

Silence settled around the table.

"There's been a lot of unrest near Dormshire." There was a heaviness to Freya's voice that bled into her words. "Disturbing attacks on Shay there by Bleck Larin in black armor, following someone they call the Wyvern King."

There was another thick silence before Rae spoke again. "Wyvern King?"

"Yes. We're fairly certain we know who the Wyvern King is, but without irrefutable proof, Belkin has been loath to formally address the situation." Freya's tone had shifted to one of frustration. "I fear with this news, he'll need to take action, and I've offered him whatever support the Shay can provide, but our people are tired and skittish when it comes to crossing the border." She sighed. "There's still so much work to do to bring Rhend together again."

"These things take time." It was the Shay man's voice, smooth and deep. His aura was strange to Neith, a blend of something not quite pure but not evil by any means. "I'm sure with this news, His Majesty will step in. He's not the type to let a threat to his people go unchecked."

"To think only half a year ago, you were strategizing against him, Bow." The warmth of a smile lit Freya's voice. "And now you speak of him as though he's your own king."

"In all practicality, he is."

Silence again; perhaps there was an exchange of smiles.

"Never mind this, Bowrhem," Freya said with a stern lilt to her voice. "Neith, tell us, where are you from?"

Neith pressed her lips together, wishing she could sink into the seat of her chair. She squeezed her hands together under the table until her knuckles hurt.

"Dakarai." She knew a one-word answer, while accurate, would likely not be enough. "I was traveling to Kekk when I was chased by one of the creatures of the deep and saved by Zennor."

More silence. Without being able to see Freya's facial expression and those of the man named Bowrhem, she wasn't sure if they were satisfied. Angry? Saddened? Curious?

"Were you traveling alone?" Freya asked gently.

Neith nodded, not sure she could trust her voice to hide the emotions suddenly roiling around in her stomach.

"She was, but she has me now. Us." Zennor stumbled on his words. "She has Rae and me to help her."

Again, silence, before she felt Zennor's hand cover her own, the heat of it soothing.

"There's more we need to discuss," Rae said, drawing Freya's attention.

Praise the Elder Gods. Neith could feel the moisture nearly over-flowing from her eyes. She hadn't cried since Zennor had found her. To cry now seemed embarrassing.

"Things that Noe-eb explained to me while I was in the Eishtala realm."

"Of course. Perhaps we should make these two comfortable first," Freya said.

"That's probably a good idea." Rae paused. "Is my dwelling—"

"It remains empty. If you wish to stay there, I can have it readied for you."

Neith tried to swallow the sudden fear of being too far away from Rae. She'd thought she'd be fine as long as she had Zennor with her, but now she wasn't so certain.

"Can we stay with Rae?"

Fabric shifted, perhaps heads turning in Neith's direction.

"Certainly! I'll have supplies sent over."

Rae wouldn't let anything happen to her here. Rae would keep her safe. Rae and Zennor both would make sure she was taken care of, and she would want for nothing. It was a strange certainty, one she'd never dreamed would have been possible in all her life.

+——— ———+

Even though it was becoming more common to see a Shay brought before the Bleck Larin court, it was still jarring when unexpected. There were a handful that had settled in Parth and even a couple that had attended the citizen hearings. So, when a tall Shay was led into the throne room, neither Gastel nor his brother were paying full attention.

Once the Shay spoke, however, Gastel was out of his seat before Dulanii could finish his sentence.

"Hail, Majesty."

"Dulanii!" Gastel didn't wait for permission; he clasped the man in a strong embrace. The kind a brother gives another brother after having been apart for years. "Gods, how are you?"

Gastel pulled away, but Dulanii didn't let him get far. He held him at arm's length by his shoulders.

"You're awake!" Dulanii's stormy eyes were rimmed with tears. "After Belkin's coronation, I...I feared you'd never wake."

"I'll always wake. Here's hoping I won't sleep quite so long next time."

"Next time?" Dulanii's smile slipped away, but Gastel couldn't stop grinning.

As if remembering why he'd come in the first place, Dulanii squared his shoulders and faced Belkin, who'd remained on his throne, watching the warm reunion between friends.

"There have been multiple attacks north of Dormshire. Freya sent fortifications to the area to ensure the safety of the civilians, but they were attacked as well. Massacred..." He choked on his words before he continued. "Several were...crucified at the edge of the Oracles along the Eastern Pass."

Belkin was off his throne in an instant. Gastel wondered if others could feel the anger radiating off him.

"Crucified?" Heads turned as Belkin's voice echoed off the stone walls.

Dulanii nodded with a solemn frown. "It was..." Dulanii stared down at his feet, trying to move through the horror of finding his people hanging from wooden posts, their bodies left to be picked away by scavengers.

"I'll kill him."

Belkin's rage was unfocused, and Gastel needed to lock him down before he spoke too freely. The throne room suddenly felt very small as the last few of the council members loitered, eyes shifting to the boiling king. It was not common knowledge that Roulin was the Wyvern King.

With a kind hand, Gastel managed to get his brother's attention, and for a long moment, Belkin held his eyes, some unknown anguish swimming in their depths. The knowledge that he would have to punish his own brother—likely put him to death—was a taste that would linger on his tongue for the rest of his life.

"Freya is concerned that...she worries that—"

"That there will be retaliation," Belkin said, his voice having an unnatural calm to it this time.

Gastel could still see the anger simmering below the stern set of his lips. It burned behind his eyes like hot irons before being pressed into flesh, but the mask of a calm king had been slammed over his features.

"I shall call a small force to arms to protect the Shay and the city of Dormshire."

"Thank you, Your Majesty." Dulanii bowed before he righted himself and took the few steps forward to take Gastel back into a rib-crushing hug. "Gods, Gastel, you have no idea how good it is to see you on your feet."

Heat flooded Gastel's cheeks as he noticed the eyes of a handful of council members still dallying at the back of the throne room.

"I've been trying to build my strength back, but you're about to snap my spine."

Dulanii eased, but the massive smile across his lips remained, showing his charming, crooked teeth.

"I think your brother was tired of entertaining me."

Gastel must have made a face because Dulanii roared with laughter.

"Not that kind of entertainment." The Shay was bent over, hands on his knees from laughing.

Gastel glanced over his shoulder at his brother, who seemed to have eased from his anger and had allowed the tiniest smirk to cross his face as he shook his head, amused.

THIRTY-NINE

Greatest Enemy

It was an uncharacteristically warm morning. Gastel plopped down beside Dulanii in the grass near the training arena. Even though the Shay insisted on leaving early, Gastel had managed to convince Dulanii he should stay for the morning meal. He missed him—his smile, his ability to pull Gastel from his melancholy—there was a spark in Dulanii that he dreadfully needed more of in his life.

"Your kingly brother probably doesn't train much these days, does he?"

Gastel glanced at the sweaty Shay. He'd just taught him a Bleck Larin sword form that had challenged Dulanii's instinctive fighting style.

"Not as much, but he still enjoys destroying me as my strength recovers."

Dulanii lay back, folding his arms behind his head. "So...*has* your strength recovered?"

"I think so, though, if you'd asked me a week ago..."

Dulanii gazed over at him, but his eyes focused on something in the distance. He sat up, his expression turning serious. "Speaking of His Majesty."

Sure enough, Belkin crossed the garden from the castle stronghold, a stoic mask set across his face, steps confident.

"This could be interesting," Gastel said as he sprung to his feet, Dulanii struggling to do the same.

Belkin pointed at Tildimin before making a circular motion with his hand. As quickly as Gastel managed to get to his feet, Tildimin gathered everyone in attendance to attention. When Belkin pointed at Gastel, he couldn't hide the sudden apprehension from slithering down his spine.

"Time to test your battle readiness, Little Brother," the king said, his jaw set as he scooped a practice sword from the ground and threw it to Gastel.

Gastel turned his head toward Dulanii. "Looks like you'll get a demonstration," he said before he stepped into the arena.

"I hope you're fresh." A slight smile crossed Belkin's lips. "Because this is going to take all your stamina."

Gastel took a deep breath. It had been nearly two weeks since he'd broken free from his mind. He'd spent every day since desperate to recover fully, as he was thrust into an advisory position at Belkin's side. Every moment had been another challenge. Especially since his Anam seemed to be taking longer to return than his physical strength.

He knew Belkin wouldn't go easy on him. And he didn't want him to. The conditions of Rhend were too chaotic. Gastel had to be ready to handle anything Belkin needed him to. He could no longer use opening a rift as an excuse for weakness.

His brother approached him with metered steps. "On the battlefield, you must simultaneously recognize and ignore your surroundings. Your enemies won't wait for you to be ready before they attack you. They won't stand by patiently while you're distracted by someone else's fight." Belkin walked around him, hands clasped behind his back. "You must be able to switch from enemy to enemy intuitively. Zero hesitation. Zero thought."

Gastel swallowed. Whatever Belkin had planned for him, he was sure to be sore when they were done.

Belkin waved at someone behind Gastel, then stepped back. "We'll start with two at a time."

Before Belkin had finished speaking, Gastel could hear their footsteps on the gravel. He hadn't had a chance to prepare. He figured this was part of the training. The first two were easy enough for him. He spun, blocking before disarming the first of the assailants; the second took another two maneuvers.

"Disarming isn't enough, Gastel." Belkin raised his voice, but Gastel didn't get an opportunity to glare at him. Two more rushed in. "Kill them, or they will kill you."

The arena seemed to fade away around him. For him to let go, to allow himself to fight with all his capabilities, he risked truly hurting someone. But this was training. He had a wooden sword in his hand instead of steel. As if in slow motion, he saw them coming, and he let his apprehensions go.

He ducked, swinging up and hitting one of the assailants with a sickening crack across her ribs. She sank to the ground with a wail of agony, clutching her side. But Gastel didn't stop. He twisted past the next man's practice weapon, slicing hard across the back of his legs and sending him to the ground.

Two more came. Two more were taken down. Then three. Gastel tripped one man, sending him into another, their swords tangled. Before they could extract themselves from each other, he had slashed across their backs, then spun, catching the third under her chin.

Again, Belkin sent his fighters in twos and threes. Again, Gastel struck them down. Another and another. Sweat beaded at his brow, but his body still had more to give. More strength. More energy. Gastel found his rhythm. Every sickening crack of his wooden practice sword across another assailant. Every killing blow went from leaving him hollow to igniting morbid pleasure in his chest. Every time he managed to dodge multiple weapons at once, every time he slipped under a swing meant for his head, a spark of satisfaction spurred him faster.

Still, Belkin sent more in. "At some point, you'll slip up. Your energy will wane." Belkin's words seemed filtered through a long tunnel of stone, echoing and syncing with Gastel's heartbeat. "Your strength will fail. Your vision will blur. That moment..." Three more assailants, three more down. "That is the moment you die."

Gastel gritted his teeth in anger as he was scraped across his bicep, barely slipping past unscathed. Too close. He needed to move faster, push harder, and drive himself until he no longer thought about his next move, the next assailant, the next swing. Three more, their faces no longer registering as anything other than amorphous gray flesh.

"Ignore the pain."

Two more. He narrowly blocked a jab to his face. Three more.

"Ignore the noise."

Three more. Two more. Men and women sprawled out around the arena as he struck each one down as quickly as his body could move.

And then it was Belkin in front of him.

Gastel stopped short, the sweat chilling on his skin, his chest heaving.

"Until it is only you and your greatest enemy left."

The cold calculation in Belkin's eyes was something he'd feared his entire life. Gastel had beaten him in duels, but this felt different. This was the warrior Belkin, the deadly high general. In a split second, Belkin was swinging at his head.

No thought. Not his brother. His enemy. This was life or death. Gastel slipped past another swing meant for his abdomen. The crack of wood hitting wood, the bone-shattering force with which their practice swords came together over and over, was all he could hear, mixing with the ragged breaths that ripped past his lips. He was nearly spent, and Belkin was fresh.

Two more swings; Gastel blocked one, dodged the second, side-stepped, blocked, blocked, deflected, blocked. Belkin landed a superficial slice to Gastel's leg, but he rolled clear of Belkin's next strike, swinging up to block his brother's next three moves. A pattern! Gastel had spent his entire life trying to find the pattern in Belkin's fighting style, but there had never seemed to be one. But here it was. Three swings, backstep, two strikes, block, block. Belkin shifted in and out of a strange dodge-then-strike cadence.

Gastel let the pattern settle over him as sweat dripped down his face, his short hair clinging to his damp temples. Block, sidestep. His vision blurred; two Belkins stood before him, and he needed to focus on the real one. He was caught across his left arm and yelped in pain, certain the wood had drawn blood. He couldn't lose. Not now.

Not ever.

He growled as he threw the last of his strength into a combination he'd seen Belkin use already, but he changed up the last move. Not a low strike—he went high and nearly caught Belkin across the face, but his brother managed to spin away, swinging through with a cutting blow that nicked Gastel's right elbow.

Ignore the pain. Ignore the noise.

The pattern was there again, but Gastel was out of energy. Belkin managed a hard slice across the back of his leg, taking him to one knee. He ducked under the next, rolling clear before cutting up and catching Belkin across his knee. His brother rolled to the side, sliding back to his feet, but Gastel was spent. His arms were too heavy to lift. He tried to push himself up but stumbled to his back, defeated.

He'd lost.

Again.

The world spun as Belkin stood over him, pressing a practice sword under his chin.

"That, my brother, was perhaps your greatest performance."

"I still lost."

"Everyone loses eventually. That's our greatest enemy. The fear of losing." Belkin reached a hand down to help Gastel to his feet. "Once you know it will happen someday, you can laugh in its face every time you defeat it."

He wobbled, his head spinning from the exertion, all the pain he'd tried to ignore rushing over him at once. He winced as everyone in the arena cheered. If he'd had any energy left, he would have smiled, he would have acknowledged with a nod, but he couldn't. He sagged against Dulanii, who had pulled one of Gastel's arms over his shoulder. His head hung, sweat dripping from the ends of the hair that hung in his face.

"Again tomorrow, and you'll be ready," Belkin said. "For now, go clean yourself up for breakfast."

Gastel allowed the Shay to help him back to his room, where he collapsed on his bed with an unceremonious flop. He wanted to sleep and bathe, then sleep some more.

"Two things," Dulanii said as he stood at the window beside Gastel's bed.

Gastel rolled to his back and pushed himself up on his elbows to gaze at the man.

"First..." He turned to face Gastel with a serious expression. "I'm sorry I have to leave so soon." The somberness melted from his face as he smiled a wide, toothy grin. "Second, that was perhaps the craziest thing I've ever seen a single elf do." He looked down at his hands. "And that's saying something. I've seen Rae slaughter two dozen in minutes."

Gastel fell back on the bed, no longer able to hold himself up. He'd managed to keep her from his thoughts, but this gave him a moment of sadness so thick he had to squeeze his eyes closed against the memory of her blushing cheeks and curious eyes.

The mattress moved as Dulanii lay on the bed beside him.

"I never thought I'd say this about anyone, but the two of you would have been perfectly matched."

His throat tightened. *Perfectly matched.*

She'd been his balance, and she was gone.

Dulanii rested for a moment before he sprung to his feet. "I need to go. And you need to get cleaned up and down for the morning meal. I'd hate for you to upset His Kingliness. He seems to love concocting torturous obstacles for you."

Gastel grumbled. The last thing he wanted to do was eat, but a soak in a hot bath sounded amazing. "I thought you were staying for breakfast."

Dulanii gazed over at him. "I will if you promise me something."

Gastel rolled his head to face the Shay. Dulanii's voice had taken on a dark note.

"Promise me, if you actually fight against this Wyvern King, that you won't get your ass killed."

Gastel hated that Dulanii was leaving again. Between Belkin's constant pushing and Dulanii's short visit, he'd never felt so much like himself. Exhausted but stronger than he'd ever felt.

"I promise."

FORTY

Things in Baskets

A kind of peace washed over Roulin as he stood in the receiving hall of the stronghold at Korthan. In his haste to read, he'd crumpled the slip of parchment and was forced to smooth it on the wall in order to make it out.

Her handwriting was still as beautiful as he remembered—her words just as manipulative. She hadn't changed, and the realization that she never would was both infuriating and reassuring. Mostly because he would never change either. But he'd learned, and he was continuing to do so. He couldn't get what he needed from her anymore anyway. Now, he only needed the satisfaction of returning all her devious favors.

Smiling to himself, Roulin paced the room. He'd sent Tace to retrieve his brother's mistress as soon as the letter had been placed in his hand. He didn't need to read it to know that it was time. The last of the troops and weapons were secured. His contacts in Raggethan had finally come through. Correspondence was prepared so it could be sent to all the strongholds. There were more council members who had a choice to make.

"You requested my presence, Highness?"

Her voice drew a ribbon of longing from Roulin that caused him to stand a little straighter. Venna was beautiful, but the longer she spent at the stronghold with him, the less he knew about her. Other than the fact that she never smiled for him.

She *did* smile. He'd seen her when she spent time with the coven of women Roulin had collected to entertain himself with. She smiled at the guards who locked up the stronghold each night. She'd even smiled at Tace when he wasn't drunk and undressing her with his eyes.

But she'd never smiled at Roulin.

"I've kept you here for a very important purpose." He stepped forward, letting his eyes follow the contours of her body, pausing at each provocative fold of her velvet dress and intentional exposure of soft, gray skin. She tipped her chin up, her eyes firmly adhered to the center of Roulin's chest.

"And what purpose would that be?"

Consent was a blurry concept with whores. He'd tried to behave himself, but he'd be lying if he said he hadn't dreamt of breaking her more than once. He was perfectly content to wear that hunger in his eyes now.

"You'll be delivering a declaration of war."

Her eyes snapped to his, wide with fear.

"Now that I have the weapons, the support, and the allies I need, I shall challenge Belkin for the crown." He closed the distance between them, gripping her chin and tipping her face to his, watching the color drain from her cheeks. "And who better to give him this than a woman he trusts."

"If you mean to make him think I betrayed him, he'll know I had nothing to do with your plans."

"Oh?" Roulin slid back from her, watching as the muscles in her neck tightened more and more with each breath.

"I've shared his bed for decades."

Ah. As Roulin had feared. Venna had been Belkin's mistress before the conflict with the Shay. Their relationship was likely far more intricate than he'd anticipated. He took a deep breath, understanding what he'd need to do flowing through him. He'd hoped it wouldn't come to this.

"And you think your relationship is so ironclad, he'd never suspect you of espionage?"

"Why would I do such a thing? What advantage would I have?"

"Money. Power."

"Money is worthless to someone who needs it for nothing. And if I desired power, why would I choose the lesser brother when I already have a king?"

Fury ignited within Roulin, searing through him as he wrapped his fingers around Venna's delicate neck.

"You're so certain." He squeezed, relishing how a tear slipped down her cheek, and her eyes fluttered as she tried to stay strong yet faltered. "So certain he wouldn't throw you away when he's done with you?"

He released her, stepping back as she gasped for breath, then emptied her stomach.

"Thank you for helping me with my decision, Venna." He sneered at her as she panted, hunched over in front of him. "I was struggling with how best to return you to him."

He'd hoped for a different outcome, but alas, things didn't always work out as one originally intended. Roulin was well acquainted with disappointment.

Rae had forgotten how brazenly hostile Freya's advisor, Tor, could be. She sat as calmly as she could with her hands folded as he threw a tantrum about new translations of the prophecy.

"Be reasonable, Tor." Freya seemed to be at the end of her rope. "She has not meant to cause you such strife."

The situation might have been comical if the information wasn't so important and Rae wasn't struggling to remember it. She hadn't been sober when she'd read from Mesmal's copy of the prophecy, leaving her with fuzzy memories. Not to mention, they usually came with thoughts of a certain king she'd rather not dredge up on top of a swift flush of sorrow for having left Gastel's side. Her guilt was unyielding. None of it was pleasant.

"Over a millennium, Freya." Tor was on his feet, hands in the air, his seemingly calm Bleck Larin countenance shattered. "Mesmal has had over a thousand years to share this text with the rest of Rhend, and yet he let it grow mushrooms in his library."

"Perhaps he didn't know what it was?"

Tor glared at Freya, the heat of a hundred fires in his amber eyes.

"Perhaps he forgot about it entirely. A thousand years is a long time."

"He's an idiot. I knew he was an idiot when he sent troops to Dormshire. No! Before that. When he thought there wouldn't be dire consequences for breaking a promise in bonding to that monstrous Gemma."

Freya rolled her eyes and turned to Rae, reaching motherly hands in her direction. "Don't fret, Rae; we'll figure this out. We always do."

Rae's cheeks heated. "I'm not proud of myself. Wine was involved."

"Exactly how could one allow themselves to be inebriated when prophecies are involved?"

Rae cast her eyes at her hands. If only Tor could understand. She hadn't expected to find Gastel as he was, and seeing him lifeless was more than she'd been able to handle without intervention. "I didn't exactly know I was reading something that could be contradictory to all the other available translations."

He crossed his arms and slumped onto a chair, his lips pinched.

"So, what *do* you remember?" Freya asked.

Rae closed her eyes to give herself a moment to recall without the visual distraction of Tor's disappointed face.

"There was a large focus on the number three. The Reborn, the Restored, and the Returned. When the worlds are at their thinnest. Something about the dissolving of a sacrifice." She glanced at Freya. "It was very cryptic."

"As every copy seems to be." She tapped her fingers on the strategy table. "I don't remember anything about a sacrifice in the others we've studied. Or the focus on threes." She reached for a manuscript.

"How hard would it be to get this copy?" Tor interrupted. "Could it be brought here for me to review?"

Rae leaned her folded hands against her lips as she thought. "I'm not sure how Mesmal would feel about it. It's his grandfather's copy."

Tor threw his hands in the air as he paced behind where Freya sat. "Impossible."

"Perhaps we need to venture to Parth—"

"And take all these other copies?" Tor motioned to a few stacks of manuscripts in the middle of the table.

"It wouldn't be impossible," Freya said.

Rae glanced between them, feeling the tension growing. "I was hoping to leave tomorrow morning. I'd be happy to discuss it with Belkin and Mesmal when I return."

"So soon?" Freya asked.

"I'm sorry, Freya, I need—"

"I know." She smiled. "I don't blame you."

Tor cleared his throat with exaggerated emphasis. "Perhaps the two of you aren't so concerned about the end of the world, but I certainly am." He pressed his hands together and motioned at the table. "Can we focus?"

Freya gave Tor her full attention. "What I think you're saying is that we need to invite ourselves to Parth." She winked at Rae. "We can send correspondence with Rae tomorrow, giving King Belkin time to prepare for our arrival."

Grumbling with absolute disinterest, Tor gathered some loose papers before tapping them on the table to straighten them.

"It's nearly time for the evening meal anyway, and I'm sure Zennor and Neith would rather not sit in Rae's dwelling with nothing to do." Freya glanced at Rae, her lips pursing in thought. "Neith doesn't see with her eyes, but she seems to have some awareness of things in space or, at the very least, where elves are. Does she—"

"Have the gift of Svet?" Rae tried to keep her face as innocuous as possible. "She does, but she doesn't know how to use it." She wasn't sure how much of Neith's past she wanted to share with Freya.

"She's very young. From my knowledge of Svet, it takes significant age to allow them to control it." Freya squeezed Rae's hand. "Be gentle with her. She needs guidance and protection, but I fear too much of the latter, and she may self-destruct."

It was a strange way of talking about a teenage elfling, but it pulled all of Rae's own feelings forward. She had begun her battle training at Neith's age. Not by choice but by Gemma's decree. If she'd thought she could run, she would have, but there'd been nowhere to go to escape her stepmother. Rae's world had been so much smaller than Rhend seemed now.

"Let's fetch your friends, shall we?"

Rae nodded with a grin, and she and Freya left Tor brooding in the strategy room.

———

Morning light spilled over the dying grass and heather of the moors. The brilliant blooms of late summer were long gone, leaving a sense of foreboding as the world began its descent into winter.

Belkin folded his arms over his chest. He'd thankfully grabbed a warm jacket before heading to the training arena. Gastel would join him soon, but before then, Belkin had some thinking to do. His youngest brother would be furious with him when he learned Raemian was alive and Belkin hadn't told him. How would he react if he ever learned Belkin had kissed her?

The memory of her lips—her breath on his skin—warmed him a little.

Withholding information felt wrong. Their father had kept so much from Gastel that Belkin had promised himself he wouldn't do the same, and here he was, already breaking that promise. At least Gastel had recovered his strength quickly. Belkin doubted things would have gone the same if Gastel had fled to chase after the Shay woman. He'd been right to do everything he could to keep him in Parth a little longer.

"Good morning." It was Gastel's soft baritone voice as he jogged to join him.

"Morning, Brother."

Gastel rubbed his strange white hands on his biceps to ward off the chill. "Just you to break me this morning?" he asked with a smirk.

Belkin had been preparing him for warfare the last few days, throwing all his elite warriors at him in waves to simulate the battlefield. If he'd doubted his brother's recovery, he couldn't anymore. He'd never seen anyone destroy so many elves in such a short span of time. It made what he wanted to speak with him about this morning all the more ominous.

"Before we start training…" Belkin hesitated. This wasn't exactly the best place to come clean. While most of the weapons were wooden, Belkin was fairly certain his youngest brother could still kill him. Especially if he drew upon his Anam. "There's something I've kept from you."

Gastel tightened, dropping his arms to his sides, jaw clenching. Of course he was angry. Belkin would have been as well. All the lies he'd been forced by their father to tell the boy growing up. All the times he'd wished to explain himself.

"I promised myself I wouldn't withhold from you, and yet here I am."

"Just tell me."

"It's…R—"

A scream split the calm morning in half. Belkin turned to find the source as he drew his saber, the heat of battle flashing through him for the first time in months. Heavy hooves on stone, something large and wooden clattered to the ground with more screams of concern.

He and Gastel were running toward the sound before either of them knew what was going on, meeting a massive horse as it erupted from a line of hedges near the stables. The rider, clothed entirely in black, clung to the reins as the horse reared, then shot across the lawn in Belkin and Gastel's direction at a reckless speed.

Going against a horse while on foot was certainly not ideal, but seeing as how the rider had yet to draw a weapon, Belkin was confident he wasn't there to kill them. In fact, as the rider drew closer, Belkin could see that he carried a basket instead of a sword.

Belkin slid to a stop as the horse reared in front of him. Shouts and the clanging of weapons against armor echoed off the stone of the stronghold. There must have been more of these black-clad riders, but Belkin could only focus on the one directly in front of him. The rider turned his horse, positioning himself so he could thrust the basket toward Belkin.

"A gift from His Majesty."

His Majesty?

Instead of taking the basket, Belkin took the reins of the horse and yanked, throwing the rider off balance as the horse lurched. Belkin dragged the man from the saddle and threw him to the ground, realizing the rider was unarmed.

"Who sent you?"

"I think that was already established." There was bitter resentment in his voice, muffled by a black mask that concealed everything but his eyes. "The Wyvern King sends his regards."

Belkin flipped his saber under the man's chin, tipping his head up so he could glare into his eyes.

"There is no Wyvern King."

"Is that like there is no Shay Queen?"

A chill of concern rippled up Belkin's spine. There *was* no Shay queen. Gemma had abdicated very publicly. There was only a regent, and if anything had happened to Freya...

His eyes dropped to the basket, a slip of parchment had been tied to the topside. Belkin ripped the paper, cracking the black wax, which was adorned with a serpentine depiction of a wyvern in flight twisting around a sharp letter *R*.

His eyes flowed over the words, reading them but not wanting to. All the things he'd feared at his coronation were coming to fruition.

Gastel's hand on his upper arm brought Belkin back to himself.

He handed Gastel the letter as he reached for the rider's collar, yanking the basket closer. With shaking hands, he grasped the lid, taking a deep breath. Based on the size, he could assume what was in it, and the mention of a Shay queen gave him reason to think he knew whose head it held. But when he lifted the lid, black hair and gray skin greeted him.

Of Monsters and Kings

It was the handwriting that Gastel noticed first. The same as the note that Raemian had found in Tremire about the Sundering. He knew he'd recognized it.

Roulin. He'd been sending messages to Gemma. He knew things Gastel could only begin to understand.

Belkin was still staring down at the contents of the basket, his body rigid, the muscles of his face tight. Gastel leaned, noticing dark hair. A head? A woman's head!

The brutality of the act was made all the more evident when Belkin whispered a name.

"Venna."

"You knew her?"

He nodded, thrusting the basket back to the black-clad rider.

"She's been my mistress for decades. There were only a few people who knew this." Belkin's glare leveled at the rider. "And none of them would have willingly given up this information."

"Perhaps there are more than you realize who want a coward and usurper of a king stripped of his crown."

"Usurper?" Gastel spat, not expecting the flood of rage that ignited his insides. Thankfully, his brother held him back with a firm hand on his shoulder.

The rider pulled his mask down and sneered at Belkin. "The Wyvern King wants to know what you've done with Mesmal?" He cocked his head to the side. "Said he looked threatened and forced at your charade of a coronation. Not to mention sickly, like someone's poisoned him."

Goosebumps blossomed down Gastel's arms as he watched his brother's stoic expression melt away, revealing the angry Belkin he'd known his entire life. The warrior, the cold, impenetrable general who had kept the Bleck Larin territories safe from the Shay for decades.

"Not to mention your complacency with allowing the Shay, who have killed our people, to just roam our lands?" The rider dropped the basket at Belkin's feet, sending the head of the Bleck Larin woman rolling across the grass. "Perhaps there are more who think you're an entitled prick who doesn't know the difference between his whore's pussy and a sow's ass."

Belkin snatched the letter from Gastel's hand and pinned it with shocking speed to the side of the man's head with his dagger, blood oozing around the smooth blade where it protruded from his skull. The rider went stiff, then slumped to the ground, twitching as though his nerves hadn't yet realized he was dead.

Gastel's brother glared down at the rider, hands clenched into fists, jaw set.

"Have his body sent to Roulin at the stronghold in Korthan with my formal acknowledgement of his declaration of war." Belkin turned away but stopped, glancing back to Gastel, the fire of a thousand deaths blazing in his golden eyes. "And ready for battle."

There was nothing Gastel could say. Belkin refused to be talked out of his madness, but the sense that it was the worst possible thing he could choose to do was overwhelming. The reality that if something happened to Belkin, Roulin would have every right to claim the throne was entirely too real. Especially since that was exactly what they were trying to avoid.

Belkin paced the strategy room, incessantly tapping his fingers along the edge of the map table as he passed. Gastel had never seen him this way, his simmering rage untamable as he clenched and unclenched his fists.

"Please, Belkin. You're the king. Kings don't go to war; they send their generals." Gastel didn't know what to say to keep his brother from donning his battle armor.

"I may be a king, but I'm the high general first." He pointed a menacing finger in Gastel's direction. "A warrior and defender of our people until death."

Gastel grabbed Belkin's arm as he passed, stopping him for a few seconds.

"Let me lead your army." Gastel had no experience leading anyone, but if it would keep Belkin from making the worst mistake of his life, he would do it. "Or send Tildimin in your place. You can trust him; he's fought at your side for centuries."

"Roulin called *me* out—not you, not Tildimin." Belkin managed to school his angry expression into one of indifference. "This is personal. Roulin challenged me, and I'll not send anyone to fight my battles in my place."

Gastel shook his head. Whatever anger burned in his eldest brother now, there was no taming it.

Tildimin slipped into the strategy room and leaned to whisper something in Belkin's ear. His mask slipped as he turned toward Gastel, a second of fear flashing in his eyes before he disguised it with fury.

"We don't have time to wait for Treina's troops," Belkin said, running his hand over his hair. Whatever Tildimin had said hadn't been good.

"Belkin, this is madness. Roulin's playing you at your own—"

"I'll not send anyone to fight my battles!" Belkin exploded, directing every drop of his anger at Gastel. "It was *my* mistake for not having addressed Roulin sooner."

"I just think—"

"I know what you think, and you're wrong." Belkin left no room for negotiation.

Gastel swallowed hard as his brother straightened, lifting his chin in defiant confidence. If Gastel couldn't keep him from going, at least he could stand with him.

"Then, I fight at your side."

Belkin flashed a wicked smile, but it faded quickly, his brow pulling forward, likely thinking of the battle to come. They had precious little time and still needed all the planning, preparations, and strategy. It was possible they'd be heavily outnumbered with only the forces they had readily available to them in Parth. Most of the Bleck Larin army had been sent home or to the garrison in Raggethan, which Treina apparently couldn't get to them in time. It felt daunting, and for the first time since Raemian's death, Gastel was crushed with the dread of what tomorrow would bring.

Belkin pointed at Tildimin, who straightened. "Have Gastel fitted with battle armor and call every reserve available to arms. We leave tomorrow."

They weren't moving fast enough. Time was slipping through Rae's hands like the white sands of the Eishtala realm. She rushed poor Zennor and Neith across the highlands and through the heart of the Middlelend Forest as quickly as they could move. She wished she'd left them with Freya to come later. If she'd been alone, she could have traveled faster. But she hadn't been thinking straight. She'd only thought of getting to Gastel.

She'd been gone for a couple of weeks—longer than she'd wanted. Now, the feeling that something terrible was happening seared in her chest, making it hard for her to focus. She struggled to remind herself that neither Zennor nor Neith was prepared for the reckless pace she forced upon them. Zennor's heavy steps were a constant reminder of their exhaustion.

"What's that?" Zennor's voice yanked Rae from her worries as they broke the northern line of the Middlelend Forest late on their second day.

"That's Parth. More accurately, that"—Rae pointed at the glorious stone structure protruding out of the moors on the eastern edge of the city—"is the castle stronghold, the seat of Bleck Larin power and where we're headed."

Zennor picked up his pace, perhaps renewed now that he knew they were almost to their destination. Rae was happy for it. The closer they got, the hotter she burned to see Gastel, though a small piece of her wondered how Belkin would receive her.

"So, the king of the Bleck Larin lives there?"

"Yes. King Belkin."

Zennor glanced over at Rae, brows scrunched in thought. "King Belkin? I thought his name was King Mesmal?"

Rae nodded. "Mesmal stepped down for his eldest son, Belkin."

"The war general?"

"The very same."

They were admitted into the castle stronghold, and Rae led Zennor and Neith to the throne room only to find it empty. After Zennor helped Neith from the sling on his back, Rae ushered them down the main hall at a swift pace, her nerves in a tight ball. The halls seemed emptier than usual. She knocked three times on the door to Mesmal's study. After a few seconds, she opened the door and poked her head in to find Mesmal alone in his chair, shoulders hunched over with weariness.

"Raemian!" He stood, a sudden boost of energy reflecting in his amber eyes. He approached with uninhibited warmth. "You've brought friends."

His eyes fell first to Zennor and then held on Neith, who likely knew full well behind her eye coverings who this Bleck Larin stared at.

"This is Zennor and Neith." Rae hesitated, remembering how Neith felt about her Svet powers, but it was important that Mesmal knew. She'd already explained to Mesmal what she'd learned in the Eishtala realm. She trusted he'd never use such information for nefarious purposes. "Neith has the gift of Svet."

Mesmal's lips slowly turned up into a warm smile as he stepped forward. "Ah, the gift of Svet. Rare and wonderful." He stopped a few feet from Zennor, who held Neith's hand protectively. "Welcome to Parth, Zennor and Neith."

He bowed to them, and Rae watched Neith's posture change, the skin of her forehead shifting as her eyes grew wide under the cloth covering them.

"Your Grace." Neith pulled her hand from Zennor's and came closer, prostrating herself before Mesmal, her face touching the cold stone, her straight, white hair fanning out around her in near-perfect symmetry.

"Such courtesy is not necessary, sweet Neith. I am no longer king, and even when I was, I never required such veneration."

"Your soul holds the reverence of one who has spent millennia in the service of your people. I am humbled by your serenity." Her words were crisp and honest. More words than Rae was used to hearing the girl speak all at once.

Mesmal closed the distance and helped Neith stand, taking her hands in his own.

The contrast between them was sharp. He towered over her as she was a mere four feet in height if that. Mesmal's stony gray flesh against her pale white. She wore only a simple gray cotton shift, and he was adorned with glorious royal robes in a deep red, embroidered with lavish depictions of dragons in silver trim along his sleeves.

Neith didn't shy away from him. Rae realized her ability to see his life force likely gave her all the information she needed about Mesmal. A true test of his kindness. His soul could not lie. Not to Neith.

"Forgive me, Your Grace, has..." Rae faltered, fearing the answer to her question. "Has Gastel...?" She swallowed hard and wished that, in that moment, she could see her own soul through Neith's eyes. Would she see the heartache that she tried to smother with the hope she felt at finding Neith?

Mesmal's amber eyes seemed to glow with happiness. "He has."

Rae let out a breath.

"But he's left with Belkin." All the joy that had been in Mesmal's expression melted away. "There is great unrest in the east. Roulin seeks to usurp the throne and has amassed an army of like-minded Bleck Larin."

Goosebumps rose along Rae's arms.

"Now, we wait for my sons to battle one another in a civil war."

Civil war? It wasn't something she'd considered when she'd thrown herself at the task of stopping Gemma's vengeful campaign.

"I fear Belkin and Gastel are wildly outnumbered. There were desperate requests to call additional forces from Raggethan. Roulin holds himself fully fortified at the stronghold in Korthan." His eyes dropped again to Neith as his hands slipped from the girl's. "Our world may be very different after tomorrow."

"How long does it take to get to Korthan?"

Mesmal glared at her; he knew exactly what she was thinking. After a long moment, he let his eyes drop to Neith's face, and a sadness settled over his expression.

"If you ride hard, it's a little less than a day to the east."

She would need to leave before the sun rose if she was to get to them in time. Mesmal must have seen the change in her thoughts, the calculation of time. If she got a few hours of rest, she could possibly make it before the battle started.

"Your friend is here," Mesmal said, interrupting her thoughts. "He's likely sleeping. He returned today, injured and weary from bringing the latest news from Dormshire."

"Friend?"

"I believe you call him Freckles?"

Rae was moving before Mesmal had finished speaking. She wasn't even sure what room he was resting in. It didn't matter. She needed to hug Freck more than she needed to breathe, and she likely knew the exact room.

Sprinting through the main residence hall of the castle stronghold, she ran directly to the room she'd last stayed in, ripping the door open without knocking. A startled Freck glanced in her direction, yelping when he saw her.

"What in the Gods' names?"

"Freck." She ignored the way he scrambled from where he'd been sitting, backing up and slamming against the wall as she flung her arms around him.

"How the fuck are you—"

"Just shut up and hug me, Dulanii."

He wrapped her in his massive arms, squeezing until she squeaked. She'd never felt so at home. She nuzzled into him, squeezing back as hard as she could.

"You're dead. I saw you... Gastel and I both watched you fall into the rift." He pushed her back and held her out at arm's length by her shoulders, his cheeks wet with tears. "How are you here? How is this possible? How are you...just how?"

Her own eyes grew dewy. "It's a long story." She pulled away, looking him up and down, her attention snagging on multiple bandages on his right arm. "Mesmal said you were injured."

He clenched his jaw. "Roulin's men have been persistent. It's nothing, though. I'll be swinging my sword again in a week."

"Idiot." She smirked.

"Yeah." He yanked her back against him, holding her in his unyielding arms. "Someone decided to die and leave me all alone to my own devices."

Gods, she'd missed him. The realization that she'd likely need to leave him behind again hit her like a blade to the chest. If he couldn't swing a sword, he'd only be in danger. Plus, it was very possible Belkin had left him behind on purpose. Roulin's black-clad soldiers had thus far ruthlessly targeted Shay.

"Did you speak with Belkin and Gastel before they left for Korthan?"

"I did. They're going to be very outnumbered, Rae." She didn't miss the dark tone of his voice. "Belkin ordered me to stay with Mesmal. It's twice as dangerous for a Shay."

"I'm leaving after a few hours of sleep. I'm going to try to catch up to them."

He pushed her away again; this time, the expression on his face was one of anguish. "Rae, you shouldn't—"

"If they're so outnumbered, every sword matters."

He shook his head. "Rae—"

"No, I'm going. Don't fight me on this."

He looked down at his feet, his eyebrows drawn in frustration. After a long moment, he smiled as he pulled her back into a hug. "So stubborn. Elder Gods be damned, I love you."

"I love you, too, Freck."

Brothers

When Gastel glanced at his brother, he knew they were doomed. It was written across Belkin's face—the same chilling, stoic expression he'd worn after Raemian had beaten him in their father's study. The acceptance of death in defeat. Belkin's throat bobbed when he swallowed. Likely, unspoken terror simmered in his veins just as it boiled in Gastel's.

The army that lined the front of the city of Korthan was a shocking size. Clouds made the exact time of day impossible to discern, but it was nearing midday based on how long they'd loitered in position.

Their singular advantage was that Roulin was the only soldier with a mount. Otherwise, they were easily outnumbered two to one. How Roulin had come by such numbers was unfathomable. Was it so hard to imagine a world where Bleck Larin and Shay existed together in peace?

Or had these men and women been told the same lies as the rider who'd delivered Roulin's declaration of war with Venna's head?

"I always knew one of my brothers would be the death of me. I guess I'd assumed it would be you," Belkin said.

Gastel's attention snapped back to his brother, and he saw a strange half-smile turn up his lips before he pulled his helm over his head. His cuff stood up through slits in the back like the wings of a dragon. Belkin didn't wear their father's cuff. He wore his old one, the one that matched Roulin's. It seemed fitting that they should wear the same cuff on such a day.

Gastel took a deep breath. He had no battlefield experience other than the intense training Belkin had submitted him to. Even that had likely not fully prepared him. He'd need to use all of his training. He might need to use his Anam as well, but it would be far too easy to drain himself of his life force before realizing how close to death he'd come. He knew one thing for sure: he would use every part of himself to keep his brother alive—to keep Rhend safe.

In some dark part of Gastel's mind, he wished he could challenge Roulin to a duel. It'd been well over ten years since Roulin had been able to beat him in one-on-one combat. Instead, they would throw Bleck Larin soldiers—*solid, elite* Bleck Larin soldiers—at one another until the field was strewn with bodies and the grass stained with blood. He closed his eyes, taking a deep breath, despising the scent of mud and horses and sweat.

And soon, death.

When he opened his eyes again, he traced the ranks of men across from them, jaw set in bitterness and frustration. At least one brother would likely die on this day. Only the Elder Gods knew which one. And Gastel would throw everything into this battle to keep it from being his king.

Belkin glanced over at Gastel one last time and gave him a nod before he urged his steed to approach Roulin, who was already riding toward the center on a massive black stallion. They would make one final attempt at negotiations.

A shiver ran up Gastel's spine. There was something so terrifying at the sight of his brothers across from each other, not as friends but as foes.

The Bleck Larin King and the Wyvern King.

Brothers.

Enemies.

She could see the dust kicked up by hundreds of feet, the evidence of a battle in the distance, the sound of cries and metal slamming into metal. She spurred her horse faster. Every moment, every second longer, was more lives lost, more opportunity for Belkin or Gastel to be hurt or killed.

The minutes dragged as she ascended another hill. She wasn't fast enough. After riding through the night, she'd dreaded exactly this—being too late to help. The cries and grunts, the moistness of a blade slicing flesh, a mace crunching through bone. The thwack of an axe carving through armor. As she crested the hill, the battle came into view. The warriors sprawled along the shallow valley that nestled between her and the city of Korthan. It was a sight she'd seen before, but the colors that painted the field were so very different. It was a blur of Bleck Larin royal red armor and the midnight black of the Wyvern King. Bleck Larin fighting Bleck Larin in civil war, just as Mesmal had said.

She tore along the right flank of the battle at a reckless speed, searching for anything that could help her identify Gastel or Belkin, but there were too many soldiers, making it hard to see more than the outer edges of the fighting. She wasn't entirely sure where the line of battle began, but once crossed, she was instantly targeted by the soldiers in black, her pink flesh and red hair standing out like a fire on a clear night.

Her blade was in hand before she was in any real danger, deflecting a handful of sloppy, half-hearted blows before she found herself challenged by three soldiers at once. They slashed at her horse, and she was thrown, landing on her side and rolling out from under the blades that sought to slice into her leather jerkin. Tragically out-armored, there was little she could do now but join the fray.

Once on her feet, she let the years of experience take over, and the world slowed to a crawl. She was careful to target the soldiers in black armor, tearing through her foes with a fervor that had been stifled for weeks, the lust for battle drawing her deeper into the depths of the fighting. She sliced through each enemy with efficiency, her motions sure and crisp. She tapped into the innate fighting instincts she'd worked so hard in her youth to hone. Blocking, twisting, lunging. It was a dance, and she was so terribly good at it. Dare she say, it was almost calming in its familiarity.

Rae made quick work of nearly a dozen soldiers, removing limbs and finding weaknesses around armpits and necks. She finally found an opening in the fighting and sprinted toward the center of the battlefield, desperately hoping she'd find Belkin or Gastel among the tangle of soldiers.

And find them, she did.

FORTY-THREE

Against All Odds

War was not like sparring. It was loud and spread out. There were no rules of decorum, and Gastel learned very quickly that no one was going to wait for him to be ready. The training Belkin had given him was exactly what he'd needed, but nothing could have truly prepared him for the reality of what he'd face.

It was chaos of weapons and armor and limbs. The senseless death and constant movement was mind-numbing. He glanced toward Belkin, but his brother was gone. Gastel found him running toward a cluster of enemies.

Before he could follow, he was knocked to the ground, the pressure of the blow blasting the wind from his lungs. As his vision refocused, he had just enough time to block an axe from embedding itself in the center of his visor. He was on his feet a second later, sneaking his blade under an unprotected armpit and deep into the man's chest. There was no time to think, prepare, or change strategy; he was on to the next, careful to target only soldiers in black armor.

Somewhere in the madness, Gastel found a rhythm. There was never only one soldier. There were always multiple. He refused to think about the warm blood that splattered between the slits in his visor or the smell of hot excrement. Instead, he focused on finding the space between armor plates, shifting out of the way of swinging blades, and staying three steps ahead of the next wave of enemies.

At some point, he heard Belkin's voice, crisp and clear through the din of metal on metal, and he took a chance to glance in his direction. He couldn't understand what his brother was saying, but at least Gastel could see that he had Tildimin with him, and they ran their swords through one elf after another after another, like red waves crashing onto a black beach without ceasing.

He watched for too long and was caught off guard, managing to flinch back from a blade aimed at his neck. While it missed the softness of his flesh, it took his helm with it, knocking him off his feet and nicking his cheek.

"For fuck's sake, Gastel, get up!" Belkin yelled from several yards away.

Gastel let his instincts take over, blocking two sword strikes from his back before putting his blade into this latest enemy's eye socket, twisting it out the side of the woman's skull. When Gastel looked again, Belkin was barreling toward him, a black-clad soldier following close behind. He clambered to his feet, taking his eyes from his brother for only a second, but a second too long.

Belkin's unmistakable cry of pain drew his attention. His king was locked in the grasp of a black-clad soldier. They glared at each other until the soldier's strength gave out, and Belkin nearly sheared the man's head from his shoulders, blood gushing in crimson rivulets.

Belkin staggered back, looking down at himself as Tildimin blocked another soldier's blade from reaching their king. Frozen and helpless, Gastel could do nothing as his brother ripped a dagger from under his arm, bringing a stream of blood with it.

"Belkin!" Gastel didn't check to make sure the path was clear. He sprinted toward his king as another soldier snuck around Tildimin, her twin short swords swinging at Belkin's legs.

"Fuck," Belkin spat as he buried his saber in the woman's chest, but not before one of her blades deeply lacerated the inside of his thigh.

Gastel slid in beside his brother, helping Belkin to his back.

"It's fine. You'll be fine," Gastel gasped between breaths. He glanced up at Tildimin, who had moved off toward the left, taking some of the enemy soldiers with him. "It's going to be fine," he said more to himself this time as he pulled his brother's helm from his head to make it as easy as possible for him to breathe.

Belkin's face was pinched with agony as Gastel tried to press his left hand under his brother's armor. Baring his teeth in a feral growl, Belkin dropped his head back and squeezed his eyes closed. When he opened them again, they were glassy, but they focused on something beyond Gastel.

"Behind—"

Gastel swung his blade up as he returned to his feet, shearing off the arm of a soldier who hadn't expected him to react so quickly. He kicked the woman away as she writhed in pain, the stump of her shoulder spraying blood around her.

This was not how things were supposed to go. Gastel was supposed to give his life for his brother, not the other way around. He readied himself for the next wave of soldiers sprinting through the dust kicked up by hundreds of boots, swallowing hard as he came to terms with the fact that there was a very real chance they wouldn't be winning today.

Rae's breath caught. Belkin was on his back, holding his side where blood poured through his fingers. His face was ashen, and his eyes rolled as he focused against the pain. Gastel stood over him, a feral sneer across his lips as he defended his king. The sight of them gave her a momentary spark of joy that washed away when she recognized what she saw.

Brothers desperately trying to keep each other alive against all odds.

Once she'd found them, her eyes refused to leave Gastel, as if she might lose him again if she pried them away. He'd lost his helm, and his hair was plastered back, away from his face, with sweat and blood, and yet, in that moment, he was the most beautiful man Rae had ever seen.

She'd never witnessed his speed as he let his instincts take over, sinking his blade into any exposed flesh he could find, a spectacle of pure battle perfection. If he'd fought against Rae in the war, it was very possible many of those battles would have had very different outcomes. The strength with which he was still able to deflect his enemies' blows was mesmerizing, considering he'd been fighting for several minutes by the looks of the field.

She shook her thoughts away, knowing this wasn't the time to marvel at the man whose amber eyes had brought her from the depths of her lost memories. She could reflect on that when the battle was won. Instead, she relieved Gastel of two soldiers who were trying to flank him, and it wasn't until she swung and beheaded a third that he looked at her and truly registered who she was.

She saw the moment in his eyes, watched him lower his guard, his face contorting with agony before he snapped back to the world where they currently existed, just in time to deflect a killing blow to his unprotected head. As she managed to finish off another soldier, he was still half stunned by her presence, his focus no longer where it needed to be.

It was dangerous.

She should have thought of this, but she'd assumed Belkin would have had the sense to tell Gastel that she was alive.

"Rae?" His voice was strained, tainted with some mixture of battle lust and the headiness of hope. "What magic is this?"

She heard Belkin cough, reminding her that he was gravely injured and, without intervention, would likely bleed to death in the next minute. She slid to her knees, meeting the king's foggy eyes.

"Where are you injured?"

Belkin glanced up, looking through her.

"My side. I got greedy. I…" He motioned with his hands.

"No need for that now. Brace yourself. This will be excruciating."

He blinked a handful of times before her words sank in.

"What are you doing?" It was Gastel's anguished voice as he ran back to them after clearing the general area of any black-clad soldiers.

"I'm healing him."

"I don't understand…"

She looked up at him, willing a stern expression that seemed almost impossible with the joy she felt in her heart for having found him and his brother alive.

"There's no time. I'll explain later."

He stepped away, eyes holding her another moment before finally turning back to the battlefield, understanding that his role at that moment was to keep them defended.

She took a deep breath, her fingers finding the sparse tufts of grass that littered the battlefield. With a deep breath, she pulled the life force into her, opening her eyes in time to see the last of the blades of grass within twenty feet wither into brown, brittle straw.

Groping along Belkin's side, she found the place where a blade had snuck through an opening in his armor, and she placed her hands as close as possible to the injury. Another deep breath, then she pushed with all her strength.

Her Eishtala was reckless as she willed the flesh around the wound to knit back together. Begging the blood to stop its incessant flow. Praying that the Elder Gods would grant her this gift of healing so the king might live.

His head fell hard to the ground as his eyes rolled, and he clutched at her wrist with a strength that she thought might shatter the bones of her forearm. A cry of absolute agony left Belkin's lips as he likely felt the full pain of his injury all at once. Not until he relaxed did Rae risk meeting his cloudy gaze. He looked drunk with pain and blood loss.

"Thank you. For saving my life...again." He breathed deeply and pushed himself to a sitting position, not wasting any time. "One of these days, I should return the favor."

She allowed herself a timid smile and stood before holding a hand down to help him up. "Let's hope you never have a reason to."

Once Belkin was on his feet, there was no time. Gastel was taking on multiple assailants, and Rae threw herself back into the fight, dispatching a soldier approaching Gastel's backside with a brutal slice to the nape of the man's neck. Before the body could hit the ground, Rae was moving to the next, quickly drawing the attention of another two black-clad soldiers as they rushed in. Somewhere behind them, Belkin managed to mount his horse as the current wave of enemy soldiers ebbed.

Gastel's eyes found her and held. There was so much in that gaze, so many questions, but as she was about to approach him, to give him just one answer that burned in his eyes, they were met with an impossible sight as the dust began to settle.

Another hundred or better soldiers lined up along the front of the city gates.

Despair, like lightning, struck the surface of her soul. There was no way even the Elder Gods could help them take on so many. Rae glanced around, noting that perhaps no more than forty of their own remaining were either injured or exhausted. When she glanced at Gastel again, his eyes hadn't left the staggering ranks across from them, his jaw set in a strange, determined way that sent a shiver down her being.

She knew that look. He would sacrifice himself. For her, for his brother. She'd seen this same determination when he'd stood at the edge of a dark rift—willing to give every last scrap of himself. A feeling she knew so very well. He took his sword in both hands and closed his eyes as he ignited it in brilliant white flames.

Anam Wielders were not used in battle for an important reason. It was too easy for them to expire their souls without realizing how close to death they came. Rae couldn't let him do this, no matter how strong his Anam was or how much he wished to save his king. He'd spent months unconscious because he'd used too much of his life force opening a rift. She wouldn't allow it, though she knew there was little she could do to prevent him.

"Gastel, you can't."

He didn't look her way; he only shook his head slowly, determination and anger darkening the skin around his eyes.

"I can."

"It's too dangerous."

"We die today if I don't."

He was right. She knew he was right, but that didn't change the way her heart screamed "no" over and over again.

"Then let me help you." She pulled her falchion, holding it in front of her with both her hands. She pressed the last scraps of Eishtala she'd pulled into her body to heal Belkin into the blade, washing it with a green glow that seemed to sizzle and twist around it like bolts of lightning.

Even tempered with magic, two blades would not cut down a hundred soldiers. One killing blow at a time would be too slow. A thought of something more obvious nagged just beyond her reach. Perhaps something Noe-eb had taught her that she'd forgotten but was determined to remember.

She sheathed her sword, extinguishing the green glow, and she took the five or so steps so she was close enough to touch Gastel. There *was* something she could do. Something that she'd done without realizing as she'd trained on the top of the monolith. Eishtala was the manipulation of living things, grass and trees and bushes. It could be used to heal or redirect. Pressed into the branches and roots of trees, it could form beautiful creations.

If it could be transferred into trees, why not into an elf? And if it was given to an Anam Wielder without the expressed purpose of healing, how would that change the Wielder's power?

"Let me give you more life force." She watched his face soften as he lowered his sword. His gaze moved across her face, passing between her eyes as he thought about the meaning of her words.

She let him stare, the questions growing on his furrowed brow.

"I don't know if it will work." She did her best to keep the fear and desperation out of her voice, but she failed, and the clenching and unclenching of his jaw confirmed it. "But please, let me try."

He nodded, his lips forming into a tight line before he sheathed his sword and squared his shoulders in her direction, evening his weight on both legs. There was a desperation in his eyes that shifted into a softness. A deep sorrow in his solemn expression that caused her breath to catch in her throat. He leaned forward and rested his forehead against hers, placing his hands on her arms. With his eyes closed, he seemed lost in the moment before his gentle voice broke through the din of war cries wafting from the cusp of Korthan.

"Together." Gastel pulled away smiling even though the ranks of soldiers across from them had broken into a charge and were only moments away from them. "We can do this together."

They turned to face the wave of soldiers, their fate sprinting toward them, kicking up clods of soil as boots tore up the surface of the earth. It took Rae a split second to center herself and hold firm rather than turn and run in absolute terror at the sight of the army that bore down on them.

She closed her eyes, blocking out the battle cries, blocking out the roar of hundreds of feet, ignoring Belkin's sharp voice as he ordered his men to arms. She reached with her mind and felt the living world around her—the grass, the trees in the distance, the scrubby shrubs dotting along the city walls. As far as she could reach.

And she pulled.

When Eishtala Meets Anam

Rae took it all in—all the life force she could—drawing it, collecting it, and directing it like drops of melted snow into a mountain spring. She yanked it into her being with a reckless, unfettered haste that left her lightheaded and her hands trembling, bathed in the faintest green light. She opened her eyes in time to see the farthest trees wither and die, stripped of life.

The reflection of the green glow danced across the surface of Gastel's armor as she placed her hand on the back of his exposed neck. Taking a deep breath, she focused on the energy's current that vibrated through her. It twisted and pulsed, bleeding into every corner of her body, flowing through her veins, oozing from her pores. She held it as she'd held the wraiths in the Eishtala realm, feeling the power change within her. This wasn't energy made of souls that had been ripped from the Sheol. This was natural and pure—trees and grass and *life*.

She closed her eyes again, praying that her plan would work, that this time if she directed the Eishtala into something rather than letting it slip away, she could give Gastel the life she felt coursing through her. She looked over at him as he waited, trusting her without a doubt, even as their death sprinted toward them. She took another deep breath, and with a silent prayer to Noe-eb, she released her Eishtala like a raging waterfall of raw essence.

There was no resistance, no restraint. Gastel's back arched as the surge of power writhed through him. He gasped from the pain, scorching pain Rae was certain had to be akin to the pain of healing, and she cursed herself for not having warned him.

He swayed but caught himself as white fire rippled out and engulfed him before he could focus the power into his hands. The concentration of it was so intense that Rae had to turn away for a moment or risk being blinded.

Gastel harnessed the new, uninhibited power. The muscles in his neck strained as he focused it into a thin line of concentrated light horizontally in front of him, shaping it and sharpening it into the edge of a blade. He pressed and solidified it with more and more Anam until it seemed to vibrate the air around them with an angry heat that burned Rae's face and eyes.

The soldiers behind them shifted nervously as they fell into formation. The pathetic few remaining lined up, ready to fight until every last drop of their blood was spilled. They watched Gastel with fearful curiosity, ready to give their lives when this new tactic didn't work.

Gastel held his strange Anam blade as the black-clad soldiers sprinted across the battlefield toward them, waiting for the perfect moment; his mouth twisted in a snarl, growling with the strength it took.

Forty yards: He twisted his fingers over his creation, pushing more of himself into the blade than Rae imagined possible. He shook from the effort as it solidified, turning a terrifying black at the center.

Thirty yards: His hands were ashen claws before him, holding the Anam firm. He swayed on his feet, eyes rolling to the back of his head before centering again. Rae let her fingers rest on the back of his neck, reminding him that she was there and she would do anything she could to help him.

Twenty yards: The black-clad army was nearly on top of them, their raging war cries enough to shred a man's bravery from his bones.

Ten yards: Their burning orange eyes blazed over their face masks, weapons ready to slice into Rae and Gastel with unforgivable fury.

Five yards: Gastel released.

The blast of Anam was so loud that Rae crouched, covering her ears as it sliced out. It exploded from Gastel like a sword made of molten metal, unyielding in its course. It seared across the field, unstoppable, severing anything and everything in its path. Bleck Larin were rent in two; torsos severed like a hot knife through bloody wax. Pieces of unidentifiable armor flew free from disembodied extremities; weapons fell from hands no longer attached to anything. Neither shields nor breastplates could protect against such power.

The blood within the veins of soldiers boiling with the rage of battle a moment before soaked the earth, splattering like mud in a river of red. Rae squeezed her eyes closed and clenched her teeth. Bile rose in her throat. The wet sound of it would be something she'd never forget. It was the sound of a hundred or better men and women being sliced in half.

And then there was silence.

Deafening, torturous silence as the last of the black-clad soldiers succumbed to their end, and the soldiers behind them stood in dumbfounded horror at what Gastel had done—what they had both done.

Gastel stood perfectly still. Finally, after an impossibly long moment, he fell to his knees, held up both hands before his face, and screamed, lifting them to the sky. It was a twisted wail of absolute despair. She feared for a moment that he would collapse, whether from the strain of Anam on his body or the shock of what his power had done. She took his head against her stomach and held him upright, his arms falling limp at his sides.

Gods, what had they done?

What had Gastel created? And what had she given him that could allow for such absolute destruction, such immense and terrible power? They weren't questions Rae could answer; even if she could, she wouldn't. Not now. Not in this moment stained red around the edges of her vision. Not when Gastel was crumbling before her.

"What..."

It was Belkin's withered, dejected voice touching the cliffs of Rae's consciousness as she held Gastel, his shoulders shaking as he wept. He leaned against her with dead weight.

"What did you... *How*? How did you...?" Belkin let the questions waft away, out across the field of horror that sprawled between themselves and Korthan. Bodies upon bodies marinating in a lake of their own blood and excrement.

Not even the Elder Gods themselves could answer his questions.

For Every Question

It had been like shaving away a part of Gastel's soul. After checking for survivors and proceeding through the heart of Korthan to the stronghold, Raemian had been given quarters on the far end of the hall with the other warriors. Nowhere near where Gastel had been taken—his suite was positioned beside Belkin's. The feeling of walking further from her was akin to wrenching away his heart, tearing it from his bloody chest, and slamming it onto the cold stone floor. He'd lived the last six months thinking she was dead. The thought of letting her out of his sight now was almost too much to bear.

"Gastel."

He wasn't expecting Belkin's door to be open as he passed. A servant was pulling his brother's armor off piece by piece as he winced from his side injury. The laceration to the inside of his thigh was worse than originally thought, and he compressed it now that his cuisses were removed.

"What exactly was that on the battlefield?" His usual cantankerous tone had returned. Something Gastel hadn't been certain he'd ever hear again when he'd seen the grass stained red below his brother.

He wasn't prepared to answer the question. Not yet. Not until he had a chance to speak with Raemian. Truth be told, he wasn't sure she would know better than he. She'd been responsible for some strange transfer of life force that he neither understood nor had known existed until today.

"Belkin, I…"

Belkin's eyes had a strange edge to them. It wasn't anger, but it was close, and Gastel didn't like being on the receiving end of it. He was certain that most of his brother's frustrations were because they had yet to find Roulin, the cause of all this disruption, but it still made him shiver with some unnamable fear.

Belkin glanced away. "Get cleaned up. We'll have a banquet to attend."

Of course, there would be a banquet. There was always a banquet after a major battle, and this had certainly been a major battle. The Bleck Larin had very nearly lost both their king and their youngest prince.

Gastel bowed, saluting his brother before stepping back out into the hall.

"And Gastel." He looked over his shoulder at Belkin, whose expression had softened again into the new gentle king, eyes turning glassy along the corners. "Thank you. For everything. There are no words strong enough. I truly thank you, Brother." He bowed *to Gastel*. Something a king rarely did, and Gastel smiled before he nodded and slipped out into the hall, continuing to his own rooms.

Once he closed the door, exhaustion took hold. Perhaps some part of him had been able to keep his legs under him, but that part was gone, and he fell back against the door, his head hitting the wood as he let his eyes slip closed. There, behind his eyelids, was the battlefield, the black-clad soldiers of the Wyvern King, the river of blood that flowed through the center of his morality.

How could he have single-handedly killed so many people?

When he opened them again, he tried to see the room around him—a generous bed with soft pillows and warm coverings. The curtains had been pulled back to let the last scraps of the waning light stain the wall with white that reminded him of the Anam he'd wielded. A servant busied himself with preparing a bath in the washroom to his right, but what was across the room caught his eye.

A great gilded mirror hung over a dressing table nestled between the windows. He was drawn to it. He ripped his weary being from where it pressed against the door and trudged toward it. The apparition within the mirror grew. The image of himself in full, heavy armor was otherworldly. He stared at his reflection for a few moments, remembering the first time he'd seen himself with his hair cut short. Now, his face was splattered with some nameless gore and armor dulled by the blood of elves. He saw power and strength and death in that reflection.

He broke free from his thoughts and removed his gloves before taking another look in the mirror, wondering where exactly to start. He fumbled with the complicated buckles, puzzled by the order of removal.

"Allow me, Highness." The servant was there before he could stop him, unbuckling his pauldrons and pulling them away, helping Gastel shed one piece of armor at a time until he was left in his arming doublet. The servant started to move away, but Gastel grabbed his arm.

"Thank you..."

The man bowed. "Telfin, Highness."

"Thank you, Telfin. For your help and the kind welcome we've received."

Telfin beamed from ear to ear with the most earnest smile Gastel had seen all day.

"Thank you for your sacrifice on this day to keep our world at peace, Highness."

The words settled over Gastel as Telfin ducked out, leaving him alone to clean up.

Sacrifice.

The lives lost, not just of Belkin's fighters, but Roulin's. This had been a war between Bleck Larin. Bloody and senseless. Built on one man's need for domination over his family and a millennium of tradition.

Gastel made a mental note of Telfin's words before he crossed to the bathing room, unfastening his arming doublet as he walked and letting the red quilted material fall to the ground. He'd pick it up later.

Steam wafted from the tub Telfin had prepared, leaving the room muggy and smelling like wet stone and mountain sage. It clouded Gastel's thoughts with a headiness that permeated every pore. He sank into the delicious water, the heat almost too much for his skin, but it soaked into his muscles and eased the tension in his neck and shoulders. He washed away the gore before he allowed himself a moment to soak, leaning his head back against the rim of the massive copper basin.

Raemian was alive.

Alive.

When he'd first seen her, his initial thought had been that he'd died and the Elder Gods were granting him his final wish: to see her one more time before he burned for eternity on the Great Sheol for the lives he'd taken. The proficiency with which she'd wielded her sword had been mesmerizing and terrifying at the same time. He was thankful he'd never been on the receiving end of that blade.

When her fingers had touched the back of his neck, he'd almost given up entirely and turned to her so he could spend his last moment in her arms. Never in his life could he have imagined what she was going to do—what she was going to give him. The agony that had gripped his bones when she'd transferred every last shred of life force she'd been able to scrape from the earth around them.

The way the magic had vibrated through him, the strength it had taken to hold it in place. All of it was a mystery. How he'd been able to do any of it could only be explained by his need to protect his brother and *her*. He'd been given a second chance to keep her alive, and he refused to squander it on weakness.

He lifted a hand from the water and glared at it, stretching his Trove-white fingers apart. When it could not answer his questions, he let it plunge back into the water before he pulled himself from the tub.

He dried and dressed in the clothes Telfin had left for him. A pair of brown pants and a red shirt that was too large. It would have to do. He ran his fingers through his wet hair a few times before he turned and glared at the bed with its welcoming coverings, exhaustion settling in him. He could sleep for days.

A soft knock startled him. He hadn't had a chance to tie the laces of his shirt. He fumbled with the strings as he crossed the room, opening the door to whom he thought would surely be Belkin rushing him along for the banquet. Instead, he met Raemian's glittering eyes.

FORTY-SIX

The Things One Misses

How was she here?

"Raemian."

How was she alive?

She'd washed and changed into a simple yet elegant black silk gown that somehow managed to accentuate every curve of her toned body in an unnerving way. Her damp hair was pulled back into a braid, allowing a few strands to fall loose around her face, curling against her powder-pink skin.

"I..." Her hesitation was disarming.

As fierce and confident as she'd appeared on the battlefield—the warrior he'd craved to see—she seemed so timid and...

"I wanted to make sure you were..." Her hand reached for his face, her cool fingers brushing near the laceration on his cheek. "Does this hurt?"

"Not anymore."

Her eyes faltered and fell to the open laces at his neck. "I came to see if you needed anything."

He pressed his lips together to keep from saying aloud what he wished to say—that he needed *her*. Needed her to stay. Her being here with him stained his thoughts with heat, wicking through him and spreading into his abdomen, where it ignited and destroyed him. Instead, he could do nothing but marvel at the fact that she was here.

Alive.

They were both alive even when faced with impossible odds a few hours ago.

"How? How did we do that today? How are you here?" The words flooded from him, and he was powerless to stop them. "How is any of this possible? I watched you fall into the rift. I... I reached for you. I tried to save you..."

He pulled his hands up as if to provide some indisputable proof, and her eyes traveled across them, wandering over the way his flesh faded from stony gray to pale white at the tips of his fingers.

"You're..." His eyes filled with tears. Hot tears that he tried but failed to hold back. "You were dead, Rae."

She reached up and cradled his cheek in her hand. Her eyes searched his, their ocean-blue depths were the same ones that had plagued his dreams for months.

"I'm sorry, Gastel." She swept a tear from his cheek, her fingers lingering on his skin. "I fell into the Eishtala realm. I had no memory of who I was or how I got there." She shook her head, her eyes hovering on his chest. "I was taught to manipulate Eishtala, to use it in ways I never thought possible. I was told I must find you and a Svet Priest. That the three of us can stop the Sundering."

Her words were too fast, spilling out of her like a bleeding wound. He tried to focus. She spoke of Eishtala and Svet Priests and things he didn't understand. He clenched and unclenched his jaw, unable to hide his confusion.

"Forgive me, Gastel. It was only seven days for me. But here? It's been so much longer."

She took a deep breath as her eyes flooded with tears. He wanted to take all her pain away, right all the wrongs against her. He pulled her to him, tucking her head under his chin and squeezing her against his chest as hard as he dared.

"I'm so sorry," she said, her voice muffled against his shirt.

"You have nothing to apologize for."

She pulled away, leaving a cold place where she'd been pressed against him.

"I do. I broke my promise at the rift. I shouldn't have been so reckless. I wouldn't have fallen into it in the first place."

Gastel shook his head. "I think we both know you didn't realize exactly what you were promising. And I never should have asked it of you." He swept a tear from her cheek with his thumb, then followed her jaw line. "I should have trusted your instincts. It was reckless of *me*. I thought I could protect you by sacrificing myself, and that...that's just..."

She searched his eyes before tucking herself back into him and wrapping her arms up his back. The feeling of her pressed against him, her warmth, was like a slice of paradise. He cradled her head in his hand, savoring the scent of lavender soap and the coolness of her damp hair on his palm. He needed another moment in her arms—another five moments—but he wouldn't get them—not yet.

"I should see if anything's to be done for this banquet Belkin insists on having."

But Raemian didn't move; instead, she nuzzled against him harder, and he buried his face in her hair. Elder Gods be damned, he needed another ten moments, twenty moments.

"I'm so sorry, Gastel." She pulled back from him.

"What could you possibly be sorry for now?" He shook his head, a grin gracing his lips at the sight of her cheeks turning a brilliant shade of pink. "I refuse to forgive you," he said with a tilt to his head.

Her eyes grew wide.

"For something you didn't do wrong," he finally said.

She smirked, pursing her lips and drawing a thread of longing from him. Gods, those lips. The memory of their kiss in the Court of Tremire was enough to set fire to his insides.

"If you won't forgive me, then let me make it up to you."

A million different ways she could make it up to him passed through his mind as the smile washed from his face. He couldn't speak any of them aloud without being entirely inappropriate. His cheeks heated under her heavy appraisal as his mind conjured reminders of his sultry dreams.

"What do you wish of me?" she said, tipping her chin up with challenge.

It was a dangerous question. He had but to lean forward to capture her lips with his own. Her eyes traced over his neck and shoulders slowly. She was likely committing all of him to memory, every inch, melting his heart into a puddle of red-hot wax at her feet. It was those eyes that had captured him first, seeing all of him.

She met his stare, raising a single eyebrow in a curious way he'd never seen her do before. He couldn't help but wonder what thoughts flooded through her mind. He swallowed as the ache within him forged into hunger the longer she stared. He needed her. Needed to know she was real. Bringing a hand to the nape of her neck, his other melting into the silk at her waist, he pulled her against him, kissing her as her fingers mapped the lines of his arms.

He pulled away, pressing his forehead to hers. "I lost you once; I can't let it happen again. I need you." His voice was tight, just above a whisper. These were words he wished he'd said so much sooner.

She threw her arms around his neck and captured his lips with a crushing kiss, not so gentle this time, her tongue running along the edges of his teeth before he opened his mouth to her. He couldn't hold her tightly enough, couldn't draw her close enough, suddenly very aware of the thin material of their clothes that separated their skin.

He clutched the fabric at her waist with both hands, yanking her hard against him and drawing a gasp from her, causing the heat in his core to sear hotter, the urgency to lick through him. The flames burning under the surface of his skin were smothering his good senses faster than he could fortify them.

He kissed a path along her jaw to her neck, filling his lungs with lavender and summer and sunshine. He'd wished so many times for this, for her to be like this with him. At the mercy of his hands and lips.

She jerked back, leaving him leaning forward, her eyes wide with shock. And then she was gone, and he was too dazed to understand what had happened. He couldn't move fast enough to stop her. His bedchamber door slammed as he stared at where she'd just been, heart pounding, hands hovering in midair.

She was gone.

Rae stood in her room, breathing hard for several minutes, fingers covering her swollen lips. Gastel's words, the way his voice had vibrated through her entire body, turning her insides to liquid fire. The hunger in his eyes, in his hands.

And then there'd been Belkin's voice echoing in her memory.

The shadow of Belkin's hands as they ran the length of her.

Belkin's scent.

Belkin's eyes.

She covered her face with her hands and sank to the floor, great sobs escaping from the depths of her soul. She'd gone to tell Gastel everything. How could she have been so selfish? Gastel deserved to know what she'd done. He deserved so much better, someone who hadn't kissed his brother while he'd been unconscious. Someone who didn't break promises or do dangerous things that hurt him. She'd caused him so much pain.

After allowing herself to wallow in self-loathing for another few minutes, she dragged herself from the floor and over to the bathing room, where she washed her face with cold water, holding her hands over her burning cheeks to cool them. So much guilt. Would she ever be rid of it? Not if she didn't tell Gastel the truth.

Rae straightened the dress she'd been loaned, smoothing the material over her stomach. She pulled her hair loose from its braid to fall around her shoulders in waves and slipped out into the corridor to find the banquet hall. She'd do her best to disguise her emotions, hide her guilt, and pray that she didn't need to explain herself quite yet. Mostly because she wasn't ready to tell him. She wasn't ready to see more pain on his face.

But the last thing she wanted was to hide anything from him.

There were too many other things they needed to figure out. Their world was spiraling toward destruction in whatever form the Sundering would take. Her own guilt at what she'd done with Belkin paled in comparison.

No, it would have to wait. And she'd need to tuck the tumultuous feelings away so she was ready when the moment finally presented itself.

Bitter Victory

Half a day ago, Belkin had been lying on his back in the middle of the battlefield, certain that death would take his soul to the Great Sheol. Half a day ago, he'd been on the losing side of a civil war that never should have been. Half a day ago, Belkin had watched his youngest brother do something that should never have been possible. And now he sat alone in his temporary quarters at the stronghold in Korthan, mulling over how and why and... *Gods.*

A tender knock at his door drew his attention. An attendant popped his head in before entering and bowing.

"The banquet hall is nearly ready, Your Majesty."

"Thank you." Belkin didn't know the man's name. This was not his usual attendant. Somewhere in the stronghold, his first lieutenant, Tildimin, and the closest person he had to a bodyguard, was probably having his wounds dressed and getting cleaned up the same way he was.

The servant lingered for a moment, then slipped back out, leaving Belkin alone with his thoughts.

It wasn't to last.

Another knock, this time drawing Belkin to his feet. His side ached where Raemian had managed to stem the bleeding but not fully heal his wound. His leg burned where another laceration had been carefully stitched and tended to as best as could be done by the healers in Korthan.

Gastel's stoic expression greeted him. It was unexpected, considering Raemian was in the stronghold. Belkin assumed the two would be glued to each other for the foreseeable future. Instead, Gastel was here, his face so much like their father's. He had fared better than most on the battlefield, wearing only a minor laceration on his cheek and a few scratches and bruises.

"I thought I'd fetch you myself." The hint of a smile brightened Gastel's eyes. "Sore?"

"Yes, but alive. I'll take that over the alternative."

Gastel stepped aside for him to pass into the hall first. They strode side-by-side toward the banquet hall. Servants flitted in and out of doors around them, walking so quickly they looked as though they could burst into a run at any moment. The soft lilt of a harp wafted from the far end, joined by the tinny sound of a lute.

"Word of our victory has been sent to Father. I also took the liberty of summoning the local counselors to the festivities this evening."

Belkin glanced at his youngest brother out of the corner of his eye. It wasn't like Gastel to take up the mantle of communications. This had always been Roulin's responsibility. He must have felt the need to fill the void that their brother had left in the chain of command.

"I hope you don't mind. I didn't mean to overstep. I just assumed—"

"Thank you, Gastel." In truth, Belkin was grateful. He hadn't been in the correct frame of mind to do any of this. "Where have you left Raemian?"

Gastel lowered his gaze to his feet, a muscle in his jaw feathering. "I'm sure she'll find her way to the banquet."

Belkin smiled, still a little shocked Gastel had let her out of his sight. His smile faded when he realized he would need to address what had happened between him and Raemian, but this was most certainly not the time for *that* discussion.

Gold light spilled from the opened doors leading into the banquet hall. Tables were filled with all manner of guests. Some were lavishly clothed, while others were clearly displaced soldiers wearing whatever the servants could rummage up for them, just as Belkin and Gastel wore. The tables were hastily dressed with crimson and candelabras, set with delicate plates and crystal goblets filled with wine.

Belkin was only vaguely aware of his name being announced as he and Gastel crossed to their seats against the far wall. A roar as loud as any battle cry filled the walls, smothering all thought. He gave a demure nod without stopping, his brother confident beside him. Belkin had saved his strength for this and managed hardly a limp as they made their way. In truth, the more he walked, the better he felt.

From the sea of stony-fleshed elves, one face stood out against the rest, and he was sure that both he and Gastel stared in her direction. Raemian Starling sat calmly with hands folded on the table in front of her, and a warm smile lit her face. She looked radiant, her vibrant red hair loose in waves around her shoulders. She wore a black gown one of the servants must have found for her that only accentuated her rosy skin tone and brilliant shaymarks.

His eyes were fixed on her, and his throat tightened. He had to push away the sudden urge to sit beside her. To hold her hand in his. He couldn't help but notice that her eyes had fallen on Gastel, where they faithfully held.

With reluctance, Belkin pried his eyes from the Shay and continued to his seat, Gastel taking the chair to his right. His younger brother seemed calm, unfazed by Raemian's presence. After months of thinking the woman was dead, Belkin was shocked his brother was able to be so stoic.

Gastel leaned toward Belkin. "A few more people than I anticipated."

Belkin could only smile. It'd been a long time since they'd attended a victory banquet. There had been so few of them.

"Just a few," Belkin said.

Servants poured in from a side door bearing trays heaped with food, delivering first to Belkin's table and then to the other guests. The musicians eased their playing to calming music that faded into the conversation. Belkin's goblet was constantly topped off with wine that smelled of blooming heather. He needed a strong Bleck Larin red tonight. Something to take the edge off the pain.

The meal was delicious: roasted game, harvest vegetables, sweetcakes, cheese and bread, and berry jams. Belkin ate his fill, trying desperately not to think. His mind was a well of chaos, burning with confusion fueled by anger at not finding Roulin's body amongst the dead and his unavoidable attraction to a woman who was not his to want.

The music shifted into something more upbeat, and others in attendance rose to dance. Belkin was thrust rather harshly back to when he'd sat at Freya's side in Tremire before he was king. Before Roulin had so publicly betrayed him. He'd been bored then, but tonight, he had too many thoughts whirling around his head.

Gastel rose from his seat, turning to Belkin, a beguiling smile across his face. It was clear the boy had consumed more wine than was recommended.

"Tell me, Majesty, do you permit such frivolity in your court?"

The boy's words were playful. Gastel had not been this spontaneously happy in ages. Perhaps it was indeed the wine or the fact that Raemian Starling sat half a room away, alive and well.

"I permit that which makes my people healthy and happy, Brother."

Gastel's smile grew, lips parting to show his teeth before he fled. As sure as day would break in a matter of hours, Gastel was drawn to her like a bee to a summer bloom, pulling her from her seat and dragging her with him to the crush of people on the dance floor. Perhaps he bowed and made a show of asking her to dance or simply took her hands in his own and invited her with his eyes.

Belkin's gaze was firmly fixed on the Shay being twirled about. The shape of her gown hugged her curves, and even from this distance, he could tell her cheeks were that irresistible pink.

He swallowed the jealousy boiling up inside him, his hands grasping the arms of his chair so tightly his knuckles turned white. He was a quarter of a millennium older than Gastel and had yet to find anyone he felt so drawn to—other than Venna, who was dead, and Freya, who seemed a paltry replacement for who was right before him.

As king, at some point, he would need to take a bondmate for the good of the Bleck Larin people and sire an heir who could be forged into a proper monarch. He hoped he could find a woman half as remarkable as Raemian Starling, half as intelligent, half as...

He was out of his seat and crossing the dance floor, ignoring the pain in his leg and side, shrugging off the inner voice that screamed at him to stop. The sea of dancers parted for him, but he hardly noticed them. His attention never left his target as she spun across the floor in his brother's arms, unaware that a king stalked in her direction.

"May I?" His burning glare never left her as she looked up, her eyes growing large and her smile fading. Belkin didn't bother glancing at Gastel; he could see his brother's frustration out of the corner of his eye.

Belkin realized how he must have looked to her. The same Belkin she was used to seeing—stern, angry. The Belkin she'd met in the throne room of the castle stronghold when Tace had dragged her from the Middlelend Forest. The Belkin who had nearly taken her life in his father's study.

Or was it the Belkin she'd taken an arrow for? The Belkin she'd kissed in a drunken stupor? He tried to ease the tension from his brows, smiling as he took her hands from Gastel. Her cheeks burned even brighter under his gaze, but he refused to look away. She was a million times more beautiful from this distance than from across the room.

Without the veneer of hatred between them, he saw her for who she was: perceptive, timid, truly beautiful. He could smell the lavender soap she'd washed away the battle with, could see the way her shaymarks accentuated her slender face. He had the distinct feeling she was memorizing the details of him, seeing every blemish, every whisper of a scar as her clear blue eyes pored over his shoulders and then his face. Her gaze hovered on a laceration to his chin, a bruise on his cheekbone.

"I owe you my life." Belkin wished he didn't sound so desperate.

She looked away, across the room in Gastel's direction. Of course, she would look for him. They were incessantly drawn to each other. He wondered if she'd kissed Gastel the way she'd kissed him. If her hands had roamed his chest. If…

"I was saving my king. I should think anyone would do the same."

"Did you feel the same when you took an arrow for me in the Middlelend Forest?"

Her eyes grew wide as they met his again, and he burned with the need to know what she was thinking. He'd been confused in that moment all those months ago. Why had she saved him? Why had she put herself in such grave risk for a man who had made no secret of his desire to see her dead? Why had he wanted to be the one to take her to the castle stronghold? To sit at her bedside for hours on end as she recovered, watching her chest rise and fall, the calmness of her sleeping face. All these feelings had been there then, and he'd pushed them away because she was Shay; she was the infamous Raemian Starling, and he was the Bleck Larin high general—heir to the throne.

He looked away, throwing a grin at his youngest brother, who sat with his back rigid, watching from the head table of the banquet hall. A sick pleasure bloomed in his chest at seeing Gastel uncomfortable and likely burning with the same need to be within reaching distance of her.

"Your help today was unexpected." The pain in his side was starting to pulse the longer he moved, but he pushed through it. When would he have another moment to be so close to her and speak so candidly? "Am I to assume you found your Svet Priest?"

She pried her attention from Gastel and met his gaze.

"I have found a Trove blessed with the gift of Svet, yes." It seemed there was more she could have said. Her words were cryptic enough that he narrowed his eyes, wondering what she was avoiding telling him.

"I suppose you'll be taking my advisor soon to pursue another rift." She furrowed her brow, and Belkin couldn't help but return her confusion with a wide grin. "I'd hoped for more time with Gastel at my side before he follows you aimlessly."

Her eyes fell to the center of Belkin's chest as she set her jaw, a flash of frustration pulling her brows down for a split second before she managed to ease her emotions from her face.

"I hope you realize the effort isn't aimless."

The music had stopped. Belkin stood with Raemian's hands still in his own, perfectly still. After a moment of staring into his chest, she glanced up, that question there in her eyes. The one that had been there in his father's study when she'd defeated him.

He wanted more time.

Another song, another moment. The seconds were moving too quickly. The pain in his side only intensified the longer he stood still.

"What did you do to my brother on the battlefield to give him the strength to kill an entire army?" The question had been pressing against the inside of his mind all evening since Gastel had dodged it before. "How was it even possible? How..."

Gastel was there in an instant, his stark white hand covering Raemian's possessively.

"Are you okay, Belkin?" Gastel's voice held a ribbon of frustration.

"What did you do today?" Belkin turned to his brother. "How was it possible? You sliced an army in half. That isn't natural. That isn't..."

Raemian's hand remained in his, and he squeezed hard enough that he felt her flinch. She stepped between the brothers to intervene, only making Belkin's heart race, that creeping feeling that he needed to draw his sword wriggling down his arms and into his fingertips, but he wasn't on the battlefield.

"Belkin, it isn't his fault. He wished only to save your life." She closed her eyes as she swallowed, centering herself before holding his glare again. "I don't know how to explain it, but I gave him the Eishtala I was able to draw from the grass and plants around the battlefield. It gave him more life force so he wouldn't entirely expel his soul using his Anam."

"What does that even mean?" Belkin rolled his shoulders, trying to stand up straight and failing. His side was blazing. He was losing more than his patience. "Eishtala and Anam and transferring life force. Gods be damned, you both slaughtered a hundred elves in seconds! That shouldn't be. *You* shouldn't be," he said as he thrust away her hands.

She'd been dead for months. She shouldn't be standing before him, fighting in battles and dancing at banquets. She was dead. Whatever magic had been used to bring her back wasn't natural.

"You shouldn't be here!"

The entire banquet hall had gone silent, and Belkin became disturbingly aware of how he must look, pointing at a Shay who had, in essence, allowed his brother to save all their lives.

He didn't care. He was right. She shouldn't be there. She was dead, and part of him wondered what the course of things would have been if she hadn't shown up.

"Belkin, come and sit." Gastel took him by the upper arm and started leading him back to their seats, leaving Raemian standing alone.

"And you, why in all of Rhend would you think it was okay to put yourself in such a situation? Thinking Anam was the answer?" Belkin asked, his voice still raised.

Gastel clenched his jaw, possibly trying to keep himself from saying something he'd regret. He helped Belkin sit before turning and sitting back in his original seat.

Belkin leaned hard against the back of his chair, the pain in his side almost unbearable. His vision was blurry, and the noise of the banquet hall was suddenly overwhelming. He reached for his goblet of wine, but his hand shook so much that he spilled half of it on the way to his mouth. Gastel was on his feet, wiping away the crimson liquid before a servant swept in to assist.

"Brother, forgive me for saying this, but we're alive, and for that, I refuse to apologize." Gastel stooped beside Belkin to wipe more wine from the floor and glared into his eyes. "Save your anger for Roulin, and let Raemian and I figure out how we managed what we did."

With his head still swimming, Belkin nodded, the throbbing in his side and leg turning to searing pain. "Help me to my quarters."

FORTY-EIGHT

Lies Upon Lies

Gastel was beyond thankful for the servant who helped haul his brother back to his room. Belkin shouldn't have pushed himself so hard. What had possessed him to dance, and with Raemian? Whatever he'd said to her, Gastel had seen her terrified expression from across the hall.

"Just leave me alone," Belkin growled as he attempted to make himself comfortable on the sofa in his guest suite instead of his bed. "I need—"

"What the fuck was that?" Gastel wouldn't have been able to stop the words if he'd tried. The boiling anger that seemed to sneak into his chest when he wasn't vigilant was there, hot and ready to burst from his skin. "The last person in all of Rhend you should be scolding is Raemian. She saved our lives today."

"Seems she has a habit of doing that, doesn't she?"

"Thank the Gods she does!" Gastel stood in front of his brother, his king, hands on his hips. He refused to back down. It didn't matter who Belkin was—he was being a selfish asshole. "You need to rest, and you should apologize to her in the morning." Gastel turned to leave.

"That's not advisable."

He stopped mid-step, turning to face Belkin. "What isn't?"

"Me. Talking to Raemian."

Gastel was certain the confusion was ripe on his face. He made no attempt to hide his emotions. Belkin deserved every sour expression Gastel could throw at him. "I'm sorry, but how would apologizing to the elf who saved your life because you berated her for no reason in front of the entire stronghold *not be advisable?*"

Belkin struggled to pull himself to his feet, standing as straight as he could. Gastel was certain the pain down his side and in his leg had to be truly terrible for him to visibly struggle.

"Because she's avoiding me."

Gastel pinched the bridge of his nose. "She danced with you; *clearly* she's not avoiding you. You need to rest."

"You need to stop patronizing me. I'm your king."

Gastel straightened. Something wasn't matching up. "What's going on? Why are you acting like this?"

"I kissed her."

Everything stopped. It took Gastel a moment to understand what Belkin was saying—whom he was talking about. That Belkin was referring to Raemian. That Belkin had kissed *Raemian.*

"She'd spent days at your bedside, wasting away. Reading to you, talking to you, falling asleep at your side." He hunched over, clutching his ribs before straightening up again. "I went to ask her how I should handle the situation with Roulin. She'd consumed an entire carafe of wine and was in no condition to make the journey back to her own room, so I carried her."

Gastel was paralyzed. There were so many things about what Belkin was saying that he couldn't quite fit together—time he'd missed while unconscious. Events had taken place, *once again,* that he'd not been privy to.

"She called me by your name." Belkin took a sharp breath, drawing Gastel's attention. A tortured expression washed over his oldest brother's face. One he'd never seen before. This wasn't Belkin. He was as hard as the blocks of granite that encased them. "She thought I was you, and I didn't stop her. I should have, but... I couldn't. I—"

"Stop." Gastel tried to keep his cool, but there were questions he never imagined he'd have swimming around inside him, burning holes in his chest. "How long have you known she was alive?"

Belkin looked down at his feet, his eyebrows drawing together in pain before he looked back up, guilt plain in his eyes. "If I had told you, you would have run after her, and you were in no condi—"

"How long, Belkin?" Heat seared through Gastel's entire body, and he wondered if he'd combust into white-hot soulfire right then and there.

"A week before you woke."

Gastel's vision turned red with fury. A week? It had been over two weeks since he'd opened his eyes. She'd been alive this entire time? Wandering around Rhend doing only the Gods knew what. And Belkin had been aware and hadn't told him? Another secret!

Another lie!

He forced a shattered breath past his lips, time standing still as he shook his head. "You lied to me."

"You were in no condition to run after her, and we both kno—"

"When will you stop *lying to me*?"

"It was for your own goo—"

"Who are you to know what's good for me? *She* is good for me. I thought she was dead." His voice cracked as he pressed the words from the depths of his soul. He grew increasingly irate the more he let it spill out, no longer able to hold anything back. "First Father's affair, Gemma, my mother, the Culling, my Anam, and now this? How do you ever expect me to trust you again?"

"Gastel—"

"No. This is important. This is real. I offered my life for you today. The least you can do is tell me the truth. *Always the truth.* Not when it's convenient or keeps me from doing something you think I shouldn't do. Or know something you think will hurt me. You're not protecting me by lying, Belkin."

His brother stood perfectly still, his face settling into the composed mask of the Bleck Larin king, taking a tall breath and letting his shoulders ease.

"What can be done to make you understand I didn't intend to hurt you, only protect you?"

"Please don't protect me anymore. Your form of protection is—"

"What can be done?"

"Never lie to me again," Gastel spat. "That's what can be done."

"I give you my word as your brother and king. I shall never lie to you again."

The silence was thick between them, and Gastel knew Belkin was likely about to collapse from pain. It was another thing that angered him. Why was Belkin so stubborn? It didn't matter if he was a prince or a general or a king; he could be killed. He felt pain like anyone else. To hide that from Gastel felt like yet another lie.

Gastel shook his head, a fake smile sneaking onto his lips. "Go lie down and rest, for the Gods' sakes. In your bed, preferably."

But Belkin didn't move. He just glared at Gastel with that empty expression. "You're still angry."

"I'll be angry until I know I can trust you again." Gastel took a deep breath, desperate to keep himself from exploding. "You lied to me; you took advantage of a drunk woman. What do you want me to say? That I forgive you?"

"Yes." His face remained a mask of reticence. "I *need* you to forgive me."

"I *need* you to stop lying to me!"

A sly smile broke across Belkin's lips, and it only stirred up the fire in Gastel's stomach again.

"That's what you're mad about? I kissed her. Let her push me down and straddle me. And you're mad because I *lied* to you?"

Gastel let Belkin's words sink in. He could see her with him. Her perfect curves pressed against Belkin's hard body. They both possessed a battle grit Gastel could never cultivate—the way their swords matched perfectly in strength. They were well suited. Raemian deserved someone who could lead an army—lead an entire kingdom.

Gastel swallowed, the rage of a moment ago evaporating. "Rest, Belkin. Please."

"Not until you forgive me."

There was something so brazenly manipulative about Belkin's demand that it ignited a spark of pure fury. Without another thought, Gastel punched his brother square in the face, sending him back onto the sofa. When Belkin glanced up at Gastel, his eyes were wide with shock.

"Never lie to me again."

Gastel turned and left, catching sight of a sly smile that broke across Belkin's bloody lips.

⁘

Neith sat at Zennor's side, carefully listening to the conversation between him, Dulanii, and Mesmal. They were friendly words, which at times still seemed so strange to her. Tonight, Mesmal had insisted they relax in his study together as they waited for news of the battle, and Neith was not one to refuse. Mesmal's soul was so pure and kind that she was drawn to it, wishing every moment to be in the man's presence. There was something so *right* about him.

Her initial thoughts of Bleck Larin were mixed. They were a stiff and judgmental people. Not nearly as easygoing as the Shay she'd met thus far. The servants were overly formal, quickly moving away from her. She was very rarely spoken to, and she had yet to determine whether it was because they sensed her strangeness, because she was a Trove, or because she spent most of her time at the side of a Shay.

Dulanii's soul emitted a brilliant sense of honesty that made him endearing, but a strange, darker, less morally sound core kept Neith at arm's length. He and Zennor were fast friends, and even now, their warm laughter brought a chill to her arms. She ran her hands across herself to smooth away the goosebumps.

"Are you cold, Neith?" It was Mesmal's gentle voice, so deep and rich and full of a love she didn't deserve. "I can fetch a jacket."

"No, thank you." But again, that chill.

Neith perked up as the still air of the castle stronghold shifted, a door opening in the distance.

"Seems they've returned," Mesmal said, hearing the same. He rose from his comfortable chair, the others following. "We should greet my sons!"

Zennor touched Neith's shoulder before he took her hand to guide her from the study. The four of them stepped into the hall as booted footsteps echoed off the stone walls to greet them. The distinct rattling of heavy armor, a sword being drawn from a sheath.

The hair on the back of Neith's neck stood on end. She could see the color change in Mesmal's soul, a deep fear radiating from him, so terrible that it shifted the contents of her stomach.

Something was very, *very* wrong.

"Hello, Father." The voice was cold, scathing. It sliced through any courage Neith may have had as she felt Zennor's hand tighten around hers. "You keep such strange company these days."

"Roulin." Genuine shock bled through the usual calm of Mesmal's voice. "Am I to assume you have been victorious against your brothers?"

A dry chuckle wafted toward them. "I left before the decisive battle. I had more important things than to watch your precious heir and pitiful bastard elfling get torn to shreds." The condescension in the man's tone was grating. "It's a wonder Belkin managed to keep himself alive for this long if I was able to defeat him with a handful of my soldiers."

A wave of snickering broke through the ranks of soldiers, then a long pause of sickening silence fell between them before Neith heard more armor shifting. She dared to reach her mind forward and pulled away when all she saw was death and evil in their souls.

"I've come to take my crown. Do be a kind old man and hand it over."

Neith swallowed hard as Zennor shifted his weight, pulling her away from the Bleck Larin soldiers across from them. He seemed to need himself between her and the threat of this rogue, Prince Roulin.

Mesmal had told them of his middle son. Angry, spiteful, and entitled. He was why poor Rae had thrown herself on a horse and raced away as soon as they'd made it to the castle stronghold.

"The crown is no longer mine to bestow."

"I don't fucking care if it's yours to bestow; it's mine to take."

More shifting of armor. Neith could sense the other Bleck Larin behind Roulin pressing closer, impatient, more weapons sliding from sheaths. The scent of sweaty anticipation bled down the hall.

Mesmal must have turned his head toward Neith because his voice was clear and crisp, though barely above a whisper. The words seemed to flood from him with desperation.

"Take Neith and run."

Zennor pulled her away, but she didn't want to leave. She reached for Mesmal's hand but missed as Zennor swept her into his arms. Her eyes filled with tears, wetting the fabric covering her eyes as she was whisked away, carried easily in strong arms.

Soon, she could only hear Zennor's heavy breathing and his soft footsteps on the stone floor as he ran.

Unforgettable

Rae couldn't sleep, couldn't stop thinking about Gastel. She couldn't stop thinking about the pain on his face when she'd pushed out of his arms and fled before the banquet. She couldn't stop thinking about the fire he'd ignited in her blood with his kiss, his hands, the way he'd greedily yanked her against him.

She'd wanted so much more of him, to stay with him, to hold his hand through the banquet, to never leave his side. When he'd invited her to dance, her heart had nearly exploded with whatever this bubbly, fiery energy was that seemed to squeeze at her heart and squeeze and squeeze and *squeeze.*

And then Belkin had taken her from him, prying her fingers from Gastel's. She was reminded yet again of what she'd done. Of how the king had made her feel in her drunken state. A flash of warmth simmered in her stomach when she heard his words echo in her head. She hated how flighty and undecided it made her seem when she'd never been this way before.

She hated herself for it.

A low growl erupted from her throat, cracking the silence of her room wide open. She needed some way to destroy the blurry memories of Belkin branded across her skin. She'd avoided wine, but Gods, she could use the numbness it provided, stripping away concerns and consequences.

Instead, she dragged herself from bed and let her feet carry her out into the dark hall of the stronghold. It was silent other than the faint sounds of sleeping elves. On this floor, some of Belkin's more trusted warriors had been given rooms near Rae's. Gastel and Belkin were on the far side in suites reserved for the royal family. The majority of the warriors were housed on a lower floor in barracks near where the servants had their rooms.

She avoided all of these and headed to the main level, where the massive dining hall was located. Her feet were silent on the stone. She had no reason to hide but didn't want to wake anyone. Once her toes found the soft wool of a rug, she let it guide her through the darkness. This level only had a handful of small braziers burning through the night. There was no need for light, no reason for anyone to be here at this hour. Plunging into the shadows, she made her way until she stood in front of the massive doors that led out into the courtyard.

There she stood, staring and staring.

Her mind was in a thousand places. Things that needed to be done, places she needed to go. A strange urgency nagged at the back of her mind, knowing that every moment dragged them closer to the Sundering. If she borrowed a horse and left now, she could be to Parth by midday. She could focus on figuring out how to rid herself of unwanted thoughts of kings, to avoid explaining painful things to Gastel a little longer. To get back to trying to figure out what needed to be done to repair the magic of the Wastelands.

"Rae?" Gastel's sleep-stained voice startled her.

She turned, finding him at the end of the hall. His dark skin and hair blended into the blackness of night so perfectly that she could barely see him. Only the white streak through his hair was plainly visible. And his eyes. Those haunting amber eyes that had given her hope when she hadn't even known her own name.

"Couldn't sleep?" he asked as he seemed to float toward her, his steps smooth and confident. The usual Gastel, unhampered by nervousness or the soreness of battle.

"No," she said, wishing her voice hadn't sounded so uncertain.

"Neither could I."

He stood inches from her before she realized he was shirtless. She swallowed, unable to keep her eyes from raking over his chest to his strong shoulders and neck. His hair hung around his face, messy and beautiful. She wanted to run her fingers through it, down to his neck, remembering how soft his skin was. She wanted to swim in the depths of his amber eyes, a spark of heat searing through her the longer he stood staring at her. She couldn't look away, trying to build the strength to tell him everything, to rid herself of this guilt. Let him hate her, because the Elder Gods knew she already hated herself.

"Belkin told me everything," he said. "That he—"

"He did nothing," she blurted out before he could continue. "I did everything. I'm to blame."

Gastel shook his head but refused to look away, his face an annoying mask of reticence. "You were drunk."

"He didn't force himself on me, Gastel. I made a choice. I made the first move."

"You were not of sound mind."

It was Rae's turn to shake her head, glaring at Gastel and that calm shell he wore. The only thing that gave away the roiling frustration within him was the muscle that feathered in his jaw.

"Gastel, I…" Her eyes welled with tears without her permission, the words stuck in her throat. They'd been there on her tongue when she'd sat at his bedside, watching his sleeping face. They'd been there whenever she held his hand, touched his face, or begged him to wake. And now they escaped her along with her courage. "I…I missed you so much, and I was stupid and confused and lonely and…"

He took a step forward; the tilt of his head and hunger in his eyes caused her breath to catch in her throat. She backed away, and he followed until she bumped against the wall.

"I wish I could take it all back. But I can't, and I don't deserve your forgiveness." Her words were rushed as he leaned into her space. One hand splayed on the wall; the other sank into her hair. She took a breath to finish what she was going to say, but he closed the distance, his lips grazing along her jaw.

"You didn't do anything wrong," he whispered in her ear, his breath brushing her neck—the sultry depth of his voice settling in her core.

In a moment of guilty panic, she pushed him away, unsure how she managed the mental fortitude to do so.

"I don't know what he told you, but you're mistaken—"

"Rae. It doesn't matter." He eased back into her space, pressing his forehead to hers and taking her head with both of his hands. "It happened. But it's done. And if we're to discuss mistakes, he failed to mention that you were even alive." He sighed, stepping back to meet her gaze, his hands sliding down her arms to her hands.

"Everyone makes mistakes. After today, I refuse to dwell on them. You're here; you're alive… We're both alive. I don't care what you've done. I don't care who you've killed or who you've kissed. I don't care that you're Shay or half Shay or half Bleck Larin." His throat bobbed with emotion. "I only care that you're here now. With me."

These last words were quiet, a whisper she wondered if he'd meant for her to hear.

"I don't deserve you," she whispered back.

"I don't deserve *you*," he said as he leaned his head to the side, kissing a tear from her cheek that had betrayed her.

When he didn't move away, she risked tipping her head to meet his lips. He kissed her soft and slow, warmth sinking into her core as he opened his mouth to her, his tongue claiming her. With unyielding arms, he pulled her against him before tracing the length of her. She let her hands wander over his shoulders, his skin like warm silk under her fingers—firm muscles flexing beneath her touch. The summer scent of him emptied her mind of everything but his smile, his laugh, *him*.

When she pulled away, he refused to go far, pressing his forehead to hers once again.

"Gastel, I—"

A thunderous pounding interrupted her, and they both flinched back from the door. Rae reached for a sword that wasn't there as Gastel stepped forward, a protective hand pushing her behind him. The pounding came again, sounding a lot more like knocking the second time.

Gastel reached for the heavy latch, but Rae stopped him.

"Without a weapon?"

His eyes glittered in the dim light. "I am the weapon." His soulflame ignited between them, illuminating the wicked smile that crept across his face.

The lone man outside was soaked and shivering from the frigid autumn rain that had settled over Rhend. He held his arm where blood soaked through his sleeve, a large gash oozed high on his cheek, and one of his eyes was swollen and bruised.

"Please, a message for King Belkin." The man stumbled forward, and Gastel caught him, helping him into the warmth of the stronghold.

"He's sleeping. You can give the message to me," Gastel said with an authority Rae hadn't heard in his voice before.

The man shook his head, looking again at Gastel and seeing who he was for the first time. "Pardon, Highness, it must be given directly to the king."

Gastel glanced at Rae before they led the man through the stronghold.

Rae helped him stand upright while Gastel woke his brother. After a few moments, Belkin's face emerged from the darkness, his tired eyes falling first to Rae and then to the man.

"What's this message that couldn't wait?"

The man fell to one knee, barely able to hold himself up. "The Wyvern King..."

Rae's blood ran cold. They hadn't found Roulin's body. It was very likely that he was still alive, hiding somewhere or worse.

"The Wyvern King has infiltrated the castle stronghold."

Unforgivable

Rae spurred her horse beside Gastel's. He rode with unbridled haste, a determined set to his jaw and his eyes wild with rage. The sky above matched their mood. They raced toward angry clouds. Sheets of rain moved across the horizon, concealing any hint as to how much farther they had before reaching Parth.

There was no rest for the weary. Behind them, riding at a much more comfortable pace for his injuries, Belkin rode with Tildimin and a small retainer of his remaining elite warriors. They didn't don their battle armor. They hadn't sharpened blades before leaving. They hadn't said goodbye to their gracious hosts.

They'd had no time for these things.

Rae tightened her grip on the reins as Gastel passed her, breaking through a thick curtain of rain that plastered his shirt to his trim torso. The soft cotton tunic Rae wore did little to protect her from the pebbles of frigid precipitation. It was so cold, Rae questioned if it wasn't, in fact, ice. Thankfully, her horse didn't waver and plunged into the storm with a fearless confidence she did not share.

Without looking back at her, Gastel set a hazardous pace. Adrenaline burned through Rae, coursing with terror and anger as she tried to keep up with him. Once hooves touched cobblestone, however, he seemed to lunge forward even faster, winding through the streets of Parth with a lifetime of familiarity that she didn't possess.

Elves dove out of the way as the two tore between the stalls of a market and then down a busy thoroughfare. Rae wondered if Gastel saw any of them or if he was so focused on making it back to the castle stronghold—to his father—that they were nothing more than faceless obstacles.

The castle stronghold's gate had been left unguarded, and Gastel cursed loud enough to turn the head of a lone servant who sat cross-legged in the rain, blood stains evident down the front of her frock. She sat beside a lump of flesh dressed in Bleck Larin royal red.

Gastel slid from the saddle before his horse came to a stop. He didn't bother to look back. Rae scrambled to do the same, still desperate to keep up with him, as he threw the front doors of the castle stronghold wide and disappeared down the hall.

Rae let him pull ahead as she took in the disheveled contents, the slashed paintings, tapestries, and doors to various rooms left ajar. A cold shiver writhed up her spine.

This had been a massacre.

Ahead of her, Gastel slipped as he turned through the open doors of the throne room, nearly falling but managing to catch himself with a single hand. He stared down at the ground as he stood before he looked up again and slowly entered, his hand falling to the grip of his sword.

Before she stepped into the throne room, her eyes snagged on the same thing he'd looked at. He hadn't slipped on water. He'd slipped on blood.

And it was everywhere.

The walls. The floor. Splattered up the pillars and soaked into the cushion resting on the empty throne. Rae was no stranger to gore, but the dark crimson against the polished granite walls seared through her bravery like a hot blade. She was frozen in place at the entrance to the throne room, unable to take a single step in.

The ground was littered with stony flesh and royal red armor, empty amber eyes staring into nothingness. The stench of entrails and urine and musty blood was overpowering. Gastel went from body to body, frantic in his search for his father, but Rae couldn't focus on him because pinned to the wall beside the throne was a very familiar pink-fleshed elf with cropped white hair, arms outstretched.

Bile rose in her throat. Whatever fear had gripped her feet in place withered at the sight, and she rushed past Gastel, moving with purpose, stepping over the pieces of the dead. She slid on a smear of blood as she took all three of the steps to the dais at once.

"Freck." Gods, it couldn't be.

But it was.

He was nailed in place with swords through his arms and shoulders, his legs left to dangle. His chest was a mess of shallow slashes, carving a cruel letter *R* that stretched down to his abdomen. Above him, a familiar short sword was speared through a length of hair that stretched over Freck's shoulder and into a heap on the floor. It could only be one Bleck Larin's hair.

She didn't wait to see if Freck was breathing; she started yanking blades from his body, frantic and chaotic.

If she'd taken him with her.

If she'd been faster.

Her breathing was ragged as she struggled to remove them from the granite wall, panic writhing through her muscles with each blade she freed. Her vision blurred as her eyes filled with burning tears.

If she'd hugged him tighter.

"Please, no."

If she got him down, she could heal him.

She didn't pause when Gastel came to help as Freck's lifeless body fell forward. He took Freck's weight, and Rae continued to work to free him, one agonizing blade at a time, catching on bone and muscle on the way out.

If she'd never been separated from him all those months ago.

If she'd said she loved him more.

If she'd never left his side.

If she could go back and make the choice to leave to help Belkin and Gastel again, would she choose any differently?

Gastel lay Freck on his back as Rae knelt beside him, unsure what to do, where to start, how to help. If she *could* help.

"No. Gods, *please!*" Her voice trailed off to a whisper as she touched his face, his neck, his chest, his shoulder, his stomach. Every inch of him was bloodied, no part of him spared by Roulin's cruelty.

"Freck, please," she said as she pressed her ear to his chest. *"Please."*

She was breaking, and there was nothing Gastel could do.

Because he was breaking, too.

She collapsed in a heap on Dulanii's lifeless body. The Shay was dead. There was no way he could still be alive. Not after the blood he'd lost, the hours of being crucified to a wall, the torture he'd endured at the hands of Roulin and his fighters.

Raemian's shoulders shook as she cried, and Gastel fell to his knees beside her, his eyes welling with tears, his arms wrapping around her shoulders.

Dulanii hadn't deserved this. When Gastel had needed to be pulled from his sorrow, he'd been there. When his hands had been two worthless lumps of scar tissue, Dulanii had been there. But when Dulanii had needed him most, Gastel had been feasting and dancing at a victory banquet.

That strange pulling of magic tickled the edge of Gastel's consciousness as he realized Raemian was trying to heal him.

"He's dead, Rae," he said, his voice cracking.

She didn't budge, and he straightened as the Eishtala moved around him and into her. She placed both her hands on Dulanii's chest and, without warning, released all her power at once. But he didn't move as the magic pummeled him, the wounds on his chest slowly knitting themselves back together.

If he'd been alive, the pain of that healing would have been excruciating. Gastel knew it well. Dulanii would have arched his back, clutched Raemian's hands, wailed in pain, *something*. But there was nothing. Raemian forced every last drop of her magic into Dulanii until she fell forward, exhausted, onto his healed chest.

"Please, Freck," Raemian whimpered.

Gastel reached for her, wrapping her in his arms. "I'm sorry, Rae," he whispered, his voice unable to speak any louder as his own heart shattered.

He didn't know what else to say. He didn't know how to fix this—or if it could be fixed. Perhaps if they had a Svet Priest, they could try to resurrect Dulanii now that his broken body had been healed, but other than the Svet Priest at the Vail, Gastel didn't know the first thing about where to find one—or whether it was already too late for such magic.

She sobbed against his neck as he held her, his eyes traveling around the throne room. This had been a mass execution. The Gods knew how many fighters Roulin had brought to attack an unarmed stronghold. And what had Roulin done to their father? It was clear he'd sheared Mesmal's topknot away, but the blood on the cushion of the throne was foreboding. What had their father done to deserve this? What had any of them done? These guards looked as though they'd been brought into the throne room and lined up before being slaughtered.

So much senseless death.

But was it any more senseless than what Gastel had done on the battlefield the day before? When he'd quite literally sliced an entire army in half?

Gastel squeezed tears back, turning his head into Raemian's hair as he struggled to keep from weeping like an elfling. After only a few seconds, she pushed away from him, her eyes wide with terror. At first, Gastel thought he'd done something wrong, but she stood, looking around the throne room, taking the steps down from the dais all at once.

"Where are Neith and Zennor?" she asked.

"Who?"

FIFTY-ONE

Regret

Room by room, Rae searched, frantic to find them. Neith would be terrified. Rae could almost feel the fear permeating the air. But there was nothing—no sign of them, just the occasional body of a guard or servant slaughtered like all the others.

It was clear that Roulin's fighters had taken this same route, killing anyone who might have been a threat, and as Rae retraced the Wyvern King's steps, her eyes pooled with tears again, bathed in wretched guilt that she knew she shouldn't feel. The Wyvern King's claim to the Bleck Larin throne would have been indisputable if she hadn't gone to the battlefield.

But at what cost?

Freck was dead. It seemed Mesmal had been taken. Neith and Zennor were missing. She wrapped her arms around herself in despair, freezing in the hall, too choked up to take another step.

"Rae." Gastel caught up to her, pulling her into his arms, heat melting through his wet clothes and into her skin. "It's going to be okay."

She sobbed against him. It wasn't going to be okay, though. They already had enough to worry about trying to open the last rift and stop the Sundering; now, they also needed to find Mesmal, Neith, and Zennor. Not to mention, the Bleck Larin royal army was currently in a state of absolute disarray as they faced the potential of more civil war. The majority of the elite fighters that hadn't been sent home after the war with the Shay were dead or in no shape to fight. And Roulin's soldiers were, Gods knew where, slaughtering anyone in red armor or with pink flesh.

She glanced up into his eyes, seeing a mixture of fury, concern, and sadness staining his furrowed brow, mesmerized as his emotions played out on his face. She wrapped her arms around him as he pressed his head against her shoulder, shaking as he cried—broken like she was. She squeezed him closer, thankful that, at the very least, she had him. They'd put this back together somehow.

+——— ———+

He should have stayed. He should have sent his soldiers with Gastel and Tildimin. If he'd stayed, Belkin had every confidence he could have managed to dispatch whatever force Roulin had brought—if they'd bothered to attack at all. Instead, he'd been greedy and hadn't listened to his youngest brother's sound advice. Kings didn't go into the battle. Kings sat on their throne. Kings sent their generals to war.

They rode painfully slow, but he wasn't sure he could handle going much faster. His side and thigh were already throbbing. As they finally breached the bailey of the castle stronghold, he was ready to be off Jore. He was helped down by Tildimin, who'd ridden ahead with a few other fighters to ensure his safety.

With a tempered limp, he swept down the main hall as quickly as his injuries would allow, trying to ignore the destruction Roulin had left. His eyes remained trained on the opened door of the throne room, where the light of late afternoon cascaded from the massive windows within. A dark stain caught his eye as he approached. A pool of blood smeared with footprints led into the space, and as Belkin's eyes rose from the puddle, they caught on the smears of it on red armor and dark flesh.

Bodies were everywhere. Some seemed to remain where they'd fallen; others were lined up in a row with their hands folded over their chests. Gastel and a couple of servants were sorting through them, preparing them to be taken away. Rae was wiping down the dais with a pink-stained rag. A sword protruded from the wall beside the throne with a plait of black hair with a familiar white streak.

"Fuck."

Gastel glanced up, springing from the deceased soldier he was trying to move, and rushed to Belkin's side.

"Where's Father?" Belkin asked as he searched the throne room, his eyes not missing the smears of blood on the wall, the discarded weapons, the bodies.

"We can only assume that Roulin has him."

Gastel's words were like a sword to the gut, leaving Belkin to bleed out slowly, painfully. He swayed on his feet, and Gastel clutched his arm to steady him.

"We'll get him back," Raemian said as she stepped toward them. Belkin looked at her, the knees of her pants dark with stains, the front of her shirt streaked as well. A swipe of blood smeared across her cheek, and still, she was gorgeous. He wanted to fall into her arms and weep like an elfling.

As she stepped closer, she reached for Gastel's hand and entwined her fingers with his. It was intentional, and Belkin let his eyes loiter on their joined hands for longer than necessary. Jealousy was for the weak-minded; and right now, he was very, *very* weak.

He glared at Gastel with the heat of all his frustration, and to his youngest brother's credit, Gastel took all of it and tucked it away, swallowing but holding Belkin's eye contact.

"Was there no one left alive?"

"Some of the servants, a handful of the staff from the stables."

Belkin stared at his father's braid, still mounted to the wall like a trophy, the blood boiling in his veins. If his father had been hurt, the pain he would inflict on Roulin would be intense and pure. He'd have no mercy for him. As far as Belkin was concerned, Roulin was no longer his brother. He was an enemy of the Bleck Larin people.

At the end of the row of the dead, a single pink-fleshed elf stood out amongst the others. *Dulanii.* Eyes closed, his white hair plastered back with blood. He hadn't deserved this. Not after everything he'd done to establish peace, to keep innocent elves safe. As much as Belkin was loath to admit it, he'd liked him.

"We think he took my friends as well."

Raemian's voice was soft, and he'd be lying to himself if he didn't admit he wanted to curl up with that voice. To bathe himself clean with it. Then he realized...

"The Trove elf?"

She swallowed, nodding, her eyes falling to her friend's corpse lined up with the rest of the dead.

"Dulanii was...mounted to the wall with Father's braid," Gastel said, his words tight with anger. "He was tortured." Gastel glanced at Raemian.

She continued to stare straight ahead, a silent tear escaping her vigilance.

Belkin pushed his grief away to process later. There were bigger problems. Much bigger. He'd lost too many of his fighters, his father, and potentially his control of the Bleck Larin territories.

"We'll get Father back." Gastel's voice was dark with foreboding. A raw edge of anger in every syllable. "*I'll* get Father back."

Belkin had seen what Gastel could do with his Anam, and Roulin deserved nothing less than to have his skin peeled off his body with a blade of flames.

"You'll be killed if you run headfirst into whatever trap Roulin has laid for you," Raemian said with a cold voice.

She was too calm. The years of war had given her an unnatural ability to school her fear into strategic thinking.

"He deserves to be crucified. He deserves to be flayed alive—"

"Enough." Belkin shocked himself with the authority in his voice. Several sets of startled eyes settled on him. "We collect ourselves." He wasn't sure he agreed with himself, the visceral fury still fresh under his skin. "If I've learned nothing else from all this, it's that we can't underestimate Roulin again."

FIFTY-TWO

Cruel Eyes

Neith could sense him staring with his cruel eyes. She'd never actually seen them, but she knew the depths of their depravity. He was nothing like his father. Roulin was a monster in Bleck Larin skin. His soul, a filthy stain, seemed to pulse with anger every time someone spoke with him.

After dragging her across a barren land with her hands painfully bound, he'd yanked her away from Zennor and Mesmal. She was terrified Zennor had been hurt—or worse. Roulin and his soldiers had called him lower than the mud that clung to their boots. She shivered every time they mentioned "the pig." She knew to whom they referred.

And Mesmal? Roulin had treated him like a common criminal. While Neith could completely understand such vengeful actions directed at a father, Mesmal was perhaps the furthest from deserving.

After shivering in a room flooded with so much light that even three bindings around her eyes couldn't prevent the agony, she'd been snatched up and roughly directed through the winding halls of this new place. It was deathly cold, with walls that echoed in a way that drove her sensitive ears to pain. Neith kept her mind tucked away, terrified of what other depraved souls she might find here. She longed to touch Zennor's or Mesmal's calming auras, even if it was for a single second, but was too scared of what she'd find instead.

"Where are you from?"

The disgraced prince paced incessantly, his leather-soled boots slapping against the floor tiles, driving her to madness. She made herself as small as possible, trying not to panic as she squeezed her legs against her chest.

"I'm speaking to you, Trove," he said with undeniable frustration. "I know you can talk. I heard you screaming when we snatched you from that Shay pig you were clinging to."

She pressed herself back, scooting until she smacked into the wall behind. She wished she could sink into the stone itself. Anything that might take her from this place. She'd rather be facing down another tendron in the depths of basalt on her way to Kekk. Those monsters killed their prey quickly. Roulin promised only torture.

His footsteps drew closer, and she turned her head away, certain he would strike her like he'd beaten Mesmal. She couldn't see his face, but she could imagine what it looked like. The same as her father's—bitter anger and narrowed eyes, lips curled up in a snarl.

His hot breath touched her cheek. It reeked of spoiled meat and wine.

"You'll come to find I'm not a patient person," he said softly. "And I have ways of getting elflings to talk." The air moved with him as he stood. "I'll be having a...shall we say *friendly* conversation with your Shay friend next. I'm giving you a chance to spare him a lot of pain."

She scrambled away from the wall toward Roulin's dirty soul on her hands and knees.

"Please, no." Her voice shook with terror, and she immediately regretted it. But she couldn't help it. Not Zennor. Anything but Zennor.

"Ah, you do speak." Roulin was half a room away from her, tapping his toe on the tile. The rhythmic sound synced with her racing heart. "Where are you from?"

"Dakarai."

"Your parents?"

"I came alone."

Roulin was silent for a moment; his tapping had stopped. "You're young to travel alone, aren't you?" He started to approach her again. "How did you come to know the Shay?"

"Zennor saved my life after I was attacked by a tendron in the tunnel to Kekk. I was...fleeing from my father." She'd given more information than she'd wanted. She was desperate to spare Zennor from whatever these monsters planned to do with him.

More silence. Neith reached with her mind, seeing the way Roulin's soul seemed to shift in color as he considered her words. Something changed in his ruthless and evil demeanor. There was the tiniest bit of compassion hidden beneath a vast ocean of treachery.

"And how did you come to be in Parth?"

"Rae found us and brought us with her to Tremire and then to your fath—"

"Stop!" Roulin shouted.

Neith sank against the wall as Roulin's voice bounced around the room.

"He is no longer my father," he said between clenched teeth. His voice was nearly a whisper. "For someone who has fled from her own father, I should think you would understand. Cruelty comes in many forms."

The silence that followed was heavy, and Neith eased into it, hoping perhaps Roulin was finished with her and would return her to whatever room it was he'd originally thrown her in. The burning light was better than this. Or better yet, perhaps she would be allowed to be with Zennor or Mesmal—or both of them. She doubted he would, though. This didn't seem like something Roulin would do. A compassionate gesture toward a terrified girl? He was much better at torture and inflicting fear.

"So it's true that the Starling brat is alive."

Neith remembered the excitement in Tremire when Freya and her people had received them, but Neith hadn't thought to ask Rae about it. Something so profound had happened in Rae's past that everyone thought she was dead.

"I guess I have more things to consider." He tapped his foot again, the sound like a drum on Neith's head. "I hope she enjoyed the condition I left her muscly, idiot friend in."

Dulanii. Neith shivered. She wouldn't be able to forget his wails of agony. She and Zennor had been found quickly and dragged back to the throne room as Roulin's men tortured him. It had crushed her, and she'd tried to comfort his soul with her mind, clinging to it to hold it in place as long as possible. She hadn't been aware she was capable of such magic until she'd done it. Dulanii was perhaps one of the friendliest people she'd ever met. He'd defended Mesmal and the others without question even though it was more than obvious the odds were impossible. He could have run, but instead, he'd accepted a painful death. A very painful death that Neith might have unwittingly made worse by attempting to keep his soul firmly inside his dying body.

"What do I do with you now?" he seemed to consider aloud.

It wasn't like Neith hadn't faced death more than once in the last several weeks, but it would always be terrifying. As Roulin walked closer, she turned her head again, trying to fade away, to be anywhere but in front of him. He yanked her up by a wrist, holding her so she couldn't reach the ground, her muscles stretching to their limit. She writhed in his grip, grabbing his wrist with her other hand, unsure of what he planned to do with her.

"Feisty little thing." He placed her on her feet before taking her by the upper arm and leading her away. "I'm wondering if you'd like to hear your Shay friend's final moments—or if you'd rather return to your cell until I've figured out what I'll do with you."

They walked quickly. She practically jogged to maintain his pace, his footsteps echoing down the long hall. She thought she could hear the faintest sounds of screaming, but it was hard to tell. A moment later, they stopped. The squeak of hinges was the only warning she got before she was thrown to the cold floor with a yelp.

"Marinate in here for a while. I'm sure I'll think of something appropriate."

The door slammed, reverberating for several seconds before silence crept in around her. At least it was dark in this room. She risked pulling the bindings from her eyes. It was a small space, bare of furnishings other than a single chair in the center of the room. Strange position for a chair, but she ignored it because she could hear the sound of someone screaming. And the voice was very familiar.

✦ ✦

Roulin glared down at his father sitting on the floor of a small, stripped-down bedchamber used as a holding cell. From farther down the hall, the distinct sounds of the Shay boy's screams echoed. Part of him longed to be present for the questioning, but he'd allow Tace to have his fun. They'd have the pig healed before they'd start again, and again until Roulin was satisfied they'd wrung every last drop of hope from the Shay's putrid pink flesh.

Mesmal looked strange without his topknot. If it weren't for his sallow face and the dark rings under his eyes, he'd look like an elfling. He was a father who thought he'd lost two of his sons. But in truth, he'd only lost one. The one standing in front of him.

Roulin refused to call the man his father ever again. And he'd decided not to share the news he'd been given after being informed they couldn't return to the stronghold at Korthan. Belkin and Gastel were very much alive and likely finding the remains of Mesmal's castle guard.

"What exactly did you know about Niminea's powers before you fucked the whore?"

Mesmal's broken eyes glared up at Roulin, a sadness deeper than death itself in the man's face. "Why does it matter?"

Roulin clenched his teeth. This was where Gastel got his petulance. Such insolence wouldn't be tolerated. Didn't Mesmal know the position he was in?

"I'll ask again. What did you know about Niminea's Anam capabilities?"

Mesmal glared, unrelenting, his lips never moving.

A searing anger boiled to the surface of Roulin's soul, and he reached down, taking Mesmal by the collar and dragging him to his feet. He was shockingly light. At least he knew the poison he'd paid to be slipped into Mesmal's wine over the last several months was working.

"I asked you a question, old man." Nose to nose, Roulin glared, but still Mesmal said nothing.

He thrust him to the ground, drawing a cry from Mesmal's throat. Served him right.

"You'll rot in here until you find the answer." He stared at the man he'd once called father for a little longer, the way his sheared hair hung around his shoulders. The white streak on the left side, a sharp reminder of Roulin's bastard brother, Gastel. A living, breathing reminder of all the things Roulin hated most about the world.

Games within games. Lies and intrigues and stolen crowns. It was all just a parade of blood and politics, and it was disgusting. He was done with it. Done with all of it.

"What have you done with the elflings?" Mesmal asked.

Roulin's insides boiled over. The fact that this man worried more about two elflings he'd known a handful of days over answering a few harmless questions was infuriating.

"This is what you care about?" Roulin took a step closer. "Two worthless elflings?" He paused because he wasn't sure how much he wanted to share with Mesmal.

"Dead. Will that help you start answering? They're dead," he lied.

Mesmal's face twisted with anguish, and he dropped his head into his hands in grief.

"You seriously care so much that it brings you to tears?" Roulin stooped down so he was at Mesmal's ear level. "If it helps, I made it fast for the girl. But the Shay?" he whispered. "I made it slow and agonizing. May his filthy soul wander this realm for an eternity and never find peace."

When Mesmal's tearful eyes found him, Roulin's rage bubbled to the surface once again. He stood, taking deep breaths to keep from killing the man. Then he turned, slamming the door behind him as he fled. He'd deal with him later when he could think more clearly. For now, he needed more information. He'd been given vague, unsubstantiated details about the final wave of soldiers. It had been a strategy to try and give Belkin a reprieve before he was annihilated. A final "fuck off." Belkin had used the strategy once before when fighting in a larger-scale battle. He'd remember.

When Korthan had been declared off limits, they'd gone to the next best place, where Roulin could regroup his men and discuss the next phase of his plan. The next piece he'd been priming in his conquest puzzle.

He'd gone to the Vail.

Rayken was waiting for him in a lavish sitting room tucked away down a small corridor off the main hall. The Master Wielder looked like death warmed over. He didn't wear his age nearly as well as Mesmal. The flesh drooped down his face, drawing far too much attention to the nasty scar across his neck.

As he stepped in, Rayken rose and bowed. Good. The Wielder understood. Roulin wasn't going to take any more chances. He needed Bleck Larin who were loyal. All others would be systematically eliminated once Roulin learned all he could from them.

"How was it accomplished?" Roulin saw a moment of panic in the old man's eyes as he likely tried to figure out what he was asking about.

Let him sweat.

"Forgive me, my lord, do you refer to the events of the battle outside Korthan?"

Roulin rolled his eyes. Must he spoon-feed everyone? "Yes, obviously. Why else would I ask *you*? I was informed that a hundred or better of my fighters were quite literally sliced in half with what clearly looked like soulfire."

"Anam is a strange device." Rayken gazed at his hands as he rubbed them together in thought. "Perhaps the princeling used some technique, but to have such strength behind it, he should have drained his soul, even for the Great Wielder Returned. I wouldn't be surprised if he killed himself."

"I have it under good authority that he did not, in fact, kill himself." Roulin grew suspicious that this old idiot had no idea what he was talking about. "Is there no combination of Wielders that can produce such an attack?"

"Without having witnessed the Anam, my lord, I cannot say."

Roulin's frustration snapped, and he lunged forward, ripping the old man from his seat and bringing him to his face.

"I can send you into battle next time. Perhaps then you can witness this power for yourself. The front lines would be the best place." He held Rayken firm, noticing the yellow rings around his aged irises, the maps of wrinkles that snaked across his sagging flesh. "Or…" Roulin eased, letting Rayken plop back down in his chair, a delightful expression of shock burning across the old Wielder's face. "You can figure it out before I need to."

A Nice Night for a Stroll

Gastel sat cross-legged on the throne room floor, his head in his hands. Three days ago, he'd been living in a very different world. He'd stood at his window, admiring the fall colors of the heather. He'd had the morning meal with his father. He'd trained with Belkin. Raemian had been dead.

And then? Everything changed with a single head in a basket.

He'd been fitted with battle armor while his stomach flipped with nervousness. He'd raced across the wilds on a borrowed horse beside his brother—his king. He'd ridden into battle for the first time in his life. He'd felt the chaos of death spilling over him in angry waves.

Failure hadn't been an option. If he failed, Belkin failed. If he died, Belkin died. His brother. His king. He hadn't seen any of it, just the blur of black as it slammed into him over and over and over.

And now? He was sitting in the silence of the castle stronghold after he'd helped scrub it of blood and gore. The bodies of the lost had been taken away. He'd held Raemian's head against his chest when her greatest friend had been carried to the burial pyre.

How could so many things have changed so completely in three days? Everything whole had been broken. Everything broken had been made whole. Three days ago, Raemian had been dead. He was still certain he'd wake to find all of this a dream. But what was worse? That he would wake to find Raemian dead and his father safe...*or this*?

He glanced over at the length of hair still pinned to the wall with the Starling short sword and swallowed. It was killing him that Belkin had forbidden him from going after Roulin. Every moment was another moment his father could be tortured or killed. Was he still alive, or did Roulin just want them to think he was?

Gastel sprung to his feet. He needed to do something or risk the growing rage within his chest destroying every last scrap of his sanity. After stalking the halls, glaring at the destroyed tapestries and broken furnishings, he needed some fresh air.

Part of him hoped he'd run into Belkin, but his brother was likely still working through strategies with Tildimin and a handful of other soldiers. They were trying to determine how they were going to hunt Roulin down, how quickly they could pull the reserves back into action, and whether they'd be able to rely on Treina's troops from Raggethan.

The size of Roulin's army had been shocking. So many Bleck Larin were unhappy enough with the current conditions that they'd tied their loyalty to a man who would see nearly half the elves in Rhend put to death for the color of their skin.

No one stopped Gastel as he pushed through the front doors of the castle stronghold; no one seemed to see him. Before he realized where he was going, he was in the bailey walking toward the main gate with no intention of stopping.

It was late; the sun had long set. The rain that had followed them from Korthan had passed, but the clouds still hung low in the sky, holding the light against the earth. Parth itself seemed tucked away for the night. Other than the occasional pub, the shops were closed.

He let his feet guide him down the streets he'd ridden with dangerous haste earlier in the day. He'd moved through the city on instinct alone, the terror of what he'd find burning a hole through him. Now that hole was full of molten rage, simmering and waiting to tear Roulin's flesh from his bones.

The city wall loomed in the distance, the moors beyond. When Gastel was young, his father told him the walls of Parth were ornamental, that no one had ever laid siege to the city, and no one would ever dare to. In a way, he'd been right. Roulin hadn't attacked Parth. He'd walked into his home.

Gastel clenched his fists as he approached the gate. The two guards on either side respectfully nodded as he passed through the open gates. Even after what had happened within the castle stronghold, there was still such careless security. Roulin could just as easily march back in and finish what he'd started.

The ambient light from Parth dissipated quickly beyond the gate, but Gastel didn't need light. He struck his soultorch and continued walking, following the same road they'd ridden in on. He didn't know where he was going or why he felt the need to walk. His mind had things to work through.

A shiver lanced through him as he realized that every single time he'd left Parth, he'd faced another danger, another unthinkable challenge. Perhaps his father had been right to keep him locked away. Maybe it was him that caused such chaos in Rhend.

Movement caught his attention back near the edge of the city wall. A dark void shifted and changed shape as it traveled several inches above the ground. He stopped to watch as it undulated and grew several feet only to condense back down to its original size. The strangest thing was that it was close enough to the wall that light should have reflected from it, but it seemed to soak up every drop. It was a nothingness, and rather than continuing his aimless walk away from Parth, he turned toward it.

It must have sensed his approach because as soon as he started walking again, it shifted in his direction, continuing to grow and shrink and shift as it slinked along the outside of the wall. Once he was close enough, he realized there was nothing to see. It was little more than a black blob of smoke.

The hair on the back of his neck stood on end as it morphed and took shape, towering over him—a bipedal creature with extra wide shoulders and a waistline slenderer than any elfling's. Its arms nearly touched the ground, and as the form sharpened, talons formed on each finger, long enough to make his dagger look like a plaything. On instinct, he drew his blade and pushed his Anam through it, igniting it with white flames, but even the light from his sword was soaked up by the blackness. Two blazing magenta eyes opened and glared at him as the thing stood to its full height.

He was frozen. He didn't believe in monsters. They were elfling stories. Rhend was free of such things—other than elves themselves. Monsters were contained to the Wastelands, where the powerful magic of the Elder Gods bound them.

The Wastelands! Gastel tried to recall the stories of the wraiths. Dark, insubstantial things that could shift into whatever monster their prey feared most. In their raw form, they were more like skeletons with smoke for flesh and braziers for eyes.

The monster shied back from Gastel's sword, bringing its taloned hands in front of it defensively.

"Who are you?" Gastel asked.

But the thing only glared at him, its ghostlike form seeming to flow loose around the more stable shadows of its legs.

"What do you want?"

Gastel thought it might stand there glaring at him for the rest of the night. He was about to sheath his sword and walk away when it opened its mouth, which was lined with jagged teeth and illuminated from deep within by the same light of its eyes.

"We've come for your nightmares."

Its voice was a wet whisper scraping across Gastel's flesh.

"We've come for your dreams, Princeling."

The thing shrank into itself until it was no taller than Raemian, the shadowy form condensing until it seemed almost solid. Again, it opened its glowing magenta eyes, which had changed into the shape of a girl's.

"We've come for your wishes."

"Who's *we*? Are there more of you?" Gastel didn't risk looking around.

He couldn't because the thing morphed again, this time into something that could only be described as a horse with its two front legs replaced with those of an elf. A long tail snaked from its hindquarters, coiling on the ground beside it until the pile of tail was nearly as tall as it was.

"There are infinite. Just as there are infinite wishes."

It morphed again, back into the taloned thing that towered over him, all shadows and chaotic teeth.

Without warning, it shrieked, exploding into a cloud of black mist and pulsing toward Gastel with limbs that reached for his arms and legs. He wasted no time, spinning as he evaded, and plunged his flaming sword through the shadowy monster.

When Gastel looked back, he saw he'd nearly cleaved the thing in half. It was a short-lived victory. Gastel shifted his weight to run toward the gate as the two halves fused back together, reforming the wraith-like figure.

"What the—"

"Wielder. We know your kind."

Gastel ducked out of the way of a taloned swipe and swung his sword again, this time severing an arm, which floated in the air beside the rest of the monster's body before it reattached.

He'd get nowhere at this rate. He would run and hope the guards at the gate knew how to handle things. Surely, it wasn't the first time the shadow monsters had wandered around the outskirts of the city. He sprung into a sprint, but ahead of him, another wraith shifted from the shadows and solidified, its head slightly smaller, its talons morphing into two massive pincers for hands.

He slid to a stop as he glanced over his shoulder to see the first wraith approaching at a leisurely pace, drifting on a nonexistent breeze.

"Your nightmares are delicious," this new wraith crooned. Its voice was higher in pitch but just as coated with decay.

"Gastel!" Raemian's voice cut the night in half.

Gastel glanced over to see her sprinting toward him at full speed from the gate.

"They can't be killed with blades."

She spun around the smaller wraith, drawing her own sword as she did and slicing off one of the monster's arms without breaking her stride.

"What are they?" Gastel had stopped as she ran past him toward the original wraith, clapping to get its attention.

"Dark One, I am *your* nightmare!" Raemian yelled.

Gastel felt the pull of magic so strong that he swayed on his feet. It was the same feeling he'd had on the battlefield when she'd drawn Eishtala all at once. It was the yanking that was the weapon, not the magic itself. The wraith closest to her screeched and clutched at its throat as it seemed to slide toward Raemian, snagging claws on the turf to keep from being completely consumed. The thing stretched thin as it dissolved into nothing more than wispy threads of smoke that Raemian absorbed into herself.

She was frozen in place, hands fisted at her side, her eyes squeezed shut. Then she screamed as she released the energy all at once, sending a green wave of Eishtala rippling across the moors. It blasted through Gastel, knocking him back several steps, and ripped through the second wraith behind him, shredding the shadows into a mist that wafted away.

Gastel looked up in time to see Raemian sway on her feet. He scrambled toward her as she slumped to the side, managing to catch her before her head hit the earth.

FIFTY-FOUR

Broken Magic

When Rae's eyes popped open, she was looking up at the underside of Gastel's chin, the line of his jaw inches from her. He was talking, the soft vibrations of his voice soothing, though she couldn't make out what he said. Time itself had stretched and twisted. He looked down at her, and she recognized her name on his lips, mesmerized by the shapes of the words as he spoke. So beautiful. He was so beautiful.

She squeezed her eyes tight, trying to clear the smoke, letting the roar of the world coalesce, the rumble of Gastel's voice pulling together until she recognized a single word.

"...okay?"

She nodded as he swept a lock of her hair away from her face with gentle fingers before looking around again, leaving her with that maddeningly delicious view of his Adam's apple.

"We need to get back to the castle stronghold." His words were crisp this time, the clarity almost too sharp as she started to remember what had happened. He looked back down at her, his amber eyes burning with concern.

She nodded, unsure if she could speak but at the very least able to understand what he was saying. She leaned up, but he stopped her.

"How did you know where to find me? How did you..." He squeezed his eyes closed as if to press the words into a coherent sentence. "How did you even know I needed help?"

Rae shook her head, not wanting to say. She hadn't been able to stop thinking about the death in his eyes as he'd left her to rest in one of the undamaged guest suites. She'd spent less than five minutes trying to turn off her thoughts when she'd realized it was a lost cause and had left her room. She'd been watching him, worried he'd sneak off to try and confront Roulin alone. He'd looked the way she'd felt so many times when she'd made rash decisions.

"I followed you."

He glared at her, the muscle in his jaw flexing. The last thing she'd wanted was to upset him more, but if she hadn't followed him, his encounter with the wraiths may have turned out significantly differently.

He helped her up but winced with his first step and dropped to one knee.

"Gastel?"

Rae's breath caught when he brought his fingers away from his leg. Blood. He'd been wounded. A soft memory of Noe-eb's voice caused her to stand up a little straighter.

Their talons have the power to destroy your soul.

"Is that from the—"

"I think so," he said as he stood up straight and tried to walk again. He limped but managed.

"How bad?"

"I'll be fine enough to get myself back to the castle stronghold."

She shivered, hoping Noe-eb's words had referred to the wraiths in the Eishtala realm and not *all* wraiths.

Belkin was weary of discussing where Roulin had likely gone. There were too many options. The Bleck Larin territory was entirely available to him. In truth, so were the Shaylands. They would need to wait until they had better information. Tildimin tried to be helpful, but the past two days weighed hard on Belkin's shoulders.

"If we're to recover your fa—"

"I'll not hunt Roulin down like an animal," Belkin said, cutting Tildimin off short. "He'll come to me with his demands." Belkin rubbed his temples; exhaustion had long set in.

"I just think we shou—"

"I said, we wait." Belkin glared at Tildimin until the man crossed his arms. "We wait until Roulin comes to us."

Tildimin nodded before shifting the correspondence sprawled across the tabletop between them. "Treina will arrive tomorrow evening with the bulk of the western division. The rest of our troops in Korthan are planning to relocate to the barracks on the north side of Parth." He paused, seeming to work through his words. "I'm sorry, Belkin. I'm not as good at coordinating as—"

"It's fine." Belkin was done dwelling on it. "You're fine." He just wanted a hot bath and his bed.

The main door to the castle stronghold slammed shut, and Belkin looked up at Tildimin, trying to register what was happening. The two of them scrambled around the table and out into the hall in time to see Gastel limping in their direction with Raemian at his side.

"The magic of the Wastelands." Gastel's voice was strained, and his eyes had a wild look. "It's broken."

"Come again?" Belkin wasn't certain he'd heard him correctly. It sounded like Gastel had said the magic was broken, but if that were the case, they had larger problems than finding Roulin.

"I was just attacked by two wraiths on the outskirts of the city wall."

"First, how do you know it's the magic of the Wastelands?" Belkin said as calmly as he could, though he knew the answer to this question. Rhend was not known to have wraiths of any kind just wandering about. They *only* existed on the Wastelands. They were creatures created by the magic of the Elder Gods. "And second, perhaps more importantly, why the fuck were you outside the city wall at this hour?"

Gastel looked exasperated by the second question, but Belkin ignored this, instead focusing on Raemian, who looked pale with terror despite having just been running.

"Freya mentioned reports of wraith sightings at night," Rae said, her voice confident if a bit rushed. "She seemed to think it was related to the Wastelands, and after this, I have every inclination to believe her."

Belkin took a deep breath, giving himself a moment to process her words. "If the magic of the Wastelands is broken..." He looked from Gastel to Raemian and back again. The prophecy was becoming entirely too real for his liking. Things had been so much easier when it had been only a fairy tale. "You need to open a third rift."

"What about Fa—"

"We can't focus on one elf, Gastel." Belkin tried to school his voice into the soft calm their father always used when giving crucial orders. "We're talking about the fate of Rhend."

Gastel grimaced and turned to leave but winced, falling to one knee.

"I need to see your wound." Raemian was bending down at his side in an instant, pulling at his pant leg.

"Wound?"

"One of the wraiths must have sliced my leg." Gastel stood, trying to put on a strong face. "It's nothing."

"Fucking idiot," Belkin spat—because it wasn't *nothing*.

His youngest brother stared at him, eyes round with shock.

"Their talons are..." Belkin glanced at Raemian. She knew. Her face was anguished as she looked up at Belkin from where she kneeled beside Gastel. "Can you cure it?"

She closed her eyes, taking a deep breath. "I can try."

"Wait, cure what?" Gastel asked.

"The wraiths' talons have the power to destroy souls," she said with a quiver to her voice.

Belkin clenched his jaw. May the Elder Gods be damned, but he refused to lose another member of his family.

✦

Gastel couldn't take his eyes off Raemian as she took a deep breath. The dark circles under her eyes reminded him that she'd used Eishtala multiple times already that day and was likely exhausted. He'd suggested having a healer clean the wound instead, but when they'd arrived at the infirmary, it had been empty, the healers either having fled or been taken.

The familiar tug at his soul as she drew the life force into herself would always feel strange. The chilled autumn air tightened around them as Raemian soaked up the warmth of life, and Gastel shivered.

"Are you ready?"

He nodded and allowed himself to watch her as she closed her eyes to focus. The softness of her face, the way her shaymarks danced along her temples. The way her red eyelashes rested on her cheeks. Her lips parted as she exhaled, a burning heat seeping into his leg as the flesh knit itself back together. It was nowhere near as painful as healing his hands or the agony the rifts had inflicted when he'd opened them. Only the slightest burning radiated from the laceration before it dissipated. When she was done, there was nothing but an angry, dark line.

Gastel ran his fingers over the scar. It was hotter to the touch than the rest of his leg, but otherwise, it was completely fine. He met her gaze with the slightest smirk, then pushed himself up, testing his weight.

"How does it feel?"

"It feels...fine. Better than fine. You and Belkin worried for nothing."

Raemian looked away from him, and he could see she wasn't convinced. Her shoulders were rigid, the muscles in her neck tight.

"I'm still worried there's more to this." She stood, and without so much as looking in his direction, she left the infirmary, calling back to him, "I want to see if there's any information in your father's library."

He stood perfectly still for another moment, alone in the infirmary, confused by her coldness yet relieved by it all the same. He needed the distance. Now that he'd dwelled on his father, it seemed his mind would torture him further by hyperfocusing on what his brother had confessed to. He'd be lying to himself if he said he wasn't upset. Every time he saw his brother's face, he imagined him kissing her. His hands roving down her body and hoisting her onto him.

Could he trust no one? Even Raemian seemed content to only tell him what she thought he needed to know.

Closing his eyes, he leaned his head back, taking a moment to just *be*—to savor the anger that still simmered under his skin. It was almost comforting in its familiarity, smoothing out all his other emotions into manageable layers.

There were still so many things he needed to figure out; dwelling on these jealous feelings only made things worse. He shivered as he remembered he had one more rift to open. And then after that was done, he and Raemian would need to figure out what, if anything, could be done to fix the magic of the Wastelands and stop the Sundering.

He spread his strange Trove-white fingers apart, looking at them as though they could provide the answers to all his questions.

He'd given his hands for the first rift. He'd given two months of his life that he could never get back for the second.

What would the final rift cost?

FIFTY-FIVE

Strange Allies

The Vail was nothing like the stronghold in Korthan. Roulin found it dreary and frigid. If he'd missed the sumptuousness of his existence at the castle stronghold before, he now understood how much worse things could truly be.

He would make the best of it, though. Rayken was a powerful ally. When Roulin learned the old Wielder had custody of a Svet Priest and an Eishtala Master, he was happy to endure the inconvenience for the opportunity to discuss the next phase of his plans.

After he'd managed to delay General Treina's troops in Raggethan, he thought he could actually destroy Belkin. And things had been going so well until Gastel had used his Anam. The question still lingered as to what he'd done to make his power so strong. Even Rayken seemed to be confused as to how he was still alive.

Roulin took a sip of his wine, letting the bitter liquid coat his mouth before he swallowed, his thoughts wandering.

The Trove girl was perplexing. When she'd spoken of her father, Roulin had tasted her fear—had seen the agony transform her tiny frame. It made him want to protect her in a way he couldn't explain. He'd never felt this way about anyone other than his mother, and it scared him. He didn't want to care about anyone. He *couldn't* care. Caring was akin to a stubborn splinter that festered until the infection spread through his body, poisoning his blood, and killing him. It was a liability he'd learned he couldn't afford.

Tace interrupted his ruminations. "The Shay Queen has arrived, Majesty."

Finally.

It had been decades since Roulin had seen Gemma in the flesh. It had taken him a fair amount of planning to sneak her out from under Legion Bowrhem's watchful eye. How long would it take for anyone to notice she was gone? He followed Tace down one of the labyrinth-like halls. Everything in this place looked the same. He actually found himself commiserating with Gastel's early exit from the place.

They entered a room he'd been using as a study. Gemma stood with practiced elegance in the center of the room, purposefully avoiding any of the comfortable chairs that had been dragged from their previous locations to provide seating. Her hair was loose around her shoulders, cascading in waves of platinum blond to her perfect backside. It partially obscured her pale blue gown, which did little to conceal her luscious curves. It was made of layers of silk shaped to hug her breasts and hips, allowing for slices of her pink flesh dappled with lacy shaymarks to peek through. Behind her, a terrified lady's maid cowered in nothing more than a simple gray tunic and leggings, wild eyes darting around the room from the bare walls to Roulin and back to Gemma.

"I see your taste for opulence hasn't changed," Roulin said, his eyes following her length until landing quite abruptly on her left eye. Her face had been healed flawlessly, but the eye itself had been replaced with a smooth gem as blue as the afternoon sky.

"Like what you see, Roulin?" Gemma asked, her torturously gorgeous red lips turned up in a sultry smile.

"Always," he said, letting the *s* draw out like a soft whisper.

She tipped her chin up so she could look down her nose at him. "Am I to assume that you've forgiven my little indiscretion?"

"Indiscretion?" he said with willful sarcasm. "Oh, you mean when you snubbed me and requested a lifebond with my unfaithful father after our years of negotiations so you could solidify a crown you already possessed? The indiscretion that could have undermined the countless alterations to historical documents I painstakingly coordinated so you could take the easy way around killing off the remaining members of the House of Starling?" Roulin let his fingers dance over the back of a chair in a suggestive manner. "I think you learned your lesson the hard way."

Her smile widened, and she took a few steps toward him, allowing him to more clearly see the gem that was now her left eye.

"The rumors are true. The Starling bitch slashed your eye before you cowered at her feet."

A flash of anger marred Gemma's perfect face, gone in an instant. Roulin reminded himself she didn't take losing well. Pointing out her shining mistakes was probably not the best way to solidify their relationship—no matter how gloriously she'd failed.

"Eishtala healed you well."

"It can't heal everything, unfortunately," she said, a bitter note to her voice. "How I wish the little whore were still alive so I could punish her properly."

This grabbed Roulin's attention. The news of Raemian Starling's miraculous return from the dead hadn't reached her yet.

"But she *is* alive."

Gemma's attention snapped to Roulin, throwing her hair in a wave of white around her.

"Excuse me?"

"I'm shocked the news hasn't reached you."

"Of course, she's alive." Gemma sneered. "Seems nothing can kill her. How perfect."

"It is perfect," Roulin said as he took another step so he was close enough that she had to look up to see his face.

She smelled of summer blooms and the wilds. Anger burned in her good eye, sending a flash of heat into his core. She always wore her fury with the grace of a God. It was perhaps her most gorgeous feature. How he wished he could wrap his fingers around her neck and slam her against the wall. Instead, he ran a single finger along her jaw to her chin before tipping her face to meet his gaze.

"You shall have your revenge, My Queen, but first, the Sundering must be endured."

Acknowledgements

I haven't written enough acknowledgements yet to keep them short, and I refuse to apologize for the length of this one.

In April of 2024 I did two crazy things. I self-published *The House of Starling*, my debut novel, and I quit my job as an art director (a fancy title for a graphic designer). I left behind sixteen years of brand knowledge, a consistent salary, and financial comfort. I hugged my amazing coworkers—some of my very best friends—and promptly crashed from burnout.

I didn't do this because I thought my book would cover my income. No, I knew it would do no such thing. I did it because I've talked about making this change in my life for more than ten years and it was time. I did it because the most special people in my life agreed with me that it was time. And I did it because I knew that if I didn't, there wouldn't be another time until I retired.

Tim, Timmy, love of my life, my mad scientist, the only person I want to annoy for the rest of my life, as much as I like to say I'm making my dreams come true, you...you have made them possible. While I've had an incredible number of people supporting me, it was you and your encouragement that made me know without a doubt, no matter what, I would be okay—*we would be okay*. Without your love and support I wouldn't have made this jump. And frankly without your nagging to keep me motivated, I wouldn't be on my current trajectory. Thank you for dealing with me while I recovered from truly stupendous career burnout. Thank you for being my home base as I navigate the waters of freelance and publishing. Thank you for giving me this opportunity to try and make my lifelong dream of "arting" for a living come true. Fingers crossed, some day (hopefully sooner rather than later) it will be me steering the financial ship while you jump into the treacherous and terrifying waters of following your dreams. I love you with all my cold black heart.

Myra, I'm crying in the den as I write this, hoping you don't come down and interrupt me (again), because you'll want to know why I'm crying, and I won't be able to explain. Being a mom is weird. I never in my life thought I'd have the relationship I have with you. There are so many things I want to teach you, show you, correct you on, protect you from, tell you not to do, tell you to *absolutely* do. I want to help you see that sometimes it's scary to follow what your heart is telling you to do, but it makes it so much easier when you have the ones you love most at your side. Thank you for putting up with me being the weirdest mom on the planet, for listening to me when I want to blab on and on about a world that only exists in my head and my books. Thank you for your love and unconditional support and for being (almost) as invested as I am in Rae and "Backpack Girl's" story. But most of all, thank you for being the absolute most amazing daughter on the planet. I don't know how I got so lucky, and I try not to ask, because I'm afraid the powers that be will realize their mistake and drop you off with some significantly more normal parents. I love you forever. Even if you follow your dreams and move a 9-hour flight away for college. Especially if you follow your dreams and allow me to be there for you like you've always been here for me.

To my Alpha readers, who didn't shy away after The House of Starling's cliffhanger, I have to thank you about twenty times over. I don't have a developmental editor, and for my first book I worked with a critique partner who taught me so much about crafting an interesting story. But I didn't have a critique partner for this book, and I had about seven million doubts. I was convinced I couldn't create something worth publishing. Your feedback, and encouragement helped me overcome some of the worst imposter syndrome I've ever had. When it felt like no one was reading my first book, your words made me keep going. So to you, Amanda, Ashley, Jackie, Jay, and Selena, from the bottom of my heart, thank you!

I know I left some names off that list, and it was very intentional.

Sara Burton, there are times when you come across people that change the way you think about yourself, and you are definitely one of those people for me. You've given me more confidence in my writing than might be healthy though, so *calm down*! Thank you for finding all the little nuggets of world building, for catching the nuance that a lot of people have missed, and for loving these characters (almost) as much as I do. Never, ever, ever change, or I will ship you a gallon of glitter loose in an amazon box. I'd send Belkin over to set you straight, but you'd like that too much, and let's be honest, he'd probably like that too much, too. Also, we seriously need to make a writing retreat happen.

Allison, I realized recently that when you finally read this acknowledgement you will have read this book four times. *FOUR*. I have no idea how many times you ended up reading *The House of Starling*, and soon you'll already be on your second time reading my next book. You've read more of my words than anyone other than myself. If you ever get annoyed with me bugging you to read through something, tough cookies, cause you're mine now. *Forever.* Your feedback has been truly invaluable, especially when it comes to digging in on where I need to do more work, add a little more, get rid of this, clarify that. Thank you for the time you've invested in my writing and in me as an author. I am truly honored to have you with me on this journey.

Katrina Robinson, I know when we first met on zoom (what was it two years ago?) I told you I was looking for an editor I could work with through this whole series. A long-term relationship, if you will, and I meant it. Sorry, not sorry, you're stuck with me now, and while Book 3 isn't coming in as hot as this one did, I have another fun project coming your way very soon. Thank you for helping me make another book baby all it can be!

Laura, my "proofreader." I put proofreader in quotes because you were essentially another editor for me and your feedback was so very helpful! Sometimes you start chatting with random people on Instagram and things just click. That's you for me. I hope I can drag you along with me as I muddle through this crazy world of authoring. If not as my proofreader and editor, at least as my friend! Because now you're fucking stuck with me!

To my Beta Readers: Selena, Mariella, Bethany, Chantel, Morgan, Jeff, April, (breath) Jayne, Maaike, Emily, Allison, Crystal, Edith, Lisa, and Amanda! You guys are seriously the best. I had way too many of you for this book, but it helped me find some places that needed more work, and for that I am eternally grateful. Some of you beta read for me on *The House of Starling*, and I hope you come along for Book 3 as well. I won't lie though, getting to the ending of this story is going to be hard. I refuse to apologize for what I'm about to do to these characters, but I promise I won't kill everyone. <side eye>

To my readers. It's weird for me to say I have readers. It's even weirder to call myself an author. I appreciate every minute you spend in the world I've created. To every one of you who has reached out to me on social media, seriously...thank you! Your words mean everything! Never stop bugging me with your unhinged yelling when my endings crush your soul. They crush my soul too. I know the ending of this story and I hope I make it worth every scrap of pain.

Okay, I know this is already long, but there are two people in particular who have, quite literally, changed my life. Not just my writing career, but my soul. It's hard to make friends as an adult. It has not been hard making friends with both of you. Zaid and Essie, I have shared more of my writing, and my past, and my weird life with you than with anyone else. You two have helped me get through some serious doubts when I was stupid and read my reviews, or at the bottom of the imposter pit. You two are the first people I run to when something cool or crazy happens and you have never once been dismissive or negative. I can send you anything: Myra painted something cool. Timmychunga said something funny. I needed to cry about life. You are there and I seriously can't thank you enough. I'm not sure how you both stay so positive when you deal with me sending you my chaos around every corner. And then, after we've laughed and cried, you trust me to read your early drafts, the ones when you are most vulnerable. I hope I never forsake that precious trust. But seriously, we are identical triplets separated by life. When I say gicks, you say vagills. When I say traveling, you say anal. You are both the most special humans on the planet and unfortunately you are stuck with me. Also, because I feel it needs to be said: "Breasts, end scene."

I'll see you all at the end, in *The House of Rhend*.

Glossary

Aequus | {*AY-kwiss*} An elf of any race holding no allegiance to any one sovereign.

Amfithere | {*AHM-fih-theer*} One of the prominent Great Houses of the Bleck Larin.

Anam | {*A-nahm*} A form of magic used by Bleck Larin elves. Anam is created at the cost of an individual's soul, making it incredibly powerful depending on the Wielder's capabilities, but also very dangerous and impractical in battle as the cost to wield is quite literally one's life force. Proficiency is only possible for a small percentage of Bleck Larin. However, all Bleck Larin possess a minor form that allows them to ignite a heatless flame (see Soultorch).

Bleck Larin | One of the three elven races of Rhend. Usually tall, almost always over 6 feet in height, and very slender, making them deceptively strong. They are pale blue, green or cool gray fleshed elves with black, dark blue, or violet hair occasionally streaked with white or silver. Eye color ranges from yellow, to amber to warm orangish brown. They have much longer lifespans than Shay by several hundred years.

Bonded | A formal coupling of two elves akin to marriage.

Bondmate | A title bestowed to one another once bonded.

Dormshire | {*DORM-sheyer*} A Shay held city previously shared between the Bleck Larin and Shay before the current war conditions.

Effrin | {*EHFF-rin*} Training overseer of Anam magic.

Eishtala | {*EESH-tah-lah*} - A form of magic used by Shay elves. Eishtala is the influence of outside life forces such as plant based or non-sentient living things in order to manipulate organic materials into desired structures or shapes. It can also be used to heal wounds of any severity, but at the cost of the outside life force. Generally thought to be possible for nearly a quarter of the Shay population to a minor degree, only a select few have enough skill to train to become masters of healing.

Rhend | The land of the elves, separated from the human domain by a magical and physical barrier known as the Wastelands, put in place by the Elder Gods after the 100 years war.

Shay | One of the three elven races of Rhend. Usually creamy pink or pale pink fleshed elves with platinum blonde, white, or red hair. Most of them have some form of red birthmarks (see shaymarks). They have pale blue almost silver irises, sometimes greenish blue or deep blue. Closer to average human height, they are naturally muscular and extremely strong. Even female Shay have defined muscles and are nearly as tall as the males. Average lifespan of around 1000 years.

Shaymarks | Bright red birthmarks possessed by Shay elves, usually lacy patterns or large freckles that run along the sizes of the face, neck and torso, sometimes down arms and rarely on to legs.

Soulfire | A general use term for the white fire Anam magic creates.

Soulflame | An advanced level of heated soultorch created by Anam magic.

Soultorch | A light source created by a simple form of Anam magic that can be created by most Bleck Larin.

Svet | {*Sveht*} A form of magic used by Trove elves. Svet can banish or return a life force to a corporeal body. While mostly associated with the resurrection of deceased sentient beings, it is also associated with having the ability to sense or "see" the life force of sentient beings. Those gifted with Svet are incredibly rare. Because Trove elves tend to isolate themselves from the other elves, there are very few Svet Priests known. Svet paired with Eishtala healing can fully restore one from death. Svet paired with Anam can destroy a life force and permanently kill.

Tendron | A giant freaking underground spider, that uses clicking sounds to navigate their environment. (see also, nightmare on eight legs.)

Tremire | {*Treh-MEER*} A Shay held city. One of the prominent Great Houses of the Shay.

Trove | One of the three elven races of Rhend. Pale violet or white fleshed elves with only silvery white hair and pale almost white eyes. Much smaller than both Shay and Bleck Larin in stature, they are thin and petite in all aspects. They rarely grow to be taller than 4 feet. They live underground and have exceptional low light vision. They rarely come above ground unless needed and choose to isolate themselves from the other elven races. Lifespan is unknown.

Character Guide

Gastel | {*Gas-TEHL*} (Bleck Larin, age 32) Confident, Curious, Naïve. Chaotic Good

Dulanii, Freck | {*Doo-LAH-nee*} (Shay, age 34) Friendly, Loyal, Kind-hearted. Chaotic Good

Belkin | {*BEHL-kin*} (Bleck Larin, age 284) Battle hardened, Unwavering, Complicated. Lawful Neutral

Tildimin | {*Til-dih-min*} (Bleck Larin) Loyal, Intimidating, Steadfast. Lawful Neutral

Mesmal | {*MEHS-Mehl*} (Bleck Larin) Calm, Patient, Impulsive. Neutral Good

Kalbasen, Kal | {*Kal-bai-sin*} (Bleck Larin) Calm, Intelligent, Respectful. Neutral Good

Jore | {*Jor*} (horse) Loyal, Trusting, Steadfast. Belkin's trusty stead

Sebinson | {*SEHB-in-son*} (Bleck Larin) The innkeeper at The Aubridge

Roulin | {*ROW-lin*} (Bleck Larin, age 267) Prideful, Bitter, Instigator. Lawful Evil

Venna | {*vehn-AH*} (Bleck Larin) Belkin's mistress

Inara | {*Ih-nar-ah*} (Bleck Larin) Timid, gentle, Respectful. Neutral Good

Tace | (Bleck Larin) Arrogant. Chaotic Neutral

Raemian Starling, Rae | {*Ray-MEE-ehn*} (Shay, age 35) Observant, Moral, Timid. Neutral Good

Noe-eb | {*NOE-ehb*} (Elder God) The patron of the Sheol of Life. True Neutral

Lorilay | {*Lor-ih-Lai*} (Shay) Gentle, Motherly, Intelligent. Chaotic Good

Rayken | {*Ray-Kin*} (Bleck Larin) Shrewd, Strict, Prideful. Lawful Evil

Kresha | {*Kresh-Uh*} (Bleck Larin) Seductive, Vicious, self serving. Neutral Evil

Bowrhem | {*Boe-ray-him*} (Shay) No-nonsense, Strategic, Moral. Lawful Neutral

Freya | {*Fray-Uh*} (Shay) Aequus, Matronly, Understanding, Perceptive. Chaotic Good

Solena | {*Soe-lehn-uh*} (Shay) Sympathetic, Moral, Stern. Lawful Neutral

Neith | {*NEEth*} (Trove) Overcautious, Fearful, Loyal, True Neutral

Zennor | {*Zehn-her*} (Shay) Nurturing, Protective, Shy. Lawful Neutral

Geri | {*JAIR-ee*} (Bleck Larin) Aequus, Naive, Inquisitive, Trusting. Neutral Good

Tor | (Bleck Larin) Aequus, Geri's father. Lawful Neutral

Telfin | {*Tehl-fin*} (Bleck Larin) Servant at the stronghold in Korthan

Gemma | {*Jem-Uh*} (Shay) Self Centered, Ruthless, Manipulative. Neutral Evil

9 781963 524024